TORN

Tony Webster

Edited by Elaine Elizabeth Webster

Unlocked Publishing

Dedicated to the memory of

Stacey Leanne Clarke

who lives on in all the lives she touched.

She was truly a force of nature,
and the most powerful example to all.

Her light shines on.

7th November 1984 - 16th April 2022

COPYRIGHT

First paperback edition 2023

Editor: Elaine Elizabeth Webster

Book design and cover by Tony Webster.

ISBN 978-1-7393361-0-3
(Paperback)

Published by:
Tony Webster
Lockdown Publishing
Wigan

A catalogue record for this book is available from the British Library.

Thank you to Darton Longman and Todd for allowing the use of text extracted:

From The Jerusalem Bible © 1966 by Darton Longman & Todd Ltd
and Doubleday and Company Ltd.

AUTHOR'S NOTE

Where to begin? Life teaches us all many lessons. Some are learned, some are neglected or avoided, and some take us down entirely misleading paths until we discover the reason for the detour. I was educated in a time and place, when, and where, I was told on a regular basis by different people in authority that I, and my life, would amount to nothing. It's fair to say that alongside the doubters were the encouragers. But, for some reason, when I was young, the positive voices seemed to be less convincing.

One of the doubters was a teacher, an educator, a person who, I imagine, was trusted to bring out the best in his pupils; he was a person I respected, even when he made what I now see as a life changing statement: 'You'll find yourself behind bars, Webster.' Growing up as best I could in working class Wigan, Lancashire, and the rough and tumble of a Catholic secondary modern school, it came as something of a shock to me.

The detractor did indeed turn out to be right. In a way. I actually spent 19 years of my life 'behind bars,' but not as he had suggested. Instead I became a prison officer. I think one of the reasons was to serve those who may have been condemned by similar put-downs, but unfortunately never got the chance, through better life circumstances, to prove them wrong. There by the grace of God! However, I must acknowledge that man's influence in my personal growth.

I have sometimes found inspiration for this story in the darkest of places, the most painful of experiences, and in the suffering of those I would have swapped places with, at the drop of a hat, to free them from their pain.

Among the people I want to thank are my daughters, Claire and Zara, my grandsons J.W.D. and O.B. And, of course, R.J.S. Each of you has inspired me beyond anything you could ever imagine. I find your determination and courage humbling. I am truly blessed.

I owe also a great debt of gratitude to those who have offered their assistance and expertise in the completion of this book. They are my sister-in-law, Elaine, who selflessly gave her time and literary skill in the editing process over the three years of writing, and my older brother, Stan, who encouraged me and challenged me to find other dimensions in my writing and within my real-life storyline. My younger daughter Zara read and offered guidance and support through the early rewrites. My elder daughter Claire spent hour upon hour listening to the unwritten original version and also challenged me to make painful decisions on behalf of the characters, who are now real people to all of us.

Thank you also to 'first readers' Ronnie Marsden and my niece Helen Webster for their helpful comments and observations.

It has become clear to me during the editing process of *Torn* that all my life I have been fighting a form of dyslexia, never diagnosed, of course, which has tried to hold me back. With gratitude I salute the technologies of autocorrect and computer programs that can transform dictation into the printed word. You may notice more than usual spacing between paragraphs. This was to help me read my own book, and I hope it will be of assistance to others with similar problems.

Last, but not least, I need to 'thank' the dreamscape from which I woke, early one morning during the first Covid lockdown in 2020. I had a big question in my head. In an attempt to answer the question, I embarked upon a mission, and that was to tell the story of Jennifer, David and Father Seth.

EDITOR'S NOTE

You are about to read a story that - I believe - will live on vividly in your memory. The characters in Torn have become utterly real people to Tony and to me. They are people who have, like us all, experienced overwhelming feelings of love, joy and pain.

I would like to thank Tony for his incredibly generous and calm attitude to my oft-used 'red pen'. I could sometimes be brutal, too, because editors have to be. I have edited many things during my life, including most of my own writing, and I have always had to be particularly brutal with that.

Tony has also been very generous in allowing me to get inside his characters' heads, and to get to know them almost as well as he does. My suggestions have been met with equanimity and gratitude, even when preceded by much animated discussion. We have found a great common ground of understanding in caring for the people who inhabit these pages.

When I began combing through the earliest manuscripts, I could not have known that something would soon happen in my own life - unexpected and amazing in equal measure - that would directly mirror events in the story I was editing. To say what that was would be to spoil the story. But let me just say this, that the people who trot out that old saying about life being stranger than fiction, well, they can be utterly believed.

E. E. W.

CONTENTS

Chapter 1

Arrival

The journey through the Transvaal had been long and tiring for the two travellers.

Waiting by a black saloon at the busy Johannesburg Park Station was a young man with dark good looks, curly-haired, tall, slim and tanned. He was peering uncertainly into and beyond the crowds.

Scanning the latest batch of passengers hurrying through the ticket barrier, he soon spotted them, a large, black-clad man and his young, female companion, both wheeling cases. She stood out, even at this distance, a dainty young nun dressed in white, not a regular sight hereabouts. She might even be pretty, thought David, narrowing his eyes. He tried not to squint too hard in her direction, though he dearly wanted to.

Father Seth Rossouw was always easy to pick out in a crowd. A tall, imposing priest with more than three decades in the pulpit, he was still handsome with a jawline that hadn't surrendered to jowls, bespectacled hazel eyes that missed nothing, and wavy, greying hair, smartly parted to the right.

He no longer had the trim figure of his youth, but his well-cut clothes hid his portly torso well. He had the look of a man who regularly enjoyed good food and wine. Well over six feet tall, healthy, strong and, in his full cassock of black, he struck an intimidating figure.

'David,' he said in a monotone, nodding proprietorially and omitting any greeting.

With an obedient smile, the younger man bowed his head of black curly hair, keeping his eyes low. He turned his face away from them and then stooped even further to avoid their gaze.

The priest had spoken only his name, but it carried a thousand meanings, a voice disconcertingly deep, with its undertone of threat. David almost flinched, hearing it again after the short break he'd had from it. This was the same voice he had heard all his life, employed at length and with great effect from the pulpit, imposing the fear of hell fire and retribution into anyone unfortunate enough to be listening.

The parish priest of St Brigid's took pleasure in berating his flock for their real or imagined transgressions, and David had often been the parishioner in closest proximity, living as he did in the presbytery. Most of them dreaded going to confession, so these days, fewer and fewer did. Young and old, when they spoke of him, it was with whispers and cautious looks. He had alienated and angered so many over the years that some hadn't stayed after childhood, rejecting their faith or finding religious comfort elsewhere. Enough of them remained to keep Father Seth in a job.

'Hello.' Again, one word, but a bigger contrast could not be imagined. A light voice, this time, sweet and gentle, from the young woman in white.

David glanced at her, smiled again, and quickly looked away. This girl, barely a woman, was not just pretty, he decided, in an instant. She was a natural, dazzling beauty, even dressed like this. Her head, showing just wisps of auburn hair, was covered by a starched wimple which contoured the glowing skin of her forehead and high cheeks, leading to a delicate, dimpled chin. Her eyebrows were rich auburn, curved and sleek, highlighting blue eyes that glistened in the light. It had been the swiftest of glances, but David took it all in.

She was small, and even though her habit was designed to cover her body modestly from shoulder to toe, he could still make out the shape of her. He felt suddenly hot, and then had to add guilt, shame and embarrassment to his list of personal difficulties.

In spite of the effect her presence must have had on most people she met, the young woman seemed innocently unaware. She unconsciously ran delicate fingers through the emerald-coloured rosary beads which hung from her belt. She smoothed down the material beneath it with her other hand. David was entranced by her simple movements, but dared not show it. He didn't trust himself to answer her greeting, apart from a polite nod of acknowledgement.

As they stood by the car, awkwardly, a crowd of mostly young women bubbled through the station forecourt and the three of them turned round at the noise.

'Oh, it must be…' said Sister Jennifer, on tiptoes now, smiling and spotting a tall black figure at the centre of the moving crowd.

Father Seth interrupted her, impatient to get going. He brought her attention back, announcing that, as David should already know, this was Sister Jennifer on leave from the convent in Cape Town, and that he had been to Newcastle in KwaZulu-Natal province to collect her from her home. David had also gathered that the visitor was visiting Johannesburg to meet the archbishop before taking her final vows, and that she was the daughter of an old family friend, one whose name he'd overheard in many telephone conversations.

The novice smiled at him and concurred with a nod. David, stealing another glance, shifted so awkwardly that she immediately sensed his shyness and discomfort.

She stared at the skinny young man before her. He must be about her own age, she thought, maybe a little younger. She decided he had the saddest brown eyes she had ever seen and he looked, well, burdened, by something. She wondered why.

He was definitely good looking, though, in spite of the burden he was carrying, she was certain of that, and maybe he was all the more fascinating because of it. Perhaps she could make him smile before long, and light up his serious face. She delighted in making people smile and forget themselves.

David opened the boot of the car and reached for their cases, glad for a distraction. Without need for further pleasantries, Father Seth passed his suitcase. Sister Jennifer, smiling, let David pick up her case, then placed her lighter hold-all to the side of it in the boot. As she did so, her hand brushed his back. It was the slightest, accidental touch, but he felt it like an electric shock and reacted by moving sharply away.

'Oh, I'm sorry,' she said, this time with a broader, reassuring smile, concerned at his overreaction. He acknowledged with a half nod. She looked at the young man with curious eyes. She looked over to Father Seth, and then back at David, wonderingly. She had just witnessed something different in the priest she had known since childhood. This seemed like a different Father Seth to the one who had bounced her on his knee and gently encouraged her vocation.

David stood up stiffly and went to open the rear door of the car for Sister Jennifer but Father Seth climbed in instead and closed the door. Obediently, he made his way to the other rear door and opened it to allow her to get in on that side.

To his great surprise, Father Seth instructed him to offer her a seat in the front. He said, firmly, 'Why don't you acquaint yourselves. Sister will be with us for a little while.' David's anxiety deepened. He'd never had such a directive from the man who had given him virtually all the directives in his life. Father Seth had never wanted him to acquaint himself with anyone.

The journey was only a few minutes from the station, but it felt like a lifetime. She spoke to him gently and quietly as they pulled away from the kerb and joined the city traffic. Aware that he was painfully shy, she took charge of the situation and talked about the thunderstorm they had witnessed during the journey from Ladysmith. It had been spectacular.

He nodded and mumbled in what he hoped were the right places, trying to display a level of interest in spite of his nerves. She was just about to fill in more time by telling him about the minor commotion caused by a well-known athlete entering their train carriage when they pulled into the drive of the presbytery.

It wasn't a moment too soon for David. He hastily jumped out of the car and opened the door to allow Father Seth to alight, always having given him precedence, unless of course the archbishop was visiting.

'No, assist Sister Jennifer,' the priest instructed, somewhat irritably. David immediately went to open the front door and stepped back to allow her out of the car. She reacted with surprise to the tone of the priest's voice and twisted round from looking at him to look into David's anxious face. Distracted, she placed her weight uncertainly on to the newly gravelled drive and her sandal slipped. She reached out and grasped his hand to save herself from falling.

It was not the most graceful of arrivals. 'Whoops!' she cried out, nearly ending up fully sitting down in a cloud of gravel dust. 'Clumsy me!'

He had tensed his arm partly due to the touch of her soft hand, still in his. It was as he pulled her to her feet that he raised his gaze and dared to look into her eyes for the first time. She threw back her head and gave a full, throaty laugh. He laughed too, unable to stop himself, at the spectacle of her scrambling to regain balance. Father Seth broke the spell of the moment. 'Boot, David, get our suitcases and Sister Jennifer's hold-all.'

David obeyed him in a daze.

Chapter 2

Steps

Ethel came out to meet them. She was a black South African, less than five feet tall, but with her rotund build and efficient manner, she was obviously a powerful force in the small world of St Brigid's parish. The younger woman sensed it immediately.

Ethel had brought five children into the world and, as a widow for over twenty years, had relied on her income from her work at the presbytery to support her family. Hardworking and staunch in equal measure, she was blessed with a great sense of humour and didn't hesitate to use it.

However, in the presence of Father Seth, she was serious, dutiful and accommodating. Having witnessed the strange, almost comic arrival of the young nun and its effect on David, she pretended to ignore the event and simply said, 'Tea, Father?' She knew that she was in danger of laughing at their antics as much as the young woman but judged accurately, glancing at Father Seth's serious face, that it was not a joke that could be shared in the present moment.

Father Seth nodded peremptorily and made his way to the dining room with the housekeeper bustling behind him, leaving David and the new arrival in the hallway. She looked quizzically at David. Raising her eyebrows and contorting her deep red lips, she gave a puzzled shrug of her shoulders and a slight shake of the head. He felt an uncontrollable smile fall across his face. The priest didn't see.

Calling to Ethel, he said, 'Excuse me, Mrs Gumede. Where is erm, Sister Jennifer to go?'

'Oh, Room 7, didn't I say?' she replied over her shoulder, as she hurried away. A mischievous smile spread across the young woman's face as she said quietly, 'What shenanigans!'

'Take her up, boy!' shouted the priest, striding towards his study. 'Show her to her room, and whilst you're doing that, you can take my suitcase to my bedroom.'

David looked at his patient charge and nodded towards the foot of the sweeping ebony staircase that led to the first floor. She reached out and retrieved her hold-all from him, their hands again momentarily touching as she did so. He dared to feel, this time, that he liked the soft, gentle touch of her skin but was immediately overwhelmed by the familiar sense of guilt. A well of frustration rose up inside him.

They made their way up the staircase, David carrying both cases. Fourteen steps in all, each step made of thick, black ebony, the spindles depicting different stations of the cross, all carved in ivory.

As they slowly went from step to step, she touched each one and whispered, 'So beautiful. It must have cost a fortune.'

Then, with further thought, she said, 'Such wealth, though, in a world of poverty and suffering. When this was built, I mean. I don't suppose the poverty is any different today, not really.' Then, self-consciously she added, 'Oh, please excuse me for running on. Sometimes I think aloud.'

David nodded but remained silent, not wanting Father Seth to hear any comments about the church and its wealth. He completely agreed with her and thought that a simpler house for the parish priest could have sufficed, but any collusion on that subject would most certainly land him in trouble.

The landing separated left and right. Directly facing them was Father Seth's bedroom. The gold numeral at the top of the solid oak door indicated it was Room 1. He opened the door, entered and put the priest's large case onto a red sofa in the corner by the window then exited.

David then reached out to take the young nun's hold-all, which she'd balanced on the top of her case. She stopped him and said, 'No, it's all right, thanks. I'll carry it.'

For the first time, he spoke to her directly, looking straight into her eyes.

'It's just that the staircase to your room is a spiral one and it's quite narrow. I wouldn't want you to fall.'

She made a wry face. 'Well, of course you don't. You've seen already how clumsy I am!'

She seemed so at home in her own skin, David thought. And it was beautiful skin, too, the little bits he could see, anyway. Did she know how lovely she was? He banished the thought.

She handed the hold-all to him with a smile of appreciation. He felt a roll of excitement in his stomach as she looked at him, gratefully, but the guilt of the feelings she was triggering also raged through him. This was not good. He needed to rid himself of them. He'd go and do some hard digging in the garden later. That's what usually worked with uncomfortable thoughts.

They made their way further down the landing, the young woman looking all around, taking in the rich red Axminster carpet and the gold framed pictures. It felt like a comfortable old manor house.

There was a door to the left, marked PRIVATE.

David explained, 'This is Father Seth's personal bathroom, for his use only.' She nodded. It was to be expected that the parish priest would have such a luxury.

To their right, across the landing was another door. Room 2. David said, 'This is one of four en-suite guest rooms, the other three are at the other end of the landing, 4, 5, and 6. I'm not really sure why you have been allocated Room 7, because it has a shared bathroom with Room 3. I'm sorry about that.' He was squirming inside but trying not to show it, because he knew that Room 3 was his, and had always been his, and Father Seth knew this perfectly well.

'Oh, that's OK. I'm used to sharing,' she answered, lightly.

David tried to breathe normally through his discomfort and led her further down the landing to the foot of the narrow, twisting staircase which led to Room 7. He signalled to her with a slight nod of his head but could not trust himself to catch her direct gaze again. She started to make her way up the staircase with him behind her, contorting his torso in the effort of carrying her suitcase and hold-all through the tightly confined space.

'Oh, thank you' she said, realising the difficulty of the task and the ease with which the fit young man accomplished it.

They reached the small, square landing at the top of the stairs. There was a roof light, a pane of glass framed and set in the pitched roof, lighting the landing and the access to two doors, a bedroom and a small bathroom, obviously for her use now, as well as David's.

She entered the room. It was picturesque and old fashioned. Set beneath the pitched roof was an old cast iron single bed, with a small wooden wardrobe, a chest of wooden drawers, and an otherwise empty bookcase, except for a copy of The Jerusalem Bible. Under the alcove window and the pitched roof stood a desk and chair and an old, green, enamelled reading lamp. The room was brightly but simply decorated, with clean, folded towels laid out on the freshly made bed, a jug of water and a glass on the small bedside table.

'It's lovely, thank you,' said Sister Jennifer. 'May I see the bathroom, please, David?' she asked with a soft, encouraging smile.

Dreading this, he went out onto the landing and opened the bathroom door. To her obvious surprise, there were David's toiletries on a glass shelf over the sink, a razor, shaving foam, toothbrush, toothpaste, deodorant and a bottle of aftershave.

'Oh, is there someone already in Room 3?' she asked.

'Well, yes, me, actually,' he stuttered, the game up at last. 'Room 3 is my room, I'm really sorry. But I can ask Father Seth if some other arrangement can be made while you're here.'

'Oh, no, it's perfectly fine,' she replied after a moment's reflection. 'We can lock the door, can't we?' She smiled again. She smiled a lot, he thought, relieved by her answer. It was a lovely smile.

He nodded in embarrassment, knowing the difficulties of the bedtimes and the mornings to come. Father Seth must have known about this inconvenience. Surely there could have been a better allocation of rooms, he thought.

'Lunch is ready!' shouted Ethel from the kitchen. She had a powerful voice that carried easily up two flights of stairs. David was relieved to be rescued from his current discomfort.

He started down the staircase before her. Needing to warn her of the narrowing of the steps to their right and the obvious danger of her long habit, he advised, 'Be careful to stay to the left, Sister.'

'You're very thoughtful, David. 'But please, just call me Jennifer.'

Jennifer. He could call her that. Wow. He felt suddenly privileged. He nodded and hid a small secret smile as they slowly descended the creaking steps.

Now on the landing and making their way to the main staircase, she asked, 'Do you work, David? Do you have a job?' Her question seemed to put him on the spot.

He looked at his feet and replied with some embarrassment. 'No not really. I do the gardening here. I also help maintain the presbytery and the church and help Father by picking people up from the station or the airport and running errands. I don't really have what you'd call a proper job.'

She raised her eyebrows. 'That sounds very much like a proper job to me.'

'It's not a job as such. There's no official arrangement. I don't have a wage. I just live here for free. It suits me. I get a small allowance for personal items, but I don't really need much,' he said, suddenly feeling the need to explain himself.

A look of disbelief crossed her face as they made their way down the stairs and into the dining room. He started to feel apprehensive and fearful that she would say something about their conversation to Father Seth. He wished fervently that he had stayed silent.

His worries were interrupted by Ethel as she greeted Jennifer with a broad smile. 'So, welcome to Johannesburg, Sister. I'm sorry it's a little belated! I was rushing around to get things ready. How is your room, dear?'

'It's both fine and comfortable, thank you,' answered Jennifer.

'You will have to share the bathroom with David,' Father Seth interrupted, pointing at him as though he were an exhibit in a museum.

He continued, 'I am expecting other guests, and all the rooms will be full. Four seminarians are going to join us tomorrow. I'm afraid they take precedence.'

Here we go, thought Jennifer, though she smiled politely. Good old church misogyny in action, yet again. She was well used to the ways of older priests, but also knew there was little point in tackling them head on. She trusted the ways of the old faith would change in time.

'I understand Father. The church is very blessed with those young men,' she replied generously, with a smile.

David avoided the priest's piercing stare, as she continued, fearlessly, 'But in my opinion, Father, the church is equally blessed with those who labour with little or no reward. At least those young men from the seminary will be rewarded with a generous stipend.'

She looked at David, reassuringly. She wasn't going to pass over the issue of his employment status, or lack of it, especially given this golden opportunity. She had often gently challenged Father Seth, the old family friend, on many subjects over the years. He usually took it well, coming from her.

'Those who do God's work with no earthly reward will be rewarded in heaven,' Father Seth replied, following her gaze, perfectly understanding the meaning of her words.

'That's also true' the young woman replied, about to launch further into her cause.

She was interrupted by Ethel who, having heard the latter part of the conversation and not comprehending

Jennifer's specific meaning, added her own wisdom, 'The reward of heaven is what we all search for, Father, but some recompense in this life helps pave the way to heaven, don't you think?'

Ethel also knew the priest of old and what she could get away with. Seeing his reaction, she started to laugh at her own boldness. 'It is easy to impose the graces of poverty from a place of abundance. The reality of holy poverty is somewhat different to those that really live it,' she said with a wry face.

Father Seth was used to hearing Ethel's take on the church from time to time but he was momentarily nonplussed at this forthright and sudden alliance of like-minded women and, for once, didn't answer. He quickly changed the subject to the forthcoming visit of the seminarians and what activities were planned.

David felt a strange trickle of appreciation. He was acutely aware that the priest was being challenged and, strangely it seemed, on his behalf. However, he reminded himself that this conversation might bear consequences for him later, and he silently looked down at his plate. It was simpler that way.

Lunch ended and Ethel started to clear the table as Father Seth went to his study.

'Can I help you, Mrs Gumede?' Jennifer asked.

'Sorry, please excuse me, Sister, er, Jennifer, but I am meant to do that,' interrupted David.

'What? Another duty to add to your extending job description?' Jennifer's eyebrows shot up.

'Go to your room and rest, or solve something on your computer, David,' said Ethel, waving him off. 'It will be nice to have the company of the young lady, so go, boy, go.'

He looked at them both. They were smiling, and Jennifer nodded enthusiastically, saying, 'Yes, go, have a little time for yourself while you can.'

'Come on, dear, let's take these things into the kitchen and mind the step down. It isn't obvious if you're not aware of it.' Jennifer nodded as she picked up a tray of cutlery and crockery.

As he climbed the stairs, David felt there was something new happening in the presbytery. He had never experienced Ethel challenge Father Seth quite like that. And to hear a young woman of a similar age to himself doing so was astounding. He couldn't begin to imagine the self-possession that such a thing would demand.

He went to his room and lay on his bed but could not rest. He felt uneasy about Father Seth finding out that he hadn't helped Ethel as usual, so he made his way downstairs and into the dining room. The door to the kitchen ajar, he overheard the conversation of the two women as the crockery was being dried and put away.

Jennifer was speaking. 'Perhaps I shouldn't say this, Mrs Gumede, and maybe it's not my place, but do you know David doesn't actually get paid for what he does?'

Ethel stopped in her tracks as she took in the information. She was outraged. He could hear it in her voice as he stood listening behind the door.

'What? Nothing? Nothing at all? Gracious me, I never knew that. I thought he must pay him something,' she said. 'That poor boy works so hard for Father Seth, always has done, all his life.'

She paused for a moment and shook her head, 'You know his history, do you? Left on the step just days old, bless him? I was the one to find him! With just a note pinned to him, saying his name was Davi, poor mite. His mother was never found. She must have been desperate.'

Ethel looked sad at the memory, and Jennifer instinctively touched her arm. Ethel sniffed and rummaged for a tissue. 'We didn't know what surname to give him, and Father said he looked as if he might be of Hispanic origin, with his lovely dark hair, and olive skin, and on the note his poor mother signed herself Mamma.

'But Father said he didn't want to give him a name that might mark him out as different so he settled on David and then the surname of a Dutch footballer – Blind. You spell it like blind but you say it to rhyme with mint.'

Jennifer couldn't help commenting on the obvious irony. 'But a lot of people won't know how to pronounce that, if they just see it written down, would they?' she asked. 'Not even in South Africa.'

'I know!' said Ethel. 'When I first saw it written down I thought it a strange name to choose, too and I hadn't heard of the footballer, what's his name...Danny Blind. But Father has always loved his football, and I think it was just before some big international thing at the time, and of course he always follows the Dutch teams.

So for good or for ill, that's how poor David got his name.'

She mimed holding a new-born baby, rocking to and fro.

'Actually, we found out Davi is a form of David in Portuguese, so he really must have Hispanic blood. Father was very good, taking him in, but I think he's been very strict with him, from being very small. I think of David as one of my own, you know, but I've had to be careful how I've shown it. Father wanted to toughen him up. He used to call me Auntie in secret when he was little, but Father heard him one day and soon put a stop to that.'

Jennifer took in a deep breath as she processed Ethel's words. So all of this was probably the reason for the brokenness she had sensed in David. She was silent for a few moments, taking in the enormity of the information.

Finally she said, 'Dear God, it must be so painful never to know where you came from. How can anyone ever truly know who they are if they don't know that?'

Chapter 3

Trapped

Jennifer's words had hit him like a thunderbolt. Did he know who he was? What he was? He had spent most of his life running away from those questions, hiding from the pain of them.

David Blind had always known of his unusual beginnings, and the name he owed to a famous footballer, but his cheeks burned, and sweat broke on his brow, listening to Ethel telling his story to this self-assured young woman. What would she think of him? He felt somehow ridiculous, as though it were all his fault. He half turned on the stairs, but then resisted the urge to go back to his bedroom. He wanted to hear what was being said.

'I guess he was a beautiful child,' said Jennifer after a long pause. 'After all, he's such a handsome young man. You must have adored him. I'm not supposed to take much notice of things like that, of course...'

Ethel started to laugh, her upper body shaking with merriment. 'Oh Sister, God forgive you, but you're right, he was such a beautiful baby and has grown into a fine, strapping young man.'

'Oh, indeed, Mrs Gumede,' Jennifer said, starting to blush at her own admission and hurriedly dried the plate in her hand.

They laughed so loudly that Father Seth opened the door of his study and called out, 'Quiet please!' The tones of their voices lowered, but David could still hear the conversation.

Jennifer continued, 'Father Seth has been wonderful to Mammy and me since Daddy left us when I was seven. In fact, Father Seth is the main reason I entered the convent. He can be stern and a bit frightening sometimes, but he is a good man at heart.

Her tone changed to one of sparky defiance. 'At least, in my eyes, he will be when he starts paying David properly, and I think I might have something more to say about that.' There was a suggestion of anger in her eyes, which was something she did not easily let other people see. But injustice made her blood boil.

Ethel responded, 'You said he was handsome, Sister.' She had a twinkle and a question in her eyes.

'Please call me Jennifer, Mrs Gumede.'

'Then call me Ethel, child, and stop changing the subject.'

Again, both laughed, but this time with restraint, not wishing to incur Father Seth's disapproval.

Jennifer whispered, 'He is very handsome, and he seems very sweet too. But I have entered the convent for my love of God, and I must pursue my vocation, Ethel.'

'I understand Jennifer. I love that boy like my own, you know.' Ethel's eyes grew moist. She didn't often get the chance to tell her part of the story to someone like this sensitive young woman.

'When I found him that morning, with the note pinned to his blanket, I rushed in with him. I don't think he had been there long, and he had been placed very safely. He had just been fed, and was quite sleepy, but I knew it wouldn't be long before he'd need changing so I rushed to the shop to buy some nappies and some baby milk!

'Then, later that day, Father had been on the phone and he told me I must take him to the parish orphanage as the presbytery was no place for a baby. But only black children were ever taken to the orphanage, bless them.

'I found that instruction so hard. However, I took him out through the back door and went across the yard to that awful place. It always felt cold and unwelcoming to me. It's been closed a long time since, thank goodness. There are new houses built there now.'

Jennifer stroked the older woman's arm to offer comfort. They both had tears in their eyes.

Ethel went on, 'But it's what I was told to do, so I did it. They asked me to change him into orphanage clothing, so I spied my chance and brought his blanket and clothes back to the presbytery, washed them, and placed them in a big envelope and asked Father to put them in the safe. They were all he had from his mother, poor thing.

'Father wasn't happy about it, but I think he did it to humour me as he could see I was upset. Also, I felt I couldn't just leave David there, so I used to pick him up every Saturday and Sunday morning and he'd spend those days in the warmth of the house and I'd look after him while I worked. I'm used to that! I've had five of my own, you know.

'I'd take him back in the evening and get him off to sleep before going home. I hadn't been working here long at all.

'I just bonded with him. It was hard not to. Much to Father Seth's disapproval, I might say, those Saturday and Sunday mornings caused a lot of grief for me, but I'm a mother. What else did he expect me to do?'

Jennifer listened, enthralled by the story.

Ethel went on, 'He was a good child, thank God, but I soon came to realise that he was a very bright boy and I felt he needed more than I could offer him. So, one day I plucked up the courage to ask Father if I could have some help to give him some schooling. I was shocked when he agreed to look into it and before long, Mrs Van der Heyden, the matron from the orphanage would come across every Saturday morning.'

Ethel started to laugh, 'We didn't much like each other, I think she thought she was a cut above me. But I knew David needed the extra help so I put up with her rudeness. That continued till they closed the orphanage when he was seven, just before he started school.

'I don't think that woman knew how to love anyone.' Jennifer shook her head in disbelief at the unfolding story, but she remained quiet, realising that Ethel needed to share it, and that perhaps she wasn't often able to.

Ethel dabbed her eyes and continued, 'Over time, there were fewer and fewer children needing places. The state had started to take the responsibility of looking after the children, and David was the last in the place, poor little thing.

'When the time came for the orphanage to close, they were finding it hard to find a place for him. He was at that age where nobody would have been prepared to foster him, let alone adopt him.

'I told Father that I thought it would be the best thing for him if he could move into the presbytery until they found somewhere more permanent to go.

'So, he's been here ever since. It's been hard, no, very hard at times, but it was worth the hard work, I mean, look at how he's turned out. Father is very strict with him, as you can probably see, and he's a bit shy, I know, but he's a good boy and I'm ever so proud of him. He's always felt like one of my own. I always wanted him to know that I loved him. To me, it was the most natural thing to do.'

Ethel lowered her voice even further and went on, 'But I was also told when he was a baby that I shouldn't get too close to him because the authorities would have frowned on a black woman being physically close to...' She tailed off, shaking her head.

Jennifer closed her eyes in near despair. This was the legacy of South Africa and apartheid.

'And Father Seth has been a hard taskmaster over the years. I know he used to punish him like they used to do in the seminaries in the old days. I thought it was too much at times, but I wasn't allowed to interfere. I wish I had, but Father is a very strong man, if you know what I mean. He has a way of putting you in your place.'

Ethel went quiet, then sniffed, and a sob broke through. 'I love him so much, but I think it's too late to tell him now. He's a grown man and I don't think he'd understand.'

'Oh, Ethel, that is such a sad, sad story. Thank you for sharing it with me. I can see you are both very special people,' answered Jennifer as she moved across to hug her. They both wept.

David choked back his tears as the older woman's words burned into him. He had always looked up to, depended upon and loved Ethel, but he had always called her Mrs Gumede, like Father Seth. And the priest had drummed it into him that she had five children of her own, and they came first, and he should expect nothing more of a hardworking housekeeper.

He returned to his room, lay on his bed, and dissolved into grief. His life suddenly felt barren, wasted, and he was trapped in it.

The tears flowed freely as he hid his pain alone, but eventually one thought lit up his troubled mind. He remembered the moments with wonderment. Jennifer seemed to value him as a person. She had stood up to Father on his behalf. She'd said he was handsome! He could hardly take it in.

He fell into a deep sleep and woke only as he heard the creaking of the spiral staircase. Jennifer was going up to her room. He found strange comfort from hearing her movements, and a short time later, he heard the stairs creak again as she came down.

There was a knock on his door. He jumped from the bed and opened it.

'I'm just going to go out for a walk. It's such a beautiful afternoon. Would you join me please?'

'Er...I'll have to ask Father if that's OK...' David almost stuttered, taken aback at the latest of the day's unusual events.

She responded, smiling, 'I'll do that, I'll ask him. It's what I want, so I'll ask, David.'

They made their way to the study. She knocked on the door. The priest answered, 'Come in.'

She opened the door and asked him from the doorway.

'Would it be all right if I went for a walk with David, Father?'

Father Seth hesitated and David held his breath, not knowing what the answer would be. Then the priest replied, 'During the daytime is fine, Sister, but you must always be accompanied, day, or night, and never leave the presbytery at night unless with me or Mrs Gumede as your chaperone.'

Jennifer nodded and smiled. She opened the door of the presbytery. 'Come on then,' she called to David.

Ethel, having heard the exchange, called cheekily from the doorway of the dining room.

'Have fun, you two!'

Hearing the mischief in Ethel's voice, Father Seth shouted from his study in his usual stern voice, 'Mrs Gumede, can I speak to you about the arrangements for later this week?'

Jennifer started to quietly chuckle.

David asked innocently, 'Why are you laughing?'

'It's Ethel. She's so funny.'

He didn't understand, but felt too embarrassed to ask her what she meant. They walked for a while around the church and presbytery grounds.

Time passed, and he relaxed and became more at ease in her company, reassured by her smiles and acceptance. He marvelled at the feeling. It was the closest sustained contact he'd ever had with another human being, apart from Ethel, and it felt good. They entered the house a good time later to see a frowning housekeeper exiting Father Seth's study.

Her expression changed and she said kindly, 'Hello, children.'

They followed her into the dining room.

'I'm just making tea for Father. Would you like some?'

'Yes please,' they answered simultaneously.

Jennifer grinned. 'That came out in stereo.'

Chapter 4

Beloved

Father Seth opened the door of his study and called out.

'Is David back?'

'Yes Father, I'm here.'

'Come into my study, boy.'

David silently sighed but obeyed immediately.

'Sit down, David. We need to talk.'

The young man's heart started to bang in his chest as he wondered if he would be brought to account for some of the things that had happened since Jennifer's arrival. All the other experiences he'd had when called like this into the study were bad ones. There'd been many occasions when he'd received beatings from Father Seth for the slightest of misdemeanours.

A powerful memory was awakened. He was nine years old.

The Archbishop of Johannesburg was completing his annual visit to the parish. He was about to have lunch in the dining room with Father Seth.

David had been doing as he'd been told, to stay in his room until permission was granted to come out. Unsurprisingly, he'd become bored and just before lunch, had sneaked downstairs to the study, entering just as Father Seth and the archbishop were taking a walk in the church grounds.

There, on the seat of an easy chair in a fine, gold trimmed box, was the archbishop's new purchase, a magnificent new mitre. He'd brought it, not out of necessity on this private, informal visit, but to show off its quality and value. It had cost the collective churches of the archdiocese a few rand, that was for sure.

It was glittering and colourful and, to a child, a temptation beyond control. David could not resist picking it up, turning it around to see it from all angles, and finally trying it on. In his excitement, he walked out into the hall of the presbytery towards the mirror as the large dark shapes of the two clerics were stepping through the front door.

The archbishop looked horrified at the sight.

'Give that to me child!' he blasted out.

At the sound of the commotion, Ethel had come into the hallway, saw David, and burst out laughing.

David started to laugh too as she gently removed the mitre from his head and handed it to the archbishop.

'You should put your precious items out of the reach of children, Your Grace,' she admonished, bravely, ignoring the blazing eyes and the veins standing out on the man's head.

She was still chuckling when she took him back to his room. It must be all right, he felt, as he went back to a half-completed jigsaw, and forgot the angry archbishop.

David was called down soon after the archbishop had left. He hadn't eaten, so Ethel took him into the dining room and gave him a sandwich. She then went to Father Seth's study and told him she was going to pick up some shopping for the household.

David had heard the front door close, and almost immediately Father Seth bellowed from his study, 'Come here, boy!'

He knew from the tone of his voice that he was in grave trouble but obediently went into the study. Father Seth took off his belt and strapped him so hard that he had bruises on his buttocks for days.

To add to the injury, David felt that the priest had even enjoyed the experience of beating him.

More painful memories were swirling in his head, plucked from many down the years. He began to realise that whenever he saw Father Seth adjusting his belt, as he did often after a large meal, he was still on his guard, senses fully alert, even now as a grown man. David had seen that belt removed too many times with the purpose of punishing him, punishing him for accidentally breaking a vase, climbing a tree in the garden too near to the boundary wall, spilling hot wax on the altar cloth, forgetting to clean the chalices, dropping the sanctus bell, the list of misdemeanours went on and on...

He was jolted back into the present, and he was in that same, fearsome study, with the portentous figure of Father Seth at the desk, turning to face him.

David steeled himself. The priest started to say something, and he expected the worst, but the tone was unexpected.

'I learnt a new lesson today David, and I learnt it from two people in this house. I've given it some thought, but felt I needed to discuss it with you before making a decision.'

David felt he was entering uncharted territory. He listened keenly for what the priest was about to say.

Father Seth continued, 'You will soon be twenty-one. When you were left in my care, all those years ago, your mother's note was particular about what she wanted from me, what she wanted me to do. But unfortunately, she was not at all specific about how I should achieve that. Do you understand, boy?'

David took a deep breath. 'I'm not sure Father. I know she asked you to take care of me, to love me, and to teach me in the ways of Our Lord. But I'm not sure what you're asking?'

He felt uneasy, almost panicked, as Father Seth replied in the sort of words that had never fallen from his lips before. David had never thought he would hear such things being spoken, not to him, anyway.

'You have been like a son to me. You've always tried to do well, and tried to fulfil my needs and wishes, but I'm afraid I've missed the point. I haven't appreciated that in you enough.'

David felt a constriction rise in his throat as he started to hope that this might be a turning point in his life. But there remained in the pit of his stomach the fear he was more used to dealing with.

'Father...' he could hardly get the word out, let alone any to follow it.

The priest interrupted, shaking his head. 'I need you to start to make your own choices and decisions in life, David, and to do that, you now need to find yourself and your way. First, you'll also have to learn how to pay your way. So, take this.'

He handed him a bulky brown envelope.

'Don't open it now. Open it in private. Open it later.'

Father Seth stood up from his chair and gave one of his rare, awkward, less stern expressions, as he directed him toward the door of his study. David left the room feeling more confused than ever. He walked to the stairs and went straight to his room. He felt nervous about the envelope's contents and placed it on his bed. He would open it sometime later.

He returned to the dining room for dinner. Jennifer held his attention throughout the meal. He was aware that he had spent almost the whole time watching her across the table and tried to look elsewhere whenever he could. He hung on her every word, regardless of the mundaneness of the conversation.

He felt insanely happy at the fact that she had come into his life, but sad that he knew her religious intentions. She could never be anything more than a friend, but then, he had always banished the prospect of relationships, let alone a marriage. Romance and marriage were for other people, something he observed at mass, at station and airport farewells, in films and in books.

He asked Father Seth if he could leave the table and return to his room. The priest responded with, for him, a gentle nod, and David left the dining room. He slowly made his way upstairs to his room and entered it, seeing the envelope on his bed. He'd completely forgotten about it during dinner.

He sat on the bed and stared at the package for a while before deciding to open it. He badly needed a distraction, something to take his mind off his feelings, and the turmoil of the day, and the package provided just that.

Picking up the envelope, he opened it and pulled out a small, blue baby blanket. It smelt musty but was otherwise clean. The fibres were stiff and compressed, but he could feel something through the layers of wool. He laid the blanket on his bed, and not wanting to damage it, he unfolded it gently.

It soon became apparent to him that this was the blanket he'd been left in at the presbytery door of St Brigid's twenty years ago. Inside was a beautifully crafted, powder blue, hand-knitted baby suit and bonnet, the note from his mother of which he knew, but had never seen before. He looked at the message simply dated 14 June 1993.

It read: *My baby's name is Davi. Please love him care for him educate him in the ways of Our Lord. It breaks my heart but I can offer him nothing. Please forgive me*

On the other side of the paper was another message that Father Seth had never shared with him.

Forgive me my child my Davi. Your name means beloved. Beloved to me. I come back for you when I can.

Mamma

It was followed by a single *X*. A final kiss from his mother. Had she kissed him, held him, cuddled him, many times before leaving him? She'd been with him for a few days, he'd been told.

The last item was a small, light green card from SAFERAND Ltd. Underneath was printed: Fr S Rossouw, Account Number 59737728. Beneath that, in black ink, was written.

For David Blind (SEE SAFE DEPOSIT BOX A773).

He looked at the note again, and especially at the signature.

Mamma

Who was she, who was Mamma? He knew why he had been given the name Blind. What had her name been? Perhaps she was Portuguese herself, given the name she had chosen for him, and the fact that she'd signed herself Mamma. Or perhaps it wasn't she who was Portuguese, or Spanish, and it was his birth father who had passed on his looks. Perhaps it was both. He'd never be able to find out.

New questions flooded in. Was she married, unmarried? Did he have siblings? Who was she? Where was she? She had never come back for him so, was she dead? Question upon question filled his head. It had been a bewildering and emotional and a day of many unexpected changes for him, not least because of the contents of the envelope, but mostly because of the effect Jennifer had had on him and, of course, the realisation that Mrs Gumede, Auntie, his African mother, had always loved him.

David had few memories of his very earliest years, and there had been little recalling of them from either Father Seth or Ethel. However, he was aware that the original site where the church and presbytery stood had previously been much bigger, and, beyond the wall, and through the first of two back garden gates had stood the orphanage of St Brigid's where he had spent some of his formative years. And, behind the church and through the other gate, separated from the orphanage by a nine-foot wall there stood the fee-paying all white boys' school of St Brigid's.

He had started school, aged seven, as South African law required. Before that, he had memories of spending much of his time, often alone in the orphanage, sitting silently in a sparsely stocked playroom, finding comfort in the story books.

But, every Saturday and Sunday, he'd be in the presbytery drawing room hearing the movements of Ethel going about her duties and taking the time to talk to him and giving him affection with her special hugs.

He remembered, too, every Saturday morning, being in the company of a strict, grey-haired older lady, Mrs Van der Heyden, who taught him how to read and write, and where all the countries and rivers in the world were on a huge map. He hadn't liked Mrs Van der Heyden.

Even as a young child, he was aware of the awkward atmosphere that existed when the only two women he knew in the world were in the same room. At the time it was just strange and unsettling. In hindsight, he recognised it was born out of the ugliness of apartheid.

The pale, steely-eyed and imperious Mrs Van der Heyden looked down on the kind and lovely African woman while barking orders at her. Ethel would nod, carry herself with dignity, and do as she was bidden, never complaining or showing it mattered.

David always knew in his heart that what he witnessed was wrong. More than wrong, he thought. It was wicked.

He had a vivid memory of his first few days at school. He remembered that Mrs Gumede was charged with taking him to the gateway in the wall where the frowning headmaster, Mr Coetzee, was waiting to collect him. Coetzee was already known to him, a friend of Father Seth's.

The priest had shared with Coetzee his belief in the words attributed to Saint Ignatius of Loyola, founder of the Jesuit Order: Give me a child until he is seven, and I will show you the man. David's behaviour was impeccable, so Father Seth was obviously right, thought Coetzee.

Touch usually led to sin, the priest had further reasoned. Better to avoid it from the earliest opportunity. Surely it would make a man more self-sufficient, less likely to commit mortal sin. Divine love and the fear of divine punishment should be all that was needed to get by. Father Seth had determined that David would become, for him, the living proof of that.

It seemed he had become the priest's little experiment, not for seven, but for twenty years.

In public, and at the parish school, David had learned to stand away from others, and to avoid any natural interactions, when he knew the priest was watching. It was just easier, he'd decided that early on. He'd found out the hard way. When Father wasn't watching, he behaved as his friends did, but if he was ever caught out, he knew he was to pay the price later, at the end of the priest's leather belt.

David had never understood what it was about, or what he had done wrong, but he had endured it, knowing he had to be strong to survive.

Father Seth's belt came off more often for a while just after his ninth birthday when falling numbers in the inner city meant that, for financial reasons, the boys' school merged with the girls' school down the road, and they started to share lessons and teachers.

David had found a new ally in Angela, a chatty, clever girl who sat by him in English and maths.

Father Seth spotted their friendship almost straight away. Walking the perimeter of the playing field, they were laughing and throwing a ball to each other. Like him, she was shy, and together they appeared to recognise their differences from the other children in their class.

Within days, Angela and he had been separated. David was moved into another class, sternly reproved by Father Seth for his 'inappropriate actions' and not concentrating on his studies, and, once again, his loneliness continued.

David began to realise that his isolation was almost self-imposed, because the situation had become startlingly clear: the less contact he had with the other children, the less he got in trouble and was beaten.

Father Seth was satisfied when Mr Coetzee regularly shared a whiskey with him while reporting on the school's progress at the end of each term and described David as a model student.

His other teachers said as much in his reports. Schoolwork, and homework - while trying hard not to be always top of the class - became David's escape and sanity. Friends became something other children had, while books and, later on, computers, became his refuge and comfort.

As he lay back on his bed, his hand touching the baby blanket by his side, David's mind was bursting with memories.

He was exhausted and soon fell into a deep sleep.

Chapter 5

Accounted

David woke in the early hours of the morning with the need to visit the bathroom. He opened the door of his room, checked all was quiet, and crept up the spiral staircase.

Although it was early, the sun had just started to rise and was breaking through the roof light as he reached the landing. As he took the final step up, the thing happened, the thing he was trying to avoid. The bathroom door opened, and Jennifer stood before him wrapped only in a bath towel.

He was struck motionless by her beauty. Her shoulders glistened and her thick, auburn hair, which ended at the waist, dripped heavily onto the towel. They both stared with deep embarrassment, she because she felt suddenly vulnerable, uncovered, and he because he was still in the clothes he fell asleep in, his teeth unbrushed, his hair uncombed, his sweat unwashed. He needed to get out of her sight as quickly as he could.

'Good morning, David!' She said brightly, quickly recovering herself and giving him a shy smile as she moved round him with her back to the wall. She entered her bedroom and, in a flash, bolted the door.

He felt his face hot and flushed as he entered the bathroom, mortified, and turned on a tap as he tried to discreetly use the toilet. This truly was mortification, he thought, feeling sick to the stomach. Before, he'd always associated mortification of the flesh with the pain inflicted on him by Father Seth. But what he was feeling now was almost worse. Ashamed, appalled, unworthy but pulled to her like a magnet - he just wanted the bathroom floor to engulf and purge him, and there were no Hail Marys for this.

She slumped down onto her bed and lay there with cheeks as flushed as his. Pulling her dripping wet hair over her face to cool it, she castigated herself for forgetting her dressing gown. She decided that she must go into the city later in the day and buy a new one. At first she'd thought the shared bathroom a manageable situation, but she couldn't risk repeating the encounter with David, and wanted the feeling of vulnerability to go away and stop troubling her. She knew that many men found her attractive. She also knew that she liked the attention. It made her feel happy and regarded, and perhaps that was the legacy of losing her father at the age of seven. But she also recognised deep down that she was afraid of the emotions and needs that male attention stirred deep within her. It had been too much for her to handle as a young teenager and she had been compelled to destroy the hopes of several prospective boyfriends before taking refuge in the convent. The different memories, and how she had dealt with them, ran through her mind. They had been nice boys. Not their fault.

Right here, right now, though, this situation with David needed to be dealt with. Her mother had given her some money for emergencies and she started to think that this was just such an emergency. She needed a dressing gown. Urgently.

She wondered should she apologise but was concerned that doing so would embarrass him further. She also worried that what they had just experienced might mar their embryonic friendship. Not only that, but she realised she liked him a lot, and she didn't want the gentle innocence to be spoiled. She knew instinctively that he wasn't like other boys of his age, not any that she'd met, anyway, and she suddenly felt a responsibility to maintain the new and growing confidence she sensed in him.

David threw his head back with his hands tightly gripping the hair at his forehead and felt the shame of the moment burn again as he tried to block it from his mind. But the memory of her long, wet hair clinging to her shoulders came back to him, and her moving past him with her back towards the wall, almost in slow motion. His thoughts were interrupted by a tightening cramp in his belly as the customary, overwhelming feelings of guilt were reawakened. He hoped beyond all else that she hadn't sensed his turmoil and prayed that what had just happened could quickly be forgotten.

With a loud warning cough, he unbolted the door, waited before opening it and on seeing a clear exit, he made his way down to his room to get ready to return for a shower. He was afraid that they would find themselves in a similar situation, so he sat on his bed out of sight with the door of his room slightly open. He wanted to feel secure that she was safely downstairs before returning to the bathroom.

It was about six thirty when he heard a creak coming from the spiral staircase. He watched through the crack of his door as Jennifer's shadow passed towards the main stairs. He waited for a minute or so before leaving his room and making his way up to the bathroom. He showered and dried himself, put on his dressing-gown and returned to his bedroom to dress for the day. He made his way to the dining room and entered to find himself alone with her.

'Good morning, again!' She looked up and her sweet smile reassured him.

'Good morning, Sister'

'Jennifer, please,' she replied kindly, reminding him of how things had begun yesterday. All was well, he thought with relief.

The front door of the presbytery opened and in rushed a flustered Ethel. As she entered the dining room, she greeted them, 'Good morning, children.'

'Good morning Ethel,' said Jennifer.

'I am so sorry I am late. My bus was late. Where is Father? David, please go to his room to check if he's there.'

He made his way to the top of the stairs to Father Seth's room and gently knocked on the door. There was no reply. It was unusual that he wasn't the first up in the morning, so he made his way back to the dining room and into the kitchen where Ethel and Jennifer had started to prepare breakfast and told them that he hadn't responded.

'Where could he be?' asked the housekeeper.

'I'll check his study,' David said.

Not in the study. David quickly made his way back to the priest's bedroom and checked inside; he wasn't there either. Neither was he in the bathroom. Where on earth is he, he thought as he quietly started to feel the panic rise. This was so unlike Father Seth. He was a man of routine; you could almost set the parish clock by his daily movements.

David returned to the kitchen, and as he told them that he was not in his study, bedroom, or bathroom. He looked through the kitchen window and saw that, unusually at that hour, the sacristy light was on in the church. Hoping that he may find him there, he went over and entered the small room which housed vestments and all the accoutrements required to celebrate Mass. But the priest was nowhere to be seen, so David made his way into the church.

There, kneeling before the altar, was Father Seth in deep prayer. David stopped in his tracks and decided to return to the presbytery without disturbing him. However, as he turned toward the sacristy, Father Seth looked up and said, 'David, I'm glad to have this opportunity to speak to you privately. Did you open the package?'

'Yes, Father.'

'Good. And what did you think?' he asked in an uncharacteristic tone.

'How are you?' he added when David failed to answer immediately.

'I'm OK, Father, I have many questions floating around in my head, many that may never be answered, I think, but I feel all right.'

'Did you find a green card?

'I did. What is that for, Father?' David had never had anything other than direct instructions from Father Seth. But now, the mysteries were piling up.

Father Seth continued, 'It's something you'll need along with your ID to access further information about your personal history. You will need to go to the SafeRand Bank. There you will be given access to a safe deposit box that contains important documents that may influence your future in an important way. You will need to read them with ultimate care.

'But first you will need an appointment to see the manager, Mr Verster. He will guide you through the process, and you must take your ID and the green card with you. I will also give you the key you'll need to access the contents of the box.'

David hardly knew what to say, but thanked him and returned to the presbytery, wondering how he could possibly fulfil the priest's precise requirements without major error. What on earth was it all about? Entering the kitchen, he sealed his concerns in a brown envelope in his mind and told the women that he had found Father Seth in the church, and he was fine. The three of them sat down at the table, and he suggested they started to eat as he wasn't sure how long Father Seth was likely to be.

Ethel started to pour a cup of breakfast tea for Jennifer as the priest entered through the kitchen door and into the dining room.

'Continue,' he said as he walked through, heading to his study. 'I need to make a call.'

He emerged from his study a few minutes later.

'David, we can go this morning, and I will introduce you to Mr Verster. Anything you can't sort out today, you can arrange to sort out another time. But I will come with you to help you get the wheels in motion.'

David was startled at the speed of all these unexpected events, but privately gave thanks that he would not have to visit the bank alone.

'What time do we need to be there Father?' he asked. Ethel and Jennifer looked at each other quizzically.

'We have an appointment at ten, so we'll need to leave at about nine thirty. Go and get the green card and your identity book now.' David left the room without question.

The others finished breakfast. It was eight forty-five. Jennifer asked if she too could go into the city later since she needed to buy a couple of things.

Father Seth explained, 'I can't spare any time this afternoon as I need to be back at twelve thirty. I'm expecting my guests from the seminary. I also need to assist David this morning with some business. However, if it is a short trip and Mrs Gumede is willing and available, she may accompany you. You can go by taxi.'

'That is fine, child. I'd like to come shopping with you,' smiled Ethel.

'Don't forget the seminarians are coming to lunch, Mrs Gumede. Something simple will be adequate,' said the priest over his shoulder, as he headed back towards his study.

It was precisely nine thirty as the men made their way out to the car. The women planned to catch a cab when the dishes were dried, put back, and the tables set for lunch.

David looked even more uncertain than usual, prompting the priest to hold out his hand for the keys. David surrendered them gratefully, glad not to have to drive through the city in his anxious state. The thought passed through his mind that, in all probability, it was an action prompted more by the priest's concern for his own personal safety than David's comfort and reassurance.

A twenty-minute journey brought them within easy walking distance of the bank. Father Seth spoke to the receptionist. Almost immediately, a grinning man in an immaculately tailored suit came to the foyer to welcome them.

'How are you Father? It has been a while, almost a year.'

'It has been a busy year. How are Eliza and the children?'

'They're all very well, thank you. I assume this young man is Mr Blind?'

He was holding out his hand in David's direction.

They shook hands and David nodded. 'Yes, Mr Verster, I'm very pleased to meet you.'

Father Seth explained, gesturing towards David, 'This young man has made my life much easier in the last couple of years, Mr Verster. He has made all the parish accounting easier by designing spreadsheets to handle everything, income, invoices, outgoings. He's quite the wiz with computers. I confess, it's all beyond me these days. Give me a pen and paper and I'm all right! But David has it all sussed.'

David took a sharp intake of breath. He could hardly believe that Father Seth was talking about him in these terms. It was true. David had designed spreadsheets for parish financial records. At first it had been simple ones and then more complex ones with formulae specific to the need. Working things out on the parish computer from first principles was his hobby, his relaxation. He'd even designed the parish website from scratch and kept it updated, and knew that other priests in the archdiocese, even the archbishop himself, had admired it.

But he had never had his own bank account.

Verster asked him for his documents. David retrieved them from the inside pocket of his jacket and handed them to him. Together the three of them made their way to the safe deposit room. It was situated two floors down from the ground floor of the bank.

The bank manager stared into a camera at eye level and in a second or two the door to the safe deposit room clicked open. The other two followed him down a stuffy, windowless corridor from which, on opening the door to an even stuffier room with a pass card, he invited them to sit down at a large, square table under harsh electric tube lights. On the table were a telephone, computer, and printer.

Verster picked up the phone and asked for an attendant to come to the room. A woman in uniform arrived and invited Father Seth to go with her to retrieve the box from the locked compartments that lined the far wall.

The manager started to print documents from the computer. He explained that they would need to be signed by himself, Father Seth, the attendant and David, and he would scan and print copies for him to take away with him to keep as his record.

David watched as Verster, the attendant and the priest signed a document headed 'Authorisation to Open Safe Deposit Box A773.' Father Seth inserted his key into the top lock of the box and turned it in a clockwise direction. Verster inserted the master key into the box's bottom lock and turned it in an anticlockwise direction. They both removed their keys, and Father Seth moved aside so that David could reach to open the box. There was a brass T bar handle on the front.

Verster told him, 'Slide it up until it comes to a stop, then turn it to the right. You will hear a click as it opens. Lift the lid. It is hinged to the rear.'

David was almost overwhelmed with nerves, conscious that his hands were shaking and clammy. The simple operation seemed to take an age.

There were numerous documents stacked neatly one on top of the other. David looked bewildered as Verster said, chuckling, 'We only need to look at three or four of them, Mr Blind.'

David responded with a look of relief.

'May I, Mr Blind?' Verster said, reaching into the box and removing an envelope, a small, green book and an official looking document.

He proceeded to open the envelope as he explained that it contained photographs from the time when Father Seth had acquired the box, ranging from a time shortly after David's birth, to his most recent ID photograph.

He further explained, 'Each is signed and dated on the back by Father Seth Rossouw as being a true likeness of David Blind, and Mrs Ethel Gumede has further countersigned them.'

He then showed him the official looking document and said, 'This is your birth certificate. What is your date of birth, Mr Blind?'

'The eighth of June 1993,' answered David.

Verster nodded. 'Along with your ID card and birth certificate, we have everything we could possibly need for a positive identification.'

He proceeded to cross reference the information meticulously for a couple of minutes. Father Seth looked at his watch.

Verster asked, 'Are you in a hurry, Father?'

'Not yet,' he answered. 'It's only half past ten, and we haven't much left to do, have we?'

'There's the matter of the savings account transfer, which will probably take us about twenty minutes to complete.'

The priest looked at his watch again, nodding his head. David sat silently, taking in all that was happening.

'This is the transfer of the savings account document,' said Verster. 'Would you like the transfer in cash, a cheque, a combination of both, or would you prefer to open an account in your name, Mr Blind?'

David turned to Father Seth for help.

'Considering it is likely to be a substantial amount, David, I would suggest you open the same type of savings account,' said the priest.

He continued, looking at Verster, 'Would it also be possible to open a RandExchange account, so I can start to transfer his monthly salary from the archdiocese?'

Monthly salary? David's head began to reel.

'Is that what you want, Mr Blind?'

Not wanting to look stupid, he simply replied, 'Yes please'.

Verster passed the final document to him. 'Could you sign on the line please, Mr Blind?' David took the pen. He didn't have a practised signature, so he simply wrote his name.

'This is the application for a RandExchange account,' said Verster. How much would you like to open the account with?'

Father Seth asked, 'Would a transfer be appropriate?'

'Yes, of course, but we will just need a nominal amount if you wish to open the account today.'

Father Seth took out his wallet and handed him 5,000 Rand. 'Will this be enough?'

David was stunned to see the money appear, as if by magic, and it was going to be in his name, in a bank.

Verster turned to the attendant and asked her to go and get coffee for the three of them.

Father Seth explained to David that he would need to access the bank website on the computer back at the presbytery so that he could manage his new RandExchange account online. The young man nodded, amazed at the new world opening up to him.

Father Seth looked at his watch and said, 'I have twenty minutes before I have to leave. That's plenty of time for coffee and the final arrangements, I think.'

The attendant soon returned to the room with a pot of coffee. She poured as the men watched her, then Verster scanned the documents and handed copies of them to David. 'For your records, Mr Blind.'

He handed him a plain cardboard envelope folder to place them in and reiterated, 'Look after your savings book. Can you please remove the remaining documents from the safe deposit box?' He handed him another cardboard envelope file to place them in.

It was now ten past eleven and Father Seth, draining his cup, rose to leave. He turned to David and said, in ignorance of the way in which the morning had begun for him, and the supreme irony of his comment, 'Come on, young man, that's enough excitement for one day.'

Something squirmed in the pit of David's stomach. He said a silent prayer that all would be well.

As they left the bank, Father Seth's all-seeing eyes immediately spotted Jennifer standing by a taxi across the street. They crossed over, dodging traffic, to catch her attention.

'Where is Mrs Gumede?' he asked, pointedly, without greeting her, his mind on the next task of his day.

The housekeeper was alighting from the taxi by the adjacent kerb and heard his question. 'I'm here, Father! What a chance encounter.'

He ignored her light tone. 'Is lunch prepared for the seminarians?' Her happy face turned to one of consternation as she replied, putting her hands together in prayer, 'It is, near enough, but please forgive me, Father, the time has run away with me. Thank God for his intervention. I'll come back with you now.'

'I'm so sorry child, can you get whatever you need tomorrow?' she asked, turning to Jennifer, apologies in her eyes.

'Unfortunately not. I must get it today,' the younger woman replied, unable to prevent her expression betraying the importance of the intended purchase, while unable to elaborate further in front of Father Seth and David.

The priest, immediately grasping the situation, suggested that David should stay with Jennifer, to ensure her safe return to the presbytery, then he and Mrs Gumede could return at once. They all nodded their heads in agreement, Jennifer still pink in the cheeks.

Father Seth asked him for the documents. 'I will take them and leave them on your bed for safety. Do you have the key to your room? I'll lock your door with my master key if you do.'

'Yes, I have my key, Father.' David answered as he handed over the folders. The two couples separated and headed in different directions.

Father Seth called over his shoulder. 'Be back for six at the latest, please. We're having dinner early tonight.'

Chapter 6

Changes

'Let's go then!' Jennifer said as she touched his arm.

His belly rolled. If only she knew how she made him feel. He was sure that if she did, she wouldn't do this to him. Nonetheless, he'd started to enjoy being close to her but decided to say nothing. To tell her might mean that it would stop, and he wanted it to continue.

They walked silently for a while, before she said, choosing her words with care, 'I'm looking for something to wear. A wraparound kind of thing. I don't want to spend too much though, just something I need to make me feel a little more comfortable when I'm not wearing my habit.'

She paused, thinking to herself, have I said too much? Will he pick up on what I'm thinking when he sees what it is I'm buying? She knew her cheeks were even pinker than before.

David said, 'There's Ackerman & Sons,' pointing down the street. 'Oh, is there an Ackerman's here?' she said, delighted at the news.

David repeated what Ethel had said when alighting the taxi outside the bank, his voice almost trembling, 'Thank God for his intervention.'

They both burst out laughing.

'Does Ethel always say that?' asked Jennifer, smiling and adding, 'I like that David, and I like you. You're so nice.'

David felt a wave of sadness overcome him, his thoughts turning from the pleasure of just being in her company to thoughts of her commitment to God and the church. Furthermore, he felt terrible for feeling this way. He was loving just to be near her but realised that would have to be enough. Her vows were important to her, and that was that.

They entered the store.

'Where will we find Ladies' Wear?' she asked. 'Oh, sorry, silly me, how are you supposed to know where Ladies' Wear is?'

He spotted a sign hanging from the ceiling.

'It says the fifth floor,' he said, pointing.

They waited for the lift. As the doors closed behind them, and there were just the two of them in the small space, he started to feel awkward. Ladies' Wear was not a department he'd ever seen, let alone visited. It might have been better for him to wait on the ground floor. Jennifer was thinking precisely the same thing.

The rise to the fifth floor was a silent one as they both dreaded the inevitable. The lift arrived with a slight thud and the doors opened. The embarrassment was immediate as aisle upon aisle of lingerie stretched out before them. He started to feel hot as she began to giggle nervously.

'Oops!' She said in an endeavour to lighten her own sense of discomfort. 'Well here we are. Ladies' wear.'

He grinned. She had broken the ice, and he felt less awkward, though still worried about where this was heading.

A middle aged, white assistant came over to them and, unable to ignore the intriguing sight of a young nun and a young man in the lingerie department, she asked, 'Can I be of any assistance, miss, sir?'

'I hope so,' replied Jennifer. 'But maybe not just here.' She smiled and looked around.

'What are you looking for, dear?' asked the assistant, studying the dynamic between David and Jennifer with each inquisitive look.

'Oh, some comfortable leisure wear,' fibbed Jennifer, hoping that a later diversion to the dressing gown section would help camouflage her concerns of the morning.

'Of course. Is it for yourself or someone else?'

'For me.'

'Follow me please, miss, sir.'

They followed, David still thinking he ought to just disappear and wait downstairs, but Jennifer looked at him and beckoned with her head.

They walked through row upon row of lacy, flimsy things. Jennifer looked straight ahead and began to wish dearly that she'd agreed to come back tomorrow with Ethel, but here they were, an unlikely pairing, so must make the best of it. David kept his eyes on Jennifer's shoulders.

'What about something like this?' said the assistant, once they'd reached safer territory, and passed her a burgundy velour tracksuit. 'It's in the sale.'

Jennifer replied, 'Oh! It's lovely, but I think perhaps it would be a little too warm. Also, er, I'm looking for something more like a dressing gown. I do apologise.'

David breathed a sigh of relief. So that was why they were here.

'That's fine, dear, this way. Here you are dear,' said the assistant, handing her a thick, embroidered pink dressing gown with a floral motif.

Jennifer stared at it.

'Er, not quite what I was looking for,' she said, adding quietly to David, 'but it would suit my friend, Ethel.'

His shoulders shook as he tried to suppress his need to laugh.

'What about this?' asked the assistant, pointing to a more feminine garment in black.

'That's pretty, but a little too… '

'What size, miss? I'd guess 36,' said the assistant, quietly.

'Erm no, I'm a 34,' replied Jennifer, in a whisper.

'I'm just looking at you miss. I'd still say 36,' challenged the assistant, used to judging women's sizes at a glance.

Jennifer's cheeks grew hotter still as she glanced across at David, relieved to see him turning away discreetly. She started to giggle at the increasingly ludicrous situation.

Realising her discomfort, he walked away, casually touching a rail of long, modest, frilly nightdresses with pretend interest, too embarrassed to return any eye contact with either woman, conscious that his shoulders were gently shaking with suppressed laughter.

'Perhaps it would be wise to try some on. You can't return anything you buy in the sale,' advised the assistant.

'Thank you.'

She led Jennifer to the changing room.

'Just wait in there, miss. I'll find you something.'

'Thank you.'

David had now composed himself and stood a little way away from the cubicle. He could just glimpse the hem of Jennifer's habit below the door.

'I think she's trying to find you something. Are you all right? I'm sorry for laughing at you.'

'Don't worry, David. I'm so sorry I dragged you up here in the first place. I won't be long,' said Jennifer, as the assistant returned with a couple of dressing gowns over her arm.

'Try these, there's a 34 and a 36. You can decide what fits best.'

She placed the two pale lemon dressing gowns over the top of the door, and Jennifer started to take off her habit.

Sounds like press-studs, he thought. He cautioned himself. Why am I thinking like this? I mustn't.

He felt he had to escape the vicinity of the cubicle immediately. But before he could act, his eyes were drawn to the space at the bottom of the door.

He watched, entranced, as her habit fell to the floor, revealing her lower legs and ankles. Her hand came over the door as she retrieved the dressing gowns. Her feet turned as she faced the wall of the cubicle.

Oh my God, forgive me, he thought as she moved first her right leg, twisted and repeated the same action with her left.

He walked away before hearing Jennifer tell the assistant, 'You were right, 36 is better, but I'm not sure about the colour.'

The assistant took the garments from her as she handed them over the door and replaced them with three more. Navy blue, orange, and bottle green.

'Here you are miss, try these. They're all size 36.'

He moved well away and walked over to a stand full of dressing gowns, and to give himself something to do, he started to browse them with the barest interest. But as he flicked from one to another, the number 36 appeared to jump out at him and before he knew it, he was back outside the cubicle carrying three dressing gowns. He handed them to the assistant, saying shyly, 'For Sister.'

At that moment, the three Jennifer had just tried on were being returned to the assistant, over the door.

'They're all nice, but a little too thick and warm.'

'Not to worry, try these,' the assistant said.

David's choices were watermarked satin, kimono style with three quarter length wide sleeves, and a tied belt at the waist.

'Oh, these are beautiful, and I love the colours,' said Jennifer, immediately.

He'd chosen cream, lavender, and apricot, having seen and loved these colours for so long in the flower beds of the presbytery garden. The silken material reminded him of the falling petals he was more used to. And he knew she would look beautiful in them.

The familiar sense of guilt was surging inside him. He shouldn't be thinking or feeling these things. He walked away again to compose himself before returning just in time to hear her say to the assistant, 'It's amazing, isn't it? I would never have chosen those for myself, but I love them. I wish I could buy them all. But I've made my choice. Thank you for all your help.'

'You're very welcome, miss,' said the assistant, accepting the accolade.

He was delighted. But he could never tell her that he had been drawn to them for reasons that would cause them both embarrassment.

Jennifer tied her white shoelaces and exited the cubicle.

'How much are they?' she asked.

'Let's go to the till, dear, and I'll scan the barcode.'

'Oh, they're 775 Rand. I'm certain that can't be right, they look much more expensive than that. I must check with my manager. Just wait here please.'

She walked through a doorway behind the tills. Jennifer could hear some muffled discussion coming from the room.

'I'll come out with you and speak to the lady myself,' she heard a voice say. The older assistant returned with a slim young woman of Indian descent. Very pretty too, the thought crossed Jennifer's mind.

'Hello, I'm the manager,' she said, looking first at Jennifer and then down at the garment in her hand. Suddenly Jennifer recognised her. She'd noticed her on the long train journey into Johannesburg. Not wanting to embarrass her, though, she just smiled and said, 'Hello.'

The manager continued, 'I have some good news for you. These are end of range and have been considerably reduced. They're now only 500 Rand.

They were originally on sale for 2,500, but they're beautifully made and of quality satin.'

Jennifer was delighted. 'Oh, yes please,' she said with an enormous smile.

'Which colour?'

'Lavender please, I love them all, but the lavender one is particularly nice.'

'Take your break, Agnes,' said the manager. 'I'll put the transaction through.'

'Thank you', Agnes said, and turning to Jennifer, added, 'Your brother has excellent taste. When he brought them to me and said, for my sister, I thought what a sweet thing to do.'

Her words made him want to shrivel inside. How would Jennifer react to what she had just heard? Would she be angry, would she think his behaviour strange? Choosing satin dressing gowns for her?

Before she had the opportunity to reply, the young manager asked, 'Cash or card?'

'Card, please,' said Jennifer, presenting her RandExchange card.

Having made her purchase, she turned to leave the counter, but the manager's voice made her stop. 'Don't I know you? Didn't we share a cabin on the train from Durban to Johannesburg yesterday morning?'

'Do you know, yes, I think we did,' Jennifer replied, with a smile.

'I thought so! Well, my name is Tanu, and if you need any assistance in the future, please ask for me. I will do anything I can to assist you.'

Gratefully, Jennifer replied, 'Thank you so much Tanu. My name is Jennifer. I will.'

She and David made their way back to the lift.

She turned to him and looked him full in the face. 'My brother! How sweet,' she said with a beaming smile.

He could see that she was comfortable with the idea that he had chosen the dressing gown for her. They entered the lift, alone again. She slid her hand into his elbow and gently folded her fingers into it, and said, 'Thank you so much, David. I couldn't be more pleased.'

It was lunchtime. 'I'm hungry. What about you David?' she asked.

He started to feel anxious since he had no money and didn't want her to know. But, aware of his situation, she said, without waiting for a reply, 'Let me buy you lunch, just to say thank you for helping me today – brother!' She grinned at him. He now felt he should tell her what he'd said, since if he didn't, he would be committing a sin of omission.

'I'm sorry Jennifer, I won't lie to you. I didn't say for my sister, I said for Sister. She must have misheard me.'

She smiled and said, 'Oh, it doesn't matter! You obviously have such excellent taste, and you made a great effort to find something I'm really going to love. I'll always know who to turn to if ever I need a personal shopper.'

They both laughed at the idea.

'Come on,' she said. 'Let's go for lunch. You've earned it, David.'

They exited the lift, and she turned around immediately, leading him back into it and laughing yet again.

'Restaurant, fourth floor - it says so on the sign.' She pressed the button. They exited into the restaurant and found a table.

'What would you like?' she asked, passing him a menu.

He paused to think. 'Just something light, I think. We're having dinner early tonight.'

'Coffee and cake then?'

'Yes please.'

He saw a sign at the other side of the restaurant, indicating toilets, and stairs. An idea flooded into his mind.

'A latte for me, please, and you can surprise me with the cake. I just need to go to the rest room. Please excuse me.'

There were toilets to the left and stairs to the right. He ran upstairs and made his way to the counter of the ladies' wear department. Tanu was serving a customer at the till. She completed the sale and turned to him.

'Can I help you, sir? Oh, hello again!'

He blurted out the words as quickly as he could. 'Hello! Yes, I hope so. I was here with Sister a few minutes ago. My friend, Sister Jennifer, the one you sold the dressing gown to? I wondered if you could put the other two aside, and I will collect them in a few days. But if you should see her again before I come back for them, please don't tell her. They are a gift.'

Tanu smiled. 'Well, she is indeed blessed, isn't she? I'm sure I can do that for you, sir.'

'But there's just one problem. I can't pay anything until I pick them up,' he said nervously.

'Don't worry. I'll put them in my office. Just ask for Tanu when you return to collect them. You can pay then.'

He was delighted, grateful, and not a little excited at the prospect of giving his special purchases to Jennifer.

'Thank you, thank you, thank you!' he said, in utter relief as he turned and walked away.

He ran down the stairs and saw Jennifer's habit as she walked into the ladies' rest room. He swiftly made his way back to the table and sat down, feeling a little breathless and nervous. Not only that, but he couldn't be sure that she hadn't seen him coming onto the landing.

The door opened, and she was making her way back to the table. He was grinning broadly.

'You have a lovely smile David, such a kind face. It's lovely to see you looking so happy.'

He continued to smile uncontrollably. He had a little secret, but she would know soon enough what it was.

The waitress came over with their order.

'Two lattes and two Victoria sponges,' she said, placing the tray on the table.

'Thank you,' they replied simultaneously.

'How was your business meeting?' Jennifer asked.

'A little confusing,' he replied, grimacing at the memory. 'We had an appointment at the bank. I met a man called Mr Verster, he's the manager there, and I think he's a friend of Father Seth.

'Anyway, I had to sign some forms, and they checked my ID.

'Mr Verster gave me some old photos of me and my birth certificate. Father Seth opened an account for me. Well, he gave Mr Verster some money so that I could have my own account.'

Jennifer's eyes widened. David carried on, 'And then he also said something about a salary from the archdiocese, which would be paid every month. So much information to take in, but I have copies of everything and my own account now! Everything is in the folders he's taken back to the presbytery.'

'Wow, that's fantastic, I'm so pleased for you,' she exclaimed, wondering if her comments had had an effect on the priest, but reflecting that, no, there had to have been much preparation in what David had just described.

'A salary? I think you deserve it. From what I understand, you've worked incredibly hard for Father Seth and the archdiocese.'

'I'm a bit nervous about it all. I've never had to manage money before, well, not for myself at least. I've never had my own account, and the responsibility scares me a little,' said David.

Wanting to change the subject and trying to move away from the subject of money, she nodded and said, 'I'd love to see the photos you got from Mr Verster. From what I've learned from Ethel, you were a very cute baby.'

Smiling, he nodded his head and said, 'OK, if you must, but I'm sure I was no different to any other baby as Mrs Gumede finds all babies irresistible'.

Jennifer let his comment hang for a moment or two, looking deep into him.

He felt he could confide a little more of himself. He said, sadly, 'I used to call her Umamkhulu when I was little. It's the Zulu word for aunt. It was our little secret. But Father Seth heard me calling to her one day and said it wasn't appropriate. He always called her Mrs Gumede, so I had to as well from then on.'

'Oh, David, that's so...sad. I'm so sorry. Father Seth can be a bit of a stickler for what's appropriate, can't he? I'm sure Ethel never loved you any the less for it.'

He smiled awkwardly. It was true. Ethel had been his harbour and his anchor, through many storms.

Jennifer smiled and changed the subject, realising the pain her comment might have triggered. 'I know you must love gardening, David. The presbytery garden is delightful, and that doesn't happen by chance. I wouldn't mind spending some time doing that with you if that's all right?' she asked. 'It's just that I'm not allowed to leave the presbytery alone, and it would give me the opportunity to get some fresh air and exercise.'

'Yes, I'd like that.' David responded, hardly able to believe his ears again. What a day this was turning out to be.

She carried on, 'Then we'll start as soon as possible. I'll sort it out with Father Seth, and we can have some time together doing that.

'My vows are about a month away. They haven't set a definite date yet, because Mother Josephine has been ill and I won't be leaving until I've seen the archbishop. But Father Seth had to pick me up over the weekend as he has no free time for a few months now due to his diocesan duties, so you might be stuck with me,' she smiled.

He was relieved to hear her say 'about a month away'. It gave them more time together. But of course, it merely postponed the inevitable.

'What will you do when you've made your vows Sister, erm, I mean Jennifer?'

'I'd like to teach,' she answered. 'I've completed my education in the convent and I qualified as a teacher back at the university in Cape Town. The convent paid for my education from the moment I entered it when I was 14. I owe them and God a lot, along with Father

Seth. They've all been so supportive of me and my journey. I've applied for a posting at a school in Gauteng, which is run and administered by the convent. If I get that position, we'll be able to keep in contact, and I'll be able to visit you and Ethel at the presbytery. I really like Ethel, and you, of course!'

'I'd like that a lot,' he said.

They talked and talked, and the time flew by as his confidence grew.

Then, it was burning in him. He had to say it, utter the words, before this chance was lost.

'I need to say something, but I sometimes find it hard to find the right words...'

She reached out and took his hands in both of hers. Stroking the back of them with her thumbs, she said, looking down at their entwined fingers,

'It's OK, David. Take your time. I'm listening.'

He took a breath and didn't dare look at her. 'I know I've only known you a couple of days, and you might think this is weird, but I feel like I've known you all my life, it's hard to explain, but I feel I can trust you...'

It dawned suddenly on Jennifer that she felt the same. Trust, except in the clergy and the nuns she had encountered in her life, had generally eluded her. She certainly hadn't trusted the many boys and young men who had tried to catch her eye or ask her out when she was a young teenager. But this young man, sitting here, David, was unlike all of them. He had come from very different beginnings. She didn't feel threatened by being close to him but couldn't fully understand why.

He paused and gulped for air. His pent-up thoughts started to tumble into words. It was the strangest feeling for him.

'You seem to understand me better than anyone I've ever met. I know I'm shy and different to others of my age, but it's hard to communicate when you've been brought up like I have, in an unnatural environment.

'I've never even had a friend or been invited to parties or a school friend's house like all the other kids I went to school with. I know most people think I'm odd, but I hope you will always be my friend. You make me feel, er, normal, equal, if you know what I mean, and that makes me feel, well, good.'

'But I also don't want you to feel obliged,' he blurted out, unable to forget his manners.

He raised his head and looked into her deep, serious eyes as tears started to well in them.

She raised a hand and placed it gently on his cheek. 'How could I not want to be your friend? Why would you even think I wouldn't want that? If I'm honest with you, if the world were full of Davids, it would be a much better world.'

She leant forward, dabbed her eyes with a paper napkin and smiling at him, she continued, 'Near or far, I will be your friend. Always.'

He smiled, and whispered to her, 'I will pray for you every day, Jennifer. I'm privileged to have this time with

you, and I will always cherish you and our friendship.'
He could hardly believe the words that were flowing
out of him.

The feelings inside, though, were bittersweet as he
realised he felt something for her he had never
experienced before. Was it love? But he knew that she
could never return his feelings in the way he might
dream of.

His emotions were in turmoil as he felt happiness,
sadness, joy, and despair in equal measure and all at
the same time. But he knew it would be wrong to share
any of that with her. Her happiness was paramount to
him. Yet, he'd only known her for such a short time.
Deep within him he felt torn, an unyielding sense of
desperation awakened as he recognised what he had to
do. He had to suppress this love, and all those feelings.

Seeing his confusion but not able to read what was
causing it and recognising that they had both been
close to tears just a moment ago, she felt it kinder to
move the conversation on.

'Would it be possible to walk around the city, David? I
haven't been here before and would like to find out
more about Jo'burg.'

Relieved, he smiled. He knew easily how to answer this
one. 'I know the perfect place to take you to. Are you
all right with heights?'

'Yes' she answered, intrigued by his question.

They left Ackerman & Sons arm in arm and made the
short walk to the Carlton Centre. The monumental
building, standing over seven hundred feet tall, had

fifty floors. The top floor was dedicated to a panoramic viewpoint across the city. It was dizzying.

They spent the rest of the afternoon gazing out over the city, David pointing out places of interest that they could maybe visit in the weeks to come.

'It's like having my own personal tour guide,' Jennifer interrupted. 'Marry that with personal shopper and gardening instructor, oh and chauffeur, you're going to be exhausted David.' They laughed.

Time stood still as they found in each other an echo of themselves, and a world of discovery. They were like children swirling in a fairy tale.

Eventually a nagging feeling of responsibility made Jennifer look at her watch and, shocked to see that the time had moved on in the blink of an eye, she shrieked, 'It's a quarter past five, David, come, quickly. Where can we get a taxi?'

They made their way to the street and with great relief saw one idling by the kerb. David raised his hand to the driver, who smiled, jumped out and opened the rear door for them They climbed in, saying almost in unison, 'Thank God for his intervention!' and both burst out laughing.

The driver grinned broadly.

'Indeed! That's my mother's favourite saying, too! Where would you like to go?'

'St Brigid's Church, please,' David said hurriedly.

The man at the wheel started to laugh. 'Do you know Mrs Gumede? Ethel?' he inquired.

'Yes,' they both replied, incredulous.

'She's my mama! I'm her eldest son, Simeon.'

David looked at him hard, and then immediately saw the resemblance. Ethel had often talked about her children, and he knew all their names, although he had never met them.

Simeon obviously shared his mother's light touch on life, and laughed with a rich, throaty roar.

They spent the journey talking about her. David asked about each of Simeon's brothers and sisters, curious to know the family story from a different perspective. The journey went in a flash. They arrived outside the church.

'Do you have time for a coffee, Simeon?' David asked as Jennifer reached into her purse.

'No, but thank you,' said Simeon, shaking his head. 'And my mama would kill me if I took money from her friends.' He continued, 'Sorry, I can't accept your invitation for a coffee. I will get in trouble with my boss if I do. But thank you, anyway. Say hello to mama for me, please?' He drove away, waving cheerfully.

As they walked up the drive to the presbytery, she turned to him, squeezing his arm tightly with both hands.

'I've had a lovely afternoon, thanks to you, David. It was really wonderful, and you are obviously a very special person. I think you will always be very dear to me.'

He was dumbstruck. But thankfully there was no time for a response as they entered the presbytery. They had made it just in time for dinner. They went upstairs to their respective rooms to freshen up.

'I'll knock for you on the way down,' she said as they parted on the landing outside his room. She couldn't see as, adoringly, he watched her climb the spiral staircase. Then he tore himself away to quiet his thoughts before she could look back at him.

He entered to find the folders on his bed. He looked at them for a couple of minutes and thought, no, not now. He picked up a hand towel and quickly made his way up the spiral stairs to the bathroom. As he got to the landing, she was leaving it.

On this occasion she was fully clothed, and in her habit. That didn't stop the memory of their morning encounter from entering both their minds.

He went into the bathroom and hurriedly washed his hands and face, physically shaking the memory from his head, then made his way down to his room.

He found her sitting on his bed. It stopped him in his tracks at the doorway.

'I hope you don't mind?' she asked. 'I didn't particularly want to go down to dinner alone with all the visitors here.'

Chapter 7

Dominic

'Of course,' David said, gathering himself as he went to step back out onto the landing. As he did so, he heard the rasping tones of a familiar male voice.

'Well, well, well, are *you* still here?'

David raised his hand in warning to Jennifer as he was half in and half out of his room, indicating to her to stay where she was. She stopped and he closed the door behind him.

She heard muffled conversation on the landing, but couldn't make out what was said. It got quieter as the pair made their way to the bottom of the stairs. She opened the door quietly and peeped out onto the landing. The coast was clear so she slowly made her way to the dining room, wondering what David's warning was for.

'Aah, Sister Jennifer' Father Seth greeted her as the four new guests stood up.

'I've just told the deacons all about you and your aspirations. Please take a seat while they introduce themselves.'

Ethel was sitting at the other end of the table with her back towards the kitchen door, facing Father Seth. The four young men, recently ordained as deacons of the church, were standing either side of him. The position of Jennifer's chair next to Ethel's meant she was directly facing David. She sat down and smiled at everyone in the gathering. The first of the deacons spoke, starting with the one to her immediate left.

'Good evening everyone. I'm Martin Thompson,' said a robust voice. He had a cheerful, boyish smile surrounded by a round fresh face.

Next to him was a shy, slightly built, sickly looking young man. 'G-good evening,' he stammered, obviously nervous. 'I'm Duncan MacDonnell.' He remained standing, gripping the back of the chair.

'Sit down, man,' said the oldest of the group, impatiently. He was standing next to David's chair and had not yet been introduced.

Father Seth looked sternly at him, 'Excuse me?' The deacon was momentarily silenced.

Duncan sat down tremulously as the dark-haired, tanned, young man facing him said gently, 'Good evening everyone, my name is Luigi Bellini. I'm very glad to meet you all.'

Finally came the last and oldest of the four, who had already spoken, but without introduction. He inclined his head towards Jennifer in a meaningful way.

'Hi Jennifer, hi all, some of you for the second time, I'm Dominic Zapatero. As you can probably work out, Jennifer, I was a late calling to the priesthood. I actually used to work in the real world before I joined the God squad.' He smirked at his imagined humour.

Father Seth glowered at the disrespect but decided to keep things as even as possible. He said, 'I'd have

89

expected perhaps a more formal introduction, Deacon Dominic, considering you haven't met Sister Jennifer before. I think I need to speak to Monsignor Prince to increase your training in formal etiquette,' he said, pointedly.

Dominic responded with a mocking nod and sat down.

'David, introduce yourself, please' the priest said, ignoring the deacon's rudeness.

He wasn't expecting this! It had never happened before. David had always been glad to be overlooked. He had never been invited to introduce himself to the deacons or other clerical visitors on previous occasions. He had always been mentioned to them before as David, the parish handyman, and was just a respectful presence in the room. He shifted from foot to foot, nervously. Ethel looked up and willed him on, and Jennifer gave him a kindly smile and almost imperceptibly nodded her head at him. He saw it.

Brief was best. 'Good evening reverend deacons. I'm David Blind. I'm the gardener and handyman here at St Brigid's.'

He started to sit down but Father Seth interrupted. 'David, just tell them a little more about yourself, your hobbies and interests, for example?'

David drew a breath and steeled himself. 'Er, well, apart from the gardening, and a little landscaping, I'm very interested in computers and creating programs and spreadsheets, doing the parish website...that's all,' he ventured before returning to the relative comfort of his chair.

Father Seth explained, 'Actually, David, it's a bit more than that,' he said. Turning to the others he went on, 'I purchased our new parish computer a couple of years ago. We needed to update. So David has completely overhauled our website and created a bespoke spreadsheet for parish financial records. We couldn't find a commercial one to do the job. It's very labour saving and it's fully accepted by the archdiocese when I submit my quarterly and annual returns. It's a marvellous tool and you might all benefit from it in the years to come.'

Everyone looked at David, nodding their heads in admiration. Dominic seemed unimpressed.

Martin commented, 'That's a great skill, David, well done. Has the archdiocese introduced it in all parishes?'

'I don't think so, not yet', he responded, smiling in gratitude at the recognition, his confidence growing.

Father Seth said, 'The archbishop would have to sanction it for all parishes in the archdiocese if he thought it appropriate. As I understand it, it has great potential in centralising the archdiocesan accounts. David has explained its potential to me and I use it to maintain control over my personal finance and accounts too.

'He very kindly set up a copy of it for me, and again, I find it most useful. If he's happy for me to do so, I intend to discuss it with the archbishop when we next meet to see if we can use it for submitting official documents to the state. Who knows, it could be adopted more widely?'

David nodded but said nothing, not wishing to irritate Dominic. Jennifer looked across at him. There was a look in her eye, something he hadn't seen before.

'That's very impressive David, you're obviously multi-skilled and a great asset to the parish and no doubt the archdiocese,' she said.

'Thank you, Je...' Quickly correcting himself, he completed his reply. 'Thank you Sister.'

Luigi asked Father Seth, 'May I ask Sister Jennifer a question?'

'Of course,' he answered, 'But let's first say grace and eat, then we can talk as much as we like. Would you say grace, please, Mrs Gumede?'

Ethel answered without pausing, glad that the food was not going to get any cooler, 'Bless us, O Lord and these thy gifts which we are about to receive from thy bounty. Through Christ, our Lord. Amen.'

She went into the kitchen, returned with a large soup tureen and placed it in the centre of the table. Dominic, seeing that no one was making a move, picked up the ladle and helped himself to a bowlful. She gave out a short sigh of disapproval, to which he was oblivious. Martin politely addressed her. 'Could I get *you* some soup, Mrs Gumede?'

'Thank you', she smiled, passing her bowl. He ladled the soup into the bowl and handed it to Jennifer, who passed it to her.

'Sister Jennifer,' he said, picking up her bowl, 'May I?'

'Thank you.'

He served everyone, leaving himself till last. Dominic watched the proceedings with disinterest as he slurped his own soup and dipped his bread.

When the main course arrived, Martin took charge immediately and served Ethel first, as before. Dominic had to wait his turn, hardly able to control the impatience writ large on his face. Jennifer watched his behaviour with concern for what it might mean in a man who might soon be ministering to needful people.

There was much discussion over dinner and Father Seth made them welcome, using the bonhomie that he seemed to be able to switch on and switch off. The wine and conversation were flowing, much of it about theology, which was only to be expected, but the deacons, bar Dominic, also showed a great deal of interest towards Ethel, in honour of her excellent food and her role within the parish.

In answer to their attention, she regaled and amused them with her anecdotes, talking about the many people who had passed through the doors of the presbytery and church over the years, but was skilled at maintaining their anonymity. Her powers of description were second to none and she had everyone laughing with her stories. Jennifer had tears streaming down her face. She'd realised almost immediately on meeting her that Ethel would be good fun, but even she hadn't laughed so much in years.

Dominic had started to laugh loudly too, fuelled by the amount of red wine he had consumed throughout the evening. Suddenly, without warning, he turned to David and, almost leering, said, 'So David, what motivates you to stay here when you should be out in the world enjoying your youth? You don't drink, presumably, you don't smoke and, presumably, you prefer not to talk to people?'

David looked down at the table, unsure how to respond. Before Father Seth could stop him, the deacon continued, 'But after all, those things are often identifiable in boffins. I've been watching you all evening, and you're quiet, way too quiet, if you ask me. But they do say, don't they, it's the quiet ones...?'

Father Seth interrupted, 'Excuse me Dominic, I'm not sure your question or your presentation of it is appropriate.'

The drunken deacon replied, 'Really? Well, what a pity, perhaps you should contact Monsignor Prince about that too?'

The room held its collective breath.

'It's OK, Father,' David said, and looking Dominic in the eye, he responded, but where the words came from, he didn't quite know. 'You're correct Deacon, I don't drink, I don't like the taste of alcohol, and I don't like how it impacts on the behaviour of those who can't take it.'

Dominic spluttered with scornful laughter.

David wasn't finished. He went on, 'I don't smoke because I don't like the taste or smell of tobacco either, and I don't usually say anything until I have something constructive to say. It's been my youthful, experience as people I respect have always told me...that it's the empty vessels that make the most sound.'

The room listened in astonishment.

'So, if my silence and other behaviours are boffin-like, then a boffin I must be. As for your comment about the quiet ones...well, I apologise, because I can't answer that as the question is too indeterminate. But, if you'd care to narrow it down a little, I'll endeavour to answer it for you.'

Duncan snorted through his nose as he failed in his attempt to stop himself from laughing at David's polite but scouring putdown.

'Shut up MacDonnell,' Dominic retorted aggressively.

David looked across the table at Jennifer, at first embarrassed at his outburst to Dominic's comments and questions. He wondered what she might think. Her slow, deliberate reaction was one he hadn't expected at all, as she lifted her napkin to her left cheek to cover a silently mouthed 'Wow!' in his direction. It was accompanied by the most encouraging smile he had ever seen, and her sparkling eyes seemed to be filled with pride on his behalf.

Dominic, unaware of how ridiculous he had sounded, looked across the table to Jennifer.

'So Jen,' he said, sarcastically, 'What name do you intend to take when you take your vows?' he slurred.

'I prefer to be called Jennifer, actually, but I hope to be Sister Magdalena,' she replied politely.

He started to laugh.

'Magdalena? Oh well, that *is* interesting. Do you feel a sense of affiliation to the Magdalene via the scriptures, or is it in recognition of, how shall we say, any earthly misdemeanours?'

Flicking his hand dismissively, he added, 'Ignore the question. The answer is quite obvious.'

'ENOUGH!' bellowed Father Seth, his eyes nearly popping out of his head.

Jennifer sat still and silently stared at Dominic.

Ethel stood up, eyes blazing, and, putting her hands on Jennifer's shoulders, said, 'Come, child,' and guided her into the kitchen.

Still laughing, Dominic continued, 'Come on, Sister, you can drop the pretence, I'm sure you're more worldly wise than that. Girls of experience always are. Either way, I'd be more than happy to enlighten you?'

'Take him to his room,' Father Seth growled.

The other deacons stood and assisted Dominic to his feet. He started to resist and swore at them. Duncan soon realised he was of little assistance and stood back, aghast.

'David, help them,' ordered Father Seth.

David was much stronger than his skinny frame made him appear. Many years of sawing wood and digging in the hard earth of the large presbytery grounds had seen to that. He calmly stood to assist them, quickly taking hold of Dominic's left arm, which was flailing around. He gripped his wrist and bent the arm up his back causing obvious pain.

Dominic complied almost instantaneously, and David, along with the three deacons, escorted him to his room, where he slumped on the bed in a drunken state.

Father Seth raged to his study as David and the young men returned downstairs to the dining room.

David immediately knocked on the kitchen door.

'Who is it?' said Ethel.

'It's David.'

'Let him come in,' he heard Jennifer whisper.

'Come in David, alone, please, but please come in,' said Ethel.

David entered the kitchen and closed the door behind him.

'I need to speak to Father,' said Ethel. 'But before I go, I saw that fool enter the dining room with you, David. Did he say anything to you?'

David didn't reply.

Ethel went on, 'What an obnoxious young man. I've never seen such bad behaviour. I remember him last year, and Father Seth had to keep reining him in, but at least he didn't get drunk. But as I recall, he was very rude to you then, David. His behaviour is obviously getting worse. Tonight was like having dinner with the devil. Did he say anything to you on your way down to dinner?' Her instinct was telling her he had.

'Yes. I saw him on the landing this evening, and we spoke on the way down,' David began reluctantly.

'Was he rude to you? What did he say?'

'He started by asking me was I still here? Wasn't it time I went out into the world and stopped leeching off the church and Father Seth? I didn't see the point of answering him. I could see he was hoping to carry on where he left off last year.'

Ethel was blazing with anger. 'Stay with Jennifer,' she said.

Ethel went straight into Father Seth's study without knocking. He was on the phone talking to Monsignor Prince.

'Not now, Mrs Gumede!' he bellowed.

'I'm sorry, Father, I must.' They heard her voice rise a tone or two. She closed the study door behind her with a firm, furious hand. They could then hear muffled, raised voices coming from the study. The sound in the dining room was similar, as the disgusted deacons discussed Dominic's antics. It all went on for some time.

'Oh, please, no,' Jennifer said, raising her head. 'The last time I heard anything like that, it was my parents arguing.' Her eyes suddenly filled with tears, and a tiny sob broke through. It wasn't what Dominic said that had hurt her. It was the memory of her young childhood. David stood by her awkwardly, not knowing what to do. He found her a tissue and waited for her to recover her composure.

'I'm really sorry about all this...' he said.

'You mustn't be,' she replied, smiling, and gratefully using the tissue. 'Dominic obviously isn't suited for the priesthood. And my tears are not about him. It's the arguments, like my parents used to have. Then my Daddy left when I was seven. I don't suppose I've ever got over it.'

David wanted to put his arms around her, to comfort and protect her, but something held him back.

Ethel returned to the kitchen with a wry look on her face. She said, 'Those poor boys out there, they looked terrified of me when I came back through the dining room.'

The three of them managed a weak smile.

Chapter 8

Standoff

Father Seth walked into the kitchen. 'I need to speak to you, Sister Jennifer,' he said in a business-like way.

'Not now, Father,' Ethel responded. 'Can't you see the child is still upset?'

The priest ignored her. 'I need to speak with her, and I need to do it now.'

David started to feel rage building inside him. He knew it was a danger sign. He rarely let such anger reach his consciousness, not in the presence of others, at least.

***

The last time it had happened was two years earlier. He was gardening in the grounds of the church when he noticed a couple of men in a shady, secluded corner and walked over to see what they were doing.

As he got closer to them, one of them, rough-looking, heavily tattooed and snarling, turned to him and told him to go away in expletives. The other a younger, painfully thin man with a white face, deeply sunken eyes and drawn cheeks, looked terrified, blood trickling from his nose and tears streaming down his bruised face.

'Go away, if you know what's good for you!' the first man hissed.

'I have no intention of going away. What's going on?' asked David.

'It's nothing to do with you. I've warned you, now go away.'

The man turned to him, brandishing a baseball bat in his raised hand and started to move towards him, swinging it at his head. David ducked and punched him hard in the groin, disabling him. The other man turned and ran off.

The next thing David remembered was Father Seth pulling him away, the tattooed man's face covered in blood and the realisation that he had almost beaten him unconscious.

'Stop it, stop it, boy! You're going to kill him.'

It was enough to bring him to his senses. The priest ordered him to return to the presbytery, turned to assist the man and as he did so he kicked out and made his way to his feet and ran away.

Father Seth had returned to the presbytery and asked David in an accusatory tone, what on God's earth had happened?

'Look at the CCTV in the sacristy, Father. You'll find what you're looking for on that,' David had quietly replied. His rage spent, he was his former self once more.

Father Seth went into the sacristy and looked at the recording. He returned without a word to the presbytery and called the police.

The attacker was known to them. He was a drug dealer in the city, and this was how he dealt with those in debt. He'd almost killed three of his victims, but none would give evidence against him. David's momentary, instinctive actions and the CCTV had solved their case for them.

***

There was something of a standoff developing in the kitchen.

'Now is not the time, Father,' David said, quietly, looking straight at him, and moving in front of Jennifer.

Father Seth continued, his voice raised and his eyes blazing, 'I said I need to speak to Sister Jennifer...'

David interrupted, 'Not now, Father.'

Father Seth glared at him, his face starting to contort with anger, but he was suddenly aware of the lack of fear in David's eyes.

Father Seth's instinct immediately told him that it would be unwise to challenge it. He, too, remembered the incident in the garden, and the realisation of what could be beneath the surface in David, should he feel intensely enough. A steely cold shiver ran down his spine. He was momentarily thrown off course, not a feeling he was used to. It was evident that David was prepared to protect Jennifer regardless of potential cost to himself. The priest recognised it might be wiser in the present moment to return to his study and deal with the situation later.

The three of them waited in silence for a few moments until they heard the door close.

The housekeeper said under her breath, 'He had that coming, David, and so had Dominic. You did the right thing.'

David took a deep breath, recognising that he might just have overcome the bully of his youth.

'I'm so sorry,' Jennifer said as she recognised the side of Father Seth that she'd seen only briefly before, in his authoritarian way of dealing with people, but not like this, in its cold, calculating entirety. She looked up into David's eyes.

She immediately saw the change. The sad eyes were now bright and full of vitality. It was as though a dark shadow had lifted from the young man standing before her.

'We never know what tomorrow will bring, but the unpleasantness of tonight seems to have cleared something in this house. Thank God for his intervention,' said Ethel, gently.

Hearing her deliver her favourite sentence, David and Jennifer looked at each other and smiled at the comfort it brought them. Jennifer relaxed and gently moved away from David, saying, 'We met your son, Simeon, this afternoon, Ethel.'

'Ah, did you?' Ethel beamed. 'My Simeon, he's a good boy; he looks after his mama and his whole family so well.'

She shook her head. 'But it's not been easy for him growing up, no more than yourself, David,' she said as she looked away for a few seconds, as though examining a distant landscape.

She felt the time to explain might be now. David had always known Ethel was a widow of many years but had never questioned her for the details.

'Simeon was only eleven, you know, when his Baba, my Dingane, was taken away by the police. I don't suppose I've ever told you the full story, have I, David?'

David shook his head. He and Jennifer knew this was another important moment for Ethel. They listened in complete silence.

'His body was found three days later. He was shot through the back of the head,' she said.

They looked at her in horror. No, they could never have imagined that this had been Ethel's personal story. David had heard all her anecdotes, sometimes many times over, but he would never have guessed that she was guarding such a personal sorrow.

'There was no justice back then,' Ethel continued. 'Black people went missing all the time, some of them, like Dingane, would be found, but many were never reunited with their families, alive or otherwise.

'I'm lucky. At least I know where my Dingane is on earth, and I will see him one day in heaven. He was a good, just man, who tried to help people and do what was right. The African National Congress employed him, you know. His job was to try to find those who had gone missing during apartheid.'

Ethel suddenly smiled. 'His name's from the Zulu and it means *one who is searching*. Suited him so well. He was always searching for a better life for his family, as well as looking for those poor souls whose lives were taken.'

David and Jennifer shared a look of pain. They both knew well the evils of apartheid and the struggle to establish the new South Africa, even though they were just babies when the new state was established.

Ethel continued her story. 'Although Mr Mandela had been released from prison, people were still going missing. It was a terrible time. Dingane found out that some government officials, you know, high up people, women included, had been involved in many murders of black people.

'I think they knew that he was on to them and they silenced him. We never knew who was responsible. But it was all over the newspapers and TV at the time.'

Ethel sighed deeply at the memory. 'I was at home one day with the children, just after we lost him. I was in despair. I didn't know how I was going to manage to bring them up. I could hardly manage just surviving from day to day.

'Anyway, there was a knock at the door. It was Father Seth.' David's eyebrows shot up.

'You see, he had read about Dingane's murder and the fact that he'd left a wife and five children. The cameras were outside my house and reported his visit on the news that night.

'He told me later that he'd come to see me to offer his condolences, but when he realised there was no longer a breadwinner in the house, he offered me the housekeeper's job here at the presbytery. He'd been without one for a while.

'I remember saying to myself as I lay in bed that night in my grief, thank God for his intervention. Life has been tough, even so, working here and bringing up my kids, but I was lucky, I had the means to provide for them, thanks to God and Father Seth.'

Jennifer went to Ethel and they wept and hugged each other, united in grief, Jennifer feeling that hers was small compared with the magnitude of Ethel's suffering and struggle. David longed to join them, but something held him back, his usual reserve, but he could see the bond between the two women was growing, and he took comfort in that. One of the women had always been the most important in his life, and the other was growing in importance daily.

'Enough, child,' Ethel said. 'I have a lot to be thankful for. I have good family and a job I love, well, most of the time,' she smiled.

Sensing that the world was beginning to open up for him, in ways he could not have imagined, David said, 'Well, Simeon is a gentleman, Ethel. I'd like to meet your other children one day, too. I think I might be able to find the opportunity now.'

Ethel started to laugh. 'And my grandkids! I have eight of them you know. Dingane would be so proud.'

'How old are you, Mrs Gumede?' asked David, wondering why he didn't already know.

'You must call me Ethel now. You're all grown up, David, and Jennifer calls me Ethel.'

She went on, chuckling, 'Don't tell Father Seth. I'm 60 next birthday, so getting on a bit, but I love my job here and I don't know what I'd do with all that time on my hands if he made me retire.'

'Well,' Jennifer said, 'you look much younger than that, Ethel. I'm 21, and if I ever become as great a lady as you, I will be very proud.'

'You're a very great lady for sure, Mrs...Ethel. You always have been,' David said, his love and admiration plain to see. She was the nearest thing he'd ever had to a mother.

'And of course, so are you, Jennifer', he added, shyly, feeling that to say nothing at this point would be impolite.

Ethel said, 'She is indeed, and a beautiful one at that, I should add.'

David nodded his head smiling, but hardly daring to glance back at Jennifer.

'I'd better check on the deacons', Ethel said, with a mock grimace, as she opened the door to the dining room.

The three young men, still seated at the table, jumped up as she entered. Jennifer and David, from behind her, started to smile at their obvious concern, and Jennifer said, 'It's OK. She won't harm you.' Duncan smiled and said, 'Are you all right, Sister?'

'I'm perfectly fine, thank you, Duncan,' answered Jennifer. 'They were just words when all is said and done.'

'We're all so sorry,' said Luigi. 'His behaviour was despicable and unforgivable.'

'All is forgivable in God's eyes,' replied Jennifer, almost mechanically. Something nagged at her. She was starting to be acutely aware that as unpleasant as Dominic had been, he had touched a nerve within her.

Why *had* she wanted to take the name of the Magdalene? She knew, deep down, that she must identify with the 'fallen woman' of the Gospels, the woman whose life was changed by her need of Jesus. Jennifer had so far run miles from any romantic involvement in her life, but was that because she was afraid of its power over her, that perhaps if she gave in to her deepest feelings, she might have followed a different course?

She'd always told herself that she didn't need love, romantic or physical. But was it more, perhaps, that she didn't trust herself? She knew many boys and men had found her attractive. Some of them made it obvious. It was embarrassing. She knew she had pushed them away. It felt safer that way. Losing her father so young had damaged her trust, and she had always recognised that. All of this was something she needed to understand about herself if she were to take her vows in the full understanding of what she was sacrificing and what she was giving to a life of faith.

Damn Dominic. He had thrown her into this turbulence with his taunting. It was almost like he could see through her. She needed to pray, and soon…

'Well, providing there is repentance,' stated Duncan, cutting through her thoughts and bringing her back into the room. Jennifer nodded at his wise words.

'Now, who would like a drink?' Ethel asked, changing the subject as David and Jennifer came back to the table.

'Sit down please Mrs Gumede. I'll do it, I'll make us all coffee,' said Martin.

'Thank you,' she said, gratefully obeying. He made his way into the kitchen and found the percolator, opening cupboard after cupboard to find the coffee and the cups and saucers. He knew how to make good coffee.

They all drank it together while Ethel took a cup into the study for Father Seth.

She was in there with him for some time. He'd asked how Jennifer was and commented with displeasure that David had disobeyed him.

That was when Ethel decided it was now, or never.

She took a deep breath and said, 'What I'm about to say, Father, I say as your friend and, I hope, as your equal.'

He looked up at her, surprised, but respecting this woman's service of many years, he nodded and allowed her to continue.

'You sometimes have a remarkably staid and, dare I say it, strict approach to life, Father, and that can influence your judgement. But, in my opinion, David did exactly the right thing because he saw the need of another human being.

'In many ways, it is like your approach to my situation when I lost my husband all those years ago.'

Father Seth thought for a moment and replied, 'The circumstances are quite different, Mrs Gumede, and I am a little concerned about how he stood in front of her when I asked to speak with her. It was inappropriate, and it seemed he was taking advantage of the situation.'

Ethel looked at him askance.

He carried on. 'I must consider what needs to be done for the church's good and Sister Jennifer's vocation. I have informed Monsignor Prince of the incident earlier this evening, and he has assured me that Deacon Dominic will be offered all necessary support and assistance.'

Ethel knew she had to defend David from Father Seth's inference.

'I encouraged David to look after her,' she butted in. 'So, if you disapprove of what you saw, then maybe it's me you need to question. Not everything is as clear as it may at first appear, and I say again, Father, he did nothing wrong.

'And as for bringing into question Jennifer's vocation, well, nonsense, but I think Deacon Dominic may already have done that with regards to himself. But... I'm sure he will just be offered confession, and that will be that. Disgraceful.'

Father Seth said nothing, so there was no stopping her now. Her tone became more defiant. 'Jennifer's a good girl and an asset to the church. She deserves your loyalty. Your issues with David are about losing control of him, and that is something *you* need to deal with.

'Life is hard and unfair, but for some more than others, Father. Don't lose sight of that fact. You can have a strong and meaningful bond with him. He's a fine young man now and has been your whipping boy for far too long.'

Father Seth was startled at her boldness, but still said nothing, and listened with growing interest at Ethel's analysis.

'Yes, I know,' continued Ethel. 'I've seen more than anyone how you've treated him over the years, and had he been weaker in spirit, he may not still be here.'

She paused to let her words ring in Father Seth's ears.

'Do you comprehend me? Don't view his capacity for love, loyalty and compassion as a weakness. He has much to offer, not just to supply you with his labour, but as a man in his own right.

'We are all equal in the eyes of God, but it would appear in the eyes of men, that some are more equal than others. God knows I've experienced that for most of my life. Any suppression of one by another is wrong. We both know that to be true.'

Father Seth stared at her. He watched, silently as she stood up.

As she left the study, she turned to him with her parting shot, 'Give it some thought, please, Father, and make the decision that God would expect you to.'

He sat at his desk for a long time, thinking deeply, furrows in his brow and anger in his soul at the challenges he had just received.

Pressing his fingernails hard into the desk, he decided on his course of action.

He went from his study and into the dining room.

'Go to your rooms!' he barked.

The deacons and Jennifer stood up obediently and started to make their way to their rooms. Knowing Dominic was still in the presbytery, sleeping off his drink, David followed and escorted Jennifer to her room in the loft.

He told her, 'Bolt your door, Jennifer. I wouldn't put anything past our drunken guest. I will leave my door open tonight, and if you need me, just shout.'

He heard her bolt the door and made his way downstairs to the dining room. He entered to find Ethel putting on her coat. As she did so, she said, 'Forgive me, Father, and forgive me for saying this again, but you have a moral responsibility to get this right. I'll see you in the morning, Father. Goodnight.' She left the presbytery.

Father Seth turned to David as he closed the door.

'How, dare, you,' he said, glaring, slowly stressing the words.

David stood his ground and looked the priest in the eye.

'We will talk in the morning, Father. I suggest you send the deacons back to the seminary when they've had breakfast,' he said, and calmly exited the dining room.

'Goodnight Father,' he added, politely, as he started to walk upstairs.

Chapter 9

Apologies

David made his way up to his room. There lying on his bed were the two files he'd received from Mr Verster earlier in the day. It seemed an age ago.

He momentarily contemplated his feelings in the restaurant and the experiences of the evening, and how they'd made him realise that emotions were a foreign place to him. He had suppressed them all his life.

He was beginning to accept that they were something likely to be awakened without warning, and that scared him. His thoughts immediately turned to Jennifer.

He left his room closing the door behind him and quietly made his way up to the loft. He gently knocked on the door to her room. He heard her worried voice, 'Who is it?'

'It's David,' he answered in a whisper. 'I've just come up to see if you're all right and to see if you need anything before you go to sleep.'

He heard the bolt slide from its keep and she slowly opened the door. The room was dimly lit by the reading lamp on the desk.

'Hello,' she said with a warm smile on her face, which was still surrounded by the white halo of her wimple, her body hidden behind the door.

David reiterated, in case she hadn't heard, 'I'm sorry to disturb you, but I was just wondering if you needed anything?'

'You'd better come in,' she whispered.

He entered the room, and she closed the door behind him. He stood facing away from her as he didn't know what state of dress she was in.

'It's OK,' she said. 'You can turn around. I'm decent!'

She stood before him in her habit looking more radiant than ever in the dim light. Aware of her vulnerability in the current situation, he said, 'Maybe it's better to leave your door wide open for now, just in case anyone...' He didn't need to finish the sentence. She opened the door fully and he stepped into the doorway.

She quickly replied, 'Of course, you're right. I need to shower and get ready for bed, and I'm concerned about leaving my room alone after what happened earlier, but it would be totally inappropriate to ask you to stay here while I do that.'

'Yes, I agree. It's a ridiculous situation, but go for your shower, and I'll sit at the bottom of the stairs until you've finished.'

He left her room and opened the door of the bathroom and checked inside to check the room was empty.

He went downstairs and sat on the bottom step. He heard her leave her room, close the door, and go into the bathroom, locking the door behind her.

He heard the shower, and her occasional movements, and tried to banish the thoughts of her crowding his mind.

He looked at his watch as he heard the bathroom door being unlocked. It was five minutes to midnight.

'All done! Thank you, David,' she whispered, from the top of the spiral staircase.

'Bolt your bedroom door,' he replied from the bottom of the stairs.

'I will, of course! Goodnight, dear man,' she whispered loudly.

'Goodnight,' he replied, secretly loving her term of affection, new to his ears, and the feeling it gave him.

He walked across the landing and entered his room, leaving the door open, sat down on his bed, and a sense of unease came over him again. He still felt worried about what the night might have in store and made the decision to stay awake.

As he switched off the light in his room, there was a noise on the landing. He went to the doorway but breathed more easily as he saw it was just Father Seth going into his room.

The priest had turned off the landing light, leaving the presbytery in complete darkness.

David sat in the shadows of his room, fighting his need for sleep, but thinking all the while about Jennifer and the wonderful hours they had shared together. He just wanted to be with her again, laughing and enjoying the silly little things that had amused them earlier.

It was nearly half past two, and he was becoming drowsy, when he heard a door open down the landing. His heart pounding, he stood quickly and made his way quietly to the doorway of his room in the pitch blackness, bracing himself, adrenaline coasting through his veins. He felt sick, his muscles tensing, his hands clenched.

There was no question of what he was prepared to do, should he consider it necessary to protect her. He could hear the muffled sound of someone creeping down the landing.

Would it be best to stay in his room and wait to see what happened, or go out onto the landing and confront the person? He couldn't decide for the moment. But it was too dark to make a positive identification and the potential risk was too great. He heard the footsteps get louder and faster as they moved towards his room, so he stepped out onto the landing as quietly as he could and switched the landing light on outside his bedroom door, just in time to see Dominic step onto the first step of the spiral staircase. The deacon saw him and jumped out of his skin.

'Where are you going?' demanded David.

'I am going to apologise to Jennifer for my behaviour earlier in the evening,' answered Dominic, with his customary sneer.

'I don't think that's a good idea at two thirty in the morning, do you? Go back to your room,' David said firmly.

'I'm just going to apologise to Jennifer first,' Dominic answered, squaring up and looking David full in the eyes.

'No, you're not,' David said in a more challenging tone. 'It isn't fair to wake her to make yourself feel better, so go back to your room.'

'I'm going to speak…' Dominic was interrupted by Father Seth coming out onto the landing to see what was going on.

'What's all the noise about?' he asked quietly, so as not to disturb the others still sleeping.

Dominic responded before David could get a word out, 'I heard a noise and came out to find David going up to Jennifer's room, Father.' The priest turned to look at David, furious.

'That's a lie!' said a voice at the other end of the landing. It was Luigi.

'I heard a noise on the landing a few minutes ago, Father. Not to put too fine a point on it, I was concerned that something like this might happen, so I left my door ajar and sat awake on the chair in my room. I sat and watched for a while, but it was so dark after the landing light was switched off, I couldn't see anything, so I just sat and listened. It was obviously the right thing to do. 'Also, when David came up to bed, the light was still on and he did go up to Sister Jennifer's room.'

Father Seth turned a quizzical eye on David and then back to Luigi. 'What then?' he asked.

Luigi answered, 'I made my way to the bottom of the spiral staircase. I could hear them talking, and I heard their conversation quite clearly, Father.'

David started to feel uneasy and was concerned that the deacon had heard him go into Jennifer's room.

Father Seth asked, 'And what did you hear?'

'I wrote it down when I returned to my room, Father.'

Luigi, self-appointed policeman of the hour, pulled a piece of paper out of his pocket and read from it in a monotone.

'I heard Sister Jennifer say, "I need to shower and get ready for bed, and I'm concerned about leaving my room alone after what happened earlier, but it would be totally inappropriate to ask you to stay here while I do that.".'

'And David replied, "Yes, I agree. It's a ridiculous situation, but go for your shower, and I'll sit at the bottom of the stairs until you've finished".'

David marvelled at his verbatim recollection.

Luigi added, 'I heard David coming downstairs, so I made haste back to my room.'

'Is there anything else, Deacon Bellini?' asked Father Seth, sternly.

'Yes, Father. About fifteen minutes later and back in my room, I heard Sister Jennifer's muffled voice but couldn't make out what she said. I then heard David reply, "Bolt your door".'

'I then heard Sister Jennifer's muffled voice again, but again couldn't make out what she said, but I heard David's reply.'

'Which was what?'

'"Goodnight" was his reply, Father.' The deacon hesitated, as if about to say something more.

'Anything else to report, Deacon?'

'Yes,' said Luigi, solemnly.

He continued, 'He, that is, David, went to his room. I watched him go in. I kept watching for about half an hour or so. During that time, you came up to your room, Father, and switched off the landing light. There was no other movement. Not until I heard someone coming out onto the landing a few minutes ago. I was just about to challenge the person when the light was switched on, and David challenged him. I then realised it was Dominic.'

'Thank you Deacon,' said Father Seth, nodding his head in approval.

'Deacon Dominic, have you anything to say?'

'I just wanted to apologise to her, Father,' said Dominic in a wheedling tone.

'Then why did you lie to me?' snarled the priest. Dominic didn't answer.

'David, is there anything you'd like to add to Deacon Luigi's account?'

'No, thank you Father, Deacon Luigi's account is accurate. I have nothing to add.'

Turning to Dominic with thunder in his eyes, Father Seth said, 'Go back to your room Deacon. We work on trust in the presbytery, but I don't feel I can trust you, so I will be locking your door when you're back in there.'

Dominic turned to walk away, looked back with scorn and disgust, then returned silently to his room. Father Seth went into his own room to find the master key for Dominic's bedroom door, returned to the landing and, checking Dominic was in the room, he locked the bedroom door.

'Thank you, gentlemen, get some sleep. I'll see you both at breakfast in the morning. Goodnight.'

'Goodnight, Father,' they replied, glad to be dismissed from duty.

Jennifer was fast asleep, and thanks to her bed being away from the door and tucked under the eaves, she hadn't heard a thing.

She woke in the morning later than usual. It was a quarter past six, and the dream that had kept her asleep was vivid in her memory.

In her dream state she'd been in front of a full-length mirror looking down at her habit. As she inspected it, touched it, she realised it was made of cream, watermarked satin from shoulder to toe and the wimple was made of the same satin material but in apricot. There was a sash of lavender satin worn diagonally from her right shoulder to her left waist.

The effect it had on her was discomforting, but the colours were beautiful. Feeling foolish, and still in the dream, she turned from the mirror and paced the room, stroking the satin, wondering what she was meant to do and why she was dressed like that...

She heard a noise. A note had been slid under her door. Now fully awake, she left her bed to pick it up nervously and opened it. It was in Father Seth's handwriting.

Dear Sister Jennifer,

I hope you slept well after the turmoil last night. Hopefully, you are unaware of the incident in the early hours of the morning. However, I write to advise you that you have no need to concern yourself about Deacon Zapatero. He is securely confined to his bedroom, and he will be taking breakfast alone this morning. Please do not discuss this with anyone until I have spoken to you.

I will ask Mrs Gumede to accompany you to a meeting with me at 7:30 am in my study. Please remain in your room and only come down to meet her at 7:25 in the dining room.

She will be aware that you have been asked to do so.

Breakfast has been delayed until 8 am to facilitate our meeting, and I have asked the other three deacons to remain in their rooms until then. They are all safe and well.

Please be assured of my heartfelt prayers.

Father Seth

A sense of panic overcame her, and she was immediately concerned about David. She was indeed unaware of any incident prior to reading the note, but the only person Father Seth hadn't mentioned was David. She started to worry. Was this a sign that something had happened to her dear friend at the hands of Deacon Dominic?

The time dragged slowly. She got dressed and prayed like never before, asking that David be safe and secure.

With a minute to spare she made her way downstairs to the landing of the first floor, her eyes wide open and scanning every inch of its fabric, looking for assurance that David was safe and well. The door of his bedroom was closed, as were all the others on the landing.

She contemplated knocking at the door but felt afraid to do so in case he didn't answer, and anyway, to knock, she thought, would be an act of disobedience. Everything looked in order. There was nothing out of place, but none of this gave her reassurance.

She made her way down the wide staircase, and again everything looked perfectly normal.

She turned slightly left at the bottom of the staircase, and with an increasing sense of unease, made her way into the dining room.

'Good morning child,' said Ethel, with a smile. 'I've been waiting for you.'

'Has Father Seth mentioned anything about David?' Jennifer asked, showing Ethel the note.

Ethel read the note carefully and said, 'No dear, have faith, I'm sure he is fine, but Father needs to be more careful in what he writes.' She tutted.

It was time now, and they made their way to the study. Ethel knocked on the door.

Father Seth responded, 'Come in.'

Ethel opened it and let Jennifer pass. 'Take a seat please, both of you,' he said, his face looking strained and tired.

'Is David OK? Tell me please Father, is David...?' asked Jennifer, trying to restrain her anxiety.

'He's fine, at least he was when I spoke to him at six o'clock this morning,' the priest replied calmly. 'Why are you so concerned about him?'

Jennifer blurted out, 'Your note, Father, it's your note.' She handed it to him.

He scanned it. 'Oh, yes, I see Sister, I see what you mean. I'm sorry, that was insensitive of me. I assure you, he's fine.'

'I see our conversation last night had some positive effect Father, and thank you for your consideration,' said Ethel. 'It's a difficult time for Jennifer. There, child, I told you to have faith,' she said, stroking her shoulder.

Turning to Father Seth, she said, 'So, the incident in the early hours, Father, what happened? Please explain and...please, please be sensitive,' added Ethel, nodding her head towards Jennifer.

Father Seth gave a full, concise account of the incident and what had unfolded in the early hours of the morning.

'So, may I ask, what are your intentions and what do you propose to do, Father?' asked Ethel.

He answered, 'I'm in an extremely difficult position. No law has been broken, and we can't assume that any law was likely to have been.

'Dominic has adhered to my request and has remained in his room since the incident in the early hours. But I must acknowledge that he didn't really have any alternative as I locked him in there. That could raise some potential issues for me should he consider it necessary to report it to the police, but I would argue that considering the events, I had no alternative, and I don't believe he would want to bring his own behaviour to the attention of the authorities.

'He has displayed a propensity for disobedience, and his comments made at dinner last night were inappropriate at best, but I feel the church has a responsibility to offer some means of intervention for both you and him, Sister Jennifer. It is a sad and sorry affair, but I fear my hands are tied.'

'I understand,' Jennifer said. 'But I have some concerns Father,' she added, her voice wavering.

Father Seth ploughed on, ignoring her, 'I have spoken to Monsignor Prince, who has reassured me that he will work with Deacon Dominic in an endeavour to help him address his issues. There has been no formal written complaint from anyone, and I would suggest that any formal complaint that is deemed to be unfounded may put the complainant's vocation into question. I personally find that abhorrent, but I must warn you of any potential outcome. That is my duty.'

Ethel was getting increasingly angry and said, 'If Jennifer decided to make a formal complaint, then surely the weight of evidence would be enough to prove her case.'

He replied, 'Anyone present last night is at liberty to make a complaint. However, everyone must consider their own position. Nonetheless, if a complaint were to be made, then a full investigation would have to be completed, and my own experience tells me that it would be extremely uncomfortable for everyone concerned. So, please consider all the options.'

Ethel could hold her tongue no longer. 'Presumably his disrespect of women, formally or informally, drunk or sober, makes this man an ideal candidate for the priesthood!' she exploded.

Jennifer, looking up in alarm, moved into her usual role of peacemaker. She said, to Ethel, gently, 'I think Father is just trying to advise us to think this through properly before making a decision, Ethel. I'm sure he will have a conversation with everyone, including Dominic, to reinforce the position of the church. He has a duty to do that,'

'You're a better person than me, Jennifer,' Ethel replied, raising her eyes in a heavenly direction.

Father Seth asked if there was anything further they wished to discuss and, when they shook their heads, ended the meeting saying, 'If you feel you need any further discussion or pastoral assistance, then please don't hesitate to come and see me.'

The women obediently left the study and went into the dining room.

'Well, I'm disgusted,' said Ethel, frowning and shaking her head. 'The church needs to sort out its insensitive approach to situations such as this. It leaves the likes of you in an untenable position. It's unforgivable.'

Seeing Jennifer's placatory expression, she threw up her hands and added, 'Oh, I know, I know, everything is forgivable in the eyes of God.'

Shaking her head again and tutting, she said, in a tone of resignation, 'Now, come child, let's eat.'

Just then, the three deacons came into the dining room, followed closely by David.

They all said quiet good mornings as they saw each other.

'Help yourselves to food,' said Ethel, 'The percolator is on, and I will make tea for anyone who prefers it.'

They sat down and started to eat. Father Seth entered the room and asked Ethel to take breakfast up to Dominic, saying tersely, 'He's in Room 4.'

Martin stood up as Father Seth went back to his study. 'I'll come with you, Mrs Gumede,' he said.

'No need, I can put him in his place if I need to. I have five children of my own, and they all know about the wrath of Mama. He is the one in danger if he decides to be foolish.'

'But Ethel?' Jennifer responded in concern.

'But nothing Sister, I'll put him on his silly backside if he starts anything.'

The dining room erupted into laughter.

'Oh, well, if you're sure,' said Jennifer with a smile.

'Oh, I'm sure child, trust me, I'm sure!'

They all listened from the dining room as Ethel made her way up to Room 4, unlocked the door and opened it. Dominic, hearing her, walked over towards her.

Ethel fixed him with a stare. 'Sit at the table facing me, and I'll bring it to you, keep your hands on the table where I can see them and behave yourself. Now, sit boy, sit,' she ordered.

Sober now but feeling the after effects of the wine, he knew that he was not going to intimidate her and did exactly as he was told.

As she left to go, he said, 'Thank you Mrs Gumede, and I'm sorry.'

Ethel snapped back, 'You won't get my forgiveness, but you may get God's if you pray for it hard and long, boy.' She exited and locked the door.

Returning to the dining room, she entered, slapping her hands together in an up and down movement and grinned.

'Just as I thought, he has enough intelligence to know his weaknesses when faced with the formidable Ethel Gumede. God forgive me, I'm a tyrant,' she announced.

Again, the room filled with laughter and harmony settled on the group as they enjoyed their breakfasts.

The doorbell rang.

Ethel went to answer it. It was Monsignor Prince.

'Good morning, Mrs Gumede,' he said, cheerfully.

'Good morning Monsignor,' she replied. 'Father Seth is in his study. I assume he's expecting you. I'll see if he's ready to receive you.'

'Thank you, Mrs Gumede,' said Father Seth from the study doorway. 'Come through, Patrick.'

Monsignor Prince thanked Ethel and made his way towards the study, shaking hands with his fellow priest at the door.

'Can you provide us with coffee please, Mrs Gumede?'

'Of course, Father.'

Both priests were sitting in the study when Ethel knocked on the door. Father Seth opened the door, and she brought in their coffee asking, 'Will you be staying for lunch Monsignor Prince?'

Partly ignoring her and addressing Father Seth, he said, 'Considering the circumstances, I think it's probably not appropriate. I'm confident that Deacon Zapatero would like to escape his incarceration, and I'm mindful that he'll need to consider his position in the more familiar surroundings of the seminary.'

Ethel was outraged but tempered her words. 'Really, Monsignor, are we talking about the same Deacon Zapatero who insulted everyone here last night?'

Then, perhaps unwisely raising her voice a little too much, she continued, 'Please don't make him into a victim, Monsignor Prince. He isn't a victim.'

'Hold your tongue, Mrs Gumede. Do not insult Monsignor Prince like that,' barked Father Seth.

'Insult Monsignor Prince?' Ethel answered, unable to stop herself. 'What hypocrisy. Have you no sense of justice? What about Sister Jennifer, what about her needs, not to mention *her* rights? Or any other young woman who has the misfortune to cross his path.'

Eyes blazing, the fearless housekeeper added, 'Do not underestimate the damage a man like that can do in the church.'

She looked at their disapproving faces and couldn't resist a parting shot. 'God forbid he continues to ordination.'

'Get out! Out of my study now!' The parish priest was furious and embarrassed all in one. He felt shamed before his superior by a woman, and a serving woman at that. He had obviously allowed this hired help too much sway in his life. No more, he raged silently, but with a face like an angry ape.

Unafraid, she strode from the study, fuming silently, and returned to the dining room. As she entered, the three deacons were standing around David.

'What's going on?' she asked.

'We all heard the commotion in the study, and David wanted to come in to support you, Mrs Gumede,' said Martin.

'Thank you David, but all is fine. Where is Jennifer?' she demanded. 'She's gone into the kitchen,' Luigi said.

Ethel made her way into the kitchen where Jennifer was busying herself, wiping down some surfaces. 'I'm sorry child, I'm sorry for losing my temper, and I'm sorry for upsetting you, but I can't believe what I was welcomed with in there. I'm disgusted. I'm beginning to think that their behaviour is giving the likes of him upstairs the permission to behave in the unforgivable way he did last night. I'm so angry with them.'

Jennifer said, 'Don't worry, Ethel, I understand. Everyone has been so supportive, you, David, and the other deacons, but Father Seth is in an exceedingly difficult position too, and we must remember that.' Lowering her voice she added, 'I'm not going to pretend that this situation hasn't made me start to ask questions of myself.'

'Whatever do you mean, child?' asked Ethel, taking Jennifer over to the window.

Jennifer spoke in a whisper so the others couldn't overhear. 'Well, I had the strangest dream last night...I will tell you about it another time, but I was wearing a habit very different to this one. Never mind...it was a complex dream,' she said, shaking her head. 'But it left me this morning with some deep questions. I feel so confused.

'My devotion and love of God are as strong as ever, but, may God forgive me, I'm beginning to wonder if I could not serve him better through a different vocation,' said Jennifer.

Touching Ethel's hand, she added, 'Please keep this to yourself for now, Ethel. I need to think carefully before I make any decisions.'

Ethel looked appalled. 'Oh child, what have I done? My anger got the better of me, and now I feel you are suffering because of that.'

'No, Ethel, don't blame yourself. It's not you, not at all. It's all that's gone on. Everything happens for a reason, and my faith tells me that I must be patient and pray to find a solution. I cannot make any decisions alone, and I must ask God for guidance.'

There was a gentle knock on the kitchen door.

'Come in,' Jennifer said. Duncan peeped round the door. 'Excuse me, Sister. Would you like to join us in prayer?' he asked.

'Oh, yes, I would,' she answered. 'Ethel, will you join us please? I'll see if we can go into the church. We'll probably feel the benefit of God's peace in there. I'd like David to come too, if he can.'

'Of course I will. We all need some peace.' She heard David's voice ring clear from the dining room.

'We'll need the key. I'll go and ask Father Seth for it,' he said.

He went to the study and knocked on the door.

'Who is it?' snapped the priest, still stinging from his encounter with Ethel.

'David, Father. Could we have the key for the church, please? We would all like to spend some time in prayer.'

Father Seth opened the door and gave the key to David. He looked drained and troubled.

'We'll pray for you, Father,' he said.

'Thank you David. It is very much appreciated. Please lock up when you've finished.'

'I will. Thank you, Father.'

Chapter 10

Maureen

The six of them made their way to the church and entered via the sacristy. It was an impressive piece of early 20th Century architecture, red brick and dressed stone. It was named after Brigid of Kildare, one of Ireland's much beloved saints. There were eight granite columns, all of which had an intricate, spiral design, and a beautifully carved staircase made from ebony.

The staircase was just inside the main entrance. It led up to a second-floor veranda supported by the columns and ran around the internal perimeter providing further seating for parishioners during the holy days of the religious calendar, when large numbers would crowd in to hear the special masses. It was also used by the choir at Sunday mass and other times of celebration, gently lit during the day by natural light, which cascaded through the exquisite stained-glass windows, and contributed to the sense of tranquillity and peace.

David knew the place inside and out. He knew where every chalice, vestment, hymn book, bible and missal was kept. He knew every statue, every crucifix, every holy picture, every light switch and electric socket, having looked after the building for so long and serving as the most respectful, obedient altar boy the parish had ever had. He had learned early, from punished failures, how to ring the bell during mass at exactly the right time and hand all the sacred vessels and cloths to Father Seth at precisely the right moments during the celebration of the Eucharist.

Like the garden, it was his place of refuge and comfort.

They all genuflected before the altar and knelt at the altar rails. Luigi spoke first, asking God to send his blessings to them all. Jennifer prayed for those with mental, psychological and emotional health issues, and privately prayed for greater understanding of herself. David prayed specifically for Dominic, asking that he be sent the strength to find a path to healing, as Ethel pursed her lips and privately asked for forgiveness for her unworthy thoughts. Martin and Duncan prayed for Father Seth and Monsignor Prince. The natural harmony of the group was uplifting to them all, and they spontaneously joined hands before finishing with the Lord's Prayer, led by Ethel.

Whatever happened during the short, impromptu period of prayer, it had given them all the blessings they sought to get through the day.

They left and returned to the presbytery via the kitchen door just as the two priests were leaving the study. They all met in the dining room.

'Aah, so you're back. I hope you found that beneficial,' said Father Seth. 'Monsignor Prince is ready to return to the seminary now, so if you'd like to go and get your bags from your rooms, gentlemen?'

'Have you got the key for Number 4, Father Seth? I'll go and release the condemned man,' said Monsignor Prince, with an attempt at humour.

Ethel just looked at him, bit her lip, and started to return to the kitchen, saying her goodbyes to the three deacons as she did so. Monsignor Prince obviously had such little sensitivity to the needs of others or their feelings that it dawned on Jennifer that he would do little to assist Dominic in changing his attitudes. Furthermore, she began to suspect that nothing further would be discussed once they left St Brigid's presbytery.

She watched through the doorway as Monsignor Prince and the others, including Dominic, came downstairs. Luigi, Martin and Duncan all returned to the dining room to say their goodbyes before returning to the hallway with Father Seth.

Waiting were Monsignor Prince and Dominic in the open front door. The younger man seemed uncertain, even edgy, shooting looks into the presbytery and up the stairs. He tried to go back in but Father Seth blocked his way.

'Time to go, Dominic,' he said. Dominic acquiesced but looked past him at the others who were quietly watching the proceedings. He asked, with a mock look of hurt, 'Does no one want to say goodbye to me?'

After a few moments of uncomfortable silence, it was Duncan who murmured, almost to himself, 'Maybe some semblance of humility…?'

Dominic sneered and didn't answer as he followed Monsignor Prince to the car. Father Seth glared at him with irritation then turned to the young clerics to shake their hands and bid them farewell.

The presbytery front door closed tight in its jamb and the relief for them all was palpable.

The parish priest went into the dining room, asking Ethel, David and Jennifer to join him in his study.

'Take a seat please', he said in a formal tone as they entered cautiously. When they were all settled and their eyes on him, he began.

'I'm somewhat ill at ease with my experiences over the last couple of days, and I feel we all need some time to make a transition to an otherwise sense of normality.

'Therefore, I ask that you deal with whatever you need to deal with appropriately. May I suggest that we take some time to assess our own individual behaviours and then sit down and have a constructive conversation to seek a positive way forward as a household?'

It sounded like a very diplomatic statement, thought Jennifer. Almost political.

The priest continued, 'I am very aware that my approach to some of the issues has lacked consideration and compassion. I intend to address that with you as individuals over time. If you feel a sense of injustice at my hand, then let me apologise, here and now.'

David and Ethel each drew a breath, not expecting these words, not from Father Seth, of all people. They had expected to be reproached, scolded, and coldly sent away. Jennifer sat silently, trying not to let her fears run away with her, and listening intently.

'My role should have been one of support to you all, and I fear I have let all of you down. I recognise the need for change, first and foremost within myself, and that is where I intend to start.

'Please forgive my weaknesses and let me reassure you all that I will learn from this. Now, unless anyone has anything to say, please feel free to go about your business, and thank you.'

They sat for a moment and waited. No one spoke. It seemed right to just stand, bow their heads in acknowledgement of Father Seth's confessional speech and exit in complete silence. Ethel made her way into the kitchen and started to prepare for lunch.

Jennifer and David began to make their way upstairs, side by side, but still in complete silence. They arrived outside his room, and he put his hand out to open the door. However, she took hold of it from the side, and he turned to her. The connection was immediate as he looked down into her eyes.

'It's my turn to struggle with finding the right words, David,' she said nervously.

'Where can I begin, other than to say thank you? I'm not normally lost for something to say, but I want you to know how proud I am of you and that I will be eternally grateful for the support you have given me.

'You put everything on the line for me, and to think you did that in the knowledge that I can give you nothing in return has moved me very deeply. I told you yesterday that I would always be your friend and of course I want to fulfil that promise to you. You're the loveliest, most sincere man I have ever met. Thank you!'

He felt as though some kind of magic was streaming from her to him through his hand, still held in hers. He tried to find better words, but simply replied, 'There's nothing to thank me for, Jennifer. I didn't make a conscious decision to do what I did. I felt a sense of, well, I just had to do it.'

He ventured further, not knowing where the words came from, 'But your friendship is all I want right now, Jennifer. You have no idea how that makes me feel.'

Jennifer responded, with a smile, 'I'm in a bit of a predicament, David. There's a lot to think about, and regrettably, I can't share that with you at the moment. But please know this, I will carry you in my prayers wherever I go, and I hope you will always remain my friend, and a part of my life. Thank you for being the man you are, David.'

She added, looking straight into his eyes, 'I'll see you later, I hope?'

'Oh yes, I hope so,' he replied.

She let go of his hand and made her way up the staircase to her room. He looked at his hand. It felt like a different hand.

Almost floating on a cloud, he went into his room, and there were the folders still lying on his bed. He felt exhausted. The last 24 hours had taken much out of him, physically, mentally and emotionally. But spiritually, he felt more vital and alive than ever. He moved the folders off the bed and placed them on the desk at the side of his computer. He kicked off his shoes and lay down for a moment. He dearly needed to sleep. It was half past eleven.

A knock at the door awakened him. He glanced at the alarm clock in his room. The amber digits said 13:15. How could he possibly have slept that long? He quickly got off the bed and opened the door. It was Ethel.

'Are you all right, David? We were getting worried about you, so Father asked me to come up to see if you were OK?'

'I'm fine. I just fell asleep. I'm so sorry!'

Ethel replied, 'It's all right, don't worry, you must have been exhausted. Are you ready for some lunch?'

'Yes, I'll just go and freshen up, if that's OK? I'll be down in a minute.'

He went up to the bathroom, washed his hands and face, and then went down to the dining room. He felt his usual apprehension as he entered and saw Father Seth. 'Sorry I'm late, Father.'

The priest nodded at him, 'I'm sure you're tired. I'm going to have a lie down myself after lunch. Oh and, Mrs Gumede, can I suggest you take a little time off this afternoon? Go and watch the TV in the sitting room if you like. It's up to you. I think we all need a little time to ourselves right now. You, too, Sister, it's been a harrowing time for us all, but the stresses laid upon you have been unquestioningly of great magnitude.'

They could hardly comprehend what they were hearing, but they were glad to take whatever comfort and peace there was to be had.

Only David's stomach lurched with unease. This was not the Father Seth he knew so well.

But Jennifer snatched the moment. She said, 'Oh, Father, I was wondering if I could spend a little time with David whilst I'm here? We talked about gardening yesterday when we were shopping, and I said I'd like to get some fresh air and help him as I can't leave the presbytery alone. Also, I would be developing some new skills. Would that be all right?'

The priest let her words hang in the air before replying. 'I'm sure David would be grateful if you did. It's a very large area of work for him and I'm sure you'll be a great help. As long as you know which are weeds, and which are plants!'

She smiled. He was almost making a joke with her. It was more than she hoped for. 'Yes Father, of course! This afternoon might be as good a time as any.'

Father Seth added, looking her up and down, 'But you can't garden in your habit Sister, not practical at all. If you've brought something more appropriate to wear from your mother's when I picked you up, then that should be fine.'

She answered, 'Yes, I did actually, Father. It wasn't intended for work in the garden, but I think it would be appropriate.'

***

Lunch was a very relaxed affair and felt far less formal than it ever had before. David had rarely been late for anything in the past since he knew Father Seth didn't tolerate lateness, but today, he had seen a few changes in him, and the atmosphere was much more pleasant. Still, the changes niggled. David could not shake off his feeling of distrust.

Ethel kept shooting her employer sidelong glances. She commented that the recent events hadn't marred their relationships and how pleased she felt about that.

What was most surprising was that Father Seth had smiled at her and said, 'I agree absolutely!'

***

Lunch was over as Ethel stood up and started to clear the table. David began to help but Father Seth stopped Jennifer from doing likewise by asking her to accompany him into the study.

'You look a little preoccupied, Sister' he said as they entered.

'I am, Father, the last 24 hours have started to make me question aspects of my life which, until now, I was very certain about,' she replied, candidly.

'Please, sit down, Jennifer.' He used her name. The one he had always used before she entered the convent. The moment was not lost on her. Father Seth had always behaved like a favourite uncle, albeit quite straitlaced, ever since she was a little girl, and she guessed he was rather fond of her but dare not show it.

He looked out of the window and then turned to speak, as though it was the start of one of his sermons. Jennifer looked down solemnly at her hands in expectation of clerical, not avuncular, advice.

'I think many who enter the religious life, and indeed members of the clergy in general, often question their faith and commitment. It's not a question of belief in God. It's more a personal question of the strength of belief in self, or the capacity to hand everything of this life over to him.

'Our humanity can create many obstacles to our faith. Or, to put it another way, our imperfections and lack of faith in ourselves as individual entities can lead us to question our capacity to have faith in another or God, and why wouldn't it? For many, religious faith is very much the most unnatural path through life and all its complexities. If we're lucky, we are nurtured from our very beginnings to reach for independence. Yet, those who assist us in doing so are often the ones who suggest and indeed teach us that we can only have true independence if we base it, and all other life experience, on an unseen, impalpable God.'

Jennifer swallowed hard and let his words soak in.

Father Seth went on, 'Quite the paradox, if you give it and yourself the space to run with it and therefore develop and grow. I've been guilty at times in my life, and I may add, in the last day or so, of falling into the most natural of human failings.'

She looked up at him, arrested by his honesty.

He continued, 'Whereas, if I'd allowed my faith to lead me, then I would have realised that I have no answers other than through prayer. That gives us the gift of time. But in the rawest of human experiences, we revert to the most basic human response, or maybe reaction is a better word. That reaction denies us the most important gift of time in our impatience to "sort out" the issue before us.'

The priest paused for emphasis, looking her straight in the eyes.

'It's only in recognising this that we learn that faith is our greatest friend if we let God take the issue from us and sort it out in his own time. We mortals are impatient, so we look for instant gratification, especially at times of stress and pain.

'Simply praying and waiting for God's response is the only way forward and the true meaning of faith.

'Science can teach us so much, and not least about God and faith. Science and faith are the beacons of human experience that eventually lead to truth, certainty and understanding of everything. Why can't we accept that God is the same?'

Jennifer had listened to every word, rapt in attention. When she was sure he had finished, she said, 'Thank you Father, that has helped me greatly. I promise, I will continue to pray and return to God the questions that I can't answer with only the assistance of my own human experience. In God's time, I know I will get the appropriate answer.'

'Yes, Jennifer, you will. God indeed works in mysterious ways. The choices we make are only of value if God, in his wisdom, ratifies them. Therefore, when we choose to do things for ourselves, or in the name of another or for their benefit without God being at the centre of that decision, we will often come to a point where we must question our actions' validity. I suggest that you may be finding yourself in that place right now?'

'Yes, I think you're right Father. Thank you.'

'You're most welcome, Jennifer.'

She left the study and reflected again that he'd referred to her as Jennifer for the first time in a very long time. He gave her the prefix of Sister or just used that word singularly when talking to her or introducing her. She was intrigued by the difference, but secretly preferred it, coming from the man who was the nearest thing to an uncle she had.

She returned to the kitchen just as they were finishing the washing up, re-energised by Father Seth's words.

'Right, I'm going to my room to get changed. Should I knock for you on my way down David?'

'Yes, that's a good idea.'

Ethel started to laugh. Then she turned to them both and said, 'That's so sweet, like two children arranging to go out to play.'

They grinned at the observation. It was true.

'I'm sure we'll have fun, Ethel,' Jennifer said, smiling.

David looked thoughtful. He loved gardening, and experienced great peace tending the plants, but it wasn't usually 'fun'.

Jennifer's cheeks looked rosier than usual and, to his great surprise, Ethel pinched David's cheeks and said, 'You're so beautifully innocent, boy, but maybe it's time for you to grow?'

He felt embarrassed, exposed. They were just going into the garden to do some tidying up. She hadn't pinched his cheeks like that since he was a boy. But a part of him liked it. He felt a new closeness between him and the woman who had been the most important figure in his life, and it felt good. He had often thought, throughout his lonely times as a child, that if he could have chosen a mother, this is what she would have been like.

The younger two left the kitchen and went to their rooms to change.

'I'll knock for you then?' asked Jennifer.

'Yes, please.'

It ran through David's head, as he started to get changed, that he must look at the bank papers later. But not now. The garden, and Jennifer, and fun, perhaps, beckoned.

She found her spare clothes and carefully removed her wimple and habit. She dressed and brushed her hair, making a ponytail of it.

Then she made her way down the spiral stairs with a spring in her step and knocked on the door to David's room. He opened the door and, there she was, a vision of natural beauty, a complete young woman, no makeup, just glowing skin and eyes.

He was speechless but tried hard not to show it. She wore a plain white T-shirt tucked into light blue denim Capri jeans, walking socks and boots on her feet. But the simple clothes did nothing to disguise her hourglass figure, and that hair, the thick, glossy auburn hair he had already seen, wet and dripping.

Oh my God, give me strength. She's a nun. She's a nun, or she's going to be, he silently told himself.

'Ready?' she asked.

He had to cough to clear his throat before he could respond. 'Erm, yes, I'm ready.' He grabbed his peaked cap, took refuge in the practical, and added, 'Have you got sunscreen on? The sun is bright and hot today. I don't want you to get burnt.'

'Oh, no, I haven't any,' she said with a wry face. 'I didn't think! How silly of me. I don't spend much time out of my habit these days, and that usually provides me with all the protection I need,' she answered, now realising the risk under the hot African sun.

'Don't worry, I think Ethel has some good stuff in the drug cupboard downstairs. She gets it for the children when they do their processions in the summer months. I think it costs her quite a bit, but she adores the kids. Let's go and ask her.'

They went down into the kitchen.

'Oh, my goodness me, Maureen O'Hara!' Ethel exclaimed as they walked into the kitchen, and she stared at Jennifer. They looked at each other in puzzlement. David wondered if it was a new expression of surprise that Ethel's grandchildren had begun to use. 'Who's that, Ethel?' asked Jennifer, more straightforwardly.

'Good heavens, your doppelganger, dear,' answered Ethel. 'I was looking at you the other day when you arrived and wondering who was it that you reminded me of, and now I see you and your lovely figure, and your gorgeous auburn hair, it's easy. Maureen O'Hara!'

Jennifer stared, curiously. Ethel prattled on, happy to share her knowledge of Maureen O'Hara.. 'She was a beautiful young woman too, just like you, and your eyes are just as pretty, but hers were emerald-green, not blue, or at least they were in the pictures.'

'Aww, thank you Ethel, that's so kind of you. You know a lot about her. Is she a friend of yours?'

Ethel started to laugh. 'No, dear, she was a film star in Hollywood, many years ago, but she was born in Ireland. Her sister became a nun, I think, with the Sisters of Charity and, if I'm not mistaken, I think the sister went on to be a teacher too...'

'Really? That's so interesting. I'm of Irish descent, Ethel. My mother's family came from a place near Dublin called Ranelagh. But our family name is O'Connor. Mammy's first name is Gaelic and spelt, oh you wouldn't believe how it's spelt, AOIBHEANN, pronounced Ayveen, but she answers to Evie, which is a lot easier! She'd just had her first birthday when she came here with my grandparents.'

Ethel wryly observed, 'Then you must surely have the same ancestors as Maureen O'Hara, then, somewhere back in history, child. The likeness is quite amazing.'

Chapter 11

Storm

David was taking it all in, the vision before him, and trying to remember to ask for sunblock.

'Excuse me, Mrs Gumede, Ethel, sorry, to bother you. But do you have any sunblock for Jennifer?'

'Have a look in the cupboard Mr Blind, sorry, David,' she grinned and inclined her head towards the cupboard in question.

He went to it, at the side of the scullery.

'Here it is,' he said, picking up a bottle of factor 50. 'Perfect for you Jennifer, I should think.'

He passed it to her, and she applied it liberally to her face, arms and lower legs, wiped her hands on a towel and placed the bottle back in the cupboard.

'You haven't done the back of your neck or your shoulders,' he said, retrieving the bottle. 'Those are the bits most likely to burn when you're gardening.'

She took her ponytail and pulled it over her shoulder and bent forward.

'Oh, can you do it please? I don't want to get it in my hair' she said, aware of the effect her request might have on David but hoping it might help him overcome some of his shyness.

'Ethel, can you help?' David appealed, immediately. 'No boy, my hands are wet. You'll have to do it. No need to make a meal of it,' urged Ethel.

He accepted his fate, squeezed the cream onto Jennifer's shoulders, and she squealed loudly. 'Sorry, it's cold,' she said, laughing.

David gently rubbed the cream into her upper back, neck and shoulders with trembling hands as Father Seth came into the kitchen.

'Is everyone all right? I heard someone scream,' he said.

'It was just me, Father, the cream was cold, that's all,' said Jennifer.

'Hmm,' he replied. 'Make sure you put plenty on. We don't want Sister to burn.'

David felt the scene was unreal. He was actually touching Jennifer's skin, and nobody seemed at all bothered, not even Father Seth.

Quick, say something to make this more normal, he thought.

'Here you are, take some for the other bits that might burn,' he said. She took the bottle and rubbed a little into her neck and chest.

'All done,' she said, handing it back to him. David might have looked steady on his feet, but his senses were reeling.

He put the bottle back in the cupboard, his hands still trembling. He quickly washed and wiped them. Then with relief, he opened the door to the garden, before making his way out to the shed. Somewhere he felt more confident. 'See you later,' Jennifer said to Ethel.

'Have fun,' the housekeeper replied.

Jennifer started to giggle.

'Why do you find that so funny?'

With eyes twinkling, she tried to explain. 'When Ethel first said it to us when we were going for a walk, the tone of her voice was mischievous, and Father Seth picked up on it straight away and so shouted at her, because he wouldn't think it appropriate. The look on her face was so funny and a little naughty.'

'I'm sorry, I still don't understand?'

Jennifer realised she needed to be a bit more specific. 'I think Ethel is having fun herself trying to match make.'

Match make? What, with me and with a nun-to-be, he asked himself in some confusion. How could that be fun for Ethel? Or how could Jennifer find it funny? His face said it for him.

'So, what are we doing today then? she said, quickly changing the subject.

'We need to weed the vegetables,' he said, glad of the distraction. They went into the shed, and he handed her a pair of gloves from a shelf. 'See if they fit; they're the smallest pair I have. Shake them out first to get any bugs or nasties out.'

She watched him shake out his own pair, ten shakes holding a different finger of each glove for each shake, then he put them on. She did the same.

He picked up two buckets and several weeding tools, 'Right, let's go. It's straightforward, but if you have any questions, I'm right here. Especially if you're not sure what is a weed and what isn't I mean…'

'I will. Thank you for letting me do this with you.'

'No need to thank me,' he smiled. 'I'm glad of your company.'

They made their way over to a line of raised beds.

'Why are the vegetables planted like that? she asked. This was an area of perfect confidence for David. He said without hesitation, 'Several reasons. Raised beds are better for water retention because the water is confined within the borders of them and doesn't drain off onto the surrounding land. They give you a better yield because you grow stronger plants, and they are that bit closer to the sun.'

'Why do you have different varieties in each bed?'

'It's an old technique called 'companion planting.' It's just a method of grouping crops together to reap the benefits from each other. For example, some insects like certain plants but not others, so if you mix plants, they often work together as a natural insect repellent.'

'You're very knowledgeable, David. I'm impressed,' she said, grabbing a hand fork from his bucket of tools.

They talked a lot about vegetable gardening and how David had learnt at an early age that home grown fruit and vegetables were always nicer to eat than those from a shop. She reached for a tomato and bit into it. 'You're absolutely right about that' she said, obviously relishing the taste.

After a couple of hours' toil and talk they went into the kitchen. He put the kettle on to make tea.

'Ethel has some cake in the tin over there,' he said, looking at her. Her face was dirty and pink, and her hair was a bit messy now, but he thought, she's still so beautiful. So is this what the saying angels with dirty faces means?

He watched as the angel went over to the cake tin and helped herself to a slice of chocolate sponge. Between mouthfuls she said, 'David, I'm so pleased to have this time with you, I feel blessed to have met you, and I really feel that God has sent you into my life.'

She put the cake down, and her face turned serious. 'But I want to say something. I don't want it to upset you,'

'Don't worry, I told you yesterday that I knew you wouldn't want to hurt me, so don't be afraid, just say it,' he said.

'You're a lovely person, and I just wish...' she gazed through the window at the clear blue sky.

'Go on, say it.'

'I...just wish you could allow yourself a little more self-confidence, David,' she began, with a smile. 'You're so bright and intelligent, and I think if you had a little more confidence in yourself and your abilities, you could achieve anything you wanted.'

Bright, intelligent! He ran the words through his head. He stirred the tea in the pot and tried not to overreact. He actually wanted to run round the garden and yell to the world that this lovely girl thought he was those things.

Instead, he said quietly, 'Thanks so much, Jennifer. But you have no idea how much my confidence has grown just because of you. You treat me like an equal.'

'So, these conversations are OK with you?'

'Yes, of course, they're helping me more than you could ever know.'

'Oh good, I'm so pleased. I'd hate to say anything that would upset you,' she said, touching his arm.

'I don't think that will ever happen. You're so kind, so please don't hold back.'

'Oh, thank you. I'll be honest with you always, then. Even when it's difficult.'

'Please do,' he said with a look of sadness. 'I've never met anyone like you, and I'm beginning to think God has sent you into my life for a reason. It feels like divine intervention.'

She nodded with great understanding, smiled again, then picked up her cake and finished it.

He poured the tea and sat at the table.

'What would you like to do with your life?' she asked.

'That's rather a big question! Well, I mentioned the other night that I like to work on my computer, you know, spreadsheets and programs. I'd love to do a university course and learn all I can about integrating software and hardware to introduce into businesses or other types of organisations.'

He was talking about what he knew, so the words flowed freely. 'I already have an idea that could be useful in many different environments. I've started to research and design software that could bring many different media together to make my idea work. But I'd need to buy hardware to check the software works as I've designed it to, so that's a massive stumbling block. There's a couple of courses I've looked at, but they're too expensive, and they're three years' full-time study, so I'd have to stop working here, and I can't expect Father to support me.'

'Well, I'll pray about that for you', she smiled.

'What about you? Do you want to become prioress, a headteacher in a school, or do you have other plans?' he asked, almost dreading to hear the answers.

She spoke carefully. 'To be honest, I'm not quite sure yet. I pray a lot and hope God will show me the way. I don't have any expectations, so I won't ever feel disappointed, but I'm ambitious to live the life that God wants me to. I just need him to show me the way, so please pray for me, David.'

'Of course, I will. One good prayer deserves another,' he smiled.

'We have a deal then,' she smiled back, holding out her hand to shake his.

They went back out into the garden, but as they did there was a distant rumble, unmistakeably a storm coming in.

David said, 'Five minutes, we've got five minutes.'

She looked at him disbelievingly.

'The storm will be here in five minutes. The wind speed, direction and the distance dictate that.'

'Really?'

'Yes,' he smiled at her.' Come, quickly. We need to get in before it gets us!'

They quickly returned the tools to the shed, emptied the weeds into a brazier and ran into the kitchen just as the first rain started to fall.

'How did you do that? How did you know?'

'My little secret, I'll tell you when you're old,' he teased.

They started to laugh as they took off their boots.

'I love to watch a good storm. I love the drama,' Jennifer said.

'My room is the best place in the house. It overlooks most of the garden, come on,' he said, beckoning.

They ran upstairs to his room, leaving the door open, and knelt side by side on the window bench, side by side, looking out into the garden, as the clouds turned blacker, and the first flashes of lightning lit up the sky.

Suddenly and unexpectedly, she laid her head on his shoulder. She didn't know why she did it, but the moment felt right. She said, 'This is so incredible. Listen to the power of the thunder and see how the rain bounces off the ground.'

He moved his head gently and hardly dared to rest it on the top of hers, but he did. It felt natural, unthreatening.

They stared at the storm. 'This is one of the sweetest days of my life David, I feel so blessed,' said Jennifer. 'Please promise me you'll always be my friend. You've touched something within my spirit, and for the first time in my life, I've found another human being to touch my soul.'

She reached to take his hand and held it tight. The storm raged, and they knelt there for what felt like eternity, secure in each other's silence.

Ethel's voice broke the silence as she whispered from the open doorway, 'Ah, you two!'

They had no idea how long she had stood there, or how long they had knelt there, but they separated as gently as they had come together, and as they turned to face her, they saw tears wet on her cheeks.

'Are you all right, Ethel?' asked Jennifer.

'Yes child, there's not much that I can't find an explanation for these days, but there's an indescribable warm glow in this room right now, and I can only consider it to be of God's making.'

'Do you mean the storm, Ethel? It's a wonderful golden light breaking through, isn't it?' asked Jennifer.

'No, not that. There's something between you two that is just so beautiful. So much so, I can't find the words to describe it.'

'Oh, Ethel, you feel it, too?' asked Jennifer.

'Well, I feel something, child, and it leaves me lost for words.'

David looked down at the windowsill awkwardly as Jennifer smiled back in obvious pleasure.

'And yes, the light is lovely,' Ethel continued.

Then a serious look passed over her face. 'I'm so sorry to ask, but would you two storm chasers both come with me? I've just been tidying Room 4 after that Deacon Dominic and I've found something I think Father Seth needs to see. I'm not sure how to approach him with it.'

They stood up immediately and followed her, wondering what it could be.

Chapter 12

Substance

Ethel pointed out to them what she'd found in Room 4.

'I found two small plastic bags in the bin under the table in the bedroom and two lines of white powder on a mirror. The mirror is normally hung on the wall in the bathroom, so I wondered what was going on,' she said.

'Did you touch any of them, Ethel?' asked Jennifer, shocked.

'Yes, but I had my gloves on. I always wear my gloves when I'm cleaning.'

'What about the mirror? Have you cleaned it and put it back on the wall yet?'

'No, I left it where I found it, and the bags are on the table next to the mirror. I put them there when I found them.'

'Sounds like it could be coke?' said Jennifer to David. His eyes widened. Ethel clicked her tongue.

'Don't worry, Ethel. We'll come and see Father with you,' Jennifer added. The three of them made their way to the study. Unusually, the door was open.

'Excuse me, Father.'

'Yes Jennifer.'

'Ethel has just found something upstairs, and we think you should see it.'

'What is it, Mrs Gumede?' asked Father Seth, distracted by the paperwork on his desk, and slightly irritated.

'Some kind of white Coca Cola,' she said earnestly.

Jennifer started to laugh. 'I think you mean coke, Ethel,' she said, emphasising the word. 'Cocaine, it's a dru...'

Ethel interrupted her, not listening and becoming more agitated, 'Well, whatever they call that white powder stuff. You said, "Sounds like it could be coke".'

She railed, 'I don't like my grandkids having the black coke to drink. It's full of sugar, and it makes them as high as a kite. But I didn't know about that white stuff. I've told my children not to give it to them; it makes them jump around like springboks. My kids never had it when they were little. They had milk and orange juice. I made sure of that.' She shook her head as David looked away to control his expression.

Father Seth, his work now fully interrupted, listened to Ethel's mistaken concerns about her grandchildren and couldn't help breaking into a grin, too.

'I'm sorry Mrs Gumede,' he said, needing to take control of the situation. 'Coca Cola is the drink, Coke for short. Coke, or cocaine, small letter c, is a banned substance.

He expanded on the subject, doubting that there was something serious to deal with upstairs, right now, in *his* presbytery. He went on, 'I believe, though, in the early days when it was first invented, Coke, the drink, actually contained small amounts of cocaine which accounted for some of its original popularity.'

David and Jennifer looked at each other, impressed and not a little surprised at his general knowledge.

'Oh, I read about it in an article somewhere...' Father Seth tailed off and waved his hand. 'Now, though, I'm pretty certain it just has legal ingredients,' continued the priest, pleased with his concise explanation, but observing that it had done nothing to calm down his housekeeper.

'Back to your problem, Mrs Gumede. Are you sure this white powder isn't something more innocent, like talcum powder?'

The other two tried to suppress their amusement at the misunderstandings being played out in front of them.

Ethel, distracted by all the sidelong looks and stifled laughter, hadn't been listening properly.

Words tumbled out of her mouth as she voiced her many concerns. 'It's a white powder, and it's on the mirror in lines, Father, it's not like talcum powder at all. Why would anyone do that? I know there's something not right about it, and I really don't think it's a laughing matter,' she scolded, looking from Father Seth to David.

Father Seth looked suddenly serious. 'Well, I see what you mean, Mrs Gumede. It does sound like it might possibly be something...more than talcum powder,' he said.

'Make your mind up, Father, you're confusing me,' said Ethel. 'I'm so worried now about the grandchildren...'

'It's all right, Ethel, I don't think they're taking...,' Jennifer said, holding back her need to laugh, but recognising Ethel's genuine anxiety. 'Let's all sort this out together.'

'Thank you child,' said Ethel with gratitude and relief, while outraged righteousness seeped from every pore.

'Yes, let's go and see,' said Father Seth. 'Where exactly did you find it, Mrs Gumede?'

They went upstairs and Ethel led them into Room 4. There on the table, just as she had described, was the mirror, reflecting two lines of white powder and the two plastic bags.

Ethel launched into her long explanation. 'I found the bags in the bin, there. I took them out of the liner and placed them where you see them now. I was about to pick up the mirror to put it back, and I saw the powder in lines. It reminded me of something I'd seen on Crime Channel not long ago about white powder with razor blades. It was a documentary but I only caught a couple of minutes of it because I was rushing out of the house.

'So, I knew this wasn't right, and I didn't know how to explain it, so I left everything where it was and went to find the young ones. They were in David's room watching the storm. I told them what I've just told you. Then we came to see you.'

Ethel's account of the discovery was almost forensic in its detail.

Father Seth tried to calm her, commenting, 'You've done very well, Mrs Gumede. I think I need to contact the police. This is a profoundly serious matter.'

'The police? Oh, my goodness, and what about my grandkids? What's going to happen to them?' She started to get upset.

'It's all fine, Ethel, come with me, let me explain. I'm sure Father Seth can wait until I've explained it to you,' said Jennifer, appealing to him. He nodded.

Jennifer went with Ethel downstairs and into the dining room while Father Seth and David made their way into the study.

Jennifer sat her down and made her a cup of tea. She sensitively explained the misunderstanding to her, and once Ethel had fully calmed down and saw the irony of the situation, she burst out laughing too. Father Seth and David heard the mood change and joined them, united in the humour of the moment.

'You should call the police now, Father,' Ethel said as their laughter died away. 'That Deacon Dominic has something to answer for. How dare he bring something like that into the presbytery?'

Father Seth went into the study to make the call.

'I can't remember ever seeing him laugh like that before,' said Ethel, incredulously when he had left the room. 'But this all needs to be sorted out, for sure, and soon! Thank God for his intervention.'

'We never truly know another's burden, do we?' asked Jennifer. 'Father Seth, I mean. All we can do is love and support each other, and hopefully, things will continue to improve for us all. We could all be so much happier if we let down our barriers, don't you think?'

David nodded. 'If I've learnt one thing over the last few days, it's to trust people more, and that is because of you, Jennifer.'

'I agree wholeheartedly,' Ethel added, 'Look at what you've done for David, well, all of us. I love you, child, and I love you too, David.'

He felt tears sting his eyes.

'I love you too,' he stammered, reaching out to Ethel and taking her hand.

'Oh, child, that means so much to me, thank you.' She kissed him on the cheek.

'I've wanted to tell you for as long as I can remember, but other...influences...made it exceedingly difficult, but no more, child, no more.

'I want you to meet my family, too. It's time now. We've waited long enough,' she announced.

'They've wanted to meet you for a long time, and thanks to you, Jennifer, that can happen now. I'll make arrangements, and you can both come over.'

'Wow, I can't wait Ethel. Sort that out soon, won't you?' pleaded Jennifer.

'I will, child, I will,' she said. Then, remembering, 'Oh David, three letters came for you this afternoon. I had to sign for them. I hope you don't mind. You were in the garden at the time. Wait here. I'll get them for you.'

Ethel got up and went to the sitting room. She brought the letters and gave them to him.

'SAFERAND BANK' was printed on the top of each of the envelopes.

'I'll read them later. Thank you Mrs Gumede,' he said, forgetting their new intimacy for a moment, as his thoughts turned to the bank.

'That's too formal, child, always call me Ethel from now on, like Jennifer does,' she smiled.

'Thank you, I will, but always with love and respect. You can call me Mr Blind, Ethel,' he answered, allowing one of the cheeky responses that had often remained in his own head, unshared, to slip out and make her laugh.

They all laughed.

Father Seth came into the dining room.

'This is a happy sight and sound,' he said to their surprise.

'There have been a few little changes, Father. I've told David he could start calling me Ethel, and the cheeky devil told me I could start calling him Mr Blind, but I'll be continuing with David.'

'That's nice for you both. Perhaps I should do the same, then, Ethel?' said the priest.

'Of course Father, but if it's OK with you, I'll still call you Father, Father?'

'Of course Ethel, that's fine,' he said.

'Well, that's amazing.' Jennifer said. 'How lovely.'

David felt a familiar sense of unease run through him and settled in his stomach. Something about Father Seth's new persona deeply threatened him. How could this be the man who beat him and ridiculed him, and stopped him having friends? David wisely made sure nothing showed in his face.

'Oh Father, these have arrived today,' he said, presenting the priest with the letters.

'Aah, that's good,' said Father Seth. Mr Verster must have sent them by courier. Make sure you read them carefully, David. They're the doorway to your future.'

'I will, very carefully, thank you Father,' David replied.

'You're very welcome, very welcome indeed.'

Changing tone, Father Seth went on, 'Well, I've just called the police. They'll send an officer out as soon as there's one free. Just leave everything as it is, for now. They want to test it to identify if it is black Coke or white coke,' he laughed.

'Now behave yourself Father. Having a joke at my expense can be dangerous,' said Ethel.

They all laughed at her mock-stern face. 'I need to continue preparing dinner, and you two both need a shower. Off you go, get clean.'

They left the room and made their way upstairs.

'Father, can I have a quick word?' asked Ethel, when they had left. 'Of course,' he replied.

'I just want to say thank you for the changes you promised. It means a lot to everyone, and it was very courageous of you to be so open with us all this morning. I think you've created a much happier atmosphere, and everyone is starting to appreciate that.'

Father Seth, in his gentlest voice, said, 'I wish I'd seen the need for it earlier, Ethel, but having Jennifer here has somehow helped to open my eyes. She instinctively knows how to break down barriers.' There was a new warmth in his eyes, Ethel noticed. It looked real.

She answered, 'Yes, she does, and she has so much to give. She's a truly beautiful human being. Thank you for giving us all the opportunity to meet her.'

'Yes, but thank *you* for challenging me, Ethel. You, too, have been instrumental in the changes. You're very wise, you know,' said the priest.

'I know,' she laughed, marvelling at the change in her old employer.

Upstairs, Jennifer was taking a shower, and David had opened one of the three letters in his room. It contained the card for his new RandExchange account. He was reading the information about how to activate it so that he could return to Ackerman & Sons to pick up the dressing gowns for Jennifer.

He had almost forgotten them in the experiences of the last couple of days, but he was impressed with the service and speed of the bank. He hadn't expected to receive everything so soon. After all, Mr Verster had advised him that it could take up to a week. It was only Wednesday, and he was almost up and running and able to buy things easily. Well, providing one of the other envelopes contained his PIN number, he thought.

He had R 5000 in his account, which would easily cover the cost of the dressing gowns and leave him with, what was to him, a substantial amount. He had no idea what was in the savings account as he hadn't had a chance to look at the paperwork or book yet, and although Father Seth had mentioned 'salary', he was still unaware as to the amount and into which account it would be paid and when.

Having read the information leaflet accompanying his RandExchange card, he signed the card and placed it in his computer desk drawer. He took a towel from his bedroom cupboard and, with it, and his dressing gown over his arm, he made his way upstairs. As he reached the landing, he saw Jennifer's bedroom door slightly ajar, and so was the door of the bathroom. He pushed it wide open to enter.

'Hi.'

He heard her voice coming from her bedroom.

'David? Could you just come into my room a moment, please?' He pushed the door open and went in.

She stood with her back to him, wearing the lavender dressing gown she had bought the day before, and a towel turban.

'That colour really suits you, it was a good choice,' he said, suddenly awkward.

'Thank you!' she answered. 'I've a little request. Can I come down to dinner with you please? I mean, actually at the same time?'

'Yes, of course,' he answered, wondering why she wanted his support for that.

'So will you come back here when you've had your shower and got dressed, please?'

'Yes, certainly. But are you all right? You sound a little nervous. It's not like you,' he said, just grateful for all these special moments in her company.

'Yes, to both. I'm all right, but I'm also a little nervous. Come back soon.'

'OK, whatever it is, I'll be there for you.'

'I know. I trust you implicitly.' He left her to get ready.

Twenty minutes later he knocked on the closed door of her room and heard her say, 'Come in.' To his surprise, she wasn't in her habit, but in a pretty, floral, day dress.

'Oh, I was expecting to see you in your habit,' he said, factually, wanting to add how lovely she looked.

'That's why I'm nervous. I don't know how Father Seth will respond to me not being formally dressed.'

'Well, we'll soon find out, won't we?' he smiled.

'Do you think I've dressed appropriately, or should I put my habit on?'

'You look very respectable, and you shouldn't feel uncomfortable about not wearing your habit. Is it an absolute requirement that you wear it?' he asked.

'No, it's not a requirement. I've chosen to wear it most of the time. I'm just feeling a little apprehensive.'

He walked to her and hugged her.

'Come on, whatever happens, I'm with you all the way. Don't worry. You're doing nothing wrong. Ethel will love your dress. It's perfect, so come on, big smile, be confident.'

The irony of his advice to her was not lost on him. Be confident. He needed to listen to it himself.

'OK, I'm ready,' she smiled back at him.

They walked down the stairs and, just before they entered the dining room, he squeezed her hand. 'What's the worst that can happen?' he said. She nodded.

They walked into the dining room. There was no one there, but she could hear Ethel in the kitchen.

Jennifer walked into the kitchen. Ethel was facing the cooker,

'Hello Ethel,' she said, nervously.

Ethel turned around. 'Oh, my goodness child, you look a picture, and your hair, are those waves natural, surely not?'

'Oh, thank you, and yes, this is just how my hair has always been. I'm a bit nervous about Father seeing me out of my habit. How do you think he'll react?'

'Well, he saw you earlier when you were going into the garden with David and that didn't appear to bother him,' replied Ethel, shaking a pan.

'But I can only imagine how David will feel when he sees you. He'll get all shy again.' They both started to laugh.

'Shhhhh, stop it, Ethel. He's in the dining room.' Jennifer whispered.

'You mean he's already seen you?'

'Yes.'

'And?'

'He encouraged me to be confident and told me I was doing nothing wrong. He also told me my dress was perfect.'

'He's a very intelligent and wise young man, so take his advice,' said Ethel, hands in the sink. They heard Father Seth's voice as he entered the dining room,

'Where's Sister Jennifer?'

'She's in the kitchen with Ethel,' answered David.

'Oh, very good. Did you read your letters?'

'Just one of them Father, it had my RandExchange card in it.'

'I got one, too, from Mr Verster. I'm just reading it now,' said the priest. He sat down and continued to read.

Ethel looked at Jennifer. She could see her getting more nervous. 'OK child, you'll be fine, time to have faith. In you go, I'm right behind you.'

Jennifer opened the door and stepped nervously into the dining room with Ethel close behind her. David gave her an encouraging smile. Father Seth looked up from the letter.

It seemed an age before he said, 'Good heavens, Jennifer, I can't remember the last time I saw you in a dress.'

'Doesn't she look beautiful, Father?' interjected Ethel, quickly.

'She does, Ethel. Indeed, Jennifer, actually...you remind me of that film star, what's her name? The Irish one.'

Ethel started laughing, 'We had the very same conversation this afternoon Father! I said the exact same thing to Jennifer. She's the image of Maureen O'Hara.'

Father Seth answered, 'She's the image of her mother, too, Ethel. You are very much like your mother, you know, Jennifer. Your features and especially your eyes.'

Jennifer started to relax and felt relieved. She hadn't known what to expect. She began to realise that Father Seth had always projected a harsh exterior to the world and that that had modelled her expectations. It was as if he himself had been remodelled, and she delighted in the pleasure it was bringing to the present company.

'Would anyone like wine?' asked Father Seth.

'No, thank you,' Ethel and David said. 'Maybe just a little for me, Father,' said Jennifer.

Together they said grace and Father Seth got up to pour the wine.

Ethel went into the kitchen to get the food. 'Homemade liver pâté with Melba toast to start,' she said, delivering a tray onto the table.

'Mmm. That's delicious, Ethel,' said Jennifer, tucking into the crisp toast she had just spread thickly with pâté. Can I have the recipe please?'

'Oh, you'll be lucky to get any recipes from Ethel. She keeps them secret, doesn't she David?' said Father Seth, mischief in his eyes.

'Of course, you can, child, take no notice of him. You can have anything you want from me. Just ask.'

'You're very honoured, Jennifer. Don't you agree, Father?' commented David, carefully watching the priest's reaction. The fear of his youth still nagged at him. Father Seth's mood could change in a flash. 'Don't you start, gentlemen, or I will have to teach you a lesson,' Ethel said with a smile. David relaxed. He felt he was in the company of allies in Ethel and Jennifer.

'Now, come on, eat. Bobotie for the main course.'

'You make the nicest bobotie, Ethel.' Father Seth said, tucking in with gusto. 'We're so lucky to have you.'

'I know you are,' she replied.

They laughed and Ethel fetched the bobotie, the smell filling the room with delicious aromas of curried beef. They enthusiastically ate most of the contents of Ethel's large casserole dish and sat back with empty plates before them.

'Who is for pudding?'

'Not for me, thank you,' Jennifer said, holding her tummy. Maybe later, Ethel?'

'I'm full, too,' said David. 'I might join you in some later.'

'I might have some, thank you,' said Father Seth, washing down the last of his claret, as Ethel pulled a disapproving face at the two younger ones.

There was a knock on the front door.

'I'll go,' David said.

He returned to the dining room with a young, uniformed, black police officer, with the star-shaped golden badge of the South Africa Police Service.

'Good evening Reverend Father, good evening everyone, I'm Police Constable Nkosi. I've come about the report you rang in earlier.'

'Ah, good evening officer, please, take a seat,' said Father Seth.

'Would you like some pudding?' Ethel asked, anxious for someone else to sample her excellent baking.

He looked at Father Seth in surprise.

'Yes, that's fine, officer. We were just finishing dinner. You're very welcome to have some.'

'Well, then, yes please, madam,' the young man said, hardly able to believe his luck. Ethel returned with two large portions of Malva pudding, delicious sponge with apricot jam, smothered in custard.

'There you are, Father. And for you, young man, enjoy.'

'Thank you madam,' he said, politely. 'It looks fantastic.'

They talked between themselves as he was eating about how busy he must be but how prompt the police response had been. He nodded and made sounds of agreement, obviously grateful for the unexpected treat. He didn't take long to clear his dish then took out his notebook.

First, he asked who had discovered the substance. Ethel explained the circumstances and how she had determined the best course of action by discussing it with David and Jennifer.

Nkosi asked questions of each of the people present, their reasons for being in the household and how long they had been there. He recorded their answers with care.

Father Seth explained about the seminarians who had stayed overnight. Nkosi was obviously interested in the most recent occupant of Room 4. He asked to see the room, so Father Seth took him upstairs to the scene of Ethel's discovery.

The officer put on a pair of gloves and produced a test kit from his pocket. He explained the process to Father Seth, and using a small spatula from the kit, he scraped a small amount of the powder off the mirror and placed it into the liquid chemical vial, screwed the top tightly and shook it. The clear liquid immediately started to turn blue, indicating the presence of cocaine or crack cocaine.

He placed it in an evidence bag and recorded the details on the bag before sealing it. He removed as much of the powder as he could, using a small hand-powered aspirator system, that cleverly deposited the residue in a small bag attached to it, and then he placed the whole thing in a separate evidence bag, again recording the details.

He retrieved the two plastic bags from the table-top, put them in a third evidence bag, and completed the record on that bag. He then proceeded to clean the mirror and tabletop with a wipe that he again produced from a sealed bag taken from his pocket. He returned the wipe to the bag and sealed it.

Father Seth watched the proceedings, silently and with great interest, but not without a little dismay.

Nkosi said, 'I just need to do a quick search, Father, just to be sure there's nothing else in here.' The priest watched him as he systematically moved from left to right, opening the doors of the wardrobe and the drawers of the desk as he did so. He lifted a pillow off the bed, gently shook it over the duvet and a plastic bag containing white powder dropped out from the pillowcase.

Father Seth took a deep breath, but still said nothing. The officer calmly placed the bag of powder in an evidence bag, recorded his findings, completed his search, and they left the room.

They returned to the dining room with the evidence and mirror. Nkosi placed the evidence bags into his lockable briefcase and asked if he might wash the mirror in the sink. Ethel showed him into the kitchen.

He returned to the dining room, where the housekeeper was waiting to offer him coffee from a steaming percolator. He started to smile as he said, 'I'm not usually made to feel so welcome, but it's very kind of you, madam.'

She poured his drink, and he completed a little more paperwork. He then asked if they knew where Dominic could be located. This was the question they knew was coming. Father Seth gave him the address of the seminary and informed him that Monsignor Prince was the principal there.

Nkosi wrote it all down and then looked up, 'Well, thank you for all your help.' He said, 'I just need to tell you that even though the evidence you have found has proved positive for cocaine, it is difficult to attribute the substance to any particular individual without first obtaining any fingerprints and a blood test. The law demands that this is a voluntary exercise, so I will attend the seminary and speak to Deacon Zapatero. Also, if there is to be a prosecution, an individual would have to be found in possession of the banned substance. So it all depends on what happens.' They all breathed a sigh of relief. It was out of their hands now.

The officer stood up and thanked everyone for their openness and input. He then spoke directly to Ethel and said, 'Madam, if you didn't cook such beautiful food and make such nice coffee for these lucky people, I'd be tempted to suggest a change of career! You were very astute not to disturb the evidence.'

'Oh, I can multi-task,' she replied, smiling.

Father Seth showed him out and returned to the dining room, where Ethel felt she needed to lighten the mood.

'Such a bad boy, that Dominic. I'm not surprised he was so badly behaved, using white Coca-Cola like that,' she said, with a glint in her eye.

They all laughed.

They sat for a while, chatting, and David started to clear the table.

'Sit down David, and I'll do it,' said Ethel.

'It's no problem, Ethel, you sit down. I'll help him,' said Jennifer as she picked up some used crockery and took it into the kitchen. David was filling the sink with hot water,

'Thanks. Can you just put them there, please?' he asked, indicating the left drainer.

'Yes, I can do that. Anything for you, David.' He hardly dared feel the happiness her words gave him.

She went back into the dining room to get the last of the washing up and returned to the kitchen. 'You're very domesticated. Do you think you'll ever marry, David?' she asked, rather pointedly.

He drew a breath and chose his words carefully. 'I have never really given it any thought. To be honest, I've never really seen myself in a relationship. I was very much encouraged to keep myself to myself when I was younger.'

He scrubbed at a plate before carrying on.

'Between you and me, Father was very strict and has always been a hard taskmaster. So, I've never really had any friends because of that. I was probably quite a lonely kid. I know he thought he was doing the right thing...so, I've always struggled to communicate with people my own age, well, until a few days ago,' he looked up at her with unashamed admiration.

'So you've never met anyone you'd like to spend your life with?'

He decided honesty was best. 'Yes, I have, just the once. But she'll never know. I didn't, wouldn't, say anything to her because it's never been appropriate.'

'Oh, so you still see her around, then? Is she already married?'

He left her question hanging. 'Yes, I see her. She's a fantastic person, beautiful, too, but she's...out of reach, out of my reach, anyway.'

'Oh David, I'm sorry, that must be so hard for you,' said Jennifer, unaware of his real meaning.

'Not really. Her happiness is more important than my need. I expect I'll always have the opportunity to see her from time to time, and I've decided that that's enough for me,' he said.

The words came easily, because every one of them was true, and there was a strange comfort in saying them to her, however bittersweet.

'Well, I hope she's happy. But you never know what the future may bring, so never give up, will you? Promise me.'

'I'll never give up, I promise you,' he said.

He looked at her and thought, just seeing you happy will sustain me all my life, and it will ensure I don't complicate your life. He was used to self-denial. He understood it from the inside out. It was almost his default position.

They finished the washing up and tidied the kitchen.

'I need to say my prayers,' she said. 'I'm going to my room. I may see you later.'

'OK, say one for me please,' he smiled.

'I will.' She smiled back and left the kitchen and made her way upstairs.

David went into the dining room. Father Seth and Ethel were nowhere to be seen. He started to make his way towards the stairs when he heard the TV was on in the sitting room. He went in to find them sat watching Crime Channel together. He could hardly believe his eyes and ears when Father Seth spoke.

'Will you join us?' he asked. David hesitated, wondering if he should. 'If it's OK with you Father, I need to read those letters, so if you'll excuse me, I'll go up and do it now.'

'That's fine, maybe some other time?'

'That would be good.'

Ethel added, 'I'll be going soon, David. Simeon is on his way to pick me up. Thank you for today.'

'No need to thank me, Ethel, I want to thank *you* for today. Oh, and stay away from the black fizzy stuff, won't you?'

'Cheeky. Goodnight,' she reprimanded. He walked away grinning.

Chapter 13

Curse

David made his way up to his room and reflected on the day. He was astounded by the events flashing through his mind.

He still had two letters to open and all the paperwork from the bank to go through, a necessary chore, but it meant he would soon be able to get the dressing gowns for Jennifer.

Letter number two. He opened it and started to read through the official jargon. It was hard going, so he wasn't taking it in until he saw the words, *The balance of your savings account as of the date of this letter is R 1,190,812.38.*

He read it repeatedly. He took the new savings account book out of the envelope and opened it, shaking. There, printed at the top of page 1, was precisely the same balance. It was a huge amount. Enough to buy a brand-new car. And more. What was going on with this?

He was certain it had to be wrong. Mr Verster was going to get into a lot of trouble, he thought, sympathetically.

He ran downstairs and into the sitting room. Ethel had gone home, and Father Seth was still watching a film on TV.

'Hello David, I thought you'd gone to sort out your paperwork?'

'I had, but I think Mr Verster has made a mistake,' said David.

'What's the matter? You'll have to explain,' answered the priest. David handed him the savings book.

'So, what mistake?'

'The amount, of course, that can't be right?'

'Of course it's right,' Father Seth snapped in response.

David felt uneasy, as if he'd upset him in some way, and fell silent.

The priest rose from the chair. 'Wait a minute. Let me get the old book from my study, the one he used for the transfer.'

He left David watching TV. It was an old British film about the Second World War, *A Bridge Too Far*, about Allied attempts to liberate Holland in 1944. A scene showing paratroopers descending from a sky filled with warplanes seemed familiar. He was sure he'd come across Father Seth watching it before. He was absorbed in it by the time Father Seth returned and made a mental note to watch the film in full some time.

'OK, here's the book he used,' said the priest. I wanted to make a comparison.' He muted the TV.

Opening the books one on top of the other, he said. 'It looks right to me. Take a look.'

David's head started spinning to realise the amount was correct. He'd never had any money in his life before, and now it seemed he had more than he'd ever thought possible.

Money wasn't something he was used to having or handling. He felt overwhelmed and couldn't speak for a few seconds.

'Are you certain this is all mine?' he finally spluttered.

'Yes, I'm certain,' Father Seth answered, nodding.

David said, 'I know now why you said I needed to read everything very carefully, Father. If I need your advice and guidance, will you help me, please?'

'Of course I will, and I'm pleased you're being sensible about this. It's a big responsibility for you, but I'm sure you're up to it.'

'Thank you. I'll see you in the morning, Father. Goodnight.'

'Goodnight, David, sleep well.'

As David started to climb the stairs, the phone rang in the study. The priest went to pick it up.

'Hello,' said Father Seth, cautiously, due to the lateness of the hour. 'Oh, hello, Patrick. Is everything all right?'

There was silence while the Monsignor spoke. David paused on the stairs to check that all was well.

'Patrick,' said Father Seth, slowly and firmly, 'It was in no way a betrayal. I had to call the police. It was a very serious matter, obviously, and it was fully witnessed by my housekeeper, David and Sister Jennifer. Surely you understand that.'

The phone must have been put down abruptly at the other end.

Father Seth waited a few seconds before replacing his receiver without a word. He contemplated calling back but thought it would be better to leave the monsignor to his anger for the time being.

So, that was it. It was only because there had been witnesses to hard drugs being used in the presbytery that the police had been called, thought David. Otherwise, it would have been quietly ignored. He returned solemnly to his room and, as he sat down at his computer desk, he reflected on the many contradictions he had witnessed in Father Seth over the years. Was this latest act Father Seth again protecting the good name of the church, or was it something less honourable? Protecting himself, too? He feared the worst, which was that the changes he was seeing in the priest were skin-deep, and mainly for Jennifer's benefit. He had seemed charmed by her and had obviously nurtured her vocation since she was young. He would have to wait until she had left their orbit to find out – and that was a loss he dreaded. Not because of Father Seth, but losing a soulmate, his new hope in life.

Jennifer had just finished her prayers. She looked at her watch, and it was twenty past ten. She made her way down to the kitchen for a drink. As she passed on the landing, David's door was open, and the light on.

He looked up from the letter as she stood in the doorway.

'Hello there, I'm just going to make some tea. Would you like some?' 'No, thanks,' he replied with a smile, 'I need to read this, then I'd better get some sleep.'

'OK, I'll see you in the morning. Sleep well.'

'You, too.'

He returned to the letter. It contained his PIN, the same instructions as the card, and a reminder to go online and register to manage his accounts.

It was a matter of moments before pressing enter, and within seconds he could see both his RandExchange and savings accounts on screen. He swallowed hard. He knew he'd need to think very carefully about what he was going to do with this enormous windfall. Time for a breathing space, he told himself.

He logged out and, on a sudden impulse, typed into the search engine 'Maureen O'Hara' and clicked on Images.

He scrolled through picture upon picture of the glamorous Irish actress, famous in the 40s, 50s and early 60s. Then there *she* was. This one in particular was exactly Jennifer. It was a poster advertising a 1939 film called *Jamaica Inn*. The likeness was incredible.

He could have been looking at a photograph of Jennifer, not a Hollywood actress born in 1920. He contemplated going downstairs to tell her about it but decided it would be more of a surprise to print a copy and slide it under her door. He pressed print and clutching the paper with a smile on his face he climbed the spiral stairs and carefully slid it so it wouldn't crease. It was bound to make her laugh, he thought. He then went back to the computer and scrolled through more of the photographs. What a beautiful woman Maureen O'Hara had been, he thought, and just the image of Jennifer.

He woke in the morning and the excitement came over him almost immediately. He logged on to SAFERAND and checked his accounts to be sure it wasn't a dream. His heart missed a beat as the reality was once more confirmed. He showered and checked the time. It was still only six o'clock.

Back in his room, he started to go through the documents in the folders. Four old savings books going back to July 1993, the month after his birth, then transactions of numerous amounts until July 2008 when regular monthly payments started to appear alongside them.

It showed deposits of R13,125 every month until his sixteenth birthday, increasing annually to R16,875 a month over the next three years, but nothing after that. But of course, he had been given the transfer book by Father Seth last night. He looked in it, and the monthly payments had increased by a further R1,125 the following year. Where had all that money come from? And why had he been kept almost penniless for so long?

He went downstairs in the hope of getting an explanation. The door to the study was open again, and Father Seth was sitting in the easy chair.

'Good morning, David.'

'Good morning Father. Do you have time to talk?'

'Yes, come in and close the door. What can I help you with?'

'It's all this money, Father. I can hardly believe it. Where did...it come from?'

Father Seth paused before replying, 'Well, David, from the moment Ethel found you that morning on the step, everybody she came into contact with kept handing her money. Little bits here and there, but it soon mounted up and there'd also been numerous envelopes containing money found on the benches in church after Sunday mass, with your name on. I had no alternative other than to open the savings account.

'Then, there were birthdays, Christmas and other special occasions. People were very generous, and in the last five years since you left school, I've been putting in your salary from the archdiocese.'

David shook his head in disbelief. The priest continued, not allowing him to interrupt.

'You get a rise on your birthday each year. And on your 21st your salary will increase considerably. I used to receive the money directly and ensured that the vast majority was paid into the savings account. So, if you could please give me the details of either of your accounts, I'll get the archdiocese to pay it to you directly.'

It almost sounded logical, explained like that. But David's mind whirled as to why all the years had gone by with his having no knowledge of any of it.

'It's all come as a shock, and I didn't know any of this, Father. But thank you,' he managed to reply. The question, 'Why?' remained stuck in his throat. Perhaps all would become clear one day.

'You're welcome. Please ask for help any time, and I understand you'll have lots of questions. Come on, let's go for breakfast.'

They went into the dining room. 'Good morning, you two,' greeted Ethel, brightly.

'Good morning, Ethel,' they both replied.

'Can you go and see where Jennifer is, please, David?'

He ran back upstairs and knocked on her door. 'I'm here!' came the quick answer.

The door opened. Jennifer was wearing pink shorts and a pink T-shirt this morning. He couldn't help it. He said, 'Wow, such a lovely colour.'

'You like?' she smiled.

'Yes, I like it a lot, but you look great, too, in your habit, your jeans, and your dress. In fact, you...' he tailed off, suddenly embarrassed at his sudden garrulousness.

'You're sweet,' she said, touching his arm.

They went downstairs to breakfast.

With a little of his newfound confidence, David spoke up as he reached for a piece of bread, 'Would it be all right if I borrow the car this morning, Father? I need to go to the city.'

'I don't need it today, so that is fine,' he answered.

'Thank you,' said David. 'I need to be back well before lunch anyway to get some work done in the church. The staircase.'

Turning to Jennifer, he added, 'I think of this particular job as the curse of St Brigid's.'

She smiled, 'What do you mean?'

'The spiral staircase in the church. It's all the ebony, mother of pearl, agate and brass. It's such a beautiful, intricate design, but it all needs so much cleaning, over and over again! Actually, you've no sooner finished the lot than you have to start again at the beginning.'

But never mind the staircase today, great, he could have the car, he thought privately. Ackerman & Sons opened at nine. He could be back by 10:30. He was now free to accomplish his mission.

He quickly finished breakfast and went to get his RandExchange card. As he exited his room, he could see the back of Jennifer's head as she was coming up the stairs. He sensed that she was about to ask if she could join him.

It was the last thing he wanted on this occasion so he decided to go up to the bathroom and wait till the coast was clear, then quickly make his way out to the car. He waited for some time. He eventually crept downstairs, but as he quietly turned on the final part of the spiral, he could see her sitting on his bed, smiling.

How could he say no to her? Whenever he saw her, he melted. Whatever she may be about to ask, he knew he couldn't refuse her. He just hoped it wasn't going to be a trip out with him, right now.

'Sorry, I'm here again!' she said.

He replied quickly, still hoping to get away as soon as possible, 'That's fine. I need to get into the city and I don't have much time. I'll be back soon.'

She got up off the bed and went out onto the landing. He closed the door behind her and started to make his way towards the stairs. As he turned at the top of them, he looked towards her. He thought she looked a little dejected. She was smiling as usual, but the usual twinkle in her eyes wasn't quite so bright.

'Would you like to come?' he finally said, against his better judgement.

She immediately brightened. 'I'll just get my bag! It will be nice to come for the ride.'

She ran upstairs and was back on the landing in the blink of an eye, an eye that was delighted to see her happy face.

But how on earth was he going to get the dressing gowns now? Their car journey into the city was a relatively quiet one, as he pretended to be distracted by the traffic, and she privately debated how to mention the picture that had appeared in her bedroom the night before. It had caught her completely off guard and at first she thought it was an old picture of her mother she'd never seen. There was no message to accompany it, so its arrival unannounced under her door had seemed a little strange.

David was meanwhile commenting on the odd pedestrian or local landmark while plotting how he was going to get to the lingerie department of the store

191

without her. He had forgotten all about the picture of Maureen O'Hara in his current dilemma. He couldn't think of an easy a way out of it and was starting to resign himself to abandoning his mission.

They parked up close to the bank, just before nine o'clock. He needed to activate his RandExchange card at an ATM. He'd memorised the PIN and changed it after completing the activation and withdrew a small amount of cash. It was simpler than he had expected.

Then, with the notes in his hand, he had a flash of inspiration. 'Do you know, I think I need to buy a wallet!' he said.

She pointed towards Ackerman & Sons further down the road, smiling. They strolled down and entered the store, bursting into the day's activity, with assistants busying themselves at shelves and counters, and delivery men wheeling in new items to stock them with.

Leather goods were on the third floor. He'd seen the information displayed on the sign earlier in the week, and it now fitted perfectly into his plan. They went up by the lift and looked at several wallets. Jennifer pored over them, smelling and feeling the leather, found the one she liked best and brought it to his attention. Very nice, he thought, and straightaway bought it. Using his card for the first time, he gratefully took it from the assistant, asking for a carrier bag. The carrier bag was essential to his plan.

'How about a coffee, and it will be my treat,' he said. 'To say thanks for your help. My new wallet is great. And thank you for choosing it.'

They didn't really have much time for coffee, he knew that, but he didn't know how else he was going to get away from her for a couple of minutes.

They walked up the stairs to the restaurant. He passed her a menu, but she didn't look at it.

'Just a latte for me, please. We've not long had breakfast.' He was relieved. No waiting for food.

A server took their order, two lattes.

'Excuse me a moment, will you Jennifer? Just need…' He delicately didn't specify what he needed, and rose from the table, picking up the carrier bag containing his wallet. She smiled and quickly checked her phone for messages.

He walked in the direction of the rest rooms but diverted, ran up the stairs to the next floor and went to the ladies' wear counter. He thanked heaven for the miracle. Tanu was there, and there was no queue. She grasped the urgency of the situation just from the look in his eyes and immediately retrieved the reserved dressing gowns, stowing them discreetly into David's carrier bag and taking payment via his new RandExchange card.

By the time he returned to the restaurant and sat down, placing the bag on the chair next to him, their coffee was on the table.

David relaxed, knowing he had achieved his objective, and she hadn't suspected a thing.

They talked of the coffee, barely a rival for Ethel's, but adequate, they decided. Jennifer's eyes suddenly glittered and she reached into her bag.

'Right, David, what on earth is this?' she said finally, holding up the picture of Maureen O'Hara. 'Honestly, I nearly died when I saw it last night. I thought it was my Mammy, with the red lipstick, but then I realised it looked more like me, although I have never worn red lipstick! It is really uncanny, I have to admit. Where did you get it?'

David explained his search online. 'There must be some connection way back, don't you think? You know, the old Irish genes, like Ethel said. I thought it would make you laugh. I'm so sorry if it disturbed you.' He looked worried.

'Oh no, no, it's fine,' she said smiling, reassured now that his motives were as she'd hoped, entirely straightforward, and the lack of a message was born of his lack of social awareness.

'Yes, I suppose you must be right about the genes,' she said, turning to examine the picture again. 'We O'Broins definitely have the Irish colleen look.'

He was relieved that Jennifer had been distracted from his absence from the table, by whatever means. They agreed that they must watch a couple of the star's films together when they had the chance.

Remembering an old Irish phrase Uncle Malachi always used, she said, mimicking him in a perfect Dublin accent, 'Sure, it can't do any harm to watch some of the great lady's fillums.' David was enthralled just listening to her talk.

They arrived back at the presbytery, still talking, and went into the dining room. There was no one about. The door to the study was open, but again there was no one there. Father Seth and Ethel were in the sitting room. The young people made their way in, and Jennifer sat down.

David spied his chance, ran up to his room, and wrote her a little note. *Something I think you'll like, David X*

He had signed it with an X, just like one his mother had left for him, then wondered if it was entirely appropriate once he had put pen to paper. But he had to leave it because time was short. Sneaking up to Jennifer's room, he laid them on her bed.

Then, delighted with his achievement, he quickly got changed and went to tell them that he was going into the church. He thanked Father Seth for the use of the car and returned the keys.

The staircase was indeed beautiful, intricately carved and inlaid, a piece of great quality. It needed regular attention to ensure the natural materials didn't crack or splinter, and for the brass to look its best.

For several years now he'd been doing this monthly, always starting at the top and working his way down to the bottom. It was going to take the rest of the day to complete the task, and Ethel knew to take him drinks and food over, as he always wanted to get the job done in one go.

It was his bête noire, but also his pride and joy. It always filled him with satisfaction to see it gleaming.

He'd been working for about an hour when he heard someone walking through the church. The acoustics of the large space were enhanced when the place was empty, and he could have heard a pin drop. The footsteps were moving from the sacristy behind the chancel and through the nave. He heard the rattle of the thumb latch and the hinges squeaking as the door was opened into the vestibule.

The noise of the footsteps continued towards him. They started to move up the stairway slowly, one loud step after another.

The staircase had twenty-two steps, and in the mind of the young man now cleaning them, this was no coincidence.

Father Seth had drummed it into him. The number twenty-two is ingrained within biblical text. The Book of Revelation ends the whole Bible with its final, and twenty second, chapter.

It was a part of the Bible David could almost quote backwards, chapter and verse. Not least because the bottom rise of the staircase had the brass inlay 'REVELATIONS 22', with a border of mother of pearl, and each subsequent rise contained text from the 21 verses inlaid into them, with a frame of multi coloured, cut and polished agate.

It was Ethel. She'd brought him coffee and biscuits. It was eleven forty-five, and if he were lucky, he'd finish the job before evening dinner. But between now and then, there was the monotony of the task in hand to deal with.

Determined not to carry 'the curse' over to the following day, he decided to ask Ethel if he could have lunch a little later than usual and miss his afternoon break. She told him that was fine and would bring his lunch for two o'clock. He started to think about Jennifer and whether or not she'd found the dressing gowns.

He worked hard, scraping, scouring, scrubbing and polishing. On this occasion, the time appeared to vanish, but he had Jennifer in his thoughts, and it helped his fingers fly over the carvings.

He looked at his watch. It was five past two and he was hungry. He heard familiar echoes resonating through the church. Ethel never let him down.

He made his way down the stairs and into one of the small rooms just off the vestibule to wash his hands. It contained a toilet and hand basin, and in a small cupboard was a fold down table. He heard the door open from the nave, and the smell of hot curry and rice started to permeate into the small space.

Ethel's curry. Delicious. He'd have his lunch at the table in the usual place. There were several chairs along the wall of the vestibule. He took the table through. To his delight, carrying the curry was not Ethel, but Jennifer. He smiled and unfolded the table. She placed a small white cloth on the top, as though the whole manoeuvre were choreographed, and retrieved two foil-wrapped plates of hot food and cutlery out of a bag, placing them on the table.

'Lunch for two,' she smiled.

'Perfect,' he said, wishing Jennifer could always be here when he worked on the curse of St Brigid's. They sat down to eat. He felt blessed.

He thought he would have had longer to prepare for the conversation about dressing gowns but he realised with some trepidation that it needed an introduction right now. The dressing gowns could be ignored no longer. He asked, almost casually, but holding his breath for the answer, 'Have you been to your room since we got back from the city?'

Suddenly blushing, she said, 'Yes! I have! And I saw that a young man had left something for me, and I love them. They are so beautiful. Thank you. But are you a magician or something? How on earth did you manage to get them so quickly this morning?'

It was now his turn to blush. He felt like a hare in the headlights, trying to tell her what he'd done and how he'd done it, but trying to avoid the real reason why he'd done it. The words of explanation just tumbled out. He was almost breathless by the time he'd finished.

'So, when we were in the restaurant the other day, and I left the table...That's when I ran upstairs and asked Tanu to keep hold of them for me. Then this morning, I thought I'd be able to go back and get them alone, but you came with me, so I tried to make a plan to somehow get them for you, and so I thought if I bought the wallet and...'

She interrupted him with her laughter. She remembered the sequence of the morning's events and realised she'd been duped but in such a sweet way and all with good intentions. Not only that, but she started to appreciate that his charming, innocent, boyish personality was something that she had never experienced before in anyone, and he was touching her heart deeply with who and what he was.

'David, that is a lovely thing to do. Well, I'm delighted, and thank you. You have excellent taste, it has to be said.'

'Yes? Well, I'm glad to hear it. I was starting to get worried in case it was the wrong thing to do.'

'Well, don't. I really like them, and it's so considerate of you. I really did need a dressing gown, didn't I? And now I have three of the most beautiful ones in Johannesburg!'

He said nothing and looked through the door into the nave of the church, but he knew he must have looked ridiculously pleased. They finished lunch, and she placed everything into the bag and handed him the flask of coffee that Ethel had made, and a bottle of iced water.

'Ethel sent you this as well. It must be thirsty work,' she commented.

Jennifer told him she was going to use the rest of the day to try to find spiritual guidance. She had a few things about which she needed to pray, but hoped to see him later for another chat, if he didn't mind.

Didn't mind? His heart was bursting.

Chapter 14

Doubts

Father Seth was reading in his study. Jennifer was putting away the last of the lunch crockery and cutlery, which had been drying in the kitchen.

She had put the last spoon in the drawer, swallowed hard and thought, I just have to say it. God will help me, ultimately, but perhaps if I speak to Father Seth, he will guide me, here and now, in navigating this problem. She had been dreading this moment of revelation to him. The study door was open slightly. 'Father?' she asked.

'Come in, Jennifer,' he answered, putting down his book.

She began hesitantly, 'I've something important to ask you, Father. Well...it's, er...' She looked down at her sandals and awkwardly pulled at the bottom of her T shirt, like a young teenager.

Just say it, Jennifer, she ordered herself, as firmly as she could.

This was it. She had to say it. Now. No going back.

She started to speak, 'What it is, Father, and I'm not sure how you will take this, Father, but, well, I'm...having...doubts about my vocation, and I wondered if I could step back from a few things while I take stock? I wondered if it would be at all possible, er, to delay taking my vows until I know I'm doing absolutely the right thing?'

He didn't show a reaction, and pondered her question, while looking at her steadily. As he deliberated, and she tried to read his thoughts, she started to feel anxious, and it showed. She was hardly ever anxious, normally. The world had been mostly sweet to her.

He recognised her turmoil and spoke slowly and carefully.

'It's best to be as open as you can, Jennifer,' he said. 'Look at things from all angles.'

'I understand Father,' she answered, diffidently. 'But it's difficult because I'm scared that you will judge me. You see, I have to recognise that this may lead ultimately to my leaving the convent altogether.'

'I do see!' he said, in a louder voice. 'Still, be that as it may, please believe me when I tell you that I'm very aware that my, er, how would you say it, cantankerous side, has probably made you fearful now and, if that is the case, I want that to cease immediately.'

He attempted a kindly smile. It was not his natural expression, and she knew that, but was glad to see it, and felt reassured.

The priest's whole demeanour seemed to have shifted since she left Newcastle with him. He had been conversational, more positive, and she liked how it made her feel, and she had been optimistic about her visit to St Brigid's. Father Seth had always been a strong and ominous presence to her, when she was growing up. Even though he had always made the effort to communicate as kindly as he could, she'd always been wary of displeasing him.

She sat there, waiting for his verdict, dreading his answer. She hadn't long to wait. He thought again and nodded. 'Jennifer, I'd be happy for you to delay your vows if you genuinely think that doing so will afford you the time and emotional space to arrive at a full and considered conclusion.

'But, dear girl, unfortunately, that is not my decision to make.'

She answered, relieved. 'I recognise that, Father. I understand that I need to follow the process. May I have your permission to contact Prioress in Gauteng?'

'Yes, of course. When would you like to do that?'

'As soon as I can, please,' she said, feeling she ought to grab this passing bull right by the horns.

He looked at his watch.

'What time do they have dinner at the convent?'

'In Cape Town we eat at eight. I'm afraid I'm not sure what time they eat in Gauteng.'

'It's probably eight o'clock too. Remember your Latin? *Convent*, deriving from the Latin *conventus*, meaning to convene, to come together. Therefore, I would suggest, that wherever you go in the world, your order will all have dinner at eight, in an endeavour to maintain a sense of community around the world.'

She nodded in assent.

He picked up the phone to make the call. It was answered almost immediately, and he asked to speak to the prioress. It was a few agonising moments before Jennifer heard Father Seth speak again. Identifying himself to the prioress, he briefly explained the matter in hand and passed the phone to Jennifer. Tentatively, she began to describe her situation.

She expressed her sorrow at placing everyone in this position but felt there was no alternative. She apologised sincerely for the feeling she was letting others down. Nonetheless, she said, she felt it was the most appropriate response to her doubts, and was giving everyone, including herself, time.

The prioress listened intently to Jennifer, and surprisingly, expressed her gratitude for her honesty. She told her gently that her doubts were not uncommon but, such a well-presented explanation for them, was. Furthermore, she tried to reassure her that her decision would lead her to the correct conclusion. She thanked her for her candid and forthright interaction and asked her to put Father Seth back on the line. Handing the phone back to him, Jennifer smiled, more out of pure relief than anything else.

Father Seth started to make notes as he listened attentively to what was being said. He said extraordinarily little in return, but as the call was coming to its conclusion, he responded, 'Very well, Prioress, I look forward to your call. I'll be waiting by the phone at ten. Thank you. Goodbye.'

He put the receiver down and, to Jennifer, he said, 'She sounds very supportive. She's looking into something and will call me back later tonight. She didn't go into much detail, but she's hopeful that the convent may be able to offer you a little, how shall we say, opportunity. Nothing to try to influence your decision, you understand. But I'll know more when she calls back.'

'Thank you Father. You made that much easier than I was expecting you to. I'm so sorry for doubting you.'

'I'm not surprised you had your doubts. I've not given you much reason to do otherwise over the years, and it is a great cross I have borne, I realise now, unnecessarily. I know I have expected others to bear that cross too. But I'm trying to change that now, and as I said to you the other day, prayer affords us the time to make the right decisions.'

Jennifer let his words soak into her. He had borne a cross. And expected others to bear that too. That's what he said. She wondered at the complex emotions behind his words.

They left the study and made their way into the dining room as he whispered to her, 'Try not to worry, dear girl; you'll get the answers in good time, and remember, there's no rush.'

She wanted to hug him but thought better of it and responded instead with a smile.

***

Thank the dear Lord, that's done, he'd thought, as he admired the shining brass and mother of pearl inlay on the first riser, the last of the twenty-two that he'd polished in reverse order. He had had a few revelations of his own today, and the lunchtime visit from Jennifer had definitely been one of them. She hadn't gone into detail, but what she had revealed was that she had things on her mind serious enough to need God's intervention.

He felt confident they were not of his making. He recognised that what she had awakened in him would need his constant supervision and increased self-control. Their interactions were, after all, based on a mutual sense of trust. He wanted to maintain that and to support her for as long as she needed him.

He returned to the presbytery, made his way up to his room, and collected his towel and dressing gown, and went for his shower. He just had time before dinner, he reckoned. He could smell it cooking.

Clean, cool, and feeling achievement from the labours of the day, he made his way downstairs. Ethel was her usual busy, but cheery self as she set the table, and Father and Jennifer were still to appear.

He could hear their voices as they exited the study, the conversation ending as they entered the dining room.

David was curious to know what they had been talking about but, he told himself, it wasn't his business when all was said and done, and what was more, it was not his place to pry.

He took his seat in the dining room then stood to acknowledge Father Seth as he entered with Jennifer. The priest looked at him for once without judgement, without castigation or retribution. David thought his face seemed to have changed in the last couple of days. The stern mask had softened, making way for a more relaxed and friendly countenance. He had maintained his promise of change, and David, like all of them, was feeling the benefit. He could hardly believe the changes that were afoot all around him, and within him.

But somehow, the fear of the past still gnawed at his bones and felt heavy in his stomach. He knew his emotional development was linked to his life experience and wanted to understand how that impacted his interactions and relationships with others. He wished it were as simple as designing spreadsheets.

He knew nothing of his birth parents or personal history, and he knew that his emotional and psychological development had suffered because of that. It was beginning to occur to him that some kind of personal counselling might be appropriate at this point in his life. Now he had his birth certificate, might he at least give some thought to what, if anything, he should do? He parked the idea. Jennifer was sitting opposite him, and she transformed everything.

As dinner came to an end, Father Seth started to clear the table, and Ethel felt that of all the changes in the priest she had seen in the last days, this one would not go unchallenged.

'OK, Father, that will be enough, thank you,' she sniffed. 'I appreciate your intentions are good, but you have enough of your own work to do. Don't forget. You pay me for my time, and if you do my work for me, my hours of employment will suffer.'

He almost guffawed at that. 'Ethel Gumede, you're way too bossy these days. But it's quite charming. I take your point.' And with that he put the plates down.

'Yes, well, it's not about being charming,' she said. 'I'm concerned for my job. God help me if you learn to cook.'

Then she muttered under her breath, 'Although you struggle to boil water, so I think I'm quite safe.'

He heard the comment but ignored it. 'Well, if you insist, I'll sit and watch you instead,' he said.

'Whatever takes your fancy,' she said, winking at David.

'Can I help?' asked Jennifer.

'No child, you can't. Spend some time relaxing, go and watch TV with David, or do some work on David's gardening timetable. I can manage.'

They looked at each other and nodded. Going up to his room, relaxed in each other's company, they laughed conspiratorially at Ethel putting Father in his place. For a moment Jennifer contemplated telling David what had happened before dinner but then thought it better to wait to see the outcome. They entered his room together and she closed the door behind them.

'I'm not sure that's a good idea?' he said, looking at the door.

'You worry too much, David. They know I'm safe with you.'

'Yes, but what about me?' he ventured, knowing the comment would elicit a reaction.

'Mr Blind, what are you insinuating?' They laughed together. There was always laughter when they were together.

'I really want you to see this,' he said.

He turned on his computer and typed 'Maureen O'Hara' into the search engine.

Maureen O'Hara, said Wikipedia, was an Irish American actress and singer born in Ranelagh, Dublin, Ireland, in 1920. Jennifer exclaimed, 'My Mammy's family is from Ranelagh!'

'Then you have to be related, somehow' said David, incredulously. 'You look so alike. She could be a second cousin or something...'

'Oh, to be sure,' said Jennifer, in a mock Irish accent, 'I don't think so, I would know if she was.

Then, back in her own voice, she added, 'Evie, my mammy, she likes to name drop. She does it all the time, whenever she can. So we can't be related to a Hollywood actress! But it's an interesting thing you say, the Irish genes...' Jennifer read through the Wikipedia entry, clicking on the pictures.

'Goodness, I never knew all this stuff...' she said, scrolling down the screen.

David let her read for a while but then interrupted her, looking suddenly serious. 'Jennifer, I want to tell you something, but I don't want you to think I'm telling you for any ulterior motive. It's just something that is worrying me,' he said.

She looked up in concern. 'It's fine, tell me. You can tell me anything,' she said, privately steeling herself for what it might be. In her deepest thoughts, she feared it might be a declaration of affection that she would have to gently rebuff, knowing that David found her, well, a bit like the beautiful Maureen O'Hara.

David's answer was not at all what she was expecting. He said, 'It's my new bank accounts. I just can't believe how much money is in them, and I honestly don't know what to do with it all.'

Jennifer took a breath of relief and touched his hand. 'I'm not sure you need to tell me, but if it makes you feel better, you can,' she replied. 'It's probably easier to show you,' he said, handing her his savings book.

She opened it on the first page and read the balance. *R 1,190,812.38*. Her eyes widened. She was silent for a few seconds, and then a tear appeared in each of them.

'I'm sorry,' he said, seeing her response. 'I shouldn't have done that. It's upset you.'

'I'm not at all upset, but don't you see what this means?' she quickly reassured him. 'I'm so delighted for you.'

'I don't understand.'

'Don't you see? This really is the gateway to your future.

'Your course, David, the computer course. You could enrol at the university and pay for your tuition, and if Father lets you live here whilst you're studying, you wouldn't have to rely on him to keep you. You could pay him for your room and board.'

She saw the whole thing, laid out before her.

'It's a perfect solution. I know you're worried you might have to give your job up, but when I was studying for my teaching certificate, I only had to go into college three days a week. Think about it. There's no rush but think about what you could achieve.'

She rubbed her hand down his upper arm, stopping herself from wanting to embrace him.

She knew she felt love for him, maybe as a brother, but something was beginning to nag at her that, deep inside, it might be more than that. Her vocation, the money, David's insecurity, her own insecurity, everything. Oh, this was all so complicated, now, and she couldn't risk giving the wrong messages, or messages that could be misinterpreted.

He let out a gentle sigh and clicked open a folder then a file.

He showed her the spreadsheet that he had designed for Father Seth. He asked if she thought it could be something that might help him to keep track on his money. They looked at it together and brainstormed how he could use it for personal budgeting, both of them finding relief in the practical. David knew he could have worked it out himself easily, of course, but it was lovely listening to Jennifer's suggestions and take on things.

'I think I need to get a better phone' he suddenly said, picking up his outdated cell phone. 'This old thing can't handle the latest apps and social media, and I reckon I need to be a bit more connected now. Maybe you could come shopping with me?'

She was more than happy to talk about mobile phones. 'Well, I couldn't manage without mine now,' she said, delightedly. 'There's an app for practically everything. I use it for banking, ordering things, and to message mammy, of course, and I occasionally video call old friends at home in Newcastle and my great uncle Malachi in Dublin, who I never, ever, would have seen without it. He's 93 and video calls me! I'd love to meet him in person one day.'

'Ah, he sounds incredible,' David said. 'Yes, definitely need a new phone. This is an old one of Father Seth's in fact,' he added, wryly. 'It's just pay as you go, and it's been mostly for Father or Ethel to ring me. I know there are lots of apps I could use. I feel quite ashamed that I haven't done anything about it before now, but there wasn't the need,' he smiled.

'Getting one on a contract may be a good way,' she advised. 'Or you could buy one outright and do sim-only. Have a look sometime and check out the deals. There are lots online. I've found you can save a lot if you shop around,' she added, pointing to the screen, which was still displaying a picture of Maureen O'Hara. She leant over the keyboard, launched a search engine and typed in 'mobile phone deals'.

There was a knock at the door. 'Come in,' called David, absentmindedly, still engrossed in the screen.

It was Father Seth.

'Sorry to interrupt,' he said. 'I need to speak to you when you have a minute, Jennifer. I have some news for you.'

'I'll come now, Father,' she said, jumping up. 'See you later, David, do some good research,' she added, almost skipping, as she left his room.

David perused the numerous mobile phones available and, as Jennifer had predicted, he found a couple of deals that would suit him.

That done, and still curious at the likeness between Jennifer and Maureen O'Hara, he typed the name of the actress into the search engine again to find out more about her.

It turned out she was a remarkably interesting character indeed. A lot of the material was typical Hollywood PR, mixed with reports of interviews and descriptions of her films.

But then...? Che Guevara and Maureen O'Hara? A more unlikely pairing he could hardly imagine.

He read on, almost disbelieving. The actress had apparently struck up a friendship in 1959 with the Argentine-born freedom fighter after a chance meeting in the Capri Hotel, Havana, whilst filming *Our Man in Havana*. The two had found common ground when Guevara had explained that he, too, had Irish blood, his grandmother's birth name being Ana Lynch, his great grandfather's Patrick Lynch, and the family's having originated in Galway. The young Che had learned much of the Irish struggle 'at his grandmother's knee', according to Maureen O'Hara. He had adored the old lady.

O'Hara herself had been born into a Dublin family just four years after the 1916 Easter Rising, and two years after the island of Ireland was torn apart into two, the Irish Free State in the south and the region of Northern Ireland, dominated by Ulster Protestants loyal to the British crown. There had been much bloodshed, oppression and bitter hatred for centuries on that small and beautiful island, close to the British mainland.

So the Hollywood star had much to share with the man known to many as a hero, as just 'Che', and had been fascinated by this man of action, a real legend, not the kind she was used to on the LA studio sets. Here she was, then, in a unique moment of history, just three years before the Cuban missile crisis plunged the world into panic and fear, talking to one of the main players and learning of his motivations. He was a man who had already become the symbol for every man and woman in every country in the world enduring the oppression of poverty and discrimination.

To illustrate the online article, one picture showed a mural on the gable of a house in Derry, Northern Ireland, proclaiming 'Ernesto Che Guevara Lynch' with the flags of Cuba and the Irish Republic. There were words in Gaelic, and a quote from Guevara's father, 'In my son's veins flowed the blood of Irish rebels'.

The translation of the Gaelic was, he read with interest, *The revolutionary may die, but the revolution lives on.* Maureen O'Hara had been delighted, apparently, to observe that the famous cap her Argentine friend wore was actually an Irish rebel's cap. It wasn't an affectation. The rugby playing Doctor of Medicine was partial to the odd pint of Guinness when he could get it.

David thought immediately of the struggle that had been fought in South Africa against the abomination of apartheid. He thought of the people he knew, and their families, who had suffered under the regime. He needed to look no further than Ethel, her children made fatherless by the attempt to bring a democratic and civilised society into being. It struck another memory for him. He thought he had read something years ago about Guevara and his links to the anti-colonial forces of native Africans. Indeed, hadn't Guevara himself led Cuban soldiers into the Congo to help train volunteer fighters?

David searched again online to confirm. Yes, there it was. After leaving The Congo, Guevara went to Tanzania where he lived in the Cuban Embassy and formed alliances with other black African movements including the African National Congress. God, what a man he had been, thought David. He fought and died for his beliefs.

The forces of oppression would always have had to put an end to his life, of course they would, he thought. David read on and found the brutal details of Che's assassination in Bolivia, in 1967. The gunmen, working with the CIA, removed his hands as trophies and took them to their paymasters as proof that he was dead. His handless skeleton was exhumed from its hidden burial ground on a remote mountainside in 1997. It was a hideous end for a man of principle and honour.

David dwelled on the story, absorbing the details, imagining the scenes. His own Christian name, given to him by his mother, was obviously Hispanic. He identified even more with Che Guevara. He longed to know more of his mother, Mamma.

Jennifer seemed to know so much about her family in Dublin.

If only he, David, knew more about his own beginnings. The hunger in him grew.

Chapter 15

Crystal

Father Seth and Jennifer sat down facing each other across his desk. She was eager to hear what he had to say, of course, and gazed at him intently with wide eyes.

'The Prioress has put forward an interesting proposal,' he began. Jennifer's eyes widened and her eyebrows shot up.

He continued, 'She wonders if you would consider taking a sabbatical? There's the possibility of a teacher post in South Sudan.'

Jennifer's eyes grew even wider.

'Don't worry, I know that sounds alarming on the face of it,' Father Seth added, seeing her reaction. 'There's currently a state of ceasefire in the country, and I'm not sure if you know already, but the Sisters are trying to establish a school in Juba. It's a mainly Christian area.

'The South Sudanese Government would support the school financially and in other ways. They're in discussions with the convent as we speak, trying to determine an appropriate curriculum.'

Jennifer was taken aback at the unexpected turn of events but said nothing and nodded.

Father Seth explained that in spite of the ceasefire there remained a volatile environment across the country, including Juba. The school would be her home and her protection for the extent of her stay, should she choose to go.

There would be no freedom of movement within the country, and she would have to remain within living quarters when not teaching. A decision wasn't immediately necessary, he said, since security measures had to be agreed upon and ratified. However, it was hoped that the school would be up and running in approximately six months. There would be a nominal fee for her work. Should she choose to undertake the position, then travel, accommodation, food, and medical needs would be provided. Due to potential risks of military incursions, she would be advised not to wear a habit, which would identify her as a target.

Jennifer swallowed hard. It was a lot to take in.

In the interim, said Father Seth, she would be welcome to stay at the presbytery until she chose to make other arrangements. Nevertheless, and whatever her decision, she was now free to look for work in the community, if she so wished.

Jennifer again passed no comment. She nodded, smiled and as she got up to leave the study she thanked the priest and said, 'Thank you for all that, Father. I will give it very careful consideration. There is a great deal to think about.'

As she was opening the door, he cautioned, 'Whilst I'm confident you'd be an asset there, Jennifer, I'm not convinced you should be asked to take such significant risks. Please, do think about this very carefully.'

Phew, she thought as she climbed the loft staircase. She was exhausted, though, and just needed to sleep on it.

She quickly got ready for bed and woke in the morning feeling rested. It was Friday. She was looking forward to putting her thoughts to the back of her mind and taking a little time to relax. It was impossible. Her mind spinning from one thought to the next, instinctively she knew what she needed to do. She sought out Father Seth and asked for the keys to the church, then made her way to a small side chapel dedicated to Our Lady of Perpetual Help. Kneeling at the altar, she started to pray the rosary. Then, looking up to the copy of the 15th century Byzantine icon of the Madonna and Child, she whispered the words of a favourite, old familiar prayer, *'O Mother of Perpetual Help, grant that I may ever invoke your most powerful name...'*

She bent forward and rested her forehead on her hands which tightly clasped the precious rosary sent to her by her great uncle Malachi. She knelt for considerable time in the silence and peace of the beautiful old church of St Brigid's, only moving to breathe.

Leaving the church refreshed and at peace, she returned lighter in heart to the presbytery. She spent the remainder of the day busying herself, much of it with Ethel, helping her with cooking and cleaning. The day drawing to a close, she made her way up to bed.

It was Saturday morning and she woke early, her mind wandering to comforting thoughts of home, and her mother. She decided she would ring her later to hear her views on the new turn of events. All this will fall into place, she told herself, walking into the quiet dining room and slowly helping herself to the orange juice and cereal laid out by Ethel.

Meanwhile, David was just waking up. He went up to the bathroom and showered. Thinking Jennifer was still in bed, he crept back to his room and got dressed before going downstairs. To his surprise, he could hear everyone laughing as he was halfway down. He stopped on the stairs to listen. There was much chat and joviality and it seemed Father Seth was at the centre of it, reminiscing about some of the mischiefs he'd got up to as a child. It was obvious that he was enjoying sharing the memories, the kind of stories David had never heard him tell.

'Yes, I really did drop the monstrance with an enormous clatter...' he was in the middle of saying. 'And the bishop scowled at me, right on the altar, in front of a packed congregation.' Jennifer and Ethel were helpless with laughter.

David realised that he, personally, had no stories to tell in company that would raise a smile, let alone a laugh. His own memories were laced with the pain that had overshadowed his childhood.

He took a deep breath and continued to the dining room. As he entered, the mood seemed to change. Father Seth's story tailed off abruptly, and the laughter turned to quiet smiles of welcome. It was as though his presence had brought Father Seth back down to earth with the same painful realisation that had just dawned on David.

'Good morning!' David managed in a jovial, but forced, tone.

'Good morning,' came the replies from Ethel and Jennifer. Jennifer looked at him with sad understanding in her eyes.

Father Seth nodded and beckoned in his direction, looking deep into him. The priest then coughed, stood up, then moved past him, a glisten in his eye. He excused himself and quickly left the room.

David looked at the two women and followed the priest into the study. He could never have guessed what would come next. As the door closed behind them, Father Seth went over to the window and fell to his knees.

'What...' he choked. 'What have I done to you, David? Can you ever forgive me?'

David, dumbstruck, didn't know what to do. He see-sawed on his feet. Should he go to the priest, should he say something, anything? He stood there for many seconds.

Finally, he went to Father Seth and, more out of raw instinct, reached out his hand and helped him to his feet. Without words, he placed his hands on the priest's shoulders and his head upon his chest. Father Seth drew in a huge breath and held it for many seconds.

The priest's mind was rushing with the memories of the unnecessary beatings, the sudden acknowledgement of the cruelty of his actions against his now comforter. Why, why?

'David, I cannot justify what I have done to you over the years,' he whispered, his head bowed.

'The Jesuits always said, give me a child until he is seven and I will show you the man. But what I have done with you has gone far beyond what was necessary. I thought it was for your own good, but I see now that was my pride, and I see that I have made you suffer greatly.

'I am truly sorry. Mea culpa, mea culpa, mea maxima culpa.'

He beat his chest with his hand three times.

David, rooted to the spot, gave the moment the dignity it commanded, and remained silent.

Then he fell to his knees before the priest and said, 'Father, please forgive me, too. None of us can ever know fully the sufferings we inflict on others. We are all only human before God, and I promise you, this will be forever between us and God.'

Father Seth placed his left hand on the young man's head and made the sign of the cross with his right. David made the sign of the cross in answer and, getting back to his feet, he looked the priest full in the eyes with new understanding and a new peace in his own. Nothing more needed to be said.

In a daze, David returned to the dining room and re-joined Ethel and Jennifer who were now chatting about recipes.

'Ah, but that's my special ingredient' said Ethel as he entered the room, and they both looked at him and smiled.

***

Father Seth sat alone in the quiet study and allowed his mind to go free. He was transported to the painful memories of his own childhood, still festering, still unhealed.

He'd been born more than half a century before into a family that had emigrated to South Africa in the aftermath of World War II from the Catholic, eastern region of Holland. His parents were strict and his upbringing was centred on the strong and unforgiving teachings of the church, rather than the kinder theology of later generations. He'd been raised, the youngest of five children, with the certain knowledge that he would enter the priesthood, and it was made clear to him from an early age that this outcome was not negotiable.

This was God's will, they'd told him, and something he should rejoice in, not resist. He'd struggled with it but he had dutifully followed their bidding, aware that a wrong word might lead his father to raise his hands to him or, worse, his subservient and anxious mother.

He remembered the times she'd been struck for small misdemeanours. He'd cowered in the corner, hating his father, angrily wanting to stop him, suffering terrible guilt for his own anger and begging the forgiveness of God.

Jan Rossouw had lost himself in drink every night for thirty years and it was a relief to the whole family when he died in 1978. Seth was 18 when that cloud lifted, but another descended when his mother, seeking comfort one lonely night, confided in him that his father, a local civil servant, had been a Nazi collaborator and responsible for betraying the whereabouts of many Jews in the area. It was news he could hardly bear to hear, and knowledge she had barely been able to live with. He longed for escape.

The seminary was hardly the refuge he had hoped for. He'd had it beaten into him at home, and the process was continued by his educators in the priesthood, to accept everything and challenge nothing, so he did. But the scars went deep.

The taunts of the youngsters on the streets where he grew up were echoed by his fellow seminarians. Catholics weren't welcome in some parts of a region dominated by the Dutch Reform Church, and Dutch Catholics were regarded with suspicion in a religious order founded by the Irish. Secure in their long Irish heritage, some of the kinder boys tried not to show it, of course, but he felt it all the same.

The seminary was where he'd met Patrick Prince, later to become his clerical superior, but back then was an ally and a trusted friend. Patrick had always been destined for higher things, so much was obvious to all he encountered. But he saw something in Seth and took pains to shelter him on the important occasions, all the way through to their priesthood. They were ordained on the same day.

The newly created Father Seth suddenly became aware of his increased status in the world. He was now treated practically everywhere with respect and reverence, even by those much older than him. Furthermore, he started to realise that he now had the power to instil into others some of the fear that had been instilled into him. He'd survived it, hadn't he? He made it through, and now look at him. Pass it on, he thought. It was the sort of thing that made you stronger. It felt good. Down all the years it had somehow helped to redress the balance in his life. Until now. Something was stuck. Something nagged.

Was it seeing the innocent joy shared between Jennifer and David? He couldn't tell.

***

'Is everything all right with Father?' asked Ethel.

'Yes, I think he's tired after the events of the week. He's resting. He'll be fine,' answered David in reassurance to the woman's look of concern.

Jennifer nodded and left them, making her way up to her room. She picked up her phone and pressed 'Home' in her contacts. Evie answered almost immediately.

The first few, bravely cheerful exchanges soon dissolved into Jennifer's real feelings. It was a long and tearful conversation, covering all of what had happened in the last five days.

Evie listened, making comforting noises and comments, and when she could finally say something between Jennifer's sobs, was adamant that Jennifer should return to Newcastle immediately.

Jennifer choked back her tears at that and said quietly, 'No, Mammy, I can't do that, as much as I would like to. Running away from the situation would serve no purpose in the long term. I feel better that prioress has agreed to me postponing my vows, and I really need to pray about it.'

'But please don't go to South Sudan, my darling girl,' pleaded Evie.

'I promise I will pray and leave everything in God's hands. Thanks so much for listening to all my problems again. Don't worry about me. Honestly, I'm feeling much better now for talking to you. I love you, Mammy.'

'I love you too, sweetheart. Ring me when you need me.' They ended the call. Jennifer washed her face, blew her nose and checked her appearance.

'Would anyone like to go for a walk?' she asked, brightly, as she returned to the dining room.

'You two go,' Ethel said, waving them away. 'I want to prepare lunch, and Father has confession this morning, so I'm sure he won't have time.'

The young ones left the presbytery through the back door and started to walk through the lush garden, filled with scent and colour. Sensing something was worrying her, David contemplated asking her about it, but held back.

She explained that she'd called her mother, and they'd had a great talk. But, she added, she was worried about Father Seth because she had never seen him like that before.

David looked down, and she saw again the sadness she had seen in his eyes when she first met him.

'Are *you* all right David?' she asked. 'It's just that you said a bright good morning, but your face wasn't in keeping with it. And it still isn't.'

'You don't miss much do you?' he replied with a smile, before adding, 'I had a moment of sadness this morning and I don't want it to affect my day. But I'm OK now. Being with you makes me happy.'

She tugged his arm, playfully. 'That's all well and good, but being your friend isn't just about being happy. Remember I'm here for you, too, always.'

'Thank you, I know that. I'm fine now,' he replied. She was reassured.

'Good, I'm pleased to hear that. Have you given any thought to the course?' she asked.

He brightened. 'Well, I've been looking, and I think I'm going to speak to Father about it to see if I can maintain my job and the studying. I expect it will be hard, but I want to try, and, if I find I'm struggling, I can give Father some time to find a replacement.'

'I think that's incredibly wise of you, she said, delightedly linking her arm with his. If you need any help with anything, please ask, won't you?'

'You know I will,' he smiled.

They continued to walk and talk. It was almost lunchtime when they returned to the presbytery.

Ethel was glad to see them back in time. 'Are you busy this afternoon, child?' she asked Jennifer. 'I'm going shopping if you'd like to come with me. Simeon picks me up at two every Saturday, and we go to the local market. I know David likes to go on his computer when he can, so you can come with me if you want?'

'I'd love to do that, Ethel. We can have some girl time!'

Ethel had to laugh at that. 'OK, I can be a cool stick when I put my mind to it.'

'Er, don't you mean 'chick' Ethel?' Jennifer enquired, laughing.

'Oh, perhaps I do. Well, don't give me any stick about it! Coke, or Cola, it's all the same to me, child.'

'Ethel's the coolest stick I know,' David said, mischievously.

'Behave yourself, boy. You're not too old to experience the wrath of a Zulu lady,' said the housekeeper, with mock ferocity.

They laughed together.

Ethel and Jennifer left the presbytery precisely at two, and Father Seth was busy preparing his sermon for Sunday's Mass. David decided to do some more research into IT courses. He found one quite quickly that appealed to him. It was a BSc Hons in Information Technology, but there were only six weeks left before it started, and only two places left to fill.

He worked out that the cost at R21,500 per year was well within his budget. He looked at the timetable and course content and realised that he could indeed make it fit around his work at St Brigid's. He knew he needed to act quickly to register his application. There was also the small matter of an entrance exam if his application were accepted.

He stood up from the desk and, without hesitation, went to speak with Father Seth.

'Are you busy, Father?' he said, as he looked through the open study door.

'What is it, David?'

'It's just that...well, I've been considering doing a BSc Honours in Information Technology, and I've found an appropriate course at the University of Johannesburg.'

The priest looked up in surprise. 'That sounds good, David. Tell me more.'

David's words tumbled out because his head was full of all the information he'd just read. 'It's a certified course and is directed towards people who are working full time who want to get a formal qualification in information and cyber security. It's NQF Level 5, and you get an official certificate from the University of Johannesburg. It consists of five modules of three days each in the first year. Each module will have an exam, you have to pass all five modules to successfully complete the first year.' He was almost breathless.

'How are each of the modules broken down?' asked Father Seth.

'Well, first, I'd have to pass a subject-based entrance exam. But I think I could do that. The first five modules are classroom-based, one module per month. They're completed through three consecutive days of study, with an exam at the end of each module. I know I'll need to carry out some course work at other times, but I already use most of my spare time to work on my computer.'

'And the second year?'

'The first three modules are online based, from six to nine in the evening spread out over twenty-four dates, followed by an exam for each module. The study periods and possible venues for the last two modules have yet to be determined. Still, there are eleven dates on which study will be required, again in the evening.

'However, if you're in agreement, I'd like to continue working and taking time off to fulfil the course commitments. Also, I don't want to live on campus and would prefer to live here at the presbytery, if you feel that appropriate?'

The words just flowed from his mouth. He didn't even have to try. It seemed natural, and he was now burning to join the formerly unreachable world of the university.

Father Seth listened carefully and with respect. 'I'd be happy to assist you with all of that, David. I don't have any issues with you living here whilst you complete your studies. But I would ask that you discuss any potential visitors to the presbytery before making arrangements.'

'Of course, Father. I have calculated the cost and will pay the tuition and any other fees from the money in my savings account.'

Father Seth nodded. 'It pleases me that you're such a responsible young man David, and I'm sure you will make a success of this. When does the course begin?'

'In six weeks.'

'What? Then I suggest you get the ball rolling as soon as possible. Good luck, I'm proud of you,' he said with a sudden and unexpected restriction in his throat, not a physical reaction he was familiar with.

'I'll go and submit my application now,' David said, almost not daring to believe that he was hearing approval and encouragement.

As he stood up to leave the study, he handed Father Seth the details of his RandExchange account, asking him to arrange for his salary to be paid into it.

'How much room and board would be appropriate?' he asked. Father Seth looked at him strangely and waved him out of the study with a shake of the head, looking back at his work.

David left the study respectfully and ran upstairs two at a time. He submitted his application online and immediately got a date to sit the entrance exam. It was to be the following Wednesday at nine o'clock. He couldn't wait for dinner to break his news to Jennifer and Ethel.

***

At the market, Jennifer had decided what her future should be.

It came to her in a flash, talking with Simeon. Neither he, nor Ethel, had any idea of the proposal the prioress had laid before her.

As they wandered the shops and stalls, Simeon mentioned that he'd always wanted to be a teacher, like her, and had particularly wanted to work with children from deprived backgrounds. But, due to his responsibilities to his siblings, he had never been able to pursue his dream.

She saw the look of disappointment on his face, and she felt this was the sign she had been waiting for. She had to go to South Sudan. Who else was going to teach those little ones? It was that simple in the end.

So, decision made, she wanted to mark it by finding a gift for Father Seth. 'Is there anywhere around here I can get a bottle of wine for Father Seth?' she asked.

'Not really,' said Simeon. 'But I know a place we can call at. We'll have to pass the presbytery, but they have some nice wines, and they're reasonably priced. They also have some in gift boxes, I think.'

'Sounds just the thing' said Jennifer, gratefully.

'Why are you buying him wine, child?' asked Ethel.

'Oh, it's just a small thing to say thank you for all he's done for me over the years, and I think he needs cheering up right now,' she replied.

'Well, that's so kind of you,' said Ethel.

'That sounds perfect Simeon, if that's OK with you Ethel?'

Ethel answered in her familiar, motherly way, the one Simeon had heard countless times during his life. 'I've told you child, if I can give it, you can have it. My time is yours.'

They made their way back to the car, and Simeon drove to the winery. Jennifer found a Western Cape Pinotage that she knew was Father Seth's favourite. She'd seen him drinking it at the presbytery. It was expensive, but it was the right choice, and she asked if they had any crystal glass gift sets.

The sales assistant pointed her towards a range of glasses and explained that she could choose any and they would make up the gift set at extra cost. Jennifer chose a beautiful crystal glass and, for the gift wrapping, a white, suede effect, satin-lined box tied up with a purple ribbon. It looked beautiful. She carried it carefully out of the shop and told Ethel she would give it to Father at dinner.

They arrived back at the presbytery. Simeon helped them take the groceries into the kitchen, and Jennifer took the present she'd bought for Father Seth up to her room. She was excited to give it to him, but she needed to tell him of her decision before that. She went downstairs to the study. The door was open, and she asked could she have a private word. He invited her in, and she closed the door.

I've made my decision Father, and I want to go to South Sudan,' she said, with a light in her eye. 'But in the interim, I would like to keep it private until nearer the time, because I don't want the pressure I know I'm likely to get.'

Father Seth nodded with understanding. 'You know that people will only give you pressure because they'll be concerned about your safety, but of course, you have every right to keep it private until you're ready.'

She said, 'Yes, in their kindness and love, I'm sure their intentions will come from a good place, but I feel this is what God wants of me. Also, I've decided to find some work to help me provide for myself before I go. I need to speak to someone on Monday to see if they can help me with finding work, if that is acceptable to you?'

The priest replied, 'The prioress already made it clear that you have been released from constraints until you come to a final decision on your future concerning vows. But I must let her know of your decision, and I will do that when you leave the study.'

Relieved, she stood up to leave and, as she walked to the door, Father Seth said, 'Just before you go, I want you to know I'm immensely proud of the person you are, Jennifer, and I want to thank you for what you have helped achieve in your short time here. It takes a special person to help so many open their hearts to change. Especially when it is born out of such grave negativity and the dark place we all found ourselves in, just a few days ago.'

She spread her arms in gratitude, smiled and bowed her head, silently receiving his blessing, before turning to leave the room.

Chapter 16

Tanu

They all sat down to dinner. Saturday dinner at the presbytery had always been an uncomfortable occasion for David. Rather than sitting at table, with Father Seth's special guests of the week, he had always cheerfully volunteered to help Ethel serve the numerous clergy and local politicians who regularly arrived, academics, authors, charity organisers and fundraisers.

The list of the priest's intellectual friends and acquaintances appeared endless, and David had listened clandestinely to the conversations, generally ignored by the company, but ever grateful for that, and afterwards he ate in peace in the kitchen.

Tonight was different, quite different.

He felt excited about his news and wanted to share it with those who had become closest to him. He wanted to share it with those he loved and regarded. Jennifer, in particular, of course.

But, for some reason, he suddenly felt someone was missing.

His mother. Mamma. He'd tried to push her from his mind whenever he could for so long, but seeing the note had brought the loss of her again sharply into focus.

He didn't know what his relationship would have been like with her. But the note she'd left was written with love and regret. He imagined himself as a small boy, playing securely in her presence. Just in the way he had done when Ethel looked after him.

All his life, he had felt her absence. He had felt her missing at the milestones of his life, birthdays, Christmases, First Confession, First Holy Communion, Confirmation, the transitions through school. He saw all the other children with their mothers. He'd never known anything about his, his flesh and blood, the woman who had brought him into the world.

He yearned to feel a connection with her, to know at least what she looked like. He wanted to believe that she had loved him, if only for a moment in time. He wished she were here, to be proud of him.

David looked around the table. They had just finished the first course when he stood up and said with quiet assurance, 'If I could have your attention please?'

They all looked up expectantly.

Deep breath. He continued, slowly, 'This week has been a time for change and reconciliation. I'm sure I have learnt something about myself as I'm sure you all have about yourselves too. You all have proved the most important people in my life.'

'You may already know, a new and wonderful thing happened this week, and that was the sense of family that you have all brought.

'So,' he said, opening his arms to embrace the room, 'I want to share something with you all. It may be a small thing to many, but for me, it is a massive step. Today, with Father Seth's blessing, I have enrolled on a degree course with the University of Johannesburg.'

He paused as he looked at them in turn. 'If I pass the entrance exam I sit on Wednesday, I will start in six weeks.'

He looked at the three faces gazing at him. Ethel had the biggest smile he'd ever seen. Father Seth looked delighted, and Jennifer stared at him with pride.

As he sat down, Ethel squeezed his hand and didn't say anything. She didn't need to, because her face said it all. Father Seth got up from his chair and went to shake his hand and congratulate him.

Jennifer jumped to her feet, a tear in the corner of her eye. She wrapped her arms around him and kissed him on the cheek. David felt dizzy with the emotions coursing through him.

The young woman stood back and savoured the light in his eyes that she knew had always been there, waiting to be released.

'David, that's wonderful,' she said.

Then, feeling her own moment had arrived, she asked to be excused. David started explaining the components of the first semester of the course to Father Seth and Ethel listened as she started to clear the plates. Jennifer went up to her room to get her special gift.

Flying back downstairs and into the room like a wisp, she looked at Father Seth shyly as she handed her gift to him, and said, 'Father, I got this for you today. It's a very small token to express my gratitude for all you've done for me since you came into my life when I was seven. I have recognised that I've never really said thank you for your guidance, love, and encouragement.'

He looked at her with delight.

He turned the gift in his hands before employing his strong, thick fingers to delicately open the beautifully gift-wrapped parcel.

He almost spluttered. 'Well, I never. My favourite wine! And the glass is...exquisite. It's crystal, isn't it?' He held it up to the light and twirled it round. It sparkled, and he flicked it with one finger. It rang out.

'Yes, it is. The best!' she answered.

'I like the purple ribbon, too,' he said. 'I love the way they've created a spiral with it.'

'The colour of Advent and Lent. I chose it because of what it represents' she said. 'Penance because I'm guilty of not showing enough appreciation. It's preparation in line with what I need to do in the future. And the recognition of the need for sacrifice.'

'Ah, sacrifice' he said, turning the glass again between his fingers.

'Do you know,' he continued, his voice dropping to a low purr. 'I've gone through the last forty years of my life struggling with sacrifice, Jennifer? Particularly the sacrifices I have needed to make to maintain my vocation.'

Jennifer, David and Ethel froze at his words. They had never heard Father Seth say anything like this. Their minds ran over a multitude of possibilities.

He carried on, as though it was purely natural, and nothing should stop him now. They held a collective breath, but relaxed as his words washed over them.

'I'd always thought that I could never enjoy family life and that my dedication to the Church had to remain at the core of everything. But, tonight, I have been enlightened by you young people. Ethel, you have always been a shining beacon, but I have turned my eyes away.

'You all see, quite rightly, that family is an integral part of your lives and the single most important thing the church should embrace. Your existence appears to be based on inclusion and that's clear to witness. How you relate to each other, warmth and compassion exude from you all, and it's beautiful to see. Of course, you're all completely right. Inclusivity indeed holds up the basic principles of Christianity. Age doesn't always bring wisdom.'

'Father, I think you're wrong, there' said Jennifer, gently. He smiled. There was a new softness in him that they all could feel. Ethel went into the kitchen and returned with dishes of steaming food. She passed the pork casserole to Father Seth, and Jennifer helped herself to the vegetables. 'Mmm, this smells amazing, Ethel,' she said.

They finished dinner as most families do, chatting about nonsenses, laughing at shared jokes, and then arguing with Ethel as to who should clear away the dishes and tidy the table.

***

It was Monday morning, and Jennifer made her way to the bus stop. For her, there was still a feeling of freedom in such a simple thing after being chaperoned by the sisters in the convent since the age of fourteen.

The stop was just outside Mr De Bruyn's fuel station, set back in a lay-by across the road from the top of the cul-de-sac, where the church was situated. The bus arrived on time. She felt apprehensive as she climbed aboard, but she had a mission in her mind and heart.

She asked the driver if the bus went anywhere near Ackerman's department store. He informed her that it stopped almost directly outside the main store, and she paid her fare.

After about 25 minutes, he announced, for her benefit, 'Ackerman's, city centre.' She got up from her seat, made her way to the front of the bus, smiled at him, 'Thanks so much!' and alighted.

She entered through the central revolving doors and made her way to the fifth floor, looking for Tanu. Agnes, the older assistant who had helped her when she'd visited last week, was serving a customer, so she waited in line.

'Good morning madam, can I help you?' she asked, as soon as she was free.

'Good morning! Is Tanu available please?'

Agnes replied, 'I'm afraid it's her day for a late start, but she will be here in about an hour. Is there anything I can help you with?'

'Maybe, well, I hope so. I was…actually, I'm looking for work and wondered if there was any availability in store?'

'I see,' answered Agnes, looking under the counter unnecessarily and rearranging some wrapping paper and a stapler.

Rising up to look Jennifer in the eye she said, tartly, 'You have to be a particular type of person to work in this department, you know. Someone discreet and very trustworthy, someone who doesn't judge or, more importantly, gossip.'

'Oh, yes, of course. Well, I should fit the criteria in that case,' said Jennifer.

Agnes pursed her lips. 'You see, you get all sorts coming in here. All sorts.' She shook her head and paused for a few moments as Jennifer nodded. Then, she couldn't resist and added, 'Only last week, a young nun and a young man came in pretending to be brother and sister. Can you imagine! It was obvious to me that they were a little more than that if you know what I mean?

'Totally inappropriate, I know. But being the consummate professional I am, I sent them away satisfied with a very…well, er… pretty, dressing gown, and I haven't spoken a word of it since.'

Jennifer looked down to let her hair fall over her face and coughed to cover a laugh. 'Goodness! I'll call back later if that's OK?'

'Yes dear, you do that. I'll mention you called in. Who shall I say visited?'

'Just say Miss O'Broin. Thank you.'

'Oh, can you spell that for me please? You're like me, dear, still single?'

'Yes, indeed, I'll come back later. It's like O'Brien but with an o and i in the middle instead of i and e. Goodbye!' Jennifer left Agnes with the spelling challenge and moved away quickly. 'Goodbye dear,' said Agnes, anxiously reaching for a pen before she could forget the name.

Jennifer left the floor, giggling to herself, and made her way to the third floor to look at the shoes and handbags. She had always liked pretty shoes, though she didn't possess any. However, she would need to find something appropriate if she were fortunate enough to get work either here at Ackerman's or elsewhere.

At least an hour passed as she got carried away with the beautiful leather goods, and trying on shoes. She made her way back to the fifth floor just as Tanu was coming out of her office onto the shop floor.

Not recognising Jennifer in T shirt and trousers, she said,

'Yes miss, can I help you?'

Jennifer answered, 'Oh, hello, Tanu! I called in earlier and asked to speak to you about the possibility of a job?'

'Oh, you must be Miss O'...I'm sorry, I'm not sure how you pronounce it? Thank you for coming back. My colleague Agnes spoke to you?'.

'Yes, she did. It's O'Broin.'

'Oh, do I know you? It's just that you know my name.'

'Yes, we met on the train last week, and I came in to buy a dressing gown the following day, and you gave me your name,' said Jennifer, smiling.

'Oh, my goodness, of course. You look so different,' Tanu said, surprise on her face. 'So what's happened? Are you no longer a nun?'

'I'm awaiting a teaching post in South Sudan,' said Jennifer. 'Until that comes around, I'm allowed to work in the community, but I can only commit to about six months. I appreciate that I won't be staying for long if I'm successful in getting a job here. But it's best to be honest from the outset, and I'm hard working and extremely flexible.'

'Well, there was a position available...' Tanu said, cautiously.

'Yes, I saw the advertisement last week when I came in with David.' Jennifer responded.

'Can you give me a moment please?' said Tanu. 'I'll just need to ring HR to see if the post has been filled?'

'Yes, of course.'

Tanu returned to her office and made the call. Jennifer saw her nodding and smiling through the window and guessed the post was still open.

'I know it's short notice, but can we interview you now?' Tanu asked when she got back.

'Oh, yes, of course, but I haven't prepared...I might have dressed more formally,' said Jennifer, looking down in concern at her comfortable clothes.

'Not to worry at all. Just go into my office and wait there a moment, please,' said Tanu, smiling.

'Oh, thank you, you're so kind,' Jennifer replied, and went to sit down.

A woman soon came onto the floor and entered Tanu's office, glancing at Jennifer, but not immediately greeting her. Jennifer was suddenly nervous. The woman placed papers on the desk, sat down then smiled and said, 'Hello, I'm Amahle Gumede, HR senior assistant for Ackerman's Johannesburg.' She asked Jennifer to introduce herself.

Jennifer took a deep breath. 'I'm Jennifer O'Broin. I'm 21, and I come from Newcastle, KwaZulu-Natal province.'

The woman nodded once, waiting for more.

Jennifer obliged. 'I'm currently awaiting a posting to a new school in Juba, South Sudan, which is going to be administered by my order. I'm also a novice in the convent, based in Cape Town. I currently live at St Brigid's Presbytery here in Johannesburg.'

Gumede. Jennifer's ears had pricked up, but knew the question she wanted to ask wouldn't be appropriate at this particular moment.

Amahle went on, 'Considering the circumstances, I'm not sure we need to complete the full formal interview process. Potentially, Jennifer, there is a position, but it would be on a casual, part time basis. Tanu has told me a little about your current situation and, I'd be happy for her to complete the process and let her decide.

'Well, for my part, I'd be happy to offer it to Jennifer if she feels it fits with her needs, Amahle,' said Tanu, smiling.

'That's good, then, Tanu, just let me know what the outcome is later, please.' Amahle stood up, shook hands with Jennifer and thanked her for coming in. She said, kindly, 'I hope to see you soon. Goodbye for now.'

When the door closed, Tanu explained that she could only offer three days per week but understood if Jennifer didn't feel it were enough. She also told her that she didn't have to work any Sunday shifts, so, it wouldn't interfere with her religious commitments.

Jennifer was delighted and said she would gladly take the job. They discussed pay, working hours, and that she would be issued with uniform and comfortable shoes (one less thing to worry about, thought Jennifer). Tanu asked could she start tomorrow, Tuesday, and work on Thursday and Friday. Agnes would provide the on-the-job training.

Jennifer couldn't believe her luck and couldn't wait to get started. They stood to leave the office, and Tanu said, 'I'm just about to take my break. Would you like to join me?'

'Oh, thank you, I will!' Jennifer had to clasp her hands behind her back to stop herself from clapping with sheer happiness. This felt so right.

Tanu explained to Agnes that she was going for her break and introduced her to Jennifer, 'This is Jennifer, Agnes. You met last week when she came in to buy a dressing gown. I didn't recognise her out of her habit, did you?'

Agnes swallowed hard and stared at the young woman before her until her eyes started to hurt. Jennifer just smiled.

Tanu continued, 'She'll be joining us tomorrow as our new sales assistant, and I'd like you to give her some training, please, Agnes.'

'Yes, of course.'

They walked downstairs to the restaurant as Tanu explained that they got breaks in the morning and afternoon. If you chose to take them in the restaurant, everything was free. That was also the case for lunch and dinner, should she work a late shift.

Jennifer thought gratefully that while the pay wasn't brilliant, there were at least some perks.

Changing the subject, Tanu's curiosity got the better of her and she asked her about David. Jennifer told her that they both lived at the presbytery and that she'd only just met him, but he was a kind hearted and very genuine man.

'Wow, you must really have made an impression on him,' answered Tanu, remembering the dressing gowns, but tactfully not mentioning them.

Jennifer smiled shyly and told her new friend about his plans for university and that he had largely educated himself in his chosen area of computing. Tanu listened with interest and, thinking ahead practically, said, 'Well, if you like, he could join you sometimes in the restaurant on his breaks. You could use the family and friends card that we all have.'

Jennifer was astounded at the worlds that were opening up for both her and David. She felt blessed.

They enjoyed their coffee together, chatting about the different departments in Ackerman's, then Tanu had to return to work. As she left Jennifer at the table, she smiled and said, 'I can see I'm going to enjoy working with you. I know we'll get on really well. I'll see you tomorrow at ten o'clock. Just come to my office when you arrive.'

Jennifer left the store joyously and got the bus back to the presbytery, arriving back just in time for lunch. Father Seth, David and Ethel were already eating when she walked into the dining room.

'You'll never guess,' she said, playfully, and waited till she had their full attention, walking jauntily around the table twice in both directions.

'Guess what?' asked Ethel, in frustration at Jennifer's teasing. 'Go on then!' Jennifer delightedly told them her news.

She answered Ethel's quizzical look with a short explanation of why she was delaying taking her vows, needing some time and space to consider many things. Ethel commented that she thought she was wise, while David just smiled and gazed at her with wonder in his eyes.

Then Ethel said, 'My daughter in law, Simeon's' wife, works in HR at Ackerman's. You'll probably meet her soon!'

Jennifer started to laugh. 'Is her name Amahle?'

'Yes, why, do you know her?'

'I've just met her! She told my new boss that I didn't have to go through the interview process, and that she could make the decision. What a small world.'

'Well, you know what I'm going to say, child.'

'Thank God for his intervention,' they all said simultaneously.

***

It was Tuesday morning, and Jennifer arrived at work early. She reported to Tanu's office as instructed. Tanu took her to HR to sign some documents, and Amahle came over to greet them. She asked could she have a word in private with her and directed her to a small side room. They entered, Jennifer feeling apprehensive. But as Amahle closed the door behind them she immediately held out her arms to hug her.

'I hope you don't feel this inappropriate,' she said, 'But when you said who you were and where you lived yesterday, I could see immediately why Ethel loves you so much. She has been talking about you ever since you arrived, and she adores you. Then, last night when she got home from the presbytery, she told me she was so excited that we'd met yesterday, and so am I.'

Jennifer replied, 'Thank you, Amahle. I love her too. She's so caring and ever so funny, and she's been so supportive. But I'm just a little worried now.'

Amahle's expression changed. 'Tell me, what is worrying you?'

'Well, it's just that only Father Seth, you and Tanu know about my placement in South Sudan. I haven't even told my mother I've accepted yet, but she knows I was offered the post.'

Amahle interrupted, 'Oh, don't worry, everything you say to Tanu and me will be held in the strictest confidence. I can understand why you don't want to tell them yet. South Sudan is a dangerous place just now, and I'm sure Ethel would try to persuade you not to go. But she's told me how devoted you are, so I appreciate you want to follow your vocation.'

'Oh, what a relief! Thank you. I'm going to tell Ethel and David just before I go,' said Jennifer.

Amahle reassured her. 'Tanu is lovely, by the way, and she knew immediately yesterday when you said where you lived that there was a connection. I talk about my family all the time, and I've known Tanu for a long time too. She's been a good friend, and she's very trustworthy. But if I can warn you to be a little careful of what you say to Agnes, she can be a bit of a gossip.'

Jennifer started to laugh, and nodded conspiratorially.

She signed the paperwork and left the office with Tanu. They went to the stores to get her navy-blue suit, turquoise blouse and sensible, blue court shoes.

'You even make the uniform look glamorous,' Tanu said, smiling as Jennifer tried it on.

'What?' squealed Jennifer. 'I'm not used to looking at myself in that sort of way. We're encouraged to ignore the physical and concentrate on the spiritual, but thank you, that's very kind of you.'

Tanu commented, 'You're very pretty, but perhaps it's best if you continue to concentrate on the spiritual. After all, I don't like competition.' The mischief was plain on her face. They laughed together.

Jennifer changed back into her own clothes since the uniform needed pressing. Today was more about preparation and training, and there seemed a lot to take in. It was break time and armed with her staff card, she made her way into the restaurant for coffee with Agnes.

Agnes, predictably, probed and plied her for information about her private life. She managed in the short time they were together to ask Jennifer about almost every aspect of her life, from her upbringing to her motivation for joining the convent and her future plans. She appeared particularly interested in her 'relationship' with David. Jennifer's answers, which came in broad sweeps of innocuous facts mixed with vague indications, somehow mollified the curious Agnes but, as Jennifer slipped away from her gaze in amusement, she felt she'd dodged a bullet.

She'd had a good first day and was looking forward to going back on Thursday. She got on the bus just after six and was back at the presbytery half an hour later.

***

David had been busy in the garden all day and looked exhausted. But he was visibly glad to see her and asked if she could give her opinion about something after dinner if she wasn't too tired.

'Of course,' she said. 'I'll come down to your room when I've had a shower.'

His door was open as she walked in, and she left it like that.

He pointed to a piece of paper face down on his desk. 'It's my birth certificate,' he said, with dread in his voice. 'I haven't looked at it yet.'

'OK, let's see,' she said, calming him.

He placed his hand on top of the paper and nervously started tapping his fingers repeatedly on it. Aware of his anxiety, she closed the door, reached out and took his other hand in hers in the hope that this would reassure him. His shoulders shook and a large teardrop fell onto her hand.

'I can't do this. I can't do this,' he repeated time and again.

'Hush, hush it's OK,' she said softly, bending towards him and bringing his head to her shoulder.

She had never seen such an exposition of raw emotion and pain before. She began to feel a sense of responsibility for his suffering. She wondered if perhaps her comments to Father Seth had influenced his decision to give David the money that was due to him and the access to his birth certificate.

She hadn't wanted to be the catalyst of his pain. However, she recognised that he had a right to know his origins and, being the sensitive man he was, there would probably never be a perfect time for him to find out the truths it contained.

She let him feel the emotion and just held him. He sobbed but in that moment felt safe in the knowledge that she would never judge him or tell him how he should respond to the depth of his feelings. He knew, too, that he would one day have to forfeit his growing closeness to her. He stood up from his chair and sat on the side of his bed, and she sat beside him, her arm over his shoulder and her other hand gently touching his face.

The last thing she remembered was lying down alongside David. They'd fallen asleep together, but now he had awoken and she lay beside him, holding him as the sobs broke through. The light in his room was still on. It was 3:47 am on the digital alarm clock. Within a short time he slept again, and she listened to every intake of breath. She slid her arm out from under his neck and gently kissed him on his forehead before turning out the light and leaving his room. David's birth certificate was still face down on his desk.

It was 6:10 as he woke. He remembered that he had fallen asleep crying in her arms and suddenly felt embarrassed that he had shown his weakness to her like that. He made his way up to the bathroom and took his shower, letting the water beat out his pain.

Today was the day of the entrance exam at the university, and he felt emotionally exhausted. He exited the shower, put on his dressing-gown and had a shave. As he left the bathroom, Jennifer was coming out of her room, towel in hand and ready to take a shower herself. In his embarrassment, now reawakened, he tried to look away.

She took hold of his hand, and looking up into his sad eyes, she said, 'I hope you're feeling better this morning, David. Please don't ever avoid me for any reason, I feel privileged to have your trust, and I never want to lose that. We've come a long way in a short time, and I want you to know that whenever you need me, I'm here.'

Her words were heartfelt and honest, and as usual, she had disarmed the situation. He bent forward and hugged her, saying, 'I'm sorry, I should have known better. You told me the other day that you trusted me implicitly. Perhaps I should do the same?'

'There's no perhaps about it, I'll never knowingly hurt you, and I never want you to hurt alone. You're incredibly special to me, and if God in his wisdom has brought us together, then he, or she, has done that for a reason.' She looked up at him with mischievous, twinkling eyes.

They separated with a smile. The sadness had disappeared from his eyes.

She called over her shoulder, 'It's your exam this morning, isn't it?'

'Yes.'

'You'll do great. I can feel it. Remember, you've worked hard for this, and everything you've taught yourself over the last couple of years will hold you in good stead. Trust me, I know.'

'Thank you, Jennifer, you do have the gift of instilling confidence into people, and Ethel was so right, you do put everyone at ease.'

'Well, thank you. But today isn't about me,' she answered. It's about you, opening the door to your future, and I want you to do that for yourself. You're more than capable. What was it you said to me the other day? Big smile, be confident.'

He answered, 'I've got the car for the morning, and the exam starts at nine, so I'll leave at quarter past eight. I don't want to be late. I'm tired, but I feel reasonably confident.'

'I'm excited for you. Have a great morning. I'll see you later.'

***

He arrived at the university exam hall and was told to take a seat in the waiting area. Ten other applicants were waiting there. The invigilator explained the exam process, and they followed her into one of the smaller exam rooms. Once there, she explained that they must not talk to any other candidate and that they may leave the room at the end only. They had two hours to complete the exam. She looked at her watch and instructed them to start.

David turned over the paper, wrote his name and candidate number on his answer book and started to read through the advice and instructions text before moving onto the questions.

He then read through each question. There were fifteen in all, and he couldn't believe the simplicity of them. He was delighted and sailed through the paper well within the allotted time. He checked the questions and his answers once completed to make sure he hadn't missed anything or misinterpreted anything. He was confident that his answers were comprehensive and appropriate.

He gazed around the room and looked at the other candidates. He hoped they would all be successful as he realised how important this was to him, so he assumed they all felt the same. He looked up at the clock. It was 10:45 am. Quarter of an hour left.

His mind wandered. He thought of his new life, his plans, his hopes...and Jennifer.

'Time's up, put your pens down and close your books.' ordered the invigilator. 'Please bring your papers up to my desk and place them in a pile.'

As chairs began to move, she announced, 'As far as your results are concerned, I'm aware that the examiners are intending to mark straight away as there is only a short time before the start of freshers' week. You will get an email as soon as possible.'

David left the exam room and made his way out through the main entrance and headed for the university car park. As he walked towards the car, he could see Jennifer standing beside it. As soon as she saw him, she started to run towards him, and as she got to him, she jumped into his arms laughing.

As he caught her, she said, 'I've always wanted to do that, I used to do it when I was little, but I never felt it appropriate in my habit. I did enjoy that.'

He started to laugh and said, 'But next time, give me a little warning, will you? I'd hate to drop you.'

She grinned, 'I think I'm still a kid sometimes. There are parts of me that are stuck in my childhood. You'll never drop me. I know when I'm in safe hands. Anyway, how was your exam? How did it go?'

He shook his head. 'I couldn't believe how simple it was - unless I missed something. But I read everything twice, three times and checked my answers, and I don't think it could have gone any better. I do hope I've not made some major blunder.'

'I'm sure you haven't. I'm so pleased for you. When do you get your results?'

'They'll email. It has to be done pretty quickly.'

'Oh, that's great. I bet you can't wait. I know I can't. I'm so excited for you David,' she said with a big smile on her face.

Then she added, 'Oh, I nearly forgot. Father Seth asked me to tell you he doesn't need the car this afternoon, so if you want to stay out, that'll be fine.'

'Really? That's fantastic. I think I'll go and look at some phones. Do you reckon they have good ones at Ackerman's?'

'I should imagine so. Let's go and see.'

'Oh, you'll come with me? Thanks. I'd like that.'

'It's my day off today. After all, I can do what I want, and I'm ready for the break,' she laughed.

They made their way to the store, and he soon found a phone and deal similar to the ones he'd seen online.

'Come on, let's go and say hello to Tanu,' said Jennifer. They caught the lift to the fifth floor. Twenty minutes and much laughter later they went down to the restaurant, needing lunch.

Leaving the shop for the sunshine and the city, they walked and talked their way to Rhodes Park, strolled around the lake and sat beneath the tree canopy, just enjoying the peace of the place, until David caught sight of his watch and groaned. They both realised that the afternoon had evaporated.

'Better make tracks!' he said, reluctantly. He wanted moments like this to never end. They jumped to their feet, brushed off the grass and increased their pace to get back to the university. It was almost five when they reached the car.

Chapter 17

Cedric

It was Thursday morning, and Jennifer made her way to work on the bus.

Her eyes flitted to and fro between her fellow passengers. She loved to people watch. There were all manner of different faces to glance at, and people of multiple ethnic origins. It saddened her to think that this social mixture had only been possible in recent years. White supremacists, in their years of imposed segregation, had preached that the happy reality now clearly in front of her eyes would inevitably lead to social downfall, the rise of violence and the total disintegration of South Africa.

How wrong they were, she thought. While there was still a long way to go to end deprivation across all colours and creeds, and to stamp out the prejudice that remained, it was apparent that none of the progress made so far would ever have been achievable under apartheid. She felt proud of her fellow countrymen and women, champions of freedom, proud that they had stood together against the evil of a barbaric regime now consigned to history's trash heap.

Jennifer's eyes fixed on the black man opposite. He was holding his child tightly in his arms. The little girl, all rounded cheeks and braided pigtails, tied with pink ribbons, looked up into his eyes and the love and delight between father and daughter almost took her breath away.

A memory of her own father was suddenly awakened, and the forlornness she felt deep inside, born out of not knowing where he was, or what had happened to him.

She'd adored him and, it had seemed, he had adored her. Fourteen years on, she still missed him greatly, his smile, his gentle Irish brogue and, most of all, the loving way he could make the worst of experiences disappear as quickly as they had entered her world. Would she ever see him again? Why did he go? She'd never find out, it seemed. She arrived at Ackerman's and went up to the fifth floor.

Tanu, at the mirror in the staff room, fixing her glossy dark hair into a bun with jewelled combs, greeted her with an enormous smile. 'You're stuck with me, today, Jennifer. Agnes has called in sick.'

She went on, grinning at herself in the mirror, 'Oh dear, how terrible for me, having to work with the new girl! Tut, tut, tut! Well, if we don't know everything about each other by the end of our shift, then I won't have been doing my job properly,' she chuckled, shaking her head.

'Oh, that sounds really good!' Jennifer replied, starting to giggle. 'Oh, I don't mean Agnes being unwell, of course. I mean getting to know each other.'

Tanu started to laugh. 'Don't worry, new girl, I know what you mean,' she said, a twinkle in her eyes.

Jennifer felt the need to explain. 'I sometimes open my mouth and talk without thinking,' she confessed. 'I put it down to praying so much. I think cradle Catholics like me just can't help themselves, praying, I mean, but I definitely find it comforting. You see, I find I pray better if I just let it flow, but I need to remember that how I speak to God is not always appropriate, you know, when speaking to, how would you say... ordinary, well, mere mortals.'

Tanu guffawed at this. Jennifer's eyes opened wide, suddenly realising how comical she sounded.

Tanu was shaking with laughter, 'Mere mortals! I love it. Well, yes, I'm a mere mortal and proud of it. Oh, please don't change, Jennifer, now you've arrived in the real world of mostly mere mortals. I can see today is going to be fun.'

The time passed in the blink of an eye. They shared much about themselves, with teasing and laughter as Jennifer learned to use the till and the stock check computer program.

Removing the security tags from items of clothing without damaging them proved ridiculously tricky, with the use of a magnetic gadget but, after a few, nervous attempts, Jennifer mastered it.

It was a quiet day with few customers, and Jennifer felt thankful that the interruptions to the training were minimal.

In the middle of the afternoon, Tanu looked up from sorting a box of price tags, a sudden look of concern on her face.

'I don't know why I'm telling you this, Jennifer, but I'm at a loss to speak to anyone else at Ackerman's at the moment. I think you might understand and see this with new eyes.'

Jennifer, crouching down behind the counter to retrieve a detached security tag, could tell that Tanu needed her to pay full attention.

Tanu waited for eye contact and lowered her voice. 'Some of us can see the writing on the wall, to be honest, and we're all pretty worried. In your interview on Monday you said that you could only offer your services for about six months. I have to say, I felt relieved for you in that.'

Jennifer looked surprised.

'Please don't repeat this. I'm sorry, I trust my own judgement here. I know you won't. But, we've been having lots of senior staff meetings recently and what's happening is, well, because so many people are shopping online these days, it's really affecting our sales and profits.

Jennifer had registered for herself the small number of customers who had strolled through the department during her first shift.

Tanu went on, 'Like so many of the good stores around the world, we're struggling. I don't know if we'll even last the year, to be perfectly frank. It's been such a worrying time for the very few of us who know, and I worry for all the hard-working people here.

'Things will have to change, and we will need to build up our online business. But it's never going to be the same as being able to walk into a beautiful shop like this and browsing all the departments like you can now. And all our jobs will go. The pensions with them, no doubt.'

'Oh, no, really?' Jennifer replied, shocked. 'But Ackerman's is a Jo'burg institution, surely? How terrible to think of it closing. But look, Tanu, you can't carry the burden of that on your own. You need to talk about it.

'But, if you can't talk to anyone else, you can always talk to me, in complete confidence, obviously. I'll pray for you and everyone here. You never know what the outcome will be, but I'm sure God has a plan.'

Tanu answered, 'Well, that's comforting to know your God has a plan. Please don't think I'm disrespectful, though, will you, but I've always found the idea of the Christian God a little hard to understand, and all that Christian prayer and confession. All that kneeling in hard wooden benches in dark churches! And scary pictures and crosses!'

She smiled and added, 'But believe me, as a cradle Hindu, I've tried to understand all the gods! I've finally come to the conclusion that I'm not cut out for any religion. My family thinks I'm wayward. But I passionately believe we should all be allowed our own beliefs and opinions.'

Jennifer appreciated her new friend's candour. 'No, Tanu, I don't think you're being at all disrespectful, or wayward! In fact, I think it's important to recognise and embrace differences too. But I don't find the pictures scary, I find them comforting and deeply moving,' she said, gently.

Tanu smiled her broadest smile. 'I'm glad I haven't offended you. Needed to get that out of the way! I'd so like us to be good friends.'

'Me, too. Dare I say I feel blessed to have met you?' Jennifer answered, mischievously.

'Now that, I do understand,' Tanu said, laughing.

Before long, they were talking about a myriad of other things, life in the convent, Tanu's life growing up in Durban with her parents and older sister Viji and extended family of aunts, uncles and cousins.

She explained she was third generation Sri Lankan Tamil, her grandparents having been people of trade who emigrated to South Africa from Ceylon, as it was then known, in 1948 when it gained independence from Britain.

At that time, relations between the minority Tamil community and majority Sinhalese communities had become strained, and many Tamils felt unsafe in their homes.

Tanu explained that she struggled to understand her grandfather's decision after World War II to move his family from one place of repression to another. But, whatever his reasoning, she was now in a place where she could create a better life for herself. She'd completed her business management degree at Johannesburg University before getting her first professional role at Ackerman & Sons, entering the accelerated promotion scheme at the department store and settling in the suburbs, near Soweto, four years ago.

Jennifer listened with great interest, and shared her own story of Irish roots, the Catholic faith, and always having been drawn to Holy Orders.

Tanu listened, fascinated by it all, but had been dying to ask about David. She finally did.

Jennifer spoke freely about him, not the sadness of his childhood, because she felt that was not her story to tell, but his work at the church, his ability with computers, his personality and the warmth of his disposition. Tanu could see the delight in Jennifer's eyes as she described her friend, but wondered privately if there was not more to their relationship. Jennifer, so sweet and innocent, probably doesn't realise David is besotted, she thought, and diplomatically changed the subject.

As they chatted on, Tanu reminded her of the train journey they'd shared into Johannesburg and how she believed that they'd been brought together for a reason, in the friendly, reassuring way of people who, even when they exclude God or divine intervention, still need to find a deeper meaning in life and its coincidences.

She said, 'I don't know if it's entirely appropriate to say this to a nun-to-be, but I don't think you'll mind, Jennifer, and if you do, don't answer! What did you think about the young athlete who boarded the train at Germiston?'

Jennifer threw her hands up in mock amazement. 'Oh, you mean the Soweto, what do they call him, the Soweto Adonis, Cedric Kai! Isn't he incredible?' she exclaimed. 'What an amazing, handsome young man, so humble and friendly too. But I only got to talk to him for a short time. Well, I think he's really great, and you can see for yourself why they call him Adonis.'

Tanu couldn't resist the wind-up. 'Hmm, Adonis... I'm pretty sure it means beautiful and handsome, with all the attributes of the Greek god of that name. As for you being able to see why he's referred to as the Soweto Adonis, well, I didn't think nuns were supposed to say things like that!' she said, laughing, her targeted tease having produced a bullseye.

Jennifer grinned. 'Well, it's not a sin to find something or someone attractive or, dare I say it, beautiful? I think it would be more sinful, less human, *not* to recognise it. After all, isn't it what makes the world go around? None of us would be here if it weren't for attraction, would we?' she pointed out.

'No, you're so right,' answered Tanu. 'Actually, I think you'd nodded off when he first got on the train. He caused quite a commotion when people recognised him, but he was so warm and not at all arrogant or conceited.

'If I'd been a teeny bit younger, better looking and a bit braver I'd have wanted to pass him my number. There were lots of women thinking the same, I bet. Especially when you moved in on him like that.'

'What? Moved in on him? What a thing,' squealed Jennifer, disbelieving, as she neatly folded a pile of T shirts. They started to laugh heartily again, and Jennifer said, eyes up to heaven, 'Well, all I can say is, it must have been the wimple. No, I just woke with all the noise, and couldn't believe it was him, so I just had to speak to him. I've seen him compete many times.

'But seriously, don't put yourself down like that, Tanu. You're quite a catch yourself, you know. He was talking to *you*, wasn't he, and didn't he start the conversation?

From what the reports say, he's extremely shy, so perhaps he felt too shy to ask you for your number?'

'Yes, he did start the conversation with me, but only because you seemed to be nodding off again, but, anyway, thank you for your kind comments. I came over all girly though. In fact, I think I probably made a complete fool of myself.' she remembered ruefully. 'How do you know so much about him?'

'Oh, I love to watch sport, especially Olympic sports. He's very highly thought of in athletics. If I'm not mistaken, there's a thing at the Jo'burg Stadium on Saturday. Perhaps you should go? Anyway, how old are you, Tanu? You can't be that much older than the Adonis.'

'I'm just turned 26 and a long time single. I think he's nearly 23.' Tanu replied, unhappily.

She added, 'I'm no angel, believe me, but I've just never wanted to get married, in spite of my family's efforts! Just never met the right man, well, not until I saw Cedric in the flesh!

'Actually, I'm not working this Saturday. I'd love to see him, if only from a distance. He is amazing, isn't he? What sport is it? He's a runner isn't he? What event? Not that I would know the difference.'

'Yes, he is amazing. He's a sprinter, you know, 100, 200 metres. He's incredibly fast,' said Jennifer. 'He's tipped for the Olympics, you know, even a world record!'

'Not fast enough if you ask me,' Tanu laughed again.

Jennifer grinned. 'Well, I'm pleased you're not working on Saturday. But like you said, you're all of 26, *much* too old for the boy from Soweto. He's all of 22.'

'Nearly 23, I believe,' insisted Tanu. 'But yes, 22. Is three and a bit years too much?'

Jennifer reassured her. 'Oh, honestly, I can see he was probably scared off by your wizened complexion and widow's hump. But listen, why don't you get a ticket from the stadium on your way home tonight? If you don't, you'll only regret it, and to be perfectly frank, I don't think I could put up with all the if onlys.'

Tanu was thinking about it, but just then a customer came on to the floor, the first they'd seen in half an hour, so they both adjusted their uniforms, turned their girlish grins to professional smiles and went to offer assistance.

It was a cheerful woman in her seventies, full of life and character. She told them she had a date. Apparently she was going out for dinner that very evening with a 'young man', actually an old school friend, and was looking for an 'outfit to impress'.

Jennifer and Tanu enjoyed the lengthy and entertaining task of dressing her from head to toe. Money was obviously little object to her. She was great fun, and she spent well, but Jennifer quietly reflected that she'd been the only customer in the last two hours to actually buy something and that, like Tanu had pointed out, the loss of younger shoppers was one of the reasons Ackerman & Sons was under threat.

'Now, do come back and tell us how it goes, won't you?' asked Tanu.

'I certainly will,' the customer said, with mischief in her eyes.

They all started to laugh.

The woman added, 'And I just love this store. I knew I'd find just what I wanted. But it's hard for me to get here so often these days. Bye! Wish me luck.'

Jennifer and Tanu waved to her, as a fitting end to their enjoyable day together. It was time to go home.

'Can I give you a lift, Jennifer?' Tanu asked.

'No, thank you, you need to go to the stadium to buy your ticket for Saturday, and I'd hate you to miss the opportunity. So, I'll see you in the morning. Goodnight, Tanu.'

'Goodnight, Jennifer.'

Tanu weighed up what Jennifer had said about buying a ticket and decided she would definitely go to the stadium on her way home.

What was the worst that could happen, she asked herself, as she drove onto the car park nearest to the ticket office. She got out of the car and made her way to the queue. She stood in line for a few moments when she heard a chorus of voices and squeals about seventy-five metres beyond the ticket office, near a semi-concealed exit.

She could just make out the now familiar shape of Cedric leaving the stadium. He stopped to sign autographs for children and more than a few adults as well, his head towering over theirs, even as he bent to write.

Her legs turned to jelly as she saw him climb into a shiny, executive 4x4 with blacked out windows. Gulping with the excitement of seeing him, she finally got to the office window and asked the assistant if there had been any races today. The young man behind the glass partition said that a number of the athletes had been training and, if she'd come earlier, she could have gone in to watch for a small ticket fee, but there were no more tickets for training sessions now before the actual competition.

'Damn', said Tanu to herself, under her breath. If only she'd known. There was nothing for it, then, she decided. She wouldn't even ask the cost, she would just buy two tickets in the best seats available for the meeting itself and would invite Jennifer to join her in the morning.

***

Jennifer arrived back at the presbytery. She went up to her room and took a shower. When she made it downstairs she could hear the TV on in the lounge. Father Seth and David were watching the local news, featuring a run-up to the African Nations Competition to be held at Johannesburg Stadium.

She wondered if Tanu had gone to buy a ticket after all. She really hoped so.

Father Seth started to tell David that they'd shared a cabin with Cedric Kai last week when he'd picked them up from the station. David commented that according to the press, everyone was talking about Kai as the new running sensation, and how they thought he had a very bright future ahead of him.

Jennifer remembered that she hadn't actually told Father Seth that Tanu, the other person with whom they'd shared a cabin, was her new boss at Ackerman & Sons.

When she mentioned it, he said, 'What a coincidence! You'll probably meet Cedric Kai again next. Things happen in threes.'

Privately thinking it highly unlikely, she changed the subject to ask David how he was getting on with his new phone. He told her that he had copied over his few contacts and had been surprised to find out that Ethel had a smartphone, too. He'd never seen her using it, always preferring the landline. She always kept it at the bottom of her bag, wary of it listening to her, she said. But she knew her number off by heart and reeled it off. She also gave him Simeon's number just in case he ever needed a taxi.

Jennifer wrote down her own number for him, commenting, 'Why are you surprised at Ethel having a fancy phone? We all know what a cool stick she is.'

David grinned. Building shared memories and jokes with Jennifer felt so good.

'Take it you've heard nothing from the university yet?' Jennifer asked, tentatively.

David answered her neutrally, not allowing himself to hope so soon for the positive outcome that he dearly wanted. The waiting was going to be a lot more nerve-wracking than the exam, he thought. 'No, not yet' he said, 'and considering the time now, I expect I won't get the email today.'

He returned to the subject of his new mobile phone. He was pleased with its basic functions, he said, and particularly the quality of the camera lens. He thought he might improve on some of the pictures for St Brigid's website, perhaps even ask Father Seth to record a short welcome video. He commented that some of the programs he had written for the PC might easily be adapted for phone apps. He'd already investigated the licensing implications. His brain had begun to explode with possibilities.

His phone pinged. It was an email notification.

He clicked on the app and immediately saw it was from the university. He excused himself and left the sitting room, making his way swiftly up to his room to read it in privacy. Closing the door behind him, and clicking on the email, he read:

Dear Mr Blind. Thank you for attending the assessment centre at the Academy of Computer Science and Software Engineering, University of Johannesburg, yesterday.

Your paper has now been marked and we are pleased to inform you that you attained a mark of 95%.

Therefore we are delighted to offer you a place on the course you have applied for in the faculty. Please refer to the letter attached to this email for full details.

Please also acknowledge your acceptance of this offer by replying to this email.

Your personal tutor has been selected and you will be completing your period of study under the supervision of Professor Pingali.

We look forward to seeing you in due course.

He read it twice, before emailing his immediate acceptance, and leaving his bedroom to find Jennifer sitting on the bottom step of the spiral staircase,

'Well?' she asked, with wide eyes, displaying an uncharacteristic level of impatience.

'I've passed, and they've offered me a place,' he said, rubbing his jaw with his open palm as though he could hardly believe his luck.

She wrapped her arms around him and said, 'David, I'm so pleased for you and so proud of you too. I just knew you had it in you. You're so bright, so clever. What did you get, what was your mark?'

'Ninety-five per cent' he said, almost in a whisper.

'What? That's incredible! Incredible! Wow. Well done. Come on, tell Father and Ethel!'

They made their way downstairs to the lounge. Ethel had just joined Father Seth and dinner was almost ready.

David entered the room, shyly, without a word. Jennifer looked at him and waited, but he looked resolutely at his phone's home screen. Jennifer couldn't hold her excitement any longer and said, 'David's just got the email with his results!'

David felt his face grow hot.

Father Seth, already knowing the answer from Jennifer's inability to stand still, said. 'And how did you get on?'

'I passed, Father, and they've offered me a place.'

'Well, that's great news, David,' smiled Father Seth, holding his hand out to shake David's.

'Well, I always knew you were brighter than the midday sun,' Ethel said, laughing.

'Oh, David, you're too modest.' Jennifer said. 'Tell Father and Ethel your mark, or I will.'

He grimaced. 'Oh...I...ninety-five per cent,' David mumbled, embarrassed.

Father Seth couldn't help but look impressed. 'That's fantastic news, well done, boy! You know there's nothing wrong with being proud of your achievements. If you intend to make a living out of this, you will need to push yourself and tell people what you are capable of,' he said.

David hadn't given that any thought, but realised it was true. He felt apprehensive towards the idea of selling himself as a businessman, but also recognised that no one else would do it for him.

He was banking on the fact that there was a module covering that aspect within the subject matter of the course.

Jennifer followed Ethel into the kitchen to see if she needed any help. Ethel had everything under control, so there was nothing to do. Ethel asked if Jennifer wanted to go shopping again on Saturday, but Jennifer wasn't sure of her plans.

She explained that she liked the athletics and if they were on TV, she'd probably be watching, in particular to see how Cedric Kai got on. Ethel didn't mind. 'Of course, child. We can go another time,' she said. 'I might watch his races myself!'

After dinner, Jennifer felt the need to pray. She went up to her room and, kneeling at the side of her bed, picked up her rosary and started to say the familiar, comforting words.

'*I believe in God, the Father Almighty, Creator of Heaven and earth...*' She knelt for about three-quarters of an hour and completed a full rosary.

'*...and after this our exile, show unto us the blessed fruit of thy womb, Jesus. O clement, O loving, O sweet Virgin Mary.*'

She always felt at peace both during and immediately after prayer. Her thoughts slowly returned to Tanu. They were such different personalities, and it would appear they had vastly different spiritual footprints, yet they'd been drawn to one another like magnets. For what reason, Jennifer wondered? At this stage, it wasn't clear, and often, clarity was a long time coming. But Jennifer believed that there were few accidents of chance. So, whatever the explanation, she was confident that their poles would align.

***

It was Friday morning. She was waiting at the bus stop when a car drew up and came to a halt just beyond the lay-by. It was Tanu.

'What are *you* doing here?' asked Jennifer, in surprise.

'Get in the car, get in the car,' Tanu said excitedly. Jennifer climbed in and fastened her seat belt as quickly as she could and Tanu drove off, blurting out, 'Well, I did what you said. I went to the stadium to buy a ticket, and while I was there, I saw him. My dream man! The Soweto Adonis!'

Jennifer wasn't particularly surprised by this since the athlete was obviously training there for Saturday but she couldn't help but share Tanu's delight. 'And did you speak to him?' she asked.

'No, it will never be that simple for me,' Tanu said, dramatically, raising her eyes. 'My dreams are always elusive! I have to chase after them. My dreams, I mean, not men,' she grinned.

'Tell me what happened then!' demanded Jennifer. 'This is so exciting.'

Tanu explained, 'Well, I was waiting in line to get my ticket. There was a bit of a rumpus at one of the entrances to the stadium. Lots of people, kids mainly, started to rush towards a doorway, and there he was, the man of my dreams, the future father of my children.'

Jennifer started to laugh helplessly at that. 'Oh, my! You make it sound like a religious experience.'

'It was a bit like that! I lay awake all of the night thinking about this. It's kismet, Jennifer, my destiny. I just feel so...optimistic about it. I feel this is going to happen. He's going to see me and fall in love with me.'

Jennifer nearly choked. 'Well, I'm pleased to hear about your optimism, Tanu, and I don't want to rain on your parade, but you just said it yourself, it will never be that simple. Don't you always have to actually chase your dreams? Just how are you going to get to talk to him? We'll need to work on this.'

'We're not going to squabble over the semantics of this,' Tanu said, reprovingly.

'Yes, of course, forgive my impertinence,' said Jennifer, in a mock English accent.

'He's just so gorgeous. He's the epitome of masculinity. It's his physical presence, you see, what he awakens in me. Oh, sorry, Sister.'

'Goodness, I should think so,' Jennifer laughed.

'But I need to tell someone, and that someone just happens to be you. Have you any idea how I feel? I've been awake all night, yet I'm full of vitality, and I'm finding this so all-consuming, yet liberating. He's awakened my inner athlete.'

They both spluttered.

'He's my newfound inspiration. The yin to my yang. He's the road to emancipation from all my self-imposed confines and boundaries.'

Jennifer had tears of laughter streaming down her face. She gasped, 'Oh, stop it, stop it! My ribs hurt! So, what am I to take from this?'

'Nothing. Literally nothing, Jennifer. You won't personally take anything. He's going to be mine, all mine, and you can't have any of him.'

'Oh Tanu, you're so funny.'

Tanu was well into her stride. 'If he were here right now, he'd find me irresistible. Looking into my eyes, he'd say, let me whisk you away to a place of perfection. Say you'll be mine, Tanu. Say you find me irresistible as I do you. He'd be pleading for my love.'

'You're crazy,' said Jennifer, wiping tears from her eyes. 'I just love you.' The car came to a sudden stop.

Somehow they'd arrived at work without swerving into the paths of other vehicles. 'Time to put on the serious, professional face again, I'm afraid,' Tanu said, her eyes still sparkling. They walked the short distance to the store, trying to collect themselves.

But before they reached the door, Tanu announced, with an air of confession, 'Well, Jennifer, I know to assume makes an 'ass out of u and me', but...when I bought my ticket last night, I bought one for you too. I hope you don't mind, and if you're not busy tomorrow, I'd love you to come with me,' She pulled the tickets from the inside pocket of her jacket.

Jennifer was thrilled at the idea. 'Oh yes, please, just try to stop me. I've never been to a live athletics event before. That's so kind of you, Tanu.'

'I thought I could pick you up, if no one would mind?'

'That sounds perfect. What time does it start?'

'It says 1 pm on the ticket, but I'd like to be there early, if that's OK?'

'Then why don't we have brunch at the presbytery?' Jennifer suggested.

'Oh, yes, please. Will Ethel be there? Amahle is always talking about her. She sounds like the perfect mother-in-law. A bit like Mama Kai will be to me.'

They started to laugh again.

'Yes, Ethel will be there, and Amahle's description is not misleading. She's such a lovely and funny lady. I'm sure you'll like her.'

'Won't Father Seth mind?'

'I'm sure he'll be delighted to meet you properly, and you'll probably get to see David again.'

'That sounds nice. What time should I come?'

Jennifer said, 'Come for eight o'clock, and I'll introduce you to everyone, and if you're interested, I can show you around the gardens and church.'

Tanu said delightedly, 'Brilliant, I love old buildings, any old buildings. I'd love to see the church, and I bet the house is interesting too. I can't pronounce that word you called it.'

Jennifer scoffed. 'I find that hard to believe. I thought you'd swallowed a dictionary when you were talking about Cedric in the car just now.' Tanu had to stifle a giggle.

They took the lift to the fifth floor. Agnes was already there.

'Good morning, Agnes,' They both said to her as they went to hang up their jackets.

'Good morning,' she replied, looking surprised to see them both at once.

'Agnes, can you just come into the office please?' said Tanu.

Agnes made her way into the office and closed the door and Jennifer could hear muffled voices. A few minutes later, she was still alone on the shop floor when a middle-aged black couple arrived. They looked a little lost, so she left it a few moments and then went over to see if she could help them.

'Good morning sir, good morning madam, can I help you?'

'Oh, we don't want to cause you any bother,' said the man. 'We're just looking for an outfit for my wife.'

'Oh, it's no bother at all. It's my job, and I would be more than pleased to help you'.

'Are you sure you don't mind? To be honest, we don't generally come into the city, but there are no big stores like this in Soweto.'

'Oh, you're from Soweto, are you? Cedric Kai's from there isn't he?' said Jennifer, the athlete's name being the first one on the tip of her tongue.

The man answered, 'Yes he is. We're very proud.'

'Well, he's certainly the man of the moment,' answered Jennifer. 'We're all hoping he'll do well tomorrow. I met him on the train last Monday, actually. Such a gentleman.'

'That's nice of you to say so. He was brought up to be respectful of everyone.'

'Oh, do you know him? Do you know his family?' Jennifer asked, more out of politeness, hardly expecting the answer that came.

They smiled at each other, and the woman said, 'We are his family. We're his parents.'

Jennifer was almost dumbstruck. 'Wow, you must be so proud, Mr Kai, Mrs Kai,' she managed.

'We *are*, very proud,' Mr Kai replied.

'Well, I feel privileged to meet you. How can I help you today? What are you looking for?'

'We're going to the stadium tomorrow, and he has insisted that we should come and buy something comfortable as it will be a long day. He is a very generous son,' he added, with a nod of respect.

'Well, as I said, he's a gentleman, and I'm happy to see he's looking after his parents,' said Jennifer, finding the most appropriate words she could. 'He's a good boy. He always has been,' said Mrs Kai.

Tanu and Agnes came onto the shop floor just then, and Agnes made her way over to them.

'Can I help you, sir, madam?'

'No, thank you, this young lady is helping us just fine,' said Mr Kai, smiling.

Agnes appeared a little put out, but all the more so when Jennifer asked, 'Agnes, would you mind asking Tanu to come on to the shop floor? I need to ask her something in particular.' She knew she had to seize the moment on Tanu's behalf.

Agnes went over to the office, her face frozen in irritation. She didn't want to run this errand at all, but was obliged to fulfil Jennifer's request.

Tanu promptly came over and said, 'Good morning, madam, good morning, sir. How may I help you, Jennifer?'

Jennifer couldn't wait to see her reaction. 'Tanu, can I introduce you to Mr and Mrs Kai?' She paused. 'Cedric Kai's parents.'

Tanu stood stock still for a moment then had to compose herself before saying, 'Oh my goodness, I'm so honoured.' Jennifer could swear she nearly curtsied.

Mr Kai smiled and replied, 'The honour is all mine, my dear.'

Tanu and Jennifer worked in tandem to assist Mrs Kai in finding the right outfit, while Agnes glowered from a distance. Tanu could hardly cope, doing her best to suppress her nervous excitement and fearful of creating the wrong impression.

Keenly aware, and hardly being able to believe Tanu's quiet demeanour, Jennifer was discreetly asking them all the questions she thought Tanu would have wanted to but couldn't. Meanwhile, Tanu busied herself choosing three suit dresses that she thought would work best for Mrs Kai, and suggested she try them on, accompanying her to the changing room before waiting quietly round the corner. After much rustling, sighing and tutting, it was clear that one was perfect. Mrs Kai emerged from the cubicle.

'Oh, yes, I think this blue one, don't you, dear?' asked Mrs Kai, turning round and checking in the mirror. Tanu smiled and nodded approvingly. 'It really is a lovely colour,' she said, not wanting to sound too much of a saleswoman, 'and it's the same blue as that on the South African flag.'

That seemed to clinch the matter. Her choice made, Mrs Kai wandered over to look at matching hats and beckoned to her husband. Jennifer continued to chat easily to them both, much to Tanu's relief, and Mrs Kai soon settled on a hat. The Kais appeared completely at ease with her and started to talk freely about 'our boy', and how he'd always loved running, and had been the fastest in his school, even against older boys. Tanu smiled and listened gratefully as Jennifer comfortably worked the conversation round to tomorrow's competition, telling them that Tanu had kindly bought them both a ticket to the event.

'Oh, that is excellent. Where will you be sitting?' Mrs Kai asked.

'I'm not sure,' Jennifer replied. 'Have you got the tickets with you, Tanu?' she asked, encouraging her to go and get them from her jacket pocket. Tanu returned with them.

'We're in tier two, block 201 seats D27 and D28,' she said, reading from them.

'Where are we sitting, Joshua?' Mrs Kai asked.

Joshua Kai took his wallet from his pocket and pulled out their tickets.

'Actually, we're in the same block, just a couple of rows in front of you!' He started to laugh. 'It looks like we'll be seeing something of each other tomorrow, then,' he said, smiling.

Mrs Kai added, 'Oh, I'm so pleased you'll be there too. I'm always so nervous about going to watch Cedric run. I'm not one for big crowds, am I Joshua?'

'No, you're not, Mama, so it will be nice to see these lovely young ladies there when our boy is running.'

'What are you both called?' asked Mrs Kai.

'I'm Tanu, and this is Jennifer, Mrs Kai.' Tanu said politely, carefully folding and bagging the suit dress and hat before processing Mr Kai's card payment. She handed the large Ackerman's bags over to Mrs Kai with a beatific smile. Her earlier bravado towards the woman she had identified as her future mother-in-law had receded somewhat.

Mrs Kai replied, 'I'm going to feel so much more comfortable tomorrow now I know you'll be there. I'll wave to you both, and maybe we can have a chat at the interval!'

'Oh, yes, that will be lovely. Look forward to seeing you,' Jennifer said. The Kais made their way towards the lift and they all smiled and waved as the doors closed and then they were gone.

Jennifer looked at Tanu and nearly exploded with disbelief and laughter. 'I think something magical just happened,' she said. Tanu had happy tears streaming down her face.

Chapter 18

Race

It was Saturday morning, and everyone had agreed to wait for breakfast until Tanu arrived. They wanted her to feel welcome, and of course, they wanted Jennifer to feel that her friends were important to them too.

She arrived and rang the bell. Jennifer went to answer it.

Hugging Tanu, she said, 'Welcome to the presbytery, come on in.'

Holding Tanu's arm, she led her into the dining room. Father Seth, Ethel and David were all sitting around the table.

'This is Father Seth,' she said as he got up to shake Tanu's hand.

'We met, in a way, on the train, didn't we? It's nice to see you again, such a small world. You're very welcome to join us for breakfast.'

'This is Ethel,' said Jennifer.

Ethel went to hug her and explained that she felt she knew her already as Amahle had said a lot of lovely things about her.

Jennifer waited for Tanu's attention. 'And, of course, you've already met David.'

He stood up and smiled at her. 'I bet you are excited about going to the athletics today,' he said.

Tanu smiled, 'Yes, I've never been to a sports event before, and I was talking to Jennifer about it on Thursday, she encouraged me to get a ticket. So here I am. It's exciting.'

They enjoyed a conversational breakfast, with Tanu asking polite questions about the parish and commenting how lovely the buildings and gardens were. As they finished their coffee, Jennifer asked, already knowing the answer, 'Father, would it be OK to show Tanu around the presbytery and church?'

'Yes, of course,' he said. 'I have confession at eleven o'clock, so if you wouldn't mind starting in the church?'

Jennifer replied, 'Oh, of course, and, David, you won't mind taking us round and telling us all you know about the building?'

'I'd love to,' David replied. 'If you're ready, let's go!'

David was in his element. His knowledge of the building and of the family that had paid for its design and construction was extensive. They entered via the sacristy where he described the architecture, down to the need for the foundations to be reinforced to carry the weight of the granite columns.

He commented that, of course, St Brigid's had been built exclusively for white people at a time when apartheid and the exploitation of black people in South Africa was at its height, the very opposite of what Christianity stood for. 'Thankfully,' he said, 'that is no longer the case.'

Tanu nodded in recognition and gazed in awe at the beautiful objects, designed never to be seen by people of colour, unless, perhaps, they were being cleaned.

The cost of creating the crypt itself had cost as much to build as the church had from the ground up, David said. Tanu pretended to be interested in the financial details, but looked around and appreciated the beauty of the crypt and the columns, in spite of what they had cost.

The carved, wooden stations of the cross from which the ivory versions in the presbytery had been copied, were originally supposed to have been installed in the presbytery, he told them, and the ivory ones in the church. They would have been, too, had the builder not made the mistake of mixing them up because the wooden ones had been painted with ivory coloured paint.

David explained factually that the mistake could have been rectified, but the parish priest of the time, it was rumoured, had decided that the ivory ones were too precious for even the white parishioners to enjoy, and would rather not risk the possibility of their being stolen.

Tanu was horrified at the presumption. Jennifer grimaced.

David then took them on to the portico via a narrow staircase accessed via a small, carved ebony door in the chancel. Few would have known of its existence since the carving blended in faultlessly with the other panels.

Finally, they descended to ground level via David's 'nemesis', the curse of the staircase. He wanted them to see it from the top down, to show them how it had been suspended from the enormous roof trusses rather than secured to the walls or floor. It had been built like this for three main reasons. The first reason was to indicate the ascension of Christ into heaven, and the second to signify that of his resurrection from the dead.

David pointed out a carving of Christ resurrected, high in the apex of the roof, which was lit during the day via a small, gold-coloured, single pane, stained glass window that directed sunlight on the carving.

The third reason was achieved by a one-inch gap at its base, to represent the seamless transition of God's love for humanity and the acknowledgement that the gap between heaven and earth was about bridging small gaps through faith.

Although the building was now 95 years old, the quality of the timbers, workmanship and strength had ensured the maintenance of this gap. Plus, David claimed, tongue in cheek, that his hard work, cleaning and polishing the 'curse' had indeed maintained its continued suspension in the last few years.

As they stepped down from the final step of the staircase, He pointed up to the steel rebar sculpture of St Brigid's Cross and explained its significance to the church and St Brigid's affiliation to it.

Looking up at the sculpture that was suspended from the roof trusses above the door between the vestibule and nave, he explained, 'The cross was commissioned by the archdiocese to mark the 75th anniversary of the consecration of the church.

'The installation of the steel rebar cross was celebrated on the feast day of St Brigid, 1st of February 1993, which was the year of my birth,' he smiled then continued. 'I've always felt a deep sense of connection with St Brigid, as she, amongst other things, is the patron saint of children born outside marriage.

'St Brigid and her cross are believed to have been originally linked together by a story which has her weaving this form of cross from reeds at the death bed of either her father or a pagan Irish lord, we're not sure which. The story goes that when he heard what the Christian cross signified, he asked to be baptised.'

They exited via the vestibule and made their way around the outside of the building where David identified the names of the twelve apostles moulded into the bricks at the time of their fabrication, and, in a stone mantel above the original side entrance to the confessional, he pointed out the name and coat of arms of the family who had paid for its construction, 'O'Broin'.

'I don't believe it,' Jennifer said. 'That's my surname, how very interesting. It's not very common, spelt like that.'

'That's amazing,' Tanu said.

'Is it the exact spelling?' enquired David.

Jennifer answered, 'Yes, but I'm sure there's no immediate connection as my daddy, like my mammy, was born in Ireland, and he'd emigrated in his early twenties just before they met. It's one of the very few things I know about him,' she said with a look of sadness. 'Oh, well, I'm glad to see other O'Broins were active in the church here.'

They made their way into the presbytery. David showed them around, and they were both able to see similarities between the fabric of both buildings.

'Oh, thank you David. I'd love to come back and find out more some time. You're so well informed,' said Tanu.

'You're very welcome, anytime,' he smiled.

It was half past eleven as they got into Tanu's car, and she drove the fifteen minutes to the stadium. They were glad they'd gone early as the car parks were already almost full. They jostled through the crowds and found their seats. The athletes' tunnel was about 85 metres to their left, and the finish line almost immediately in front of them.

Jennifer asked, 'I don't want to be rude, Tanu, but how much did you pay for the tickets?'

'Why, are they not good ones?' asked Tanu, anxiously.

'Erm. No, completely the opposite. You see that tunnel to your left?'

'You mean the big hole thing that goes under the seats?'

'Yes, the big hole thing under the seats.' Jennifer replied, laughing. 'That's the athletes' tunnel, their entry point to the stadium. They'll all come into the stadium at that point.'

'So, I'll only get to see him from the side.'

'No, no, no. You've never watched athletics at all, have you?'

'No, I've never watched any sport,' Tanu confessed.

'Then it's a good job we came early. Let's see how much I can explain, said Jennifer, mischievously. 'The middle of the arena is where the field events take place. The red thing around the outside of the field, with the white lines on it, that's the running track where Cedric's event will take place.'

'Well yes, obviously,' tutted Tanu, raising her eyes to the second part of Jennifer's quick guide to athletics, and poking her in the ribs.

'And are the sand pits for the kids to play in?' she joked, while being not quite sure exactly what events they were for.

Jennifer didn't want to patronise her friend but guessed correctly that without some guidance, Tanu would miss some of the important moments of the afternoon. She laughed and explained, 'So the pits are for the long jump, and triple jump. I'll point them out when they're happening. And there are other places on the field for other events like javelin and shot put, hard to see sometimes, but we should get good pictures on the big screen when it all starts.'

'OK, the white lines around the track, with the other lines crossing them? What are they for?'

'They're lane lines. In the short distance races, like the ones Cedric competes in...Look, are you winding me up here?'

Tanu shook her head with wide, apologetic eyes. Jennifer, reassured, continued patiently, 'OK, well, they must stay in the lanes. In middle and long-distance races, they use a standing start. If it's 800 metres and over, they line up, side by side, along that curved start line. Athletes in those races can cross to the inside lane as soon as it's safe.'

'This is all very complicated. Can you just tell me what's happening as it happens?' Tanu whimpered.

'You'll get used to it. I'll try, but I won't be able to do that with Cedric's races as they only last seconds.'

'Really? That fast? Better not go for coffee, then. So, will his race start on the curved line?'

'No, can you see the first bend in the track?'

'The one with the bit sticking out of it?' asked Tanu.

'Yes, that one. There's a straight white line that crosses the lanes. If you look in the bit sticking out of it you can see the line I'm talking about. Cedric's race will start from that line. It's called the start line,' she giggled, shaking her head in disbelief.

'So, where's the finish line?'

'Can you see the straight line crossing the lanes just there almost directly in front of us? That's the finish line.'

'Oh, thank you!' Tanu said, throwing her arms up to the sky, suddenly realising the advantage of their position in the stadium. 'Cedric will no doubt see me and come running up to me and say, my wife to be, where have you been, I've been looking for you! So what's your name?'

Jennifer was highly amused at Tanu's expectations for the afternoon. She pointed. 'Look in your programme, Tanu, at the back - there's a short description of all the events.'

'Will it tell us what time Cedric is racing?'

'Yes. His heat is at four o'clock and the final, which he's bound to be in, is six o'clock,' said Jennifer, distracted by the preparations on the track.

Tanu was reading. 'Oh, look, look, look, *About the Athletes - Cedric Kai. Age 22*, it says.'

Tanu grimaced. 'I'm definitely too old. Well, maybe not. What do you think?

She didn't wait for an answer. She carried on reading, 'It says, *Born in Soweto. Lives with his parents in Soweto*... We're virtually neighbours! That's good, he has stability, and of course, I've met them, and they adore me.

'*Ambitions: To win an Olympic gold medal, to make his family proud and to be happily, married and have a big family.* Oh, I knew it! How many babies would you like, husband-to-be? Who on earth said I was too old?'

'Tanu, you're hilarious.' Jennifer burst out laughing at her friend again. Just at that moment they heard the arrival of a group of people behind them and turned to look. A suited official was coming down the steps, slowly leading Mr and Mrs Kai to their seats. As the couple passed their row, Jennifer called out to them, 'Hello there!'

'Good afternoon Jennifer, good afternoon Tanu,' said Joshua Kai, grinning broadly.

'Good afternoon Mr and Mrs Kai,' said Jennifer, while Tanu managed a smile and a shy wave, afraid to make anything but a good impression.

The Kais took their seats at the end of the row, two rows in front and once they were settled, Joshua Kai turned round and beckoned to them. Tanu and Jennifer slipped out of their seats and went forward to crouch by the Kais, Jennifer nearest to Joshua and Tanu on the step below where she could get eye contact with Cedric's mother.

Joshua said, 'We spoke to Cedric on the telephone last night, and he remembered meeting two young ladies and a priest on the train last week. But he said one of the ladies was a nun, but he didn't ask anyone's name. So, I'm not sure if he'd met you and Tanu another day.'

'Yes, he definitely met us a week last Monday,' said Jennifer. 'I boarded the train at Ladysmith with Father Seth Rossouw, who is parish priest at St Brigid's Church here in Johannesburg. Anyway, when we got on the train, Tanu was already there, and then Cedric got on at Germiston. So that's how we all met.'

'Was there a nun in your compartment too?'

She started to laugh. 'Sorry, I should have explained. It was me. I'm the nun, well I'm in the novitiate. I'm working part-time at the store till I take up a teaching placement later in the year. I've been given a dispensation to earn a little money in the community before I travel. I'm living at St Brigid's presbytery at the moment.'

Joshua replied, 'Oh, that's very interesting, Jennifer. We are a Catholic family. We're members of a small parish in Soweto. Mama insisted he get a dispensation from the archbishop when he has to race on a Sunday. They said there was no need, but Mama felt better for him doing that.'

'Ah, how lovely,' said Jennifer. 'Well, God speed him today!'

Meanwhile, Mrs Kai and Tanu were getting on well. The quick-witted African woman had already determined Tanu's ancestry and was intrigued to find out more about her culture. She was immensely proud of her own ancestry, so they were soon in deep conversation.

They spoke about Cedric, too, which delighted Tanu, though she tried not to show it too much. Mrs Kai explained that his had been a difficult birth, having endangered both their lives. The doctors had told her that the risks of having other children were too high, so Cedric was an only child. But since they'd had little money while he was growing up, he'd never been spoiled other than with love and affection, she said.

'Jennifer is from KwaZulu-Natal Province,' Tanu said, aware that she should bring her friend into the conversation. Jennifer's ears pricked up and she smiled and nodded.

Mrs Kai reached over her husband's shoulder to take Jennifer's hand. 'Really, that's lovely, Jennifer! That's where I originate from, but I've never been back in 23 years. Not even when my parents died. We couldn't afford the transport.'

Jennifer was about to express her sympathy for such a sad memory when, at that moment, the crowd rose to applause as the first athletes of the day took to the field and track. Jennifer and Tanu smiled at the Kais and went quickly back to their seats.

Long jump, high jump, pole vault and javelin were first off, with the 400 metres hurdles being the first track event.

They watched sport after sport, absorbed into the dramas unfolding in front of them. Before they knew it, they'd already watched the first three of the four 100 metres qualifying races. Next on the track would be Cedric's race, and both the Kais were getting nervous. They turned to wave at the young women behind, obviously glad to share the moment.

'Ladies and gentlemen, please welcome to the track our athletes running in the 100 metres qualifying race number four.

'Running in Lane 1, from Angola, Filipe Diogo. In Lane 2, from Zambia, Chikondi Mumba. In Lane 3, and from South Africa, Cedric Kai...'

The crowd erupted as the Soweto Adonis coolly strolled out of the tunnel. The Kais and Jennifer all clapped heartily at the sight of him, Tanu whooping a little more enthusiastically than was absolutely necessary.

Cedric looked composed and focused as he proudly donned his national colours and the pair of headphones he made a point of wearing before each race. The announcer struggled to be heard as she continued through the remaining contestants.

They limbered up, first one, then the other, practising their breaks from the blocks. They were called behind by an official after a couple of minutes and told to enter the blocks. Silence filled the stadium.

'On your marks,' The sound of the whistle indicated the need for the athletes to get set.

Bang! Bang! The runners left their blocks and pulled up abruptly, consternation on their faces. False start. Tension built as there was intense discussion amongst the officials. The warning flag was raised in Lane 8 and Zimbabwe's Patrick Tshuma was immediately disqualified.

Now all the runners were grim faced. They returned to the blocks for the second time. Cedric rolled from side to side as they were held for an uncomfortable length of time.

'On your marks.' Again, the sound of the whistle to get set.

Bang. This time they were away, and in a flash of effort and muscle it was over. A photo finish on the line between lanes 1, 3 and 7.

'Only two can make the final,' whispered Jennifer in Tanu's ear.

Everybody stared at the big screen for what felt like an age, then the result flashed up.

1st Lane 7. Moses Haruna   Nigeria   9.714

2nd Lane 3. Cedric Kai   South Africa   9.716

3rd Lane 1. Filipe Diogo   Angola   9.717

The crowd went wild in celebration. The up-and-coming local boy had made it to today's African Nations final and would be competing for the African Nations Gold Medal, but it had seemed no easy feat for him. Was he lacking form? Or was it the false start? The TV commentators ruminated the implications. Jennifer was glad she couldn't hear.

The friends went forward to speak again to the Kais.

'That was too close for comfort,' Joshua said.

'Have faith. He's kept some in the tank,' replied Jennifer.

'I hope you're right.' Mrs Kai said.

'Whatever happens, we'll all still love him,' Tanu said, suddenly becoming aware of the accuracy of her words. Not wanting to give too much away, she tilted her head and smiled broadly.

'That's all that matters.' Mrs Kai said, smiling back.

'Right, who's hungry?' asked Tanu.

'Oh, don't worry, Tanu. Cedric has arranged for us to eat in the restaurant at eight. We'll be seeing him then, and he's asked me to ask the two of you to join us.'

Tanu gulped. She didn't seem to have to chase this particular dream too hard. Things seemed to be falling into her lap. She couldn't wait to see her idol again and vowed that this time she'd have a little more self-control.

Jennifer was privately concerned that Father Seth wouldn't give her permission to stay for the meal, so she deftly excused herself and went to call him on her mobile. She got through and explained the situation. He immediately responded as she'd hoped he would.

'I'll ask David to pick you up if you need a lift back. Just call him if you do,' he said. She thanked him profusely and returned to the group.

'Well, I need a coffee, so please let me get you a snack and something to drink. It's the least I can do,' Tanu said, looking at Jennifer, hoping she would support her and go with her.

'Mrs Kai, she won't take no for an answer. What would you like?' asked Jennifer.

'You're such sweet girls, I'll have a small coffee and Joshua, and I will share a sandwich.'

'What would you like, Mr Kai?' Tanu asked.

'The same as Mama, please,' he answered. 'We don't eat much during the day, so half a sandwich is fine. But can I give you some money to pay?'

'No, absolutely not. But thank you. Now, what would you like on your sandwich?' Tanu asked.

'Any spiced meat please,' Mrs Kai said, decisively.

The young women left their seats and made their way up the steps to the concourse. As soon as they were out of sight Tanu started to grin and jump around like a schoolgirl.

'Jennifer, just wondering, is there anything we can do to make you less attractive for this meal tonight? Nothing too severe, you know, perhaps just cut your hair to a more manageable length, like short, really short, and drip sauce all over your top and round your mouth?'

They both laughed. Jennifer was beginning to dearly love Tanu's sense of humour. 'Aren't they such nice people?' she commented.

'Who, my in-laws? Yes, they're lovely, and like me, they're so unassuming.' Jennifer laughed heartily at her friend again. They found a kiosk that made fresh sandwiches and coffee. They returned to their seats with their refreshments and enjoyed the remaining events. Soon it was twenty to six as the 100m qualifying times and final lane positions flashed up on the big screen. It was immediately apparent that Cedric's qualifying time was the slowest of the eight.

Lane 1. Ameen Puddo	South Sudan	9.699
Lane 2. Farid Touati	Algeria	9.701
Lane 3. Seth Haruna	Nigeria	9.706
Lane 4. Alamini Otieno	Kenya	9.707
Lane 5. Ben Innatimmi	Ghana	9.709
Lane 6. Marcus Smitt	South Africa	9.712
Lane 7. Moses Haruna	Nigeria	9.714
Lane 8. Cedric Kai	South Africa	9.716

Jennifer turned to Tanu and whispered, 'Don't worry. His personal best is 9.645. It says so here in the programme. He's probably being tactical. I'm sure he'll give it his all now.'

'Good evening, ladies and gentlemen, please welcome today's African Nations 100 metre finalists.'

The Adonis stood behind the start line, looking every inch of his nickname, skin glistening and muscles rippling as he shook down his limbs. He looked focused and determined as the other competitors practised their starts from the blocks. His headphones were in place till the officials brought the others back behind the line. It was only then that he removed the headphones and got into position in his blocks.

'On your marks.' The whistle.

Bang. Away at the first gun.

He'd never been so quick out of the blocks. The crowd went wild as he left the competition in his wake. He threw his arms in the air as he crossed the line with a personal best of 9.605. He'd annihilated the field. The crowd chanted, 'Kai. Kai. Kai.'

A spectator gave him a South African flag to drape over his shoulders as he took a lap of honour to cheers and applause.

Jennifer and Tanu moved forward to join the Kais. Joshua rose to his feet, waved his arms in joy before kissing Mama, Jennifer and Tanu. He immediately apologised to Jennifer for forgetting himself, then kissed her again.

Mother and Tanu were jumping up and down, holding hands.

Cedric was led away for the compulsory drug test, but no one in the stadium doubted that the result had been achieved fairly.

It was 7:15 and, still wrapped in his national flag, Cedric led out the line of three to receive their African Nations medals. He stood proudly on the podium, hand on heart, as the South African national anthem 'Nkosi Sikelel' iAfrika' played and the athletics supporters sang loudly, hearts bursting.

A massive cheer went up as Cedric kissed his medal and waved to the crowd.

***

They all arrived at the stadium restaurant and were shown to their table to wait for Cedric. Joshua Kai seized the moment to exchange phone numbers with Jennifer and Tanu.

Tanu hesitated and felt reluctant because she didn't want to miss out on getting Cedric's, afterwards. But she couldn't ask everyone to do it later as it would expose her secret motive. Fortunately, just at that moment she saw the double doors open, and her hero came walking over to them. Her chest was pounding, but she managed to keep a calm exterior.

He went straight to hug his parents, a touching moment, and then Mr Kai said, 'Son, let me formally introduce you to Sister Jennifer and Tanu, although I think you met before on the train.'

'One moment please,' said Cedric, with a beaming smile.

He was gone a few seconds and their eyes followed him. He went to a waitress and returned with her white towel, giving it to Jennifer, who immediately recognised what he wanted her to do. She put it on her head and pulled it around her face like a wimple.

He offered her his hand and said, 'Good evening Sister Jennifer, it's lovely to see you again. You look quite different without your wimple.' They all laughed as she responded, 'Hello, I'm very pleased to meet you, again. Please call me Jennifer. Might I ask, though, which do you prefer, Adonis or Cedric?'

'Adonis is fine by me,' he shrugged, laughing.

'Be respectful,' Mama said, wagging her finger.

Jennifer ignored his hand and gave him a hug. She then turned to Tanu, saying, 'Meet your biggest fan, Cedric.'

He bent forward, caught Tanu in his gaze and said, 'I'm so pleased to see you, Tanu. I wasn't sure if I'd get the opportunity to see you again.'

There was an immediate energy between them, plain for all to see.

Tanu could barely croak her answer, but she somehow managed to make it sound controlled, even though the words were coming fast and furious.

'So pleased to see you again, too! I couldn't believe it yesterday when your parents came to Ackerman & Sons, and Jennifer called me through to the shop floor.

'Sorry, that's where I work, and she is working there part-time at the moment. It was so nice to see her again too when she came in on Monday looking for work.'

'Oh, so you're not old friends then?'

'No, we've only just started to get to know each other. But we feel like old friends, don't we, Jennifer? To be honest, Jennifer is probably everything you'd expect a friend to be, and a nun not to be.'

At that, Jennifer said, 'I beg your pardon,' with mock disapproval on her face.

'See what I mean? I love her already,' Tanu said, smiling.

Cedric's father was listening to the conversation closely and interrupted, 'These two young ladies have been such a pleasure to spend time with today, haven't they Mama?'

Mrs Kai replied, 'They have indeed, and I must apologise for not addressing you properly, Sister Jennifer.'

'Please, don't, there's no need. I've never been precious about titles. I'm just Jennifer,' she said.

'I'm not quite sure about my title,' said Cedric. 'But I appear to be stuck with it now, at least until I get old and fat.'

They all laughed at the thought of this handsome, slim, young man one day becoming old and fat.

The scene was set for a happy meal, with much chatter and laughter. Tanu wished it could never end.

It was about eleven as they got up to leave the restaurant. The question of phone numbers hadn't come up again and she had been privately wondering how she could broach the subject. She had decided in the end that perhaps she ought not to, even though it was nearly killing her.

Cedric escorted them to their car, and as he said good night to them both, he kissed them on the cheek before saying to Tanu, 'Would you mind if I called you tomorrow?'

She breathed a huge sigh of relief, hopefully not audibly. 'I think you might find that a little difficult. You haven't got my number,' she smiled.

'You see what shyness has achieved for me!' he countered. 'Well, would you mind giving me your number please, and would it be acceptable to you if I called you tomorrow?'

She smiled, feeling insanely happy. 'Yes, of course, and I'd be incredibly disappointed if you didn't,' she managed, with dignity, in spite of wanting to whoop with joy.

'It's been lovely to see you both again, and I hope to see much more of you in the future,' Cedric replied.

'I'm sure you will,' Jennifer said, smiling. 'Oh, and maybe I might have your number too, please Cedric? I have a friend who I know would love to meet you sometime. He's also a new friend, and, like you, he's a gentleman. I think you'd get on really well.'

Cedric smiled and they all exchanged numbers then Jennifer and Tanu got in the car. Cedric gave them an enthusiastic send off and made his way back to his parents, who were waiting in the foyer.

Tanu drove away from the stadium car park and, once she was at a safe distance, and out of sight, she pulled over, banged on the steering wheel and screamed. Jennifer covered her ears at the decibels.

When she'd stopped, she turned to Jennifer and, in a more normal voice, managed, 'He wants me to have his babies, could you see that? He doesn't know it yet, but we're going to have six boys and four girls. The eldest we'll call Jennifer.'

Jennifer was laughing again as she pointed out one of the obvious problems, apart from the little matters of courtship and marriage, 'But what if your first is a boy? You can't call him Jennifer.'

'If he's my son, I'll call him whatever I like,' challenged Tanu. They both laughed. It felt like they'd been friends for a lifetime. There seemed no walls or boundaries, just a mutual understanding and growing love and loyalty. It was a mirror of how she felt towards David.

Chapter 19

Crossroads

The time had flown since Jennifer had decided to take the offer of a sabbatical.

Five months had passed, and the friendships she had made in the first couple of weeks in Johannesburg had flourished. The three deacons had become an integral part of her world, visiting regularly to have dinner, and to talk and to walk with both Jennifer and David. The three promising young men were now ordained and serving in different parishes in the Johannesburg area.

David studied hard and worked hard at the church in his spare time. Father Seth had maintained his vow for change, and all at the presbytery delighted in his new peaceful demeanour, including Father Seth himself. The idea of family was no longer just an idea, but a reality, and Jennifer's influence had proved an enormous driving force for its continuation. David and Jennifer had met all of Ethel's family, and they often visited each other and included everyone in their day to day lives.

Then there was Tanu and Cedric. David had been introduced early on to their friendship with Jennifer, and an immediate bond grew stronger. The four of them saw a great deal of each other.

Jennifer prayed that, where David, the most treasured of her friends, was concerned, all these people she loved and cared about would fill her shoes and help him as she moved on with her decision to go to Juba, South Sudan.

David had settled well into college life, and he and Jennifer had been sharing the work at the presbytery, church, and gardens. There had been many occasions when David had struggled to keep the promise he'd made to himself. Seeing her daily, spending increasing periods of time with her, fuelled his internal battle. He longed to tell her of his love, but he couldn't, just couldn't, burden her any further than she seemed already burdened.

Their daily shared experiences were the times that he cherished above everything, even though he knew that they couldn't lead to anything beyond friendship.

The times when he wasn't in college and Jennifer wasn't at Ackerman's were spent with her around the church, working side by side and learning more about each other. David had insisted on transferring money to her account for her labour as he was still getting the same salary but working fewer hours. But as their bond grew stronger, his personal burden grew too.

Evie had been invited to the presbytery to join her daughter, and Jennifer decided that now was the time to share her news with everyone. Only Father Seth had known the gravity of the decision she had made, and she was now ready to share it with those whom she loved most and to whom she was closest. Evie was due to arrive tomorrow at midday, and Jennifer intended to take Father Seth's car to pick her up from the station since David had a study day with Professor Pingali, or, as he called it, 'another encounter with the genius'.

To the professor, the feeling was mutual since they were working together on the launch of one of David's business ideas. It had soon become apparent that David was way ahead of his classmates and often startled his tutor with his diligent yet straightforward approach to computer science. He may have come late to the world of the university, but he was truly finding his feet in the world of academia.

Jennifer had warned Father Seth that she intended to make her announcement at dinner the following day, and he was very aware that she wasn't looking forward to the emotional fallout. He had tried on numerous occasions to talk her out of her decision, but she was adamant that this was what God wanted her to do. So, unless God changed his plan for her, she was going to Juba.

Jennifer had arranged to take the day off from work, and Tanu and Cedric were going to join them.

She'd woken after a restless night worrying about everyone. In her youth and idealism, she was fearless of personal sacrifice and just wanted her dearest friends to be happy. However, she was also acutely aware that her need to pursue what she believed to be God's will, was going to cause pain for those she loved most and, of course, those who loved her.

But tonight was the night, and she couldn't protect them from the danger of her vocation and its demands.

She drove to the station to collect Evie. Jennifer made her way to the platform, excited to see her mother again. As the train pulled in, she hurriedly scanned the carriages and spotted Evie, greeting her with a smile and a huge hug as she alighted the train. They both had so much to say, and so much to tell each other.

Their conversation soon turned from the journey and how well they both looked and became very much centred on David. Evie wanted to know everything about him. It felt distinctly as though she was hanging some sort of hope on him, Jennifer thought, shifting uncomfortably. Evie was definitely showing more than a passing interest.

Jennifer wondered if her mother hoped that he had, in some way, persuaded her to forget about Juba. But, of course, David still knew nothing of her plans, and her mother nothing of her decision. She wondered if her announcement was going to be the most difficult of all for her mother to take, more than anyone else, even David. She suddenly realised that there had rarely been a phone call when she hadn't mentioned David to her. Jennifer drove her mother quickly back to the presbytery, dying to introduce her to Ethel.

Ethel welcomed her like an old friend, and they hardly took breaths between the confidences shared. The conversation almost inevitably drifted to Maureen O'Hara, and amidst all the references, Evie said she would find out all she could about the actress's origins on her forthcoming visit, as she was going to be in Ireland for two weeks.

David arrived home from college and Jennifer, keen to introduce him, welcomed him in the hallway and led him into the dining room to meet Evie. He was his usual, quietly charming self as Evie probed him almost mercilessly.

Mammy was indeed placing some unrealistic hope on him, Jennifer thought, praying for the inquisition to end. However, David didn't appear at all put out by the tirade of questions being thrown at him.

Jennifer, watching the exchange between them was reminded of just how much the once-shy David had changed and matured. Delighted with his progress and self-assured responses, she waited for a natural pause in the conversation before saying, 'I expect you'll want to freshen up and change for dinner, Mammy?'

'Yes darling, but I was just getting acquainted with David.'

'That's OK Mammy, but I know David has things he needs to do before dinner too. Perhaps you can chat later?' Jennifer, standing behind her mother, gestured to David, indicating the direction of the door.

David smiled again at Evie, amused by her relentless barrage of questions. He saw his chance to escape and proceeded up to his room.

***

It was time for dinner, and Tanu and Cedric had arrived. They'd been introduced to the Evie who, like her daughter, loved sport and was, therefore, very aware of Cedric and his increasing successes.

They'd finished the meal, and Jennifer decided that it was now or never. She remained seated and, taking Evie's hand, she took a deep breath, waited for a natural break in the conversation and said, 'Well, everyone, you're all aware that I have been praying for guidance and direction for some time now.' They all looked up.

'So, I believe God, in his wisdom, has provided me with both. In four weeks, I'll be taking up a post at a new school in Juba.'

Jennifer didn't wait for a reaction but looked around at the concerned faces at the table and ploughed on with her announcement.

'After arriving here in Johannesburg, I found myself challenged by some unforeseen circumstances. Circumstances that made me question my vocation and led me to do some soul searching.'

The room was silent. 'It's proving a tough journey, and I need more time to determine if pursuing a vocation within the order is right for me. So, after a period of prayer and reflection, I spoke to the prioress who suggested I took a sabbatical and offered me the post in Juba. I know the challenges before me are great and not without danger. But I truly feel that this is the path I should take before coming to any conclusion.

'The school has been purpose built to provide education for the very needy children of that city. I believe this to be my immediate vocation, but I will only be allowed to work there for a year, until I, with God's help, determine my longer-term future with the convent.'

'Oh, no, Jennifer! Not Juba!' gasped Evie, finally, as she started to cry.

Ethel, remembering the conversations she'd had with Jennifer after the upset created by Dominic all those months ago, decided it was time to speak up. She said, 'As a mother too, I understand your pain, Evie. We strive to protect our children and do everything we can to keep them from harm's way. But as hard as it is, we have to allow them the freedom to take the pathway they need to. God love you, it's the hardest of challenges, and believe me, I know, but we must allow them to choose their own time to spread their wings.'

Looking at Ethel, Jennifer, in a quiet, kind, but firm voice, said, 'Thank you, Ethel. I'm glad you understand.'

Turning to Evie, she said, 'Please, Mammy, I don't want anybody to be upset. I know about the dangers, and God in his mercy will determine what is best for me. So please try to be happy for me, I love you so dearly Mammy, and I'd like to know you'll pray for me and my vocation, whatever it may turn out to be. I'd like to know I have your support.'

David sat in silence, stricken, but holding back the turmoil in his stomach.

Father Seth straightened the cutlery remaining in front of him, unnecessarily lining up their handles at ninety degrees to the edge of the table.

Ethel, looking at Jennifer said, 'You have my prayers and support, child. But I feel I must ask. Are you absolutely sure this is what you want, and this is what you need to do to pursue what you believe God wants of you, Jennifer?'

Jennifer, about to answer, was interrupted as Evie dabbed her eyes, 'I'm sorry, Ethel, but nothing you say will change her mind. She has her daddy's stubbornness and, believe me when I say, there is no one more stubborn.

Turning to Jennifer, she went on, 'You have my blessing, my beautiful girl, but only because I know you so well, and the strength of your faith. May God bless you.'

'Thank you Mammy, that means the world to me,' said Jennifer, suddenly choked.

An image of her father flashed through Jennifer's mind. It was accompanied by bittersweet recollections of the man to whom she'd been so close until he left without explanation or farewell.

Tanu felt she needed to add to the moment. 'Jennifer, I want you to be safe, and I want you to be here, but I know if you stay, you'll be unhappy, and so you won't be our Jennifer. So of course, you should do what you need to do.'

Looking at Cedric, and touching his hand, she added, 'Both Cedric and I want you to know you mean so much to us, and we love you. But it's only a year, so we will wait for you.'

David, summoning up his greatest strength, spoke carefully and clearly. 'Just make sure you come back safe,' he said.

Father Seth smiled at her. 'You must follow your heart Jennifer.'

Although the emotion was plain to see on his face, he continued, 'It would be selfish of us to ask you to ignore your heart, especially considering that you have given this situation so much thought and prayer.'

Jennifer looked around at the little gathering with relief. It had been easier than she'd expected, and even though David hadn't said much, it was he who had raised her greatest concerns. He'd made so much progress in every area of his life, and she knew that he felt much of that was down to her.

She knew she would be leaving him at a time of great change, but what else was she to do? She knew there were other people in his life now who would look out for him and support him. He and Cedric had established a great friendship, and David had been invited to almost every athletics meeting around the country in the last few months.

Jennifer went to hug and thank them all before quietly excusing herself and returning to her room.

She picked up her mobile phone to plug it in to charge and noticed several missed calls. They were all from the prioress. This was unusual, thought Jennifer. She'd never called her directly before and had always previously communicated with her via Father Seth. But it was too late to call back now, so she would ring her in the morning, she decided.

She knelt by her bed, saying the rosary. It was just gone eleven, and her phone started to ring. She never liked interrupting her prayers, but she could see it was the prioress, or at least, someone from the convent dialling from that number.

She stood up and picked it up from the bedside table. 'Hello, Jennifer speaking.'

'Oh, hello Sister Jennifer, it's Sister Teresa at the convent in Gauteng. I've been trying to get hold of you all evening. I'm so sorry, it's past both our bedtimes, but it was really necessary for you to hear what I have to say.'

'I must apologise, prioress. We've been having dinner at the presbytery where I have been telling my dear friends about my placement.'

'Oh, I see. Well, Sister, that's what I was ringing about. We had some communication from Juba earlier in the day, and I know this may come as a shock, but regrettably, the school was the subject of an attack this morning. Several army personnel were killed and injured.'

She paused for the news to sink in.

'We're recalling all the sisters and, therefore, the project has been cancelled, Jennifer. I'm so sorry. I expect you'll need a little more time to consider your position with the convent.

Again, she paused for the information to be absorbed.

Then the prioress continued, 'I feel I must advise you that we'd rather you took more time than rush into something you may regret in the future. But in the interim, and in an endeavour to support you, I'll speak with Father Seth tomorrow to try to determine a way forward that can hopefully accommodate everyone.

'Don't say anything right now, there's no need. Please say your prayers, and I'm sure the right answers will come. Bless you, sister, and goodnight.'

Jennifer managed a quiet 'Goodnight, prioress, and thank you so much for letting me know.'

She put down the phone and sat down on her bed. She immediately started to think about all those who had lost their lives and, sadly, the loved ones they had left behind.

In comparison, she recognised their loss was far greater than the position in which she now found herself. She believed without question that God in his wisdom had decided that it wasn't the right journey for her. She finished saying the rosary then climbed into bed and, praying long and special prayers for those involved in the attack, eventually, she drifted into an exhausted sleep.

She woke as soon as it was light, and after her shower, she dressed slowly and went downstairs to speak to Father Seth in his study.

She explained the situation and told him to expect a call from the prioress. Father Seth nodded kindly, took her hand, and together they went into breakfast.

The atmosphere in the dining room was sombre. Ethel kept giving Jennifer sideways glances as she was setting the table, and Evie was uncharacteristically quiet. David smiled, and as she sat down, he reached over to her and squeezed her hand whilst giving her an encouraging smile.

Oh, the timing of this had been all wrong, she thought. If only she'd waited to make her announcement, it would have saved much worry for these wonderful people.

No point in waiting any longer. She said, looking at them all in turn, 'Something quite terrible has happened. I had a call from the prioress last night, and she informed me that there was an attack on the school yesterday, people killed, and they're withdrawing all the sisters. So I won't be going to Juba after all.'

Evie started to cry, but they were tears of joy and relief. Rising from her chair, she walked around to where Jennifer was seated and wrapping her arms around her and looking in a heavenly direction said, 'Thank you, thank you, thank you Lord.'

Ethel looked over to mother and daughter, and with tears in her eyes said, 'Thank God for his intervention. I know that doesn't help those poor people in Juba, and I don't know what the answer is to all that, but at least you are kept safe, Jennifer.'

David gazed at her with relief and love. He dared not give vent to his true feelings, the utter delight that she was to stay with him a while longer, but felt guilt that the unrest in Juba had claimed yet more lives.

Jennifer hardly ate and couldn't hide her restlessness. She asked David to walk in the garden with her.

They left the presbytery side by side and made their way through the garden, talking about the latest flowers in bloom, David naming them as if they were friends, even gendering some of them, and pointing out the next buds to look out for.

They reached the quietest of the garden and Jennifer suddenly sat down on the grass, motioning to David to join her.

He knew something of what she was going to say.

'David, I sense I'm at a crossroads and in some way I'm being given an ultimatum in relation to making my vows and I just know I will regret it, if I am forced to come up with a solution.' She dropped her chin onto her hands and glumly surveyed her sandalled feet.

It was then that he had an idea.

He thought it through for a few moments, then said, 'Jennifer, don't write off your vocation. You have no reason to. Look at this as a temporary measure and go to Ireland with your mother. Take whatever time you need to make your decision, and then, in God's time, you will come to the right thing, I'm certain of it.'

'Wow,' she said. 'Ireland! David, you're right. If I decide that I must leave the convent, and if God wants me to be a nun, a doctor, or work in a burger parlour, then as long as I'm doing his work, it doesn't matter where or how I do it.' She hugged him.

'Thank you. Oh, yes! I can't wait to go to Ireland! Now I just have to convince my mammy,' she laughed, the weight of the world suddenly lifting off her shoulders.

They returned to the presbytery. She went straightaway to find Evie, who was reading in the sitting room.

'What date do you leave for Ireland, Mammy?' asked Jennifer, brightly.

'Fed up with me already?' asked Evie, looking up from her book, smiling. 'There's nothing written in stone yet, sweetheart. Uncle Malachi is expecting me whenever. I've not even booked my ticket yet.'

Jennifer could hardly contain her excitement. 'Mammy, I've just had a talk with David in the garden, and he's come up with a brilliant idea, but I want to see what you think about it. He suggested that I come to Ireland with you and take as much time as I need to make my decision. The convent have made it clear that I must take my time, so, as long as I'm doing God's work, it doesn't matter where I do it or whether I do it in jeans or a habit. Whatever happens, I know he will find the right path for me.'

Evie's face was glowing. 'Where is he? David, I mean! I want to go and hug him. That's a fantastic idea. You're right. He's such a great young man. When can you leave your job at Ackerman's?'

'I can ring Tanu now. She's at work today, and if she can speak to Amahle, I'm sure they'll let me know as soon as possible.'

Jennifer made the call and told Tanu all the things that had happened since they said goodnight after dinner.

Tanu couldn't hide her joy at hearing Jennifer's latest plans. Dublin was far away, but at least her friend would be safe there. She'd ring Amahle, she said, and get back to her straight away.

She added, 'I'm not absolutely certain, but I think you should work two weeks' notice. So, you can leave in two weeks or drop it like a stone, but you won't get paid.'

'Brilliant, Tanu. I'll tell Mammy. Thanks a million!'

'You're welcome, girlfriend,' Tanu replied.

Chapter 20

Malachi

It was the night before Jennifer and Evie's departure, and David had arranged a farewell dinner at Father Seth's choice of excellent restaurant. They gathered around a large table and the air was filled with happy voices.

Ethel had decided to make a speech. She had practised it, keeping the piece of paper in her pocket for the days, going over and over it under her breath while Jennifer was out at work.

She began hesitantly. This was not the Ethel they all knew so well.

'Father, Evie, children. I just want to say a few words to mark this occasion.' She paused for a deep breath.

'I'm sure everyone here has a special place in their hearts for our dear Jennifer. She has brightened our lives with her warmth, understanding and love.

'We all know that she has had her own issues to deal with, and she continues to do that through prayer and faith. She has been an inspiration and has created an environment that I know has helped me to search for a better me.'

Turning to Jennifer, she went on, 'I'm going to miss you so much, child, but I know there are others here who also know the depth of that feeling. But at least you'll be safe where you're going, and although there is no constraint on your time away, I hope you will come home soon to the delight of all who love you.'

She turned back to the others. 'I would like to raise a glass to Jennifer and her safe return.'

'To Jennifer and her safe return.' It resounded through the room. They all stood and raised their glasses and drank before bursting into spontaneous applause. Jennifer's eyes sparkled with delight. David's did, too, but for him there was just the threat of a tear.

The sense of relief was palpable, and in the next moment of silence, Evie turned to thank David for all that he had done to bring them to this happy place.

The celebration over, Simeon took Ethel, Amahle, Tanu and Cedric in his car, and David drove Father Seth, Evie and Jennifer back to the presbytery. As they arrived, Jennifer said, 'David, would you mind taking a little stroll around the garden with me? I'm too hot and restless to go inside right now.'

Evie and Father Seth bade them goodnight, entered the presbytery and went into the sitting room.

She did what had become almost second nature when they walked together. She gently folded her fingers into the joint of his elbow.

The two of them followed the path to the wall and along to the vegetable patch where she stopped and turned to face him. 'You're so selfless, David,' she said. He looked back at her, surprised, wondering what was coming next.

'I feel so sad that I have to leave you, but happy knowing that I do that with your love and support. These last few months have been so special for me, not least because of you. I don't want you to feel sad, and I don't want you to be alone.

'Whatever happens in your future, I want you to know I'm only at the end of a phone and I want to be a part of your life. It isn't all that long since we had those conversations about friendship. But I feel ours has been heaven blessed, and I thank God for giving me the opportunity to get to know you.

She spread her other arm to encircle him and laid her forehead on his chest. 'So, my sweetest of all friends, be kind to yourself, embrace your future and know I love you.' Then, looking deep into his eyes, 'As you once said to me, big smile, be confident. You can achieve whatever you set your mind to.'

He answered, ruefully, 'I know I said to take as much time as you need, Jennifer. But perhaps I should have made it clear that you have to come back at some point!

'You've taught me so much, and I know I'll miss you like I'd miss my right hand. But in a way I'm not sad because I know you need this time to find your happiness and, when you find that, I'll be happy too. Go find what you seek, and I'll wait for you.'

They hugged each other, and again, just for that moment, all was good in their world.

They went into the presbytery. Evie and Jennifer's flight was at 1:50 pm the following day. David wasn't in college, so he had promised to take them to the airport.

He wasn't looking forward to saying goodbye again, but on the other hand, he wanted to spend as much time as he could with her because he didn't know when he'd next see her.

Early the next day Jennifer made her way down to breakfast, and spent the morning in church, taking solace in the silence.

She was up in her room finishing packing when there was a knock on her door, it was Ethel. She had tears in her eyes and a stricken expression.

She stood a little way into the room as Jennifer took her arm with concern. Ethel dabbed her eyes, blew her nose, and said, 'I'm going to miss you child. It's been so good to have had a woman in the house and you've made such a difference to us all.

'And, well, and well, you've helped David so much, he's going to miss you more than anyone, you know, but it's none of my business. I just hope he will be all right. But you need to find your own answers too and I know you've done everything you can to help him.'

Jennifer looked at her, a look of puzzlement on her face.

'What do you mean when you say it's none of your business, Ethel?'

'Nothing child, I just know how much you've helped him, and in all his life, I've never seen him looking so well, and full of life. That's down to you Jennifer.'

'Please Ethel, don't undermine him. He's very capable and that's all he needs to hear. He needs to be reassured and encouraged to chase his dreams. He needs to see that we both believe in him.'

'I'm sorry child, you're right. I'm just scared for him.'

'Please trust me, Ethel, encourage him, celebrate his achievements, don't dwell on the negatives. You know better than anyone how important that is. Have faith, Ethel, you're such a special person.'

Ethel nodded. 'Goodbye child, and thank you. I'll always be grateful to you - grateful for everything and especially grateful for the changes you have brought to all our lives.'

They hugged, safe in the knowledge that their bond would stand the test of time.

Having finished her packing, Jennifer went out onto the landing. As she opened her bedroom door, there was David, ready to knock.

'Are you ready? We need to go soon,' he said, in his practical voice.

He smiled, a natural and relaxed smile. 'Let me take your suitcase and hold-all,' he said. 'And remember...'

She interrupted, 'Stay left, you wouldn't want me to fall.'

They both laughed and made their way to the hallway,

'I'll just go and say goodbye to Father,' she said.

She walked into the study and Seth looked up from his easy chair. 'Time to go, Jennifer?' he said, smiling.

'Yes, Father, and thank you for your guidance, wisdom and hospitality. I've learnt so much since I arrived, and I've experienced so much that I don't think I would have, if I hadn't come to St Brigid's.'

He stood, and as he offered his hand, she moved past it and hugged him.

'Sorry Father, on these occasions, a handshake is just, well, not enough.'

'Bless you Jennifer,' he said as he reciprocated. Evie went to hug him too, and they had a quiet word of farewell together.

As the three of them drove to the airport, David, Jennifer and Evie, Jennifer was finding it hard to suppress her excitement at the prospect of actually meeting Uncle Malachi, but at the same time dreading the moment of farewell with David.

Reading her mind, he said, 'You must be really looking forward to meeting your uncle. I bet he can't wait to see you in person. I think he must be amazing, 93 and techno savvy. Wow.'

Jennifer answered, 'Oh, I can't wait, you're right. He's invited me so many times, and now at last I'm on my way. I'll tell him all about you, and maybe you and he can chat sometime when I call you?'

'Thanks, Jennifer, I'd love to chat to him. He sounds incredible.'

They reached the airport and as they pulled up to park, David said quietly to Jennifer, beside him, 'I guess this is it then? The inevitable.'

Before she could answer, he jumped out of the car and opened the door for Evie. She alighted, taking his hand, covering it with her own and smiled her thanks. She then walked a few yards away to read a poster, perhaps unnecessarily, but to allow the young ones to say their farewell.

David said, 'Thank you Jennifer for all you have done for me, I'll never forget it.' She looked at him, suddenly anxious. 'I told you last night what you mean to me, David. And I promise, I'll call you regularly. I am coming back, you know, but I'm just not sure when.'

He smiled. 'I know you're fulfilling a dream and I'm sure you'll be fulfilling one for Uncle Malachi too in the process. Enjoy your time with him.'

They embraced. She kissed him on the cheek as tears started to fall from her eyes. She hadn't expected them to. She had intended to stay strong and calm, to make it easier on him.

He squeezed her shoulders. His turn to be strong.

'Come on,' he said as he retrieved a trolley from the trolley park before wheeling it and all the baggage into the check-in area.

He left them there, with a cheerful wave, as they joined the queue at the KLM desk for flights to Schiphol Airport, Amsterdam.

***

Malachi was the last of the living family in Ireland. He had never married and had always adored Evie as his only niece. When Jennifer arrived in the world, he had made his one and only trip out of Ireland to see her.

He adored Jennifer, too, and had often invited her to Ireland during their regular video calls. Jennifer had always worried about going since she had little money of her own and he had insisted on paying for everything.

But now, things were different. She had her savings and she had reasons and time to visit him without feeling she'd be imposing on his generosity.

Great uncle Malachi had told Jennifer on their last video call that he'd almost given up hope of ever seeing her in person again, how he remembered her as a tiny baby and how he'd always carried the photograph of him holding her. It was time for another picture to be taken, she'd said. After all, twenty-one years was a long time.

Malachi was still independent but lived for the visits from Evie. His brain was as sharp as ever, but his heart was failing and his arthritis made moving difficult. He adamantly refused to leave his home, though, the home he'd been born in, no matter how persuasively the modern alternatives were described to him.

Then there was Oliver, his young friend and honorary grandson. Oliver was the 12-year-old son of his next-door neighbours, the O'Callaghans. Oliver, who had no grandfather of his own, loved spending time with Malachi, and wouldn't let a day pass without visiting the old man next door. He ran every errand for him with gladness. Malachi had often tried to give him a couple of euros for his kindness, but Oliver would always refuse, saying he did it because he wanted to, and he didn't need the money.

***

Jennifer and Evie arrived in Dublin on the Aer Lingus flight from Amsterdam the following day, 17 hours after leaving Johannesburg. They were tired but cheerful to see the soft Irish rain falling on the tarmac as their plane coasted to a stop.

As they wheeled their cases to the exit of the arrivals terminal, Jennifer quickly spotted a taxi driver holding up a name card, O'Broin.

They greeted him with some relief, glad that this next bit of the journey would be straightforward. The Dubliner's brogue was much stronger than Malachi's, so both mother and daughter had difficulty understanding him, and the problem was probably two ways, but his reassuring smiles were all that was needed. He led them to his taxi and, opening the boot, placed their bags and cases into it.

'You sit in the front Jennifer, you'll see more from there,' Evie said.

Her mother's instruction awakened the memory of the first time she'd met David and how Father Seth had almost barked at him, telling him to open the passenger door for her. She felt a tight knot come into her stomach, and a sudden overwhelming sense of loss. This was new to her, something she had never experienced before about anyone other than her father. So why was she feeling like this about David, she asked herself.

329

She quelled the feelings and asked the driver if he knew the address of where they were going. His response made her giggle as the only words she could make out were, 'ya mean auld Mal's cottage Ranelagh.' She looked at Evie and smiled, Evie said, 'You'll find life here is very different, everyone knows everyone, and if they don't know you today, they'll know you tomorrow. It's a friendly place.'

They drove out of the airport and within a few minutes they were driving through beautiful fields of emerald green. It really was emerald, thought Jennifer. So many different shades.

She turned to Evie and said, 'Isn't it beautiful, mammy, so green, so unspoilt.'

'It is, but we'll be going onto the M1 soon, and that's a bit different, but that's the price of progress.

'But, yes, there are some beautiful areas of countryside that are completely unspoiled. You might not remember, but north of the city is gorgeous.'

They drove through many built up areas before turning right off the main road. Immediately it felt like they'd travelled back in time. The car bounced down a potholed, narrow road which came to an abrupt end just beyond a right-hand curve that took them around an old, but well managed, coppice, and there in front of them stood the beautiful, whitewashed, thatched cottage of old memory, the home of great uncle Malachi.

It had been in the family for more than 200 years and had been considerably extended over time but maintained all of its character, charm and original features. Jennifer loved it at first sight.

They got out of the car and the driver carried their luggage to the front door of the cottage.

They entered and there, in front of the fire in an old rocking chair, was the man that Jennifer had spoken to so many times on video. As he turned his face towards them, she recognised the warm, infectious smile she'd become so familiar with. He raised his hands and, looking at Jennifer and Evie, he beckoned to them to come to him.

They both walked over and bent forward to kiss him. Silent tears started to fall from his eyes as he said in his gentle, quiet brogue, 'I'm so pleased to see you, Aoibheann, and meeting you again, Jennifer, after such a long interlude, brings me such great joy. 'Tis true to say, there's no one quite like family to warm the heart and inspire me to live another day.'

'Oh uncle, I'm so pleased to be here with mammy. I've been so excited to see you in person. I promise you'll never have to wait so long again.'

'Well,' he said, chuckling. 'I'm so pleased to hear that Jennifer. I'm not sure I have the time to wait another 21 years.'

The three of them laughed at that.

'I love the cottage.' Jennifer said. 'It's so beautiful, so quaint, and has such a homely feel about it.'

'This will all be yours one day, Jennifer,' Malachi responded, with a smile. He'd said it to her many times.

'Goodness, well not too soon, I hope,' she replied, stroking his hand and looking lovingly into his ancient eyes.

Malachi asked Evie to show Jennifer to the back bedroom and said that she was to go in the front room, as usual. He was now too weak to climb the stairs, so he had had the large sitting room converted into a bedroom and en-suite bathroom.

Evie took Jennifer up to her room.

Jennifer whispered, 'Mammy, Uncle Malachi, he worries me. Doesn't he have anyone who helps him?'

'No, he's very independent and very stubborn. There's little Oliver next door, of course. He comes to see him every day, as you know and Uncle Malachi thinks the world of him. But he's only twelve, and I know it worries him that Oliver will find him in a heap one day.

'I've tried for so many years to get him to come to South Africa and live near us. But he's always said he wants to live his days out in the place where he was born, but this is all he knows, and he's always said he has too much depending on him here in Ireland to move away. I have no idea what he means by that. As I've said, there's only Oliver. But perhaps that's his reason to stay.'

Oliver soon made his appearance to greet the visitors, and it was soon clear that the old man and the sandy-haired young boy had a delightful relationship. Malachi played chess with him, teaching him all the moves he knew and how to plan strategy, and Oliver introduced Malachi to new uploads on YouTube of Irish music and history documentaries. They both shared a fascination with archaeology and the Viking artefacts found in and around Dublin. It was moving to see them talking so animatedly. Jennifer rejoiced to see it.

But, as the days passed, Jennifer became increasingly worried about Malachi's personal safety, and his advancing age.

She decided, after a week in the cottage, on what she should do. 'I'm going to stay on for a while, mammy,' she said. 'I have my savings to support me, and if I'm careful, I can look after Malachi and convince him to get help before I return to South Africa.'

'You should discuss that with him, sweetheart. First, he's very proud, and I'm not sure he'll let you do that, but you can ask,' said Evie.

They decided to speak to him together. The conversation was difficult to broach since they didn't want to offend his pride but the thought of something happening to him when he was alone was too frightening for them.

They tried every argument they could think of, and Malachi listened patiently.

He understood their worries, and he had obviously given great thought to it. He had several provisos before he'd agree. One: he was to pay Jennifer for her time. Two: they'd get a home carer to come in during the day to help him with his more personal needs. Three: Jennifer would return to South Africa at least once a year to keep in touch with her friends and loved ones. Four: Jennifer must prioritise her own needs over his and must have the freedom to move on whenever it was appropriate for her. And all this was to happen with the agreement that he would continue to employ the carer.

It was the breakthrough they were hoping for. It was with great relief that Evie took her leave of them both after two weeks to return to South Africa.

***

Jennifer dedicated herself to looking after Malachi in the ensuing months, and the time flew by. The home care agency they chose sent Sinead, a cheerful woman in her late forties, to help twice a day with bathing and personal needs, and they were all soon laughing at the silly little things that happened, and the stories of Sinead's family life that brightened all their days.

Jennifer had enrolled with an online university for an honours degree in Childhood and Youth Studies, using the money Malachi insisted she take. The great old man was easy to open up to, wise and welcoming, and Jennifer was soon sharing with him some of her deepest feelings, worries and concerns. She spent hours talking to him about her father and the deep scars in her heart his departure had caused. Malachi's soft tones soothed her pain like never before.

Seán O'Broin had emigrated to South Africa three years before he met and married Evie, and five years before Jennifer was born. He originated from the outskirts of Dublin, too, the only child of parents who had died by his twentieth birthday, and Jennifer had never heard mention of any family in Ireland on her father's side. But then, Evie had seemed to block it all out because she couldn't deal with the pain, and Jennifer knew instinctively it would be cruel to poke the embers of her mother's trauma.

In many ways, she reflected, Malachi was like her Daddy, or at least her memories of him, gentle and loving, and he seemed able to tune in to her thoughts, even though many decades separated their life experience.

He also made her feel at ease when he told her that, although he loved her mother as if she were his own daughter, he never felt it appropriate to judge Seán for leaving the family home. On the only occasion he'd met him, he said, he had proved the most charming and considerate of hosts, in spite of working long hours as a structural engineer. Jennifer remembered seeing her father in his hard hat, and demanding to wear it too, laughing gleefully at the sight of herself in the mirror before it slipped down over her eyes.

Malachi said when he'd visited South Africa, Séan had welcomed him into their beautiful little family with open arms. He remembered saying goodbye to them when Jennifer was still tiny, feeling confident that Evie had chosen her life's partner well and was shocked and devastated when he learned of their separation, and Seán's effective disappearance.

None of us ever truly knew what troubles and challenges others had to face in life, counselled Malachi, and to judge other people only brought unhappiness to those who judged. Jennifer already knew that, so she didn't judge, either.

Malachi's stories of her father were partly reassuring, but also confusing. Did he really not know what made him leave? The mystery deepened for Jennifer. Why? Why? She just wanted to know why her family had been torn apart.

Evie had always struggled to talk to Jennifer about her father. Jennifer had noticed, though, that whenever she gave away any small snippet of information, she always did so without ill feeling, and she'd always been grateful for that.

The next time they video called, she thought it might be as good a time as any to broach the subject again.

'It's really been bothering me while I've been here, Mammy. And I've asked Malachi for everything he knows…but can you tell me what exactly happened, Mammy, when Daddy left?' she asked.

Evie prevaricated, but she realised, with discomfort, that Jennifer's curiosity was not going to die down. She'd never wanted to discuss the painful episode but she also recognised that her daughter was still struggling to understand. She needed to unlock the mental box she had archived, unlock it with extreme caution, giving as little away as possible, but hopefully enough to satisfy Jennifer's craving.

All she could really tell her, she said finally, was that she had no idea why he had left. They'd always seemed happy until a couple of months before he'd walked out, and he'd started to drink heavily some months before that. Jennifer nodded. She'd heard that part of the story before.

Evie had challenged him, but he would never enter into any conversation about what was the matter, and that was when the rows had started, she said. She added, with her voice cracking, that she'd never stopped loving him, but that she knew she had to make her life without him. She knew he wasn't coming back, felt it in her bones.

She said, 'Jennifer, he simply adored you, and I thought he did me, and you couldn't have had a better daddy. I was devastated when the arguments started, and he went, and could never understand why he went, and especially the way he went. He packed his cases and was gone before I knew it. I'm so sorry, sweetheart, it must have been dreadful for you.'

They wept together, then, Jennifer realising fully for the first time what a traumatic event it had been in her mother's life, as well as her own.

When she came off the call, she resolved to focus her efforts more strenuously to find whatever trace remained of her father. She couldn't leave the trail to grow any colder.

She first tried to trace him through all the social media portals she could think of. Nothing. Then she just put his name into a search engine. She punched in his name and pressed enter. The only reference that came up was in a news report in Cape Town in 2005, just five months before she entered the convent there. It was a picture of a new building being opened, with the designers, architects and builders all smiling for the camera. She spotted his handsome face and broad smile immediately. He was wearing a hard hat. She always remembered him with his hard hat. Hard hats everywhere, whenever she saw them, on building sites, worn by workers or maintenance crews on the rail network, they always reminded her of him. She felt bereft, knowing that he'd been in Cape Town at that time. So close. They might have seen one another, or their paths might have crossed.

She checked everything on the births, deaths and marriages registers but couldn't find any records of him after that date. In fact, the last record in relation to either parent was that of their divorce, again in 2005, so she had to believe her mother's story because she'd waited almost eight years before divorcing on the grounds of irretrievable breakdown of the marriage.

Jennifer tried every avenue she could think of, for nearly three months. All there was left after that was to try DNA. Perhaps she would be able to contact a second or third cousin or someone who might know of his whereabouts. It was a long shot, but worth trying.

So she submitted a sample and posted it to the company with the biggest database, FindMyFamily DNA, sending it off with a prayer.

She missed him so much. She now believed that this was her last opportunity to find the man who, for all of those formative years, had given her the best possible emotional start in life. She'd come to the conclusion that she was who she was, not because of something special in her, but, because he had given her the tools to love herself enough to be able to truly love others.

***

Over dinner one night, Jennifer looked over at Malachi mischievously and asked another question, a frivolous question, compared to the others she had been asking up to now, but which, she knew, would have no better answer than the one from her great uncle's lips.

'Tell me, won't you, uncle, what do you know about Maureen O'Hara?'

The old man started to chuckle as he responded, 'Maureen O'Hara? The fillum star? Now how did you get to thinking about Maureen O'Hara?'

Jennifer answered, 'Well, it's just that Ethel told me once that I look like her. I'm very flattered by that, of course! I'd honestly never heard of her. But I believe her family comes from Dublin. I just wondered if there might be any connection between the families, way back in history.

'Well, Jennifer, there may well be, but none that I know of,' said Malachi, enjoying the interesting turn this conversation had made.

He looked askance at her, his eyes twinkling. 'Do you know, I rather think you do! You do rather look like her, and your mammy, too for that matter, but to be sure, Maureen always wore the bright red lipstick for the fillums, and her hair was more, how'd you say, Hollywood-style.'

Jennifer giggled at his description, and his charming pronunciation. Perhaps Great Uncle Malachi had always had a soft spot for the local girl made good.

Malachi added, 'Her real name was FitzSimons, don't you know, and there were quite a few FitzSimons in Ranelagh and round about. She was the talk of the town many years ago!

He continued, warming to his theme, 'We were all amazed when a Dublin girl ended up in Hollywood. I mean, can you imagine! I went to the pictures to see her in the fillums. I bought magazines with her pictures in. She was very glamorous, a really big star, along with people like Charles Laughton and John Wayne, but that was way before your time, Jennifer!

'She was in a fillum called *The Quiet Man*, with the big fella, you know, John Wayne. That Hollywood lot, they were all over County Mayo. You can visit the place it was made. I went myself once when I was a bit younger.'

'Then we must watch it together!' interrupted Jennifer, excited at the prospect. 'Yes, we shall, then' answered Malachi, nodding happily at his young great niece. But he hadn't finished on the subject of Maureen O'Hara. 'Maureen FitzSimons was a true Irishwoman, through and through, you know. She never forgot her Irish heritage, and she went to live in Cork with her daughter, I believe. I saw a picture once, of where she lives. It was a beautiful house by the sea.'

Jennifer listened, enraptured. Here was a bona fide witness to the life and times of an incredible woman who captured Hollywood, if not the world, and had held them in her spell across three decades.

Malachi went on, 'So, no. I don't know of any connection with our family other than that. But the FitzSimons and the O'Connors were known for their handsome daughters, all with wonderful, strong, Irish genes. Look at them and look at you, and your lovely mammy. Beautiful, all of you, past and present.'

Jennifer blushed and went over to give her great uncle a hug and a kiss. She loved talking to him. It always filled her with happiness and peace. She was especially happy to know that her genes were Irish, and strong, just like Evie's and Maureen FitzSimons'. It helped to banish some of the sadness that seeped into her soul when she thought of her lost father.

Chapter 21

History

Over the next two years, David and Jennifer would see each other only twice when she returned to South Africa for her holiday, but they video called often and shared their news. Saying goodbye was always hard, even online. All their time together, digital or real, was delicious and precious.

Ethel and Father Seth would make appearances on David's calls every so often, and, at other times, Tanu and Cedric filled the cottage in Ranelagh with the sound of their happy stories, jokes and laughter.

David and Malachi would talk for hours at a time, too. Jennifer would sit close to her great uncle and listen in to their conversations on all manner of topics and emerging technologies. The old man, born into a world of silent films and wind-up telephones, could tune into the instant social media world of the young man, and Jennifer marvelled at their ability to communicate about the latest complex developments. She loved to see and hear them bridging the gulf between their lives and experience.

'Good morning and happy birthday Uncle,' beamed Jennifer as she entered Malachi's room, carrying a carefully wrapped gift. She walked over to him and handed it to him, along with a pile of greetings cards from Evie, David, Ethel, Father Seth, Tanu and Cedric. She bent forward and kissed him on the cheek.

'Ah, good morning, Jennifer, how sweet of you,' the old man replied with a smile to mirror the delight of that of his great niece. 'Are you sure?' he questioned. 'What's the date today?'

She grinned. 'It's the 28th of July, my favourite uncle's birthday, and I just wanted to say a special thank you. You have given me so much love and support, such understanding and kindness in the time I've been here, and I don't really know how to thank you properly. How you do all that Uncle, I don't know, but believe me when I say, you've been a godsend.'

His eyes filled up and his chin quivered as he said, 'Well, child, my Mam and Dad brought me up first to listen, never judge, and told me that would steer me well. They were, of course, always right, and I've tried to live up to that.'

Jennifer sat on his bed and gazed at him with fascination. 'Tell me more, Uncle. Tell me about your parents. I know hardly anything.'

'Are you sure you want to know, Jennifer? I know your Mammy was only two when your Granda died, and your Grandma wouldn't have known anything about our family history. She was from the north, Castlereagh it was, just outside Belfast.'

'Yes, please tell me. Mammy knows nothing of her own history, not even on Grandma's side. I don't think they ever talked much about it, and I know nothing of Granda's history either, so yes, I'd like to know, warts and all.'

'Well, there are plenty warts, Jennifer,' he smiled. 'Where to begin?'

He thought for a few moments. 'So, given this is my birthday, I was born 96 years ago today, on 28th July 1920 at 3:37 in the morning to be precise. Your great Granda was always a very precise man. He had to be, working as he did in Dublin Castle, a senior records clerk, don't you know. Although he wasn't a military man himself, he was a stickler for punctuality and precision, and a hardworking civil servant.'

'But wasn't Dublin Castle under British control, Uncle?' asked Jennifer, confused.

Malachi answered, 'It was until 1922 and the partition of Ireland into the republic and the six counties of Ulster...'

Jennifer interrupted him. 'Ah, I see, so great Granda got a job in the castle after that?'

Malachi said with a soft smile, 'No, he worked in the castle from 1910 when he was in his early twenties. He and your great Grandma met there, and they married in 1912. She was a Catholic, too.'

'Your great Grandma was soon expecting but lost the baby. She lost two babies, actually. Then it was quite a while till I came along in 1920, and your Granda was born in 1930. Just the two of us, which was unusual in those days, with all the large Catholic families in Ireland.'

Jennifer moved further onto the bed, sat cross legged and cupped her chin in her hands to listen even more intently.

Malachi let her get comfortable. 'We were very different as brothers. I was quiet, some might say shy, whilst your Granda had the red hair and the personality and temper to go along with it. I always got the impression that your great Grandma and great Granda wanted more children, but that wasn't to be, and I never thought it appropriate to broach the subject with them.

'I used to love taking your Granda out in his pram when I was 12 or 13 and took him for long walks as he got older. It would give Mam a break, and all the girls would chat to me,' he chuckled.' Jennifer looked at him with new eyes and wondered why he had never married. She could see that he'd have been a handsome man and he'd have been a wonderful husband and father.

'I bet the girls were quite taken with you Uncle, seeing you looking after your little brother like that.' she smiled. 'Anyway, how did great Granda end up working in Dublin Castle, why did he choose to work for the British?'

'The Irish story is very long and complicated, Jennifer. Your great, great Grandma's family, the MacFarlanes, owned and worked the land here. Their family originated from Scotland, they were protestant and came over during the Plantation of Ulster, centuries ago. You might have to look that up on your laptop.

'From everything I know, they were good, decent people and during the famines they shared what they could with their neighbours. Many lives were saved in and around Ranelagh because of them. That's probably why the community always remained so tightly knit.

'Anyway, long story short, Edith MacFarlane, my grandmother, married a Catholic, my grandfather, Seamus O'Connor. And she was an only child.'

'Now that makes sense,' interrupted Jennifer. 'I often wondered how the house and land was in our family. Catholics didn't often own much land, did they?'

'Yes, that's right. So, being the oldest son, I inherited Old Memory and the remaining bit of land when your great Grandma died in 1950. But I tried to make sure to be certain that your Granda got his rightful share. But he was working in Belfast, and he never wanted to discuss it with me. I'd broach the subject with him, many times, but for some reason, he would sidestep it, and move the conversation on. But I did try, Jennifer. He was a very proud, private man, your Granda.

'I tried with your Mammy too, but like your Granda, she was happy in South Africa and didn't want to know.

'Anyway, much of the land had been sold off in the late 1800s by my grandparents, and what you see now is, I imagine, very different to what was originally here. Anyway, it felt quite natural for your great Granda to find work where he could, and it just happened to be Dublin Castle. He only left there when he......' He silenced himself, with purpose, it appeared to Jennifer.

He gazed out of the window and tears pricked his eyes. 'Are you OK Uncle?' Jennifer asked quietly. She was beginning to regret asking him about family history that was obviously painful.

He nodded and took a deep breath. 'Sad memories Jennifer,'

She looked deep into his eyes, searching for a clue, some indication of what, exactly, was troubling him. He closed his eyes, took another deep breath, and began.

'My Dad, your great Granda was, like many of the Catholics living in this area. He had no personal axe to grind with the British, or anyone else for that matter. He always described himself as a peace-loving man...but he told me some awful stories just before he died.

'He was working in the castle when the rebels attacked during the Easter Rising. The castle itself was pretty much undefended at the time, and part of it was being used as a convalescent hospital for the soldiers home from France, but the British soon sent reinforcements and the rebels were forced to back off.

'A policeman my Dad used to say good morning to was shot and killed, though, God rest his soul. Often it's the innocent who pay the price.

'It was a terrifying time for everyone, and while your great Granda secretly sympathised with the rebel cause, he couldn't show it or he would have been shot too, and there was your poor great Grandma expecting her first child.'

Jennifer nodded and listened silently.

'He did many things quietly, secretly, though, to help, whether it was changing small details on this form or that form so that people could escape, or letting families know what had happened to their loved ones.

'Well, as you probably know, Dublin became a battlefield for days during the Easter Rising. You can still see the bullet holes outside the GPO in O'Connell Street. But the British Army soon outnumbered and overwhelmed the rebels, and they were taken to Kilmainham Jail and shot, one after the other.

'Terrible things happened in the name of fighting for a free Ireland, and the bloodshed went on and on, for many years. The British sent in the Black and Tans to subdue the Irish and they went from town to town, village to village, brutal they were, to anyone they suspected of supporting the IRA.'

Malachi shook his head and looked directly at Jennifer. 'So, you see, great Grandma and great Granda lived through the worst of times, and I'm convinced that with the shock of worrying about your great Granda in the attack on Dublin Castle, and how dangerous it was for him working for the British, she lost the baby she was carrying then. She always told me about that baby and wondered if I'd have had an older brother or sister.'

Jennifer hugged the old man, recognising that it was his loss, too. 'That's so sad, Uncle,' she said.

'It was sadder still for the many, many people who lost their loved ones in the fighting,' he answered. 'And that is to say nothing of all those Irish and English lads who went to the trenches in France and never came back. Do you know, I heard that some of the British soldiers who were sent here as reinforcements after the Rising didn't even know they'd landed in Ireland. They thought it was France and they were being sent to fight Germans. They didn't know why they were pointing guns. They were just following orders.

'How stupid war is. What a waste of young life.'

'Poor great Grandma, poor everyone,' said Jennifer, tears welling now in her eyes.

'Come here, sweet girl,' Malachi said as he wrapped his arms around her and comforted her.

'You know you were named after your Grandma don't you, Jennifer?' he said after a few moments.

She looked up in surprise. 'No! I didn't. Mammy never told me that. I only knew her as Grandma. I don't know my Granda's name either, Uncle. That's really bad, isn't it? What was he called, what was his name?'

'Good lord Jennifer, didn't your Mammy ever talk about family at all? His name was Aloysius.'

'Oh, like St Aloysius, the Jesuit! I always thought it a funny name,' Jennifer said, glad that she could now identify the familiar saint with a family member.

She went on, 'Well, I know that Grandma always came to mass with us whenever she visited us in Newcastle. I also remember we'd walk hand in hand to the altar rails and she would take Holy Communion, then she'd turn and smile at me and I'd cross my arms across my chest for the blessing.

'She came to my First Holy Communion too and bought me a beautiful gold medal of the Sacred Heart. I have it upstairs on a gold chain. That was a very special day for me Uncle, Sunday 20th June 1999. It was one of the last times I saw her, and Daddy had left us in September of that year too.'

'Bless you, child. That was very difficult for you, and painful, I know.'

Jennifer nodded, took a deep breath and decided they'd had enough sadness for one day, and pointed to her gift. 'Open your present Uncle.' She smiled her brightest smile.

He smiled back and started to open it. His smile broadened when he saw what was inside.

'Well, how can I fail to have a happy birthday with this? Trout River Irish Whiskey, the finest single malt anywhere in the world and 18 years old, it says on the label. Get a couple of glasses Jennifer,' he said, opening the bottle and sniffing the whiskey.

'Oh Uncle, it's only just lunchtime,' she said, laughing.

'Ah, get the glasses, girl, we need a sip to warm the cockles,' he answered, chuckling. She almost skipped to the kitchen and returned with two crystal tumblers, delighted that her gift had given him so much pleasure.

He poured the whiskey into the glasses, raised his and said, 'To you, your Grandma, your Mammy and Maureen FitzSimons and all those handsome daughters of Ireland.' They chinked their glasses and laughed, swallowing the smooth amber liquid.

'Mmm,' said Jennifer, 'the label isn't lying, is it?'

Filling their glasses again Malachi said with a grin, 'Ceann don doras.'

'Ah, one for the door,' said Jennifer. 'The Gaelic is like music to my ears Uncle, and I'm learning fast. Well considering it's your birthday, it would be impolite to refuse, but this must be my last, or I won't be able to walk to the door, let alone open it.'

'And may God forgive you, you're a terrible influence.' They chinked glasses and laughed again, secure in their special bond.

They heard the front door open and Sinead soon stood in the bedroom doorway. 'Good morning you two lovely people and happy birthday Malachi. I see you've started without me,' she observed, with a twinkle in her eyes.

'Get yourself a glass, Sinead, just to warm the cockles.' Malachi said, with a glimmer of mischief on his face.

'But I'm working,' she protested. Malachi ignored her and when Jennifer came back with another glass, he poured her a dram. Raising his own glass, he said, 'To Maureen O'Hara, Sinead and Jennifer, may their hair never fade from the auburn to the grey. Beautiful, one and all.'

Jennifer said, 'God help us, were going to have a day of it today. The O'Callaghans haven't been in yet, and nobody has video called from South Africa, either.'

A short time later, Bernadette arrived carrying a birthday cake and Feargal joined for yet more sips of whiskey, with Malachi, to warm any cockles in the room that remained unwarmed. Oliver stared on with glee. The celebrations continued into the early evening to repeated requests from Malachi, 'Ceann don doras,' his neighbours politely refusing.

Happy video calls from South Africa had completed the impromptu party. 'Have you had a nice birthday, Uncle?' Jennifer asked as Sinead helped him into bed.

'I have indeed, with the best of family and friends from here, at home, and overseas. Ceann don doras.' he said, chuckling to himself.

Malachi was soon asleep, and Jennifer made a pot of tea for Sinead who had come back to assist her to make sure he was safely tucked up in bed after his special day of celebrations.

'I'm thinking of staying here and not going home at Christmas, what do you think, Sinead?' asked Jennifer.

'You should talk to Malachi, Jennifer. Tell him, because, if you don't, he may think he's holding you back. Promise me, you'll talk to him.'

'OK, I will, but I think we both know what he'll say,' Jennifer commented wryly. They drank their tea and said goodnight.

She woke the following morning and realised she needed to grasp the nettle. She asked Malachi the question, 'I'm thinking of staying here and not going home at Christmas, uncle. Would that be OK with you?'

He answered without pausing. 'Ordinarily, it would, Jennifer. But you're going to be helping Tanu to sort out her wedding arrangements. If you don't go, she'll probably feel like you're letting her down. She's like a sister to you, so I think it's important for you both that you go. I'll be fine on my own, and Sinead and the O'Callaghans will be in and out, to be sure. So, I insist, you must go home Jennifer, you must.'

'I understand Uncle, I was just trying to avoid the journey,' she fibbed, and planted a kiss on his cheek.

***

Jennifer's holiday in Johannesburg was fraught with sadness. Malachi passed away, alone, early on Christmas Day, and poor Oliver had found him.

The gentle, dear old man looked as if he were asleep, perfectly at peace in his favourite chair, a little smile on his lips. Oliver had shaken him gently before the sad reality dawned, then he ran like the wind to get his mother and, with her, returned to sit on the hearthrug and weep.

Jennifer came back to Dublin with Evie early in the New Year to arrange his funeral, to quietly grieve and mourn his passing.

When Evie returned to South Africa at the end of January, Jennifer stayed on alone in the cottage to complete her degree. It was a welcome distraction from the silence and the sadness. But all around, she felt the presence of Malachi, his gentle encouragement, his love and his strength.

And Ireland itself. For Jennifer, it was a land of beauty, joy, sadness and self-discovery.

The memories of her father continued to bombard her mind, and Malachi's kind words echoed all around. She was haunted by them. But she was also fearful of banishing all thoughts of the man who had carried her on his shoulders as an infant, sang to her when she was sad, and told her stories to send her to sleep with sweet dreams.

To pursue his whereabouts, or to wonder what had happened to him, seemed a betrayal of her mother, who had had to forge a life alone and bring up her daughter as best she could.

What had happened? Why had he left? Where was he? Was he dead?

She couldn't wait for the DNA results to come back, and some clue she might have missed.

One day, her phone pinged with a new email from FindMyFamily DNA. She recognised the logo immediately, with its rainbow double helix design. It reminded her a bit of a spiral staircase. Like a staircase in fairyland, she thought.

She felt a flutter of excitement as she opened it up and read it. She was tired and at first the words didn't sink in, so she read them again, then again.

It said her DNA was 47% Celtic Irish. Well, she had expected Irishness, of course. No surprise there. Then, it appeared, she was also 36% North West European and 11% Scandinavian. The final portion of the pie chart was 6% Scottish.

Well, that was all a bit unexpected, she thought, but she'd already researched it and knew that people often had unusual places of origin in their DNA, even when their families had lived in the same place for generations. And she knew all about the Vikings in Dublin. Wasn't Dubh Linn the name the Vikings gave it? It meant Black Pool in in Old Norse, she remembered from her school days. She always thought that was hilarious, knowing of Blackpool Tower in Lancashire, with its Kiss Me Quick reputation for fun and frolics.

So much, so interesting. She couldn't wait to tell David. Now for the DNA matches.

It was hard to make sense of it, but she tried. Third to fifth cousins here, fourth to sixth cousins there, but no names she recognised, and the places were far flung. She'd researched the likely outcomes of heritage matches, so she knew that shared great grandparents could result in distant relatives in many different places, Canada, New Zealand, Australia, USA. And this was what the results bore out.

But nothing, nothing, to tell her where her father might be. She spotted a couple of MacFarlanes and a few distant O'Connors in her matches, but there wasn't an O'Broin to be seen.

She sighed and closed the app. Maybe not now, maybe not yet' she thought.

Chapter 22

Honour

Uncle Malachi's death, alone on Christmas Day, brought her massive guilt. Jennifer had prevaricated for weeks about going home to South Africa, but Malachi had insisted she should be there for Christmas with her mother and to help Tanu and Cedric finalise their wedding plans. Oliver and the O'Callaghans would see him right, he had said, firmly.

She reflected on the last three years. Her great uncle had been just what she needed, a wise and wonderful confidante and friend, a father figure. He had listened to the emotional turmoil as it spilled out of her and met it all with calmness and reassurance. But still she had to determine her resolution, whether she would ever be ready to take her final vows, and losing him had placed it right in front of her, a massive, towering obstacle. What was she running from?

He'd counselled her, and he'd done it with whispers of love, understanding and kindness. She missed him profoundly, and the thought of never seeing him again in this life made her bereft.

The air inside the cottage had seemed still and weary since her return to Ireland. Even the fabric of the building, like a silent witness, had started to grieve and decay since the great old man's death.

She wandered its sad rooms, reminded everywhere of his presence and her loss. Then, one day, summoning all her courage, she told herself it was now right to move on, and that Uncle Malachi would be urging her on through her doubts. So, although she was never keen on flying, especially on her own, she booked her ticket.

She couldn't miss Tanu and Cedric's wedding. It was as simple as that, and Uncle Malachi would have told her so. She was to be maid of honour. And it felt like the greatest honour of her life.

There was no simple or easy way to get back to Johannesburg from Dublin. It was approaching the Easter weekend, so travelling would be chaotic, and she prepared herself for the first leg to Amsterdam. It meant she was flying into Johannesburg from Schiphol on Good Friday, and she wasn't looking forward to the crush and the hurry. But after this penultimate journey back to her motherland, come September, she told herself, she'd be returning to her beloved friends and her home country for good.

***

Cedric's whole family was Catholic, but these days he went to Mass only occasionally, making the effort more often when he was home in Soweto, especially to please his parents. Tanu, happily of no religion, although originally Hindu, was delighted to marry him wherever he thought suitable, but when they'd asked Father Seth if he would marry them at St Brigid's, the priest had explained that, of course he would be delighted, but in order for that to be possible, Tanu should receive instruction and, if not actually become a Catholic, she must be a baptised Christian. Tanu had looked at him with surprised, wide eyes, but she wasn't going to let a thing like that get in the way of a great marriage, and the eternal meeting of two souls.

357

The ever-practical young woman decided to go the whole hog. If Catholicism was good enough for her Cedric, and her dear friend, Jennifer, it was going to be good enough for her. Furthermore, she wanted to know what she had been missing all her life, if this particular religion meant so much to two of the people she loved most in the world.

In the end she took great delight in her weekly 'instruction', which meant long discussions with Father Seth about all manner of things, discussing all the wrongs in the world, reading the books he sent her home with, and having excellent dinners with him and David, courtesy of Ethel's magnificent cooking.

Ethel's homespun explanations of Catholic devotion became a central plank of Tanu's new faith and, thanks to the redoubtable housekeeper, she soon learned which saint to ask the help of, depending on your personal dilemma. Ethel swore by a prayer for the intercession of St Anthony if you had lost your keys, St Christopher if you were travelling, but most of all, said Ethel, with her usual great candour and affection, Tanu should most often ask the help of St Jude, who was the patron saint of hopeless cases.

Cedric had asked David to be his best man. Tanu had asked her sister Viji and Jennifer to be her joint maids of honour.

After all, hadn't Jennifer witnessed their meeting on that momentous train journey where she'd also first met Tanu as she boarded the train at Ladysmith with Father Seth? Cedric had boarded the train at Germiston amidst the fervent attentions of the supporters of the then up and coming sprinter, known to them all as the Soweto Adonis. Wasn't she instrumental in the two meeting up again, having helped Tanu through the chance meeting with his parents at Ackerman & Sons? The way she had taken control of that situation was incredible, thought the grateful Tanu.

Jennifer landed in Johannesburg just after 10 pm, and there, waiting faithfully at the arrivals gate, was the sweetest and most precious of all her friends. She spotted him straightaway and, leaving her rolling trolley to make its way to a stop, she ran into his waiting arms. She'd always been happy to see him, but the emotions of the last few months spent alone in Ireland had shown her even more how important he was to her.

'Hello, you,' he said with that soft and gentle tone she hadn't heard in person for so long. 'I've missed you.'

There was confidence in his voice. It made her feel safe and secure.

'I've missed you, too,' she said, with glistening eyes. 'It's so good to be home.'

She suddenly realised she'd never used that term before, not about returning to Johannesburg, only about Newcastle. She'd always said, 'it's good to be back.' But he heard the significance of the word immediately. He knew from their many video calls that Malachi's death had hit her hard.

He drove back to the presbytery where Tanu, Viji, Father Seth, and Ethel were waiting to welcome her. Ethel was staying for the weekend since she had taken control of the reception arrangements whether Tanu liked it or not, and she wanted it to be a perfect day for everyone, but in particular, the happy couple. Tanu was more than happy to let Ethel take charge. It meant she could relax and just be the bride.

An enormous marquee had been set up in the grounds of the church. The ceremony was to start at two the following day. Police had already cordoned off the area at the end of the cul-de-sac in front of the church. They were expecting many hundreds, if not thousands, to throng the road outside to see the African Nations champion marry his beautiful bride.

As they drove up to the presbytery, Jennifer asked, 'Are you nervous about tomorrow, too, David?'

'A little, I must confess. It's a big day for the big man, and I want to do my bit to make it perfect for him. He has been a great friend to me since you went to Dublin, and I want it to be perfect for Tanu, too.

'I don't think I could have managed all the changes without them. They're so good together'.

He added, watching for her reaction, 'And of course, I get to dance with the loveliest maid of honour, and that terrifies me.'

'I'm sure Viji will be gentle with you,' she said, throwing the line away and bending to pick up her bag.

The door of the presbytery was flung open as Tanu came running out to greet her. The squeals of delight were almost deafening.

David remembered the first time he'd picked Jennifer up from the station with Father Seth and recognised how far he'd come in every aspect of his life. It was all down to the beautiful person there in front of him, bursting with love and acceptance, as always.

He felt like she'd opened him up to the possibilities that life had to offer, simply because she wanted him to achieve his potential. She'd never asked for anything in return.

He looked at her with unashamed adoration. It was plain for all with eyes to see that he would give his life for her.

He had adored her since that first moment, and nothing had changed, nothing, except for the fact that he had, over time, come to realise, and constantly reminded himself, she could never be to him what he'd dearly wanted her to be.

His love for her was unyielding and without condition, he knew that. He would continue to fulfil the vow he'd made to himself. Whatever made her happy was something for which he was prepared to sacrifice his needs, his wants, and innermost feelings.

Snapping into the practical, he took her luggage from the car and asked Ethel where he should put it.

'Room three, your old room, please David. Father is in room seven so that Tanu, Viji, and Jennifer can share the big bathroom tomorrow. Viji is in room two, and her children are in rooms five and six. Tanu is in Father's room, the best in the house, and I'm in room four, the coke den.'

They all started to laugh. Ethel was like a South African elephant. She never forgot a thing.

David took the luggage up and placed it on top of his old computer desk. His dearest memories had been made in that room: the day of the storm, the application for his degree, the realisation that he had the money to pay for it when Jennifer explained it to him. There were the happy times he'd spent there with her after they'd worked in the presbytery, garden, and church, so many beautiful memories. Then, for just a moment, there was a feeling of melancholy as he drifted into thinking of what could have been.

He shook it off, went downstairs and into the sitting room.

'Excuse me all, I need to get back to the Adelphi Hotel. The Adonis needs my assistance.'

He made a mock bow then added, mischievously, 'Hmm. The Adelphi Adonis. I'm sure there will be headlines to that effect tomorrow!'

Tanu laughed heartily at that. 'I suppose that is going to make me his Aphrodite,' she suggested. 'Or is it Venus? I always get confused.'

'Indeed, I think it will,' answered David. 'I think they're one and the same thing, really. Anyway, media circus aside, I have an extremely nervous groom to look after. I'll see you all at two tomorrow, all being well. Now try to get some sleep. Good luck Father, I think you may be kept awake tonight by all the noise.'

Jennifer stared at him with wonder. This was definitely a different David speaking, she thought. So confident and self-assured. It was beautiful to witness.

They all rose from their seats to hug him. First Viji. 'Goodnight David, it was lovely to finally meet you after all this time.'

Then Father Seth, 'Goodnight David, I'm very proud of you.' Then Ethel, 'Bend forward child. You know you're too tall for me to stretch up to these days.'

Then Tanu, 'Goodnight, you wonderful man, don't forget to bring Cedric and, whatever you do, don't let him run away, because you'll never be able to catch him.' David threw his head back and laughed at that.

Finally Jennifer, 'Goodnight, my beautiful friend, my absolute hero.' David beamed but dared not bask long in her words. He turned to the group, 'Goodnight, everyone. Sleep well.'

He made his way into the hall. He'd been followed, without his realising, by Jennifer and, as he opened the door, she touched his arm to stop him. 'David, I can't wait to see you again tomorrow. Drive carefully, stay safe. You know you mean the world to me, and I just want you to know I'll be forever grateful to you for all you've done for me.'

She kissed him on the cheek.

He walked on air from the presbytery, got in the car and drove to the hotel on the outskirts of the city. Her words were ringing loud in his head. He knew they were words of love and affection but was cruelly aware that her expression of love for him could only ever be words and a gentle kiss on his cheek. He hadn't reciprocated because he knew that if he did, it would open the floodgates to all his feelings.

The wedding day dawned, and, soon after one o'clock, the guests were starting to assemble at the church. Some of them were from the world of athletics, champions past and present, and some of today's hopefuls. Cedric had used his money and influence to establish sports clubs all over Africa for children of all ages, so there were representatives from the Cedric Kai Foundation in attendance, too.

The white limousine arrived at the Adelphi. Cedric's proud parents were escorted to it by the hotel concierge. They felt overwhelmed by the cameras of the world press and being in full sight of their fellow countrymen.

Then Cedric and David followed in full morning suits, with grey brocade cravats and waistcoats, camera shutters clicking as Cedric waved and smiled at the excited crowd, filled with black and white faces, all cheering their home celebrity. The attention was new and alien to David, of course, and he had spent weeks mentally preparing for his role. At least he was not the main focus and could stand well back, he thought with relief.

A police escort was provided to get them to church, clearing the way as they travelled through the busy city streets and into the suburbs.

All this for the humble boy from Soweto, thought David, as he watched the scene unfold. Nelson Mandela's great legacy of equality was being handed on here, like a baton in the relay, for new generations and a newly crowned man of the people.

They arrived at St Brigid's in good time, alighting from the limousine to loud applause and cheering from the thousand or so fans assembled behind barriers outside the church.

Smiling and waving, they made their way up the steps and were welcomed by Father Seth at the doorway. Cedric introduced his parents to him as they entered. They were taken to their seats by one of four South African athletes, teammates of Cedric's, all Olympic hopefuls, who were fulfilling the duty of ushers for the day. They were run off their nimble feet as guests arrived all at once like spectators in the stadium for the finals.

It was now a quarter to two, and the church was packed to the rafters, quite literally, since every seat was taken, including those in the gallery. There must have been at least 500 people of all races, colours, and creeds in attendance. It was undoubtedly the most significant event the church had ever seen. To mark the occasion, the nave, columns and altar were a sea of beautiful flowers. Planned by David, much thought and his knowledge of plants had gone into the decoration. King proteas, the national flower of South Africa and blue water lilies, the national flower of Sri Lanka, symbolised the marriage of the two young people, and of their cultures. The beautiful blooms were simply arranged with gypsophila, at the end of every pew, and surrounding the base of each column.

Rising up the columns on both sides and following the curved, spiral valleys carved into the granite were garlands of white flowered shamrock, added at Tanu's special request, as an acknowledgement of the strength of her friendship with Jennifer. The altar was surrounded by a sea of white and purple arum lily, Tanu's favourite flower, and a native of the South African countryside.

Tanu's closest male relative on her father's side, her cousin Babala, was to give her away. He'd always been more like a brother to her and to Viji, so it felt only right that the honour should go to him. He and his wife, Ekiya, and their children had flown in from Durban yesterday and were staying at a small hotel just up the road from the church.

It was five minutes to two as Tanu, Babala, Viji and Jennifer prepared to leave the presbytery. They emerged into the bright, sunlit day but were briefly shielded under the white canopy, decorated with flowers, which covered the short path to the church's entrance.

As she left the canopy and stepped into the full glare of the South African sun, the petite figure of Tanu dazzled and glittered as her traditional Tamil saree of exquisite red and green silk, bejewelled with flowers and gold, reflected its rays like fireworks.

On her head she wore a traditional papidi billa of pearls, separated by engraved gold water lilies, and around her neck were chains of gold, inset with the jewels of every colour. She wore gold bangles studded with precious stones that had been handed down by generations of brides in the line of her family history.

Most precious to her was the necklace that comprised small gold coin pendants. Tradition had it that every family bride to wear it had added a coin on the day of their wedding. Tanu had added a one tenth of an ounce gold Krugerrand. For a young woman who had been raised modestly, she had been taken aback at the combined wealth of trinkets placed upon her by the ancestors of her family. Her hands and arms had been decorated with henna, and she carried a bouquet of arum lily.

Viji had wiped a tear from her eye as she put the final touches to Tanu's hair. She said, 'Our parents would have been so proud, Tanu. You are beautiful, little sister. Walk with your head held high down that aisle.'

Tanu looked at her with a million shared memories in her eyes and quickly dabbed her eyes too before her exquisite makeup started to run.

Viji and Jennifer wore watermarked silk sarees of lavender and cream, headdresses of blue water lilies, surrounded by shamrock. Both, like the bride, carried bouquets of arum lilies. The vision of the three smiling, serene, young women appearing together for their short walk to the church was breath taking.

There were seemingly interminable photographs on the church steps. More minutes than they expected or wanted passed by, as the photographer secured his images, and inside the church, Cedric started to fidget in his seat.

The wedding congregation could hear the crowd's reaction to the bridal group's different poses but there was nothing to be done except wait and sneak looks over their shoulders, hoping for the first moment to spot the bride.

'It will be fine. Don't worry,' said David to Cedric, who replied that he felt more nervous than he had in any starting block, including in the African Nations finals. 'Understandable,' said David.

'Ready?' asked Babala as the door was opened by a smiling Father MacDonnell. The young priest signalled to someone inside the church. The first notes of '*Johan Pachelbel's Canon in D Major*' informed Cedric of the imminent arrival of his beautiful bride.

One of David's fellow students was a member of a string quartet who had been delighted to be asked to play at such a prestigious occasion. Cedric's suggestion for the bridal march had been a complete surprise to Tanu since she'd never heard it before but was happy to agree when she knew its significance.

Cedric had listened to it many times throughout his career as part of his preparation before all of his races. He'd always walked out onto the track wearing headphones, and fans and journalists alike had assumed that this was just a part of a superstitious routine, maybe even to put off his fellow competitors, since they had no idea what he was listening to or why.

The music had always stilled him and let him find his focus. It had the same effect now in the church as he stood tall and proud to welcome his bride to the altar.

Father Seth looked down the aisle and could see Tanu waiting to make her entrance. He signalled to Cedric and David to take their places in front of him as the beautiful music started to swell to a gentle crescendo.

Cedric looked at his glowing bride. The most enormous smile lit his face as he whispered a simple, but loving, hello. He'd no idea she would be wearing the traditional bridal dress of her ancestral home. He'd been expecting to see her in white. Tanu had kept the secret well. She looked gorgeous, perfect, and he felt so lucky to have her there by his side. This was better than winning any race.

David's stomach rolled as he saw Jennifer. The lavender and cream silk reminded him of the dressing gowns and the time he'd told her she looked lovely in everything she wore. She'd done it again. The saree looked amazing on her, and her headdress appeared to bring out the colour of her eyes, the eyes he knew so well. He said a silent prayer and quietly acknowledged to himself that he'd love her forever. He reminded himself sadly that he'd never be her groom.

Father Seth had been joined on the altar by Father MacDonnell, Father Thompson and Father Bellini. Each would play a part in the wedding and would assist Father Seth at the giving of Holy Communion. All in attendance would be invited to receive communion or a blessing, regardless of faith.

The age-old words of the nuptial mass sounded unique here, in this setting, with this bride and this groom. The four priests ended the mass, giving the final blessing simultaneously.

The string quartet burst into *'Beethoven's Ode to Joy'* as the wedding party made their way back into the sunshine. The crowd erupted into applause. The sun was high in the sky, and the air was still. Tanu asked the police officers to let some of the children through the barriers with their parents. She sat down on the church steps, talking to them, creating memories for those like her and Cedric who had had little in their own childhoods. The cameras clicked and filmed as Cedric, Jennifer, and David joined her.

The papers were going to be full of it tomorrow. David looked at his watch. It was time to go into the marquee, and it was his job to make it happen. They said goodbye to the children, with hugs and kisses for everyone on the steps.

Cedric and Tanu made their way to receive some of their guests in front of their table. The few they had handpicked were not the dignitaries or heads of the numerous athletics bodies. They were youngsters and their chaperones who, ordinarily, never see such grand surroundings, all members of Cedric's sports clubs. The children were dressed in new sports shirts, tracksuit bottoms, and the trainers issued to them free of charge when joining one of his clubs. The expense of their travel and accommodation had all been taken care of by Cedric.

David was dreading his moment, the best man's speech, but enormously pleased to have Jennifer by his side as he rose to make it. She squeezed his hand as he stood up, which gave him the extra confidence to get through it. He even made the guests laugh with a few late additions to his speech, telling them how hard it was looking after the Adonis in the Adelphi, charged with the responsibility of delivering him to Aphrodite, and how afraid he'd been of Cedric getting cold feet, because he knew if he ran off, he'd never catch him.

David had searched long and hard for the right words to finish his speech, the words to best describe the love he saw in Tanu and Cedric, and the words that best described his love for Jennifer.

He finally found them in a small volume of Shakespeare's Sonnets that he'd picked up in a city centre bookshop.

The wedding guests fell silent as he began to read.

Let me not to the marriage of true minds
Admit impediments. Love is not love
Which alters when it alteration finds,
Or bends with the remover to remove:
O, no! it is an ever-fixed mark,
That looks on tempests and is never shaken;
It is the star to every wandering bark,
Whose worth's unknown, although his height be
taken.
Love's not Time's fool, though rosy lips and cheeks
Within his bending sickle's compass come;
Love alters not with his brief hours and weeks,
But bears it out even to the edge of doom.
If this be error and upon me proved,
I never writ, nor no man ever loved.

There were audible sighs and cheeks dabbed. Cedric stood and brought Tanu to her feet to embrace her. Then the room erupted into applause, the guests rose from their chairs and whooped with delight.

The meal and toasts finished, everyone was free to mingle and chat. The informality of the whole occasion had made it easier to enjoy, and it was, just as Tanu and Cedric had wished for, a happy family atmosphere.

The live band and disco had arrived and had set up ready for the evening celebrations. Guests for this included the mayors of Johannesburg and Soweto, numerous religious leaders, the Metro Police Chief and representatives of numerous charitable organisations. David had met many of these people in his shy and unassuming past. More recently, he had met them in business meetings through the university. The young man who used to feel totally at odds in large groups of strangers was now a quietly confident and successful home-grown businessman.

The evening celebrations were about to begin, and the best man took to the stage. Cedric and Tanu were invited to the dance floor for their first dance as husband and wife. They'd practised their perfect waltz steps and worked in a few flourishes, to the delight of their audience.

David then stepped down to the floor and took Jennifer by the hand. Immediately they wrapped their arms around each other as if it were the most natural thing to do.

Ethel was fighting tears, just watching them together. David was so obviously in love with her, and Ethel knew in her heart that he always had been. Father Seth and Ethel, Viji and Babala and others joined them on the dance floor. The music ended, and everyone except David returned to their seats.

He went up onto the small stage and said hello to all the band members personally.

Cedric and Tanu looked at each other in surprise as David then took the microphone, tapped it, and began his special announcement.

'Thank you everyone. Today has been one of the most beautiful days of my life. I have been privileged to know Tanu and Cedric for the last three and a half years, and they have become an integral part of my life.

'You see, my best friend in the world, the friend who introduced me to them, went to Ireland three years ago and I missed her terribly. But she, along with Tanu's sister Viji, was a maid of honour today.

'I have been blessed to have these people in my life. I love you all more than you could ever know, and this is just to say thank you to Tanu and Cedric...'

The guests applauded and cheered.

David waited for quiet. 'Anyway, I have been seeing quite a lot of the band behind me in the last few months, and they have helped me find another voice.

'I'll share it with you now to thank this extraordinary couple, the new Mr & Mrs Kai. The message they have conveyed to me is captured deep in the words of this incredible song. So it's for them, on this special night of their lives, and it is for all those who love someone special.'

The band started to play, and David looked over and beyond his listeners and began to sing. No one had heard him sing before, except for the hymns in church, when his voice was mostly lost among other, stronger voices. Father Seth and Ethel stared in disbelief.

He began, at first quietly, to sing the old and beautiful song, *I Only Have Eyes for You*. He had a fine, rich tenor, which built in strength and handled the notes with ease. Even his dearest friends were taken by utter surprise, but also delight, and then tears of emotion.

It was a song that was able to deliver a different personal narrative to every listener. Tanu and Cedric gazed at each other for a long time, and then together watched David. Within seconds of the first few lines, he was looking at Jennifer and she at him. They were absorbed in the moment and each other. Everyone in the marquee could see it.

David stepped down from the stage, and Ethel went over to him with tears streaming down her face. She took hold of his hand and led him over to Jennifer, who had tears on her cheeks. She stood up and wrapped her arms around him and put her head on his chest, taking comfort in his strong embrace. A rush of emotions ran through her, and she felt safer hiding her face.

The band had recorded a disc of David singing a small selection of other songs to give to Tanu and Cedric at the end of the night. Seeing the moment was right, their lead singer flicked the button on the console, and it started to play. Tanu and Cedric got up, both choking with emotion and started to dance. Before long, the dance floor was packed as David and Jennifer danced tightly in each other's arms.

He hadn't intended to hold Jennifer's gaze for so long. He just couldn't help it. He knew he'd just shown Jennifer exactly how he felt about her. He could see her pain. She was still grieving for Malachi, he knew that. But was there more to the sadness he saw in her eyes?

He reminded himself that he must now, more than ever, remember his vow. She took his arm, and they walked out of the marquee into the warm darkness of the night.

Jennifer spoke quietly, looking out across the sunset, still just tinting the sky. 'David, I'm coming home to South Africa in September, and I won't be going back to Cape Town. I'll be staying here.'

His heart dropped. She was coming back, and that was a good thing. But she'd be staying at the presbytery, which could only mean one thing: she'd be taking her vows. Inside he wanted to scream with the pain. He knew he couldn't stop loving her. He'd made the decision to always be what she needed him to be. They walked around the grounds, arm in arm and eventually found themselves in the exact spot where he'd first looked into her eyes.

On this occasion, he wasn't speechless or nervous as he said, 'I'm pleased you've come to your decision, Jennifer, and I'm pleased that you can move forward in the knowledge that you've really thought this through. Always know I love you, as your dearest friend, and whenever you need me, I'll be there.'

She answered, 'I know you will. You've never let me down or put me under any pressure or placed your expectations on me. I've known from the first time you told me that you'd always be there for me, and that I could rely on you, and that's why we remain so strong. You truly are the sweetest man I've ever known.'

They made their way back to the marquee. The limo had arrived to take the newlyweds to the airport. They were flying out to a surprise destination on their honeymoon. It was their gift from David. He'd planned everything, but they knew nothing. They were to fly first class to Colombo, Sri Lanka, the home of Tanu's ancestors.

Tanu had mentioned to David a couple of years ago that she'd always wanted to go but didn't think she'd ever be able to afford it. However, that was before the successful young entrepreneur had been able to invest in his own business ideas and she'd agreed to marry the now reigning 100 metres African Nations champion.

They said their goodbyes, and the guests started to dwindle until the last of them were left chatting, enjoying their time together, Father Seth, Ethel and her extended family, the three priests, Duncan, Martin and Luigi, Cedric's parents and, of course, David and Jennifer.

Simeon had booked taxis for all his family, and they'd all, as planned, arrived to take them home at the same time, Ethel ensuring that they all got in the right cars before getting in the taxi with Simeon and Amahle. David was staying the night at the presbytery, and the three priests were waiting for their taxi.

It had been a perfect day. Well, almost, David thought. His heart yearned for life with Jennifer, for the one thing he couldn't have.

Chapter 23

Seth

It was Saturday morning, and David woke at his usual time of six o'clock. As he stepped up to the landing at the top of the spiral staircase, on his way to the bathroom, he was thinking only about Jennifer. It had been four months since the wedding, but he missed her every day, and the wait for her imminent return had felt like a lifetime.

She was due back for good in a couple of weeks when her final exam results came through. There was the possibility she might have to return briefly to Ireland at some point with Evie, just to finalise Malachi's affairs.

But still, she'd told him at the wedding that she'd be taking her vows. The memory of that short conversation on the evening of the wedding had left him feeling the regret of never telling her how he truly felt, but in doing so would have broken his self-made promise.

It seemed crazy to him that so much had happened in the last few years.

He opened the door to her old bedroom, walked in and sat on the bed. In some ways, the room offered him comfort as he remembered how beautiful she'd looked the first time that she'd invited him in, and he'd seen her in the glow of that old green, enamel lamp which still sat on the desk.

Alongside that memory was the incident that had led to that moment and her ultimate choice to leave South Africa. Her initial decision to go to South Sudan had been derailed by events at the site of the school in Juba. While he was delighted she wouldn't be risking her life in a war zone, he was secretly hoping that it would lead her to make the decision to leave the convent. But even if she did, if he were honest with himself, he'd probably be in the same position, he thought, unable to make her know how much he loved her. She was so special a human being, and he couldn't feel deserving of her love.

Jennifer was taking a breather in Dublin. A good class degree in Childhood and Youth Studies was what she hoped for. It had come as no great surprise to David that she would follow such a path. She adored children and loved to help people. She had the gift of putting everyone at ease. He remembered just how much she'd helped him to come to terms with so many of his personal demons and how gently and considerately she'd done that in those happy months he'd spent with her. She had helped him recognise his own gifts and abilities and gave him the encouragement to forge his own career.

He now owned a handsome house close to where Tanu and Cedric lived, and commuted into the city every Monday to Friday, where he was the CEO of his own software development company. He had created jobs for each of Ethel's children, except Simeon, who loved his taxi work and the freedom of driving around the city. David's relationship with Father Seth had become one of equals, and he chose to spend every Friday night and Saturday at the presbytery.

The priest was visibly older and had been diagnosed with prostate cancer shortly after Jennifer had gone to Ireland. He was making a good recovery from surgery and radiotherapy, and had not troubled her with his medical problems so that she could concentrate on her studies. Although he was still ministering to his congregation, he was now less active, fatigued by the cancer and shocked by the abrupt reminder it had given him of his own mortality. He was a changed priest in parish and pulpit, and the parishioners of St Brigid's continued to remark upon it with wonder.

He had now engaged a handyman gardener to cover the work that David had done for so long, and Ethel worked part-time now that she had reached her mid-sixties. Nonetheless, she still joked with Father Seth and David that her final role in life was to keep an eye on them to ensure they stayed on the straight and narrow, so they'd better mind themselves.

The priest had mellowed in every way since Jennifer had burst into his life at the presbytery. She had been the catalyst bringing Father Seth, David and Ethel closer together, and thank God she had, David thought. She was adored by them all, and in truth, they all missed her terribly, but none more than he.

All these things ran through the young man's head as he gazed around at the familiar objects and breathed in the familiar smell of the presbytery. Not threatening now, as it once had been. It felt like a place of safety and comfort.

***

David took his shower, dressed and went back to his room, where he completed some work on his laptop before making his way downstairs. To his surprise, Ethel was nowhere to be seen, and Father Seth was in the kitchen preparing breakfast. It was now a quarter to eight.

'Good morning David,' he said with a smile of welcome.

'Good morning Father.'

'Simeon has just called to say Ethel isn't coming today. She's had a bad night with her arthritis and doesn't feel up to working, so we can do something together if you'd like?'

David thought for a moment.

'Jo'burg Jags,' he said. 'I think they're at home today. Would you like to go?'

'That sounds a good idea,' replied Father Seth.

The elderly priest had played football in his youth, and at quite a high standard, but in those days, apartheid had meant there wasn't the level of competition for South Africa that was enjoyed elsewhere in the world. He had often bemoaned the situation.

However, he'd enjoyed being assistant chaplain to the 1992 team who beat Cameroon 1-0 at King's Park in Durban after they were readmitted to FIFA, having served a 16-year ban due to the protests against apartheid. At that time he was the young curate to the then parish priest at St Brigid's. Father Seth had always said that the combination of representing God and his country at the same time had been a great honour.

'Kick-off is at 1:30,' David said, checking his phone. 'They're playing Pretoria Pumas. Shall I book tickets to pick up at the stadium?'

Father Seth answered, with a look of genuine pleasure on his face, 'Yes please, David. I'll look forward to it.' David quickly made the online transaction.

They had breakfast together, and David started to wash up, Father Seth reminiscing about his playing days, and David had in his hands the beautiful crystal wine glass that Jennifer had bought for the priest on the night that David had announced his application to Johannesburg University.

Father Seth had drunk from it the night before as they were chatting in the sitting room. It was a treasured possession, and he always enjoyed using it.

As David placed the dried glass down, he knocked it accidentally and the stem snapped just above the foot of the glass. A small shard broke off and embedded itself in the soft tissue of David's right thumb.

'Oh, no', he said with dismay, more at the damage to the precious glass, than the damage to his thumb.

It immediately started to bleed quite heavily, so he wrapped the tea towel around it to reduce the flow of blood, but the blood quickly oozed through it and started to drip from the towel. Father Seth ushered him into his study and sat him down on the easy chair. He went to a cupboard in the corner of the room and retrieved a first aid kit. He pulled his leather office chair over, took his hand and rested it on the blood-stained tea towel.

'Look, I'm going to have to get that piece of glass out,' he said.

The priest took a pair of tweezers out of the kit and opened the tea towel. There was blood everywhere, but he removed the shard from David's thumb, cleaned the cut and dressed it with a wound closure strip.

'Let's see if it stops the bleeding,' he said. 'Though you might need a stitch.'

'I'm sure it will be fine, and I'm not missing taking you to the game for a small cut like that,' David replied. 'I'm so sorry about the glass. I will replace it for you, though I know it had special significance…'

Father Seth shook his head and, concentrating on the task before him, placed the tea towel and first aid kit on his desk then further cleaned David's hand with antiseptic wipes. He then went into the kitchen and washed his own hands, drying them on a clean towel, before throwing it onto the kitchen worktop next to the sink and returning to the study.

'How is it?'

'It's fine now. It's stopped bleeding.'

'Let me see.'

David held his thumb out and, indeed, it had stopped.

'Do you have a plaster or something I can put on it?'

'I have a tubular bandage - that may be better?'

'Oh yes if you don't mind. It will give a little more protection,' said David.

Father Seth dressed the wound with lint and applied a tubular bandage, wrapping tape around the base of his thumb to secure it.

'Thank you, you've done a great job,' said David, giving him an exaggerated, bandaged thumbs up.

'You're welcome. I'll make us some coffee,' said Father Seth.

He returned to the kitchen and percolated the coffee.

They sat and talked for a while in the study, drank the coffee, then David said, 'Come on, Father, let's make a day of it. Let's have an early lunch in the city, then go to the game.'

'Are you sure you're all right?' asked the priest.

'Yes, I'm fine. Shall we go?'

They drove into the city in David's car, and made for Father Seth's favourite Italian restaurant, Europa.

The restaurant was virtually next door to where a small branch of Ackerman & Sons had been, not the branch that Jennifer had worked at, but still, both that and the restaurant brought memories of her flooding back to David. This was where they'd all celebrated the night before she left for Dublin.

Ackerman & Sons, and its subsidiaries, had gone the way of other department stores, finally closing their doors for good, just as Tanu had feared, two years after her conversation with Jennifer.

There had been about 20 guests the night of Jennifer's farewell dinner, including Father Seth, Evie, David, Ethel, Simeon, Amahle, Tanu, Cedric, Father Martin, Father Luigi, and Father Duncan.

The deacons had been ordained a couple of months after their first, unforgettable night at the presbytery, and Father Seth, Jennifer, David and Ethel had all been present at their ordinations and celebrations.

'What would you like, Father?' asked David, handing over the menu.

'Surely you know that by now,' the priest smiled. He did.

Father Seth ordered his favourite Italian meal, pasta al forno con pollo, washed down with a large glass of soave classico, and David decided to join him in his choice, but drank water. Father Seth had first sampled the traditional chicken dish when he had visited Rome as a 19-year-old seminarian, and had often requested that Ethel make her own delicious, but spicier, version. He'd always done justice to her cooking, and could often manage two helpings, though here in the restaurant, one had to suffice.

Pasta al forno con pollo. It wasn't the only memory he brought back from Rome. The eternal city had, of course, burned itself into him, but the highlight of his month-long visit was meeting Pope Paul VI. He had always kept a photograph of the occasion on the wall of his study at the presbytery.

They both cleared their plates. It was nearly half past twelve as they left, and David hailed a taxi. It was Simeon's, not too surprisingly, since this part of the city, and this time of day, was his regular haunt. Father Seth got in the front and David in the back.

'Hello Father, hello, David. Where can I take you?'

'Johannesburg Stadium, please Simeon,' David said.

'Ah, you're going to the game. What happened to the thumb?' he asked, spotting the large bandage immediately.

'Yes,' grinned David, 'Oh, just a stupid accident. I cut it on a glass.'

'How is your mother?' Father Seth enquired, changing the subject.

'She's OK, thanks, in a little pain but wants to come back to work tomorrow.'

'Well, that's all right, but only if she is really able,' answered the priest.

'Have you come into the city by car?' asked Simeon.

'Yes, in my car,' said David.

'What time does the game finish? I can pick you up and take you back for your car.'

'We should be out for about 3:30,' said David.

'Say no more. I'll be waiting for you.'

'Thank you, Simeon, that's very kind of you,' David replied.

'My pleasure, my dear friend.'

He dropped them right outside the ticket office. The crowd was building, and the atmosphere electric. They walked over, and David took out his mobile and gave the booking reference. They picked up their tickets and made their way to the relevant turnstile and entered the stadium. They found their seats, situated perfectly on the halfway line.

There was a sense of enormous excitement in the crowd, and as the teams filed out of the tunnel, the noise was deafening. Jags were in their distinctive yellow strip, the Pumas in red.

The whistle blew, and Pumas kicked off, the crowd singing and chanting. They weren't to be disappointed. The first shot on goal came 19 minutes into the game and Jags went one nil up.

But it was still one nil, late in the second half as Pumas were prevented again and again in their attacks on the Jags' net. At the 83rd minute, a corner went to Jags, and the ball smashed into the Pumas' net, the goalkeeper's mid-air dive proving useless. Two nil, and the home crowd sang and cheered. The final whistle blew after two minutes of injury time.

The stadium went wild. It had been South African football at its best.

'Great game,' Father Seth said as they left their seats. 'I can't believe the pace and ferocity of how it's played these days. It was never like that in my day.'

'I'm so glad you enjoyed it. We should do it again,' said David, realising that too many such occasions had escaped their grasp.

'That would be nice.'

'Perhaps I should invite Simeon next time, or maybe all of them?' suggested David, thinking of Simeon's siblings.

'That would cost you a fortune,' said Father Seth, practically.

'I know, but I could treat it as a company day out. They all work hard, and if they think it's a work-related event, they're more likely to come'.

'I'm sure they'd appreciate it.'

'I'd want you to come too, Father, of course. You really enjoyed that, didn't you?'

'I did. I haven't seen a live game since 1992. I don't know where the years have gone,' said the old priest, regretfully.

They walked together out of the gates, and there was Simeon, true to his word.

'I've been listening on the radio, great result. Did you enjoy it?' he grinned.

'We did,' Father Seth said, a big smile on his face.

David grinned. 'I was thinking, would you and all the family like to come with us some time? I'd like to treat you all, and of course Father will be coming too.'

'Well I can ask, but it's a lot of money, David,' replied Simeon.

'Let me worry about that. I'll speak to them in the office on Monday and see what availability everyone has,' David countered, delighted with his own idea.

Simeon said, 'Is it OK if I mention it tonight, then, when they all come over? They come every Saturday night to see Mama.'

'Of course, in fact, that would give everyone the opportunity to decide when they're all free.'

'Thank you, I'll do that tonight then. Thank you David.'

They were back outside Europa restaurant in no time, and Simeon dropped them off. 'How much do I owe you, Simeon?' asked David, though he knew the answer.

Simeon started to laugh. It's more than my life is worth. You know how my mama feels about taking money from friends.'

'You must let me give you something, please?'

'No, but thank you, I'm looking forward to making arrangements for the game. Now take care. I hope to see you soon.'

'Me too, see you soon, Simeon. Take care and give our love to everyone.'

They waved farewell and made their way to the car, still talking about the game. David had invited Father Seth to go to other games in the last few years, but he didn't like to leave the presbytery when Ethel was there as he'd seen her slowing down and was concerned about her welfare. He'd suggested retirement, but she was adamant that she wanted to work for as long as she could.

He'd even stopped having overnight visitors apart from David and Jennifer when she visited from Ireland. But that had been just once a year at the most, and David ensured that he didn't create any extra work for her and would spend time at the presbytery cooking and discreetly cleaning so that the burden for Ethel was reduced.

David, like Father Seth, dreaded the day when illness or infirmity might take her, since she had been the stalwart of their lives.

They arrived back at the car, and David drove them back to the presbytery. Arriving at about five o'clock, David asked Father Seth what he wanted to eat for later.

'There are some cooked meats and cheese in the fridge and bread and pickles in the scullery, so that will be fine for me,' he said.

David went into the kitchen and prepared the meal for the priest and made a pot of tea for them both.

He placed the food and tea tray on the dining room table and went to the study.

'Ready, Father.'

'Thank you.'

They returned to the dining room, and Father Seth immediately commented, 'You're not eating, David.'

'No, I'm having dinner with Tanu and Cedric tonight, so I don't want to spoil my appetite,' he answered.

'Oh, I see,' said the priest, tucking into the cold spread with obvious enjoyment.

It was seven forty-five when David eventually looked at his watch.

'Oh, is that the time?' I'm sorry, I'll have to leave you. I've really enjoyed today, Father. And I'm looking forward to doing it again soon.'

'Me, too, David, and don't worry about the washing up. I can do that later.'

'Thank you, I'll just take these things into the kitchen to save you having to carry them in.'

'Thank you. Now, be on your way. You don't want to be late!'

David called for fuel on his way. The garage, owned by old Mr De Bruyn, was situated on the main road, almost facing the entrance to the cul-de-sac. He had known David all his life and was a long-time friend of Father Seth's. The priest and he had filled up at the station for as long as he could remember. They could buy fuel cheaper elsewhere, but this was one way of supporting the local community. David filled his car and went in to pay.

'Sorry, Mr De Bruyn, I can't stop. I'm rushing.'

'Have you had an accident, David?' the old man said, looking at his bandaged thumb.

'Yes, it's nothing much. Broke a glass. Sorry, got to go, I'm late! Goodnight, and thank you, Mr De Bruyn.' David hurried the conversation to a close.

'Goodnight, David,' said the old man, nodding him on his way.

David continued his journey to Tanu and Cedric's home, his own home situated right across the street from them. It was a quarter past eight when he arrived.

They welcomed him with hugs and smiles.

'Sorry I'm late. I've had a good day with Father Seth. We went to the football match. It was a great game, too,' he greeted them.

Reflecting on the day, he added, 'He's not as strong as he used to be, though. I feel a bit worried about him.'

'I'm sure he's got plenty of life left in him yet,' Cedric said, grinning. 'Sit down and let me pour you something.'

'He's still pretty fit,' Tanu added, to reassure him. 'What happened to your thumb?'

'Oh, I cut it. Just an orange juice, please, Cedric. Yes, he is, but the cancer has taken its toll, I think. Simeon rang Father Seth this morning to say Ethel wasn't coming. She's 63 now, you know, and I've known her, well, both of them all my life. They're the nearest things to parents I've got. It just makes you worry.'

'Stop being so morbid,' Cedric laughed.

'Yes, you're right,' said David. 'And I've been thinking about Jennifer too, and I miss her so much, so I'm probably not great company tonight.'

'Course you are,' replied Tanu, who was well into her second glass of white wine. 'And we all miss Jennifer.'

'So...' she started, then thought a little and said bluntly, 'Look, David, why don't you just...tell her you love her? Why don't you tell her you're in love with her?'

David looked up, startled. Something in Tanu had apparently decided that this was the moment she had waited a long time for, and the wine and the opportunity had loosened her tongue.

'Look, from the very moment when you came back to me in the store that day to ask me to hold those two dressing gowns, it was obvious to me you were in love with her. You've been allowing opportunities to pass you by all this time and putting yourself through what must be... hell. Well, David, who knows, she might just feel the same about you?'

He answered, grinning, 'She knows I love her, and anyway, she hasn't made her decision about her position with the convent, and I can't marry a nun.'

Tanu placed her glass down and looked at him seriously. 'But loving someone and being in love with someone are quite different things, David. I know how you really feel. It's obvious to me. You are totally besotted with her, and that's more than understandable.

'But perhaps the fact that she hasn't given her answer to the convent in three years is something of a message in itself? You've obviously thought about marriage too,' she said, giving him a coy smile. He shook his head.

'You forget, David, you're an open book, so easy to read,' Cedric added, mischievously.

David started to laugh through his embarrassment. The game was obviously up.

'OK, OK, but how could you both tell?'

'How could we not tell would be the easier question to answer,' laughed Tanu.

She went on, 'She's taken her final exams now, and what if she decides to stay in Ireland? How would you feel if the next time you spoke to each other, she told you she'd met someone? You need to act now. She's a beautiful girl and a beautiful person. Someone is bound to want her sooner rather than later. I'd hate to see you hurt.'

Cedric added, 'Tanu's right. You have things going for you, David. You're sort of reasonable looking,' he laughed. 'You're a successful businessman, even though computer programming is a bit boring, and I suppose you're not too bad a friend.'

David pulled a face and threw a cushion at him.

'OK, though, being serious now. Not only that, but you're made for each other. Just pluck up the courage and say something.'

Tanu wasn't letting him off the hook, either. 'He's right David. You're all those things and more. Just do it before it's too late before some handsome Irishman steps in and does it before you. Promise us you'll do it, we love you both dearly, and we want you both to be happy.'

David, still laughing at Cedric's back handed compliments and acknowledging Tanu's warning, pleaded, 'But what if she decides to take vows? Has she said something to you?'

Tanu replied, 'No, but she's less of an open book in that respect, much harder to read, if you ask me. But the way we see it is that you've known each other for so long, and whenever you're together, you both glow.

'Whenever she's over from Ireland, she spends all her time with you. We've asked her to stay here a few times, but she's always refused. We think it's because she wants to spend time with those she loves most, and that very much includes you. Just do it, David, please.'

'But whenever she comes over from Ireland, she always stays at the presbytery, that's why I see so much of her, and you're still not acknowledging that she hasn't made her decision,' protested David.

Tanu wasn't having any of it. 'But you don't live at the presbytery anymore, David, yet you take time off work and live there when she's over, and furthermore, the presbytery is not her home either, and her mother always has to come from Newcastle if she wants to see her. Come on David, wake up. Take off your blindfold. For a very clever man you can be surprisingly stupid sometimes!'

It was almost game, set and match.

They all started to laugh.

'But her vows. What about her vows?' David spread his hands wide, appealing for understanding.

Tanu felt it needed saying loud and clear. 'Do you remember the night of our wedding when you surprised us with that beautiful song you sang, David? I know you brought the whole room to silence, and I don't think anybody could have missed the chemistry between you both.

'The words of that song could quite easily have had a different meaning to every person in the room, but I think everyone at our wedding was moved by the love that came out of you both for one another. It was like there was no one else in the room.

'And it was *our* wedding, I might remind you.' Tanu wagged her finger at him in mock admonition.

She went on, 'It was the way you looked at each other while you were singing. The number of people who came to us both to say how touched and moved they were, we lost count. Even Ethel came to us crying and said, 'I so wish... God forgive me.' There's something so beautiful when you're together, you know, something so innocent.

'So, please David. Just tell her,' Tanu said with a tear in her eye.

David nodded, as much to shut Tanu up as agree with her.

'I promise, then. I'll tell her. But she told me on your wedding night that she was coming back to the presbytery. So if she does, then she'll obviously be taking her vows.'

'What did she say?' asked Tanu.

'She said she wasn't going back to Cape Town, that she was coming back here.'

'That could mean she intends to leave the convent, couldn't it?' asked Tanu.

'I suppose so, but I will tell her, because I'd rather she said she was staying in the convent than tell me she wanted another man. I think I'd be devastated if that happened.'

It was a sudden revelation to him. Yes. She might want someone else. If he didn't let her know what she meant to him, and she didn't want to take her vows, he might lose her forever. It had never crossed his mind that she might consider another relationship.

He could now see beyond his own naivety. Tanu was right. Jennifer might actually meet a handsome Irishman. She might already have met him. The handsome Irishman might be, might have been more, forthcoming about his feelings towards her.

David knew now he must seize the moment. It was obvious. How could he not have seen this before? He almost felt he should leave Tanu and Cedric right now and video call Jennifer, but he managed to quell the anxiety and stayed for the excellent dinner they had cooked for him.

They talked of the game, Cedric's training regime, and the new project taking much of Tanu's time, a small fashion boutique she'd opened in the city, using her redundancy payment and help from Cedric.

David's phone pinged and he automatically went to check it. He scrolled down from the top of his screen. It was a notification from News24, just a sentence. A black athlete had been stopped and arrested by six white police officers. He read it out, then apologised for interrupting their happy conversations.

'Don't apologise', said Cedric. 'I saw that on the news earlier. I've not met him, but I know of him. It's disgusting. Apparently he'd done nothing wrong, apart from being black in a mostly white neighbourhood. Oh, and owning a nice new car.' David and Tanu sighed and shook their heads.

'We've still a long way to go in some ways, I think,' said David. 'I'm sure there will be a protest. We all need to protest. They shouldn't keep getting away with this sort of thing.'

Cedric went quiet for a moment and looked blankly at the closed curtains.

'Did I ever tell you it happened once to me?' he asked.

'No, you didn't,' said David. Tanu touched Cedric's knee.

'It was about four years ago. Same sort of thing. I was driving home to Soweto from Sandton. I was followed for a while by one police car then another appeared out of nowhere in front of me and they forced me over and out of the car, while they checked me out, a couple of them aggressively. They didn't arrest me, I think, because one of them recognised my name.' He grimaced at the memory.

'It's happened to a lot of my friends over years, people I grew up with. You sort of always expected police interest, well, white police interest, from being a black teenager hanging out in the park.

'Nowadays, they wave me on because my face is well known, but, man, you never forget a thing like that.'

David and Tanu listened intently. Tanu had heard the story before and nodded. 'It happens to people with brown faces, too,' she said, sadly.

David looked at his friends with new understanding and regard. It was plain to all three that they shared a nation, but each recognised that their brave new South Africa had a way to go before prejudice could join apartheid in the dustbin of history. Maybe it never would. They could only stand proud and continue to be who they were.

David raised a toast. 'This is to who we are, and to who we always will be.' The friends drank to that and their conversation turned to happier things.

David said, brightly, 'Hey, remember the Adonis in the Adelphi?' and they all laughed. 'So glad you didn't run away, Cedric. It would have been very embarrassing for me.'

Nodding and raising her glass again, Tanu said, 'And for me! So here's another toast, if you wouldn't mind. This is to my last wine drinking for a while'

David cocked his head to one side and looked at her querying, while Cedric pulled a clown face.

'Well,' she said, very deliberately. 'Alcohol and babies don't mix, do they? So I'm just letting you know that it's time I started thinking about providing Cedric with that large family he wants.

'To babies!' They all repeated the toast, clinked glasses and Cedric gulped his chenin blanc rather more quickly than absolutely necessary. Tanu looked at them both with gleaming eyes.

They spent hours sharing memories and anecdotes and David was just about to leave when Tanu said, 'Oh, yes, I meant to ask you properly before. What *exactly* did you do to your thumb?'

'Oh, it was such a shame,' he answered. 'I cut it when I was drying Jennifer's glass this morning. You know, the beautiful cut glass she bought for Father a few years ago, the one he always drank his wine from. I feel really bad about it, and I will buy him a new one, though I know it won't be the same.'

'Oh yes, of course. Beautiful glass. Never mind. It happens. Are you OK? Have you had it stitched?'

'No. Father Seth dressed it for me. I wanted to take him to the match, and it was just a small cut, a bit deep, but I'll be fine.'

'It's a magnificent bandage, you have to admit,' said Tanu, grinning. 'All right then, David, good night. Sleep well.'

'I will. You, too.'

He left his friends and crossed the road to his house, opened the front door, turned around and waved at them.

'Night', he shouted across the street.

'Goodnight. Don't forget your promise,' Tanu shouted back.

'I'm sure you won't let me,' he laughed, shaking his head as he closed the door.

Chapter 24

Discovery

David watched TV for a while and then made his way upstairs to his room. He glanced at the clock. It was half past one, and he dearly wanted to just close his eyes and rest. It took only moments to fall into a deep sleep. It seemed like a flash before he woke up, his thumb throbbing with every heartbeat. He switched the light on to look at it. The dressing had come off and it was inflamed, hot to the touch. He checked the bedside clock. It was 4:46 am.

Sighing, he got out of bed and went to the bathroom cabinet to look for painkillers. There were none in there. He went downstairs into the kitchen and opened the cupboard where he kept other medication and the first aid kit. There were none in the cupboard either, so he checked the first aid kit. Still nothing to be found, and no tubular bandage or applicator either. He went back to bed and tried to sleep again, but the pain was getting worse, and he started to feel nauseous. There was nothing else for it, he decided, but to drive to the all-night pharmacy at the health centre. He got dressed, left the house and got into his car. It was just gone quarter past six.

The health centre and pharmacy were 25 minutes away and throughout the journey David cursed himself for having broken the glass. Father Seth's special glass, too. He pulled into the carpark and was thankful to see a brightly lit but empty shop. The pharmacist, looking up from the computer screen at the counter, took one look at his thumb and said, 'Oh, that looks painful, sir. It might be infected. Just wait a moment, and I'll see if one of the doctors will examine it for you. I'll just make a phone call.'

She made the call then told David to go into the clinic and ask for Dr Prabhu. David already knew him. He was a regular practitioner in the practice. It wasn't long before he was called into the consulting room.

'So, what happened to your thumb, David?' asked Dr Prabhu, with concern on his face.

David explained the events of the day before and how Father Seth had dressed it for him and why he had attended the pharmacy searching for pain killers.

'Yes, there's a slight infection starting to wake up in there, but it's fortunately still wet, so I can clean it out, hopefully. Sit down over here.'

Washing his hands at the sink he asked, 'When did you last have a tetanus injection?'

'Sorry, I can't remember,' said David, privately thinking of all the times he had cut his hands while gardening, without having a problem.

The doctor replied, 'It's OK, I'll give you a booster, and you'll need some antibiotics too. I'll prescribe them, and you can get them from next door.'

He proceeded to clean the wound. It was a painful process but fortunately it took only a couple of minutes before Dr Prabhu announced, 'Oh good, fresh, clean blood, and I think I've got all the nasty stuff out. It will heal better if we leave it open, so I'll just put this lint over it till it stops bleeding. Take it off in ten minutes or so and leave it open.

'OK, a slight scratch,' he said as he inserted the needle. 'Done, all done, and don't go without your script.' He pressed print on the screen.

'Thank you, that was very quick, if not completely painless,' said David, gratefully.

'No worries, David. If you have any further concerns, just get in touch, and I'll see you again, but hopefully not! Goodbye.'

David smiled then went next door to the pharmacy and picked up the prescription. It was now half past seven. It was a beautiful morning, and it looked like it was going to be another lovely day.

David, relief washing over him, contemplated calling at the presbytery since it was only a fifteen minute drive away, just off the main road, and he'd be passing the cul-de-sac anyway. But he'd started to get a temperature and sweat was beading on his brow, so he thought better of it. Some more sleep would do no harm.

***

At the presbytery, Father Seth was in the kitchen, filling the sink with hot water when the telephone rang. He left the kitchen, and went into his study to answer the phone. It was Ethel.

'Hello Father, I'm sorry I'm running a little late, but I'm just leaving home, Simeon is bringing me, so I don't have to get the bus.'

'It's perfectly fine, Ethel, stay at home. I can manage,' protested the priest.

'No, it's OK. I'll see you at eight at the latest. I've a few things to do, and I've made a big fruit cake. I'll bring you some.'

'All right then, if you insist,' he replied, still tired after the excitement of the day before to argue.

'Bye, Father. I'll see you then.'

''Bye, Ethel.'

Father Seth made his way toward the kitchen and heard the water still running. It had started to cascade down the cupboard door onto the floor. Irritated at his own forgetfulness, he hurried into the kitchen as fast as his feet could carry him but slipped, completely losing his footing on the wet floor tiles, his hands flailing and unable to catch hold of anything to break his fall. His head and neck came down with force onto the towel he had thrown next to the sink the day before.

It was almost slow motion. He felt a sharp blow to the left side of his neck and a sudden, piercing pain from the broken stem of the glass, which had been standing upright under the towel. David had placed it there on the worktop after cutting his thumb.

He fell to the floor, landing in a prone position. He thought at first he had just twisted his neck but, as he started to push up from the floor, he saw the towel moving with him and felt searing pain to the left side of his neck running into his shoulder, chest and down into his arm. He remembered the glass stem with horror.

He immediately knew he needed urgent help and managed to get back to his feet. He staggered into the dining room and then the study, blood spurting from the wound and through his fingers. He pulled at the glass still embedded in his neck but couldn't dislodge it. He reached his desk with an almost superhuman effort and picked up the phone before collapsing. He knew, as everything before his eyes grew dark, and faded into blackness, that he was dying.

The quiet of the presbytery was broken only by the trickling water and the dialling tone of the receiver. The birds still sang outside, but Father Seth could no longer hear them.

***

It was eight o'clock precisely as Simeon entered the drive. As he pulled to a stop, Ethel shook her head, handed him her key and a box with the cake. She said, 'Just tell Father I'm sorry, will you Simeon, but I really don't feel well enough. I thought I was all right when we left the house, but I can feel the pain starting again. I'm so sorry for dragging you out on your one day off.'

'Yes, of course I will, Mama,' replied Simeon. 'No need to apologise.'

'OK, then just take the key to let yourself in. Father may well be in church, and if he is, I'll ring him later.'

He took the key and unlocked the front door of the presbytery, knocking as he did so, and calling out for Father Seth. The bloodbath greeted him. He stepped back momentarily, a look of utter horror on his face and turned away to the fresh air.

Recognising immediately that something was badly wrong, Ethel opened the door of the taxi. Seeing her, he went back to the car.

'No, No, No, No, Mama, you can't go in. You mustn't go in. I think there's been an accident, now please, sit in the car and stay there.'

He closed the door. She opened it again.

'NO, NO! Please sit in the car and don't move Mama,' he shouted.

She knew by his response that it was something very bad and for once she remained quiet and stayed where she was, praying - for what exactly, she didn't know. He closed the door of the car and made his way back into the presbytery closing the door behind him.

His senses were competing to understand what lay before him. The sights, smells, sounds, his vision, taste and hearing became acute. He could see blood everywhere, all over the floor and on the walls, still slowly dripping and running like rain drops on a pane of glass, a bloody handprint on the architrave of the door to the study. The sound of water running the smell of blood in the atmosphere. Through the doorway of the study, he could see a body slumped in the chair, the head, chest and arms sprawled out on the desktop.

Heart pounding, he went into the study and over to the desk. It was only then he knew for sure it was Father Seth. The right side of the priest's ashen face was lying in a pool of blood on the desk. The blood sodden towel, lying over his upper left arm, fully revealed the stem of the glass in the side of his neck. Father Seth's right hand still held the blood-smeared telephone receiver.

In desperation he touched the priest's shoulders and tried to lift him, blood soaking his hands. The wound in the man's neck seemed not to be pumping blood any more. That means his heart has stopped, thought Simeon, the factual observation snapping him back into the world of logical thought.

As a last desperate attempt to find life, he leant over Father Seth's face to see if he could hear any signs of breathing. Nothing. Simeon was now certain that he was dead and, considering the amount of blood on the desk and elsewhere, he realised there was no more he could do to help him. He made his way into the dining room, the sound of running water getting louder. The blood on the wall and floor, in a continuous trail, led to the kitchen.

He stepped into a red pond of water and blood and went to the sink and turned off the tap. The blocked old floor drain was gurgling as the blood and water were slowly draining into it. He surveyed the scene in disbelief then, looking at his own red hands, he tried to rinse them under the tap. The blood was under his fingernails and stained the cuffs of his white shirt.

Drying his hands on his trousers, he took out his phone and dialled 112 and asked for an ambulance. Robotically, he gave his details to the operator and the details of what he'd found. The operator told him they would relay the information to the police.

Remembering his mother was still outside in the car and knowing he must tell her the awful news before the emergency services arrived, he took a deep breath, went outside, and made his way towards the car. Opening the door, Ethel said, 'It's Father Seth, isn't it? What in the name of God has happened?'

Immediately she saw the bloodstains on his cuffs. 'Oh my dear Lord,' she cried.

'It's OK, Mama, I've sent for an ambulance, but there's nothing more we can do for now.'

Her stunned response was also one of calm acceptance and, seeing the look on Simeon's face, she chose not to ask any more questions.

For Simeon, the moment had just brought back painful memories of the day when his father's mutilated body had been found, and Ethel had had to break that terrible news to her children.

The sound of sirens filled the air. Simeon and Ethel could hear them getting closer until ambulance and police arrived almost simultaneously, the ambulance pulling up near the presbytery steps. Two paramedics jumped out and one called over to Simeon, 'Where is he, please?'

'In the study, you'll see from the hall,' said Simeon, hardly able to get the words out.

The paramedics quickly pulled on overshoes and latex gloves then entered the presbytery carrying oxygen and resuscitation equipment. It was no more than a minute before they emerged.

'He's deceased, massive bleed out,' said one to the police officer. The officer looked at his watch and said, 'I make it 08:33.' The ambulance crew confirmed the time. They wrote it down, as did the police officer, in his pocketbook. He radioed in, requesting the assistance of another patrol officer and forensics.

Simeon and Ethel stood together, watching and listening to the proceedings as though through a mist.

'Do you need homicide?' came the radio voice.

'That would be appreciated,' the officer replied.

The police officer approached Simeon.

'Simeon Gumede?' he asked.

Simeon nodded, dumbly.

'And you are?' he asked gently, looking at Ethel.

'Mrs Ethel Gumede, Simeon's mother', she responded, her voice quivering.

They were joined by a young female police officer.

'Take Mrs Gumede to the police car and let her sit in it. Stay with her, but just let her be for now,' said the male officer.

The officer took her to the police car, as another started to cordon off the end of the drive with incident tape.

The officer with Simeon said, 'Sir, we need to investigate further. We need to interview you and Mrs Gumede back at the station.'

'Can I go to my mother?' asked Simeon, in distress.

'No, I'm afraid not, Mr Gumede. It's a matter of procedure. In circumstances like these, we must keep you separated. I have requested another vehicle for you. When it arrives, I will advise Mrs Gumede on the procedure. Try not to worry. I'm sure you must be in shock.'

'I just came to drop her off.'

He was interrupted. 'I'm sorry, Mr Gumede, I appreciate you want to explain, but it would be better for all concerned, if you could wait till you get to the station.'

'OK, I think I understand. Are we under arrest?'

'No, that has not proved necessary and won't be necessary if you choose to come to the station voluntarily, but...'

Simeon interrupted the officer, 'Of course, we'll come voluntarily. Father Seth is my mother's employer and has been our friend for many years.'

Forensics and homicide arrived, followed quickly by a second patrol car. A dazed Simeon was then driven to the police station and placed in an interview room.

Ethel, who had been waiting silently and tearfully in the car with the female officer, was soon making the same journey.

When they arrived, the female officer remained in the back of the police car with her. She explained gently to the trembling housekeeper why it had been necessary to take them to the station independently. Ethel nodded. The journey was quiet and sombre, and she took comfort in saying her prayers under her breath.

***

The forensics team entered the presbytery. Forensic Crime Scene Investigator Anna Van Der Merwe was relatively fresh out of college. She'd been in post in Johannesburg only nine months after cutting her teeth in Durban and was keen to ensure that she did her job to the letter.

Senior Forensic Crime Scene Investigator Erik Visser supervised her. His had been a sketchy career, saved by one or two high profile successful prosecutions that reflected well on the department. But he wasn't much respected by his colleagues, who privately wondered how he'd got so high in the job. However, Van Der Merwe was already seen as something of a trailblazer, a strong character and a stickler for detail. After all, she believed that her role was equally important to the suspect and victim alike, alive or dead.

Visser had told her to 'do the necessary, and I will point you in the right direction if I need to.' She was happy with that arrangement. She always remembered one of the first principles of her training, that not every scene would necessarily be a crime scene but, if she treated them as such, then she couldn't go far wrong. She started taking photographs and video of the scene immediately.

She photographed the area and turned on her video body camera as she exited the vehicle making sure she had photo and video evidence of the car parking area, the front door and Simeon's taxi.

In the early days of 'supervising' her, Visser became, on occasion, frustrated with the time she'd taken at some incidents. But her thoroughness had led to several convictions so far and, equally importantly, two acquittals.

She completed her initial photo and video scan of the scene and proceeded to identify, bag and tag all the immediate evidence available to her.

However, she would, more often than not, complete a second sweep of the scene before leaving. This would infuriate Visser, but she saw his response as an occupational hazard. He'd started to be more accepting of it over time, but it still irritated him.

She completed her initial collection of evidence in the immediate vicinity of the study. She moved on, body camera still running, to check out the other areas, being careful to ensure there was no cross-contamination from room to room. Eventually, she went to David's room, where she found numerous clothing items and a laptop. She bagged and tagged several items of what she believed to be clothing that had been worn so that they could be tested for traces of blood and DNA. She completed her second screening of the presbytery in reverse, finishing back in the study. The coroner had arrived and was waiting for permission to remove the body. However, she just needed to complete her process. So, he would have to wait.

She advised the coroner that the body could now be removed and was curious to know when the post-mortem was expected to be completed and when the report would be available, as she was on leave for a week at the conclusion of today's shift. According to the coroner, there was no reason why the autopsy wouldn't be completed as soon as he got back to the lab. That being the case, the report would be completed by lunchtime tomorrow at the latest.

She'd got to the end of her shift, though, and nothing had been forthcoming from the coroner's office. She felt disappointed as she wouldn't know the outcome until she returned to work.

***

David had returned home just before eight. The journey had proved an uncomfortable one, due to the increasing pain in his thumb. He'd immediately taken his antibiotics and painkillers then gone to bed, only to be woken three hours later by a loud knocking on the front door.

Two police officers asked to come in. Sleepy and confused, having woken from a dream, David led them into his sitting room. They informed him sympathetically, but factually, of Father Seth's death. They told him they'd received a call, and on attending the presbytery, he had been pronounced dead by the ambulance crew.

David, already dazed by pain and lack of sleep, reeled at their words. He held his head in his hands and cupped his ears, as if not to hear them. He shook his head in denial, and couldn't even look at the police officers. After a minute or so, it dawned fully that they were serious, and that this was real, not a continuation of his dream, not even a nightmare.

Died? How could he have died? Father Seth, the man he left safe and well yesterday, the man who had been there all his life, the man who had been his authority figure, the one he feared and the one he loved, the man who had ultimately been like a real father to him. The man who had just enjoyed a meal and a football match with him, how had he died? It seemed beyond his understanding.

He asked them the tremulous question.

They explained that they couldn't say since they were awaiting the coroner's report but would let him know as soon as the information was available to them. However, they asked could they stay in his home just to ask him a few routine questions. It was the usual type of thing in these circumstances, they said.

When had he last seen Father Seth, what had they done, where had they gone, how had the deceased seemed during this period of time, how had their last time together ended, etcetera, etcetera. It seemed interminable. David answered like an automaton, telling them everything he could to the best of his recollection.

They left. David closed the door behind them with relief, but what kind of relief was this? He sat alone with terrible and tumultuous thoughts bouncing around his head.

Father Seth, the man, his life, his beliefs, his sins, his sufferings, his successes and his failures, was gone. Everything that he had been, everything he ever was, or could be, was now suspended, frozen in a moment of time.

He must have suffered. He must have known he was dying.

There was another knock on his door. Tanu and Cedric.

'What's happened, David? Are you OK? Is Jennifer OK?' asked Tanu, the panic clear in her voice. David melted into sobs at the sound of her voice.

'You'd better come in,' he said, choking. 'It's Father. He's…. oh, dear God, he's…dead. They couldn't tell me anything, but he's dead, he's gone.' He shook his head and ran trembling hands through his hair.

They both pulled him into an embrace. They didn't know what else to do.

Cedric asked, 'Does anyone else know?'

David looked at him with horror. 'Oh my God, I forgot. Ethel, poor Ethel! I hope she didn't find him like that. She was ill yesterday and didn't go to work but said she was going back in today. Please God has spared her that.'

'Perhaps you should call her, David, or, either I or Tanu should call her.'

'No, ring Simeon instead,' said David. 'I want to be sure she isn't on her own when she finds out, if she doesn't know already. Dear God, I hope she didn't go to work this morning and find him.'

'Have you got Simeon's number?'

David found it on his phone and passed it to Cedric.

Cedric hit the dial button. Simeon's phone just kept ringing.

'It's just ringing out, David,' said Cedric.

'That's not right. I can usually always get in touch with him. He never goes anywhere without his phone.'

'Let me try Ethel,' Tanu said.

'No, no, I need to know she's not alone when she finds out,' protested David, frantic in his grief.

Tanu tried to reassure him, holding his hand. 'And what about Jennifer? Would you like me to call her, David?'

'No, as much as I don't want to, I'll have to tell her. Don't think me ungrateful, Tanu, but I feel it's my responsibility.'

'I understand. I don't think you're ungrateful,' said Tanu, stroking his arm.

'I'll do it now. Will you stay with me, though?' David asked, the grief showing plain in his eyes and voice.

'Of course,' they both said, almost simultaneously.

'What time is it?' asked David. 'They're an hour behind in Dublin,' he said, finding comfort in the small practicality.

'It's just past 12:45,' said Tanu.

He dialled Jennifer's number to video call. It rang out a couple of times, then she answered with an enormous smile.

'Hello there, my lovely man, how are you? What are…'

She stopped herself mid-sentence, seeing his expression, then continued, 'What's the matter? What's wrong?'

David somehow got the words out. 'It's Father Seth, Jennifer. He…died last night, I think, or this morning. I don't know, I'm not sure.'

Jennifer stared, disbelieving. It seemed an age before she replied, 'Oh, David, oh no, that can't be true. Tell me it's not true.'

But then, seeing his grief, she asked, 'When? How?'

He answered, 'I don't know anything, really. The police came to tell me this morning, just the bare facts. I'm really worried about Ethel. I hope she wasn't the one who found him.'

'Haven't you spoken to her? Has Father been ill?' Jennifer asked, her stricken face suddenly frozen on the screen, as the connection buffered.

David waited a moment before answering. 'Cedric tried to ring Simeon because I didn't want her to find out while she was alone. He isn't answering his phone. She didn't go to the presbytery yesterday. She wasn't well, but she said she was going today. I just hope she didn't. We had a lovely day yesterday, we went for lunch and then we went to the football match together, and he really enjoyed the day, we both did. I'm just pleased now that we had that time together.'

'Are you on your own now?' asked Jennifer.

'No, Tanu and Cedric came over just after the police left. They said they had to wait for the coroner's report before they could tell me anything. I understand that, of course, but it's hard not knowing how or why he died. I'm sorry to have to tell you all this in this way. I just wish we could be together right now. I need you so badly.' The words were tumbling out.

Jennifer said, 'Listen, David, I was just going to wait here for my results, but I'll book a flight as soon as I can.

You need me there, and I need to be with you too. I'll call you later.

'I'll have to tell Mammy when I come off this call. She only flew back to South Africa on Thursday. God knows, she'll be devastated, obviously. We've sorted out most of Uncle Malachi's outstanding affairs, but the rest will have to wait till we return later in the year. Mammy and I can return when this is sorted out. I love you, David. I'll be there with you as soon as I can.'

'I know, and I love you too,' he said.

'Goodbye, sweet man. Goodbye Tanu, goodbye Cedric. I love you all so much, and I'll see you all soon. Look after David for me.'

'We will. Let us know when you can get a flight. We'll all come for you. 'Bye.'

'Bye.' With a smile of courage, Jennifer ended the call.

David turned to speak to Tanu and Cedric just as there was a knock at the door. Cedric went to answer. It was the police.

'David Blind?' asked one of the plain clothed police officers.

His colleague corrected him, 'No, it's not. This is Cedric Kai, African Nations 100m sprint champion. Am I right, Mr Kai?'

Before Cedric could answer, the first officer said, 'Oh, I'm sorry, Mr Kai, are we at the correct address?'

'Yes, you're at the correct address,' said Cedric. 'David is inside with my wife. You must have some news about Father Seth's death. You'd better come in.'

They entered the house and followed Cedric into the sitting room.

'David, it's the police,' said Cedric.

'David Blind?' asked the first officer.

'Yes, that's right. So, please, can you tell me what happened? How did Father die?'

'We're terribly sorry to be the bearers of more bad news, but we can't at the moment go into details. Could you please accompany us to the station so that we can rule you out of our enquiries?'

'Yes, of course,' David replied, and turned to grab his phone.

'Can I follow you down so I can bring him back when you're finished?' Cedric asked.

'There's no need to trouble yourself, Mr Kai. We can bring him back,' said the second officer.

David followed them to the police car and climbed into the back. Tanu and Cedric returned to their own home and, in sadness and confusion, watched the car drive away.

***

David walked into the police station and was soon shown into an interview room. Two different officers entered, one carrying documents.

'Hello, Mr Blind,' said one. 'I am Homicide Detective Sergeant Maseka and this is Homicide Detective Constable Joubertf.' David immediately tensed. It was now obvious the police did think Father Seth had been murdered.

Maseka continued. 'Don't worry. This won't take long. We are continuing our enquiries into Father Rossouw's death, and we need to eliminate certain people from our enquiries. You will understand that the scene in the presbytery involved quite a lot of blood, and there are various fingerprints we need to identify. Would you mind providing yours, Mr Blind, and a saliva sample for DNA? It is purely voluntary at this stage, of course but it would significantly help us with our enquiries.'

David relaxed. 'Of course, that won't be a problem. My fingerprints and DNA will be all over the property since I have visited so often, and that's where I cut my thumb. But I will do anything to help. Just ask.'

Maseka answered, 'Ah, your thumb. Can you tell us all about what happened to it? Actually, we probably need to record this part of the interview, so we have it on record. Please wait while we organise that.'

When the tape recorder was switched on, David spoke freely and honestly about the incidents that had led up to his thumb being injured, the subsequent pain and the need for medical intervention. They questioned him extensively about his movements between his home and the clinic.

David was home within a couple of hours, delivered back in an unmarked police car, desperate once more to sleep. He walked into the house, and Tanu and Cedric, who had been watching anxiously, came across immediately.

'How are you?' asked Tanu.

'I'm not sure how I feel, other than sad,' David said. 'I've given them a DNA sample, and they took my fingerprints. I told them they'd probably find both all over the presbytery. They seemed extremely interested in my thumb, but I explained what happened yesterday, and they seemed happy with that. But they said they'd go to the clinic to check out what I told them this morning.'

'What happened? What clinic are they checking out?' asked Cedric, in alarm.

David explained about the infection in his thumb, the pain, the lack of sleep and why he had attended the clinic.

He added, miserably, 'I suppose it's like they said. They want to check my movements because Father died in unusual circumstances.'

Chapter 25

Questions

David's phone rang. It was Jennifer.

She said, with an attempt at normality, 'Hi there, David. Just to let you know I've been trying to get a flight, but it's proving difficult. Have you had any more news?'

He explained what had just happened at the police station. She looked afraid and tearful, and he felt helpless to comfort her.

'I've just spoken to Mammy,' she said, her voice breaking. I don't know how to tell her this...'

David said, 'Jennifer, just don't say anything more until we have something concrete.'

'Yes, you're right. I won't. See you as soon as I get a flight. I'll let you know.' They said their goodbyes.

As he came off the phone, Cedric asked, 'Have you contacted Ethel yet?'

'No, perhaps I should try Simeon again,' answered David.

'Do you want me to ring him?' suggested Cedric.

'No, I'll do it now.'

David dialled the number, but still there was no answer. 'I think I should drive over to tell them, 'he said nervously.

'We'll come with you. Cedric will drive,' Tanu instructed.

They all started to make their way out and towards Cedric's car when David heard the message tone on his phone.

It was a voice message from Simeon. He played the message so they could hear it.

'So sorry David, couldn't do anything to help him. Only glad I'd made my mama stay in the car. It was horrible. She changed her mind about working at the last minute and I went in to tell him and I found him.

'Glad it was me because I'm not sure Mama could have coped. The police have questioned me twice. I'd touched him you see and had blood on me. They've taken our fingerprints and DNA to eliminate us from their enquiries, they say.

'We're both exhausted now and sure you must be too. Mama wants to come and see you tomorrow if that's OK? We'll come 9:30 unless we hear otherwise. God bless, stay strong.'

'Poor Simeon. How will he get over this? How will any of us? Come on, let's go to our house,' Tanu said, taking David's hand and leading him to her front door.

She prepared food, but David couldn't eat. They spent the rest of the unhappy day together, sometimes talking, letting the TV fill the silences and continued to sit there sadly, not knowing fully how to comfort each other before David stood to take their leave just after midnight.

He went to bed but didn't sleep. He drifted off before waking again, startled, and then relived the horror of the day, over and over.

He got up early, took a shower and got dressed in preparation for whatever lay ahead. Cedric and Tanu came over at seven. They'd brought breakfast of eggs, bacon and crusty bread. David hadn't eaten anything since Saturday, so ate it all ravenously.

'Do you want us to stay till when Ethel and Simeon arrive?' Tanu asked. 'Yes please. I could do with you here,' said David, between grateful mouthfuls.

It was just before nine thirty, and the expected knock on the door announced the arrival of Simeon and Ethel. Cedric answered the door, and they entered the house. As they saw each other, their joint grief spilled out.

'Oh child, come here,' Ethel said. They cried in each other's arms, and Tanu comforted Simeon.

Cedric quietly went to the kitchen for a few minutes, then returned to the living room with tea and coffee for everyone.

'How did Father die? When exactly? What actually happened?' asked David, breathing hard between the questions to suppress his tears.

Simeon, surprised at David's lack of information, explained in detail what had unfolded, with a graphic description of what he had confronted. David turned away and felt physically sick. He ran out of the living room and into the downstairs bathroom, vomiting violently.

When he'd gone, Simeon apologised for sharing his experience so vividly. The others shook their heads with understanding and waited quietly for David's return.

'Don't worry Simeon,' said Tanu, kindly. 'None of us know how to deal with any of this.'

When David came back, Ethel felt she ought to tell them how invasive the police had been during her interview.

'I began to think they suspected Simeon,' she said. 'They kept interviewing him, asking him all kinds of questions about Father Seth and how he'd treated me! They even asked me what kind of a son Simeon was.'

Tanu raised her eyes to heaven.

'I told them that Father could be difficult sometimes, a bit bossy, but you all know it wasn't something I couldn't handle. And he'd mellowed these last few years, hadn't he? Oh dear, poor Father Seth gone. I still can't believe it.' She dabbed her eyes and wiped the tears from her cheeks.

'They asked me how he treated you, David,' she said, with an air of confession.

'I told them that Father had been very strict with you, and that he sometimes strapped you with his belt.' David looked up, startled.

'I don't think I should have said that, but they kept on at me. David, I'm so sorry if that makes things difficult for you. But I used to see the marks on your legs and back. It upset me very much, and I told Father about it at the time. You were such a good boy, and you didn't deserve that. I told them that too.'

David, suddenly aware of how her comments might have been construed, quelled his concern and told the fretting woman not to worry. 'None of us has anything to hide, Ethel. It's important to be honest and to tell them what they need to know to catch whoever did this. But it might also have been an accident, let's not forget that.'

Ethel and Simeon stayed for a couple of hours. Shortly after they left, David lay down and fell asleep on the sofa, and Tanu and Cedric thought it best to let him rest.

**

Jennifer was having problems booking a flight to Johannesburg. The only one available was on the Wednesday and it meant she would arrive in the early hours of Thursday morning.

David told her not to worry. Nothing could really be done anyway, the presbytery was sealed off, and they all needed to rest. Jennifer could see the sense in that, so she tried to relax and took the bus into Dublin city centre to take her mind off things. She wandered through the National Museum and up and down Grafton Street, listening to the excellent street musicians and took a coffee in Bewley's.

She walked through the beautiful gardens of Trinity College and up into the library, which smelt of varnish and ancient books. She went to see the Book of Kells and marvelled at the intricacy of the gospel illustrations, painted and gilded by medieval monks.

The beauty of them calmed her. She and her mother would soon be back with David, Tanu and Cedric, the people she loved most in the world. She knelt in the college chapel and prayed for Father Seth.

She went back to the cottage, video called David, and read, and read, and read. The time passed slowly, it seemed, but she took the opportunity to walk again among Malachi's old, familiar haunts, and then boarded the bus to Phoenix Park, the beautiful, huge hunting and deer park of former times, when Ireland owed its allegiance to the throne of the British monarch. David would love this, thought Jennifer. She decided they must return together at the earliest opportunity.

***

The days passed and Jennifer had boarded her flight, due to land in a few hours' time. She tried to sleep and to lose herself in the onboard entertainment.

In Johannesburg, the quiet of the evening was broken by a loud knock at David's door. It was Maseka and Joubertf. Cedric answered it.

'Hello, Mr Kai, is Mr Blind here, please?' said Joubertf.

'Yes, he is. Come on in. Can I get you a tea or coffee?'

'No, thank you, this won't take long.'

The men entered the living room as David stood up in surprise at their sudden arrival, and without hesitation, Maseka said, 'David Blind, you're under arrest for the murder of Father Seth Rossouw.' Joubertf handcuffed him. 'You do not have to say anything unless you choose to do so…………'

David shouted in shock and protest, 'What? No! This is wrong. You're mistaken! I didn't murder anyone! I didn't do anything to Father Seth. I would never…'

'Mr Blind, you can come quietly or make it more difficult for yourself,' said Maseka.

David's face contorted in fear, but he managed to sound calmer than he felt. 'I've nothing to hide. I'm sure we can clear this up. Can you contact Stephan Potgieter for me, Cedric? He's my solicitor.'

'Yes David, I'll do it immediately,' said Cedric, shocked at what had just taken place in David's living room. 'Stay strong my friend. We'll do everything we can, you can be sure of that.'

Tanu started to cry as they led him out to the waiting police car. David was trying to reassure them as the officers forced him into it, holding down his head to protect it. 'Don't worry, I'll be back soon. We'll go for Jennifer later,' he managed to say, with a brave smile, before the car door was slammed shut and he was removed with speed from their presence.

He was booked into custody at Johannesburg Central for questioning. He'd been in a cell for about an hour and a half when his solicitor arrived. Potgieter looked through the observation panel on the door, and saw David sitting with his head in his hands.

'Hello, David,' he said, with a serious expression. 'I'm sorry we're meeting in these circumstances but be assured I will do everything I can to sort this out for you.

'They're not obliged to release their evidence at this time, but that will normally come out during the interview. Is there anything you need to tell me, David?'

'Yes. I'm not guilty,' said David, defiantly.

'Did you kill Father Seth, David?' asked the solicitor, calmly and matter of fact.

'No, I've told you, Stephan, I'm not guilty.'

'OK, they have 48 hours from the time of your arrest to format their evidence and place it before the court. I've known you a long time, David, and you're an honest man. I'm confident you're telling the truth. So, let's get this sorted and get you out of here.'

Potgieter was briefed by the police, but not on what specific evidence they had. They did, however, say the evidence was of great significance. He took notes. David was taken from the cell to an interview room where Potgieter was waiting.

'Hi David, this is a messy situation. They have some pretty compelling evidence, according to the arresting officers. Let's see what they've got, and we'll take it from there. They'll come in to interview you soon. Please listen to any advice I give you throughout the interview and follow it to the letter. I'll only interject if I fear they are trying to back you into a corner.'

David answered, 'OK, I've nothing to hide, so I'm good to tell them whatever I can. If Father Seth died at the hands of anyone, I want to do everything I can to assist the police.'

Maseka and Joubertf entered the room. They sat down at the table and Maseka turned on the tape recorder, stated the date and time and introduced himself and all the participants in the officially approved order.

'Present is myself, Homicide Detective Sergeant Maseka, Homicide Detective Constable Joubertf, the accused, Mr David Blind, and his legal representative, Mr Stephan Potgieter,' Joubertf began. 'Is it OK if I call you David?'

'Yes,' managed David, staring at them like a cornered animal.

'OK David, we know from the Gumedes' interviews that Father Seth died between 7:30 and 8am on Sunday morning, as Mrs Gumede made a call from her home landline to the presbytery at 7:27. We've confirmed that with the phone company. The ambulance despatch unit received a call from Mr Gumede at 8:02 am. We've retraced the drive time from the Gumedes' home to the presbytery, and that takes 29 minutes.

'We've collaborated your statement with the clinic in Parktown and confirmed that you visited with an infected cut to your right thumb, and you left there at 7:30 am on Sunday morning. We have CCTV evidence of you leaving the clinic car park at 7:31 am. That gave you a period of time that we feel you can't account for, about ten to fifteen minutes in all. I'm going to show you a piece of video evidence, David.

'I'm showing Mr David Blind Video Exhibit Vid-STB'S-27/08-000029. Is that you, driving your car out of the clinic car park on Sunday morning, David?'

'Yes, that's me, and that's my car.'

'Which road did you use when you drove home on Sunday morning?'

'The Botha road.'

'Why did you take the Botha Road?' asked the detective.

'It takes about 25 minutes,' answered David.

'Is that the fastest route?'

'Yes, there are other routes, but they can take double the time, depending on traffic.'

'Correct me if I'm wrong, David, but doesn't the Botha Road pass the top of Sobukwe Close, the cul-de-sac where St Brigid's church and presbytery are situated?'

'Yes.'

How long is the drive from the clinic to the presbytery, David?'

'I'd guess about 15 minutes.'

'You said in your previous interview, and I quote, "I considered calling as it was on my way home and I was only 15 minutes away from the clinic." So, what time did you arrive at the presbytery?'

'That's a leading question, David. You don't have to answer that,' Potgieter said.

'No, it's fine, I'll answer it,' said David. 'I didn't arrive at the presbytery. I drove straight home because I had a temperature. I went home and went straight to bed. I also said that in my interview on Sunday.'

'Indeed, you did.'

'But, just to clarify, is the drive time from the clinic to the presbytery 15 minutes, or, *about* 15 minutes, David. Which is it?'

'I would estimate, *about* 15 minutes.'

'That's a little different from your previous statement, David,' Joubertf said, accusingly.

'Yes, it is. But I can't be absolutely certain, as I've never actually made that journey. But, just to clarify, it would appear that you can't be absolutely certain if the period of time you suggest I can't account for, is ten, *or,* fifteen minutes, which is it?' David asked, calmly, sure of his ground.

'I'm asking the questions, David.' Joubertf said, appearing rattled by the speed and challenge of David's response.

'So, now it's *about* an estimated 15 minutes, David?'

'Yes, estimated. It's the only answer I can give you, because, as I've just told you, I've never actually made that journey.

The interview continued, a game of cat and mouse for three hours. They paused the tape, repeating the date and time and stated who they were interviewing. They took a comfort break.

'You're doing really well, David,' Potgieter said, when the officers were out of the room.

'I find the truth easy, that's why, Stephan. Can you call Cedric and remind him to pick up Jennifer? I don't think I'll be out of this nonsense in time. Father Seth is gone, and that should be my main focus right now.'

'I'll have to do that when the officers come back. I can't leave you alone, and I'm not allowed to have my mobile phone in an interview. Have you got his number, please?'

David gave Potgieter Cedric's landline from memory. Maseka and Joubertf entered the room and sat down. Potgieter explained that he needed to make a phone call and advised him not to enter into any conversation with the two officers before he returned. He left the interview room and went to call Cedric.

He explained the convoluted situation and asked him to explain it to Jennifer when they got to the airport. He was hopeful that David would be released sometime later, he said. Cedric asked worriedly that please could he be kept informed of any progress and told the solicitor to call him on his mobile, giving him the number, any time, day or night.

Back in the room, the tape was turned on again and the formal process followed before Maseka took over the questioning and continued with the interview.

'I have several more pieces of evidence that I intend to discuss with you, David. We'll look at them when appropriate, and I will identify them for the purposes of the recording. Do you understand?'

'Yes.'

'How long did you know Father Seth Rossouw?'

'All my life. He brought me up,' answered David, without hesitation.

'Did you have a happy childhood?'

'No, not really, quite a lonely one,' answered David, truthfully.

The officers exchanged glances. 'Did he ever hit you?' Maseka asked.

David paused. 'Sometimes, yes.'

'Was he ever cruel towards you?'

'He could be, sometimes,' David said, carefully, aware that the officers were baiting him.

'I'm sure that made you angry and vengeful as you got older?' suggested Maseka.

'No, you might find this hard to believe, but it made me want to pursue a better relationship with him. I actually respected and felt great affection for him for everything he'd done for me, however imperfect, and I wanted to feel he felt the same way. In fact, that had become the case in the last few years. We'd become much closer, and we understood each other. He'd started to be able to express himself in a gentler way.'

Maseka looked at David incredulously. 'So, you felt great affection for a man who used to beat you. A man who was cruel towards you. You respected and admired him?'

'Yes, I did,' repeated David. 'I'm not a vengeful man. I'm not ordinarily prone to acts of violence and I'm not the sort of man to pursue retribution,' said David, looking him straight in the eyes.

Maseka returned his gaze. 'I'm showing Mr David Blind Video Exhibit Vid-STB'S-27/08-000063. Can you describe what you see in the video, David?'

They all watched the clip.

'Yes,' answered David. 'There are two men in the garden at the back of the church. I tackled one of them, a drug dealer who you people put away for a long time on the back of this evidence.'

'Yes, a drug dealer, who I think it's safe to say, you'd have beaten to death if Father Seth Rossouw hadn't intervened?'

'Absolutely not. Why would you even think that? There were no charges brought against me, no caution, no consequence at the time at all other than that for Ramirez, the drug dealer.'

'Isn't it indicative of the violent man you can be?'

David looked at him, weighing up the prejudice in the officer's eyes. He said, carefully, 'I'm sure we all have the capacity for violence, but I'm not ordinarily violent. I dislike injustice and especially when perpetrated against the weak and defenceless.'

'So, what you just saw on the video was acceptable?'

'No, that's not what I said.'

'OK, I am showing Mr David Blind photograph Exhibit Ph-STB'S-27/08-000057. Do you know what that is, David?'

'It looks like a cassock.'

'Can you be more specific David?'

'You don't need to answer that, David,' said Potgieter.

'It's all right, Stephan. I'll answer the question. It looks like a cassock with a large stain on it.'

'Thank you David. Where is the stain, David?'

'It's on the left-hand side from the shoulder extending diagonally to the lower quarter of the cassock and the left arm.'

'Very precise. Presumably, you know what the stain is?'

'I don't actually know, but I think you're probably going to tell me it's blood,' said David, feeling his stomach rise.

'It's Father Seth Rossouw's blood.'

David retched, putting his hand over his mouth and pushing his chair away. Joubertf handed him a sick bag as Potgieter moved swiftly away from the table.

'For the sake of the recording, Mr Blind is vomiting into a sick bag,' said Maseka.

David was violently ill as he took in the reality of the massive blood loss Father Seth had endured. Potgieter retrieved a box of tissues from a corner table and passed it to him.

They waited for him to compose himself before Maseka continued. 'It was effortless to get Father Rossouw's DNA from that amount of blood. I'm showing Mr David Blind photograph Exhibit Ph-STB'S-27/08-000042.

'Do you know what that is, David?' It was a close-up photo of Father Seth's neck, still with the glass embedded into the flesh.

David retched again. 'Do you know what that is, David?' repeated Maseka.

David squinted at the picture, still nauseous. 'It looks like a glass and a heavily blood-stained towel in a wound,' he said, wearily, fighting the tears that threatened.

'Let me show you this one, David. It's a zoomed-out photo similar to the one you've just seen. I'm showing Mr David Blind photograph Exhibit Ph-STB'S-27/08-000037.'

'Oh my God, please, no.' David started to sob into his hands.

'Yes, that's Father Seth as you left him on Sunday morning after plunging that glass into his neck with such force that you severed both the carotid artery and the jugular vein before leaving him to die, scared and alone.'

David looked up in panic. 'I didn't do that. I could never have done that. I wasn't there, I told you, I went straight home from the clinic.'

'But the evidence tells us differently, David. You know, I know, Joubertf knows, and I'm sure Mr Potgieter is beginning to realise that you murdered Father Seth Rossouw in a cowardly, cold-blooded, premeditated fashion that can only be described as evil.'

'What evidence do you have to show that my client committed the alleged murder?' Potgieter remonstrated.

'I'm getting to that,' said Maseka.

'David, when did you last see Maria, your mother?'

David looked up in pain and grief at the question. 'Maria? My mother? Is that her name? I've never seen her. I've never met my mother.'

'I'm showing Mr David Blind photograph Exhibit's Ph-STB'S-27/08-000069 to Ph-STB'S-27/08-000094. Twenty-six exhibits in total. What are they, David?'

'They look like letters.'

'Typed, or handwritten letters?'

'Handwritten.'

'One of those letters, signed Maria, says, *Thank you for letting me see my boy,* but you claim you've never met her.'

This was too much for him. He sobbed, 'I told you, I've never met my mother. I never knew her name. I've never seen those letters, and I have no idea what's in them.'

'So Father Seth never showed them to you? He never told you about your mother. Is that why you murdered him? You must have been outraged when you found them and found that your mother had been allowed to see you but you had been kept in the dark. All those years.'

'I've never seen those letters, as God is my judge,' David said, in utter misery.

'I find that hard to believe, David. There's an ongoing search of your home as we speak. These letters were found, along with other documents, in a large card envelope from SafeRand Bank. We believe you've had these letters since they came into your possession three and a half years ago.

'I've never seen those letters,' David said, looking him in the eyes.

'But what about the photographs, your birth certificate and the savings account books. The note from your mother that was with you when you were found. Have you never seen those, either?'

David was struggling to answer. It felt like he was being ripped open.

Eventually he managed to reply. 'Yes, I've seen those, but I found the birth certificate too painful, too upsetting, because I'm sure it confirms that I belong to nobody, so I never looked at anything else. I didn't feel ready to know. I always meant to do it one day, but it was too painful at the time.'

Maseka almost scoffed. 'I find that hard to believe, and also very convenient. I can only imagine how that pain became anger when it was festering inside you for all your life. The beatings, the lack of love, being kept away from your mother. And I agree, Father Seth was cruel. I understand why you'd want to kill him. In fact, you're right, we all have the ability to be violent, and I think if I found myself in a similar situation, I'd probably be angry enough to kill, too.'

'You don't have to...' began Potgieter before David interrupted him. 'I've told you. I didn't kill him. I didn't murder Father Seth! There must be another explanation,' David was shaking his head in distress and grief.

Maseka ploughed on. 'Let's return to the cassock, David. Not only did we find Father Seth's DNA on it, but we also found yours. We also found a substantial amount on the tea towel that we found on the desktop and another sample on the glass along with your fingerprints and, of course, your thumbprint.'

David came back to his senses as the words burned into him and logical thought returned. He said, 'I told you about my accident in my interview on Sunday, and I told you about the glass, the tea towel, and that Father Seth had placed my hand on his knee when dressing my wound. So, all of that DNA is accounted for.'

Maseka answered, 'You're a very clever man, David. Almost clever enough to lead us away from the reality, but you forgot an especially important piece of evidence. You didn't mention anything about the towel that was hanging out of his neck.'

David felt panic rise again at not being believed. He said, 'No, because it wasn't part of the incident.'

'That's really interesting, David, because we found your DNA on that too. Only a small amount in comparison to the huge amount of that of Father Seth Rossouw. But nonetheless, enough to back up the rest of the evidence that identifies you as the murderer of Father Rossouw.'

'I've told you. I didn't murder Father Seth. I...I...thought a great deal of him. He was a very remarkable man.'

Maseka looked at him with cold eyes. 'Murder of any kind is a heinous crime. But the brutal, what should we call it, patricide, of the man who brought you up is nothing less than evil.'

Hearing that, David felt that he was dealing with men of little understanding, and he thought they had made a basic error. He said, calmly, 'I take it you're not Catholic. When I refer to Father, it is in regard to him being my priest. As I understand it, patricide is the murder of a birth father.'

'Yes, he was your priest, and actually, yes, I am a Catholic, and surprised that he was allowed to continue as a priest if the church knew all of what we now know. It's not a pretty story, is it? A Catholic priest taking advantage of his position to seduce and leave a woman pregnant and desperate, unable to bring up her child?

441

Who exactly was Maria, Mr Blind? Where is she now? I'm sure you must know.'

David shook his head in misery, looking down hopelessly at his upturned palms.

Maseka watched him in disgust. 'But don't worry, Mr Blind, we'll find her, eventually, wherever she is, whatever name she might be using now. Someone, somewhere knows the truth.'

'You don't need to keep the dirty little secret anymore, David. We all know your priest, Father Seth Rossouw, was also your birth father. The DNA tells us that too.'

David's head shot up and he opened his mouth but no words came out. The detective's words had entered him like knives. He stared into space, unable to compute the information.

The room fell silent as the officers watched every move, every flicker of his eyes.

David finally recovered some composure. 'Father Seth told me nothing other than the gist of what was written on the other side of the note, but I had never actually seen it in all those years, and the rest of her words were kept from me. I have no idea who my mother was or is.'

Maseka waited for a few moments. 'I find all of this hard to believe. You are a very intelligent man, obviously, David Blind. But the facts seem to point to one thing, and one thing only.'

'Oh, dear, dear God,' said David, holding his head in his hands, 'This is causing me great pain. I may have had an unusual relationship with Father Seth but, I repeat, I did not kill him.' A single tear ran down his cheek.

The detectives did not reply, the interview was formally ended and the tape switched off. Maseka informed Potgieter that David would be formally charged with murder just as soon as they had completed the relevant paperwork, and he was likely to appear in court tomorrow morning. They told the solicitor he could have ten minutes with him in the presence of a uniformed officer before they locked him up for the night. It was 11:25 pm.

When they'd gone, David turned to Potgieter with terror in his eyes.

'They must be mistaken, Stephan. Father Seth is not my father. They're making the evidence fit the crime. I didn't kill Father Seth. They've obviously cross-contaminated the DNA.'

The solicitor answered, 'I'm sorry, David, but the evidence they have presented is compelling. I understand what you're saying about it, considering you gave them a voluntary interview and what you told them at that time. We have a lot of work to do to try to find something that will clear you, something that will be easily identifiable by the jury, something that will create some reasonable doubt. I'll see you in court in the morning, but I have to tell you, with the evidence they have and the way they will present it, it's doubtful you'll get bail.'

David looked down at the floor in panic. His mind was a kaleidoscope of possibilities.

Potgieter left the station as David was returned to his cell.

***

It was nearly midnight when Potgieter called Cedric's mobile. Cedric put it on speaker for Tanu to hear.

'Hello Cedric, it's Stephan Potgieter. Unfortunately, they are about to charge David with Father Seth's murder. He's due to appear in court in the morning and, considering the evidence, I don't think he's likely to get bail. It is, as the police say, compelling evidence, and we have a major job on our hands to prove his innocence. There were a number of revelations in the evidence that have somewhat put our backs against the wall.'

'Oh my God, no,' said Cedric. 'You sound like you believe the police rather than David.'

'If I'm completely honest with you, the evidence is very compelling when you hear it in its entirety, but it's my job to defend him. I have some doubts in my mind in relation to the potential cross-contamination of DNA, and if we can prove that, but it's a big if, then they may have no case. But if we can't, and I have to prepare you for this eventuality, I'm afraid he's looking at a life sentence.'

Potgieter waited for that terrible information to sink in before adding, 'Unfortunately, you can't come to court tomorrow as it's a plea hearing where the judge will most likely remand him in custody.'

Cedric couldn't believe the words coming into the room. He answered, almost robotically, 'OK, thank you for ringing, Stephan. Can you call to advise us as to what we need to do?'

'Yes, of course I will, Cedric. Goodbye.'

Cedric's voice was flat, pushing away the swirling emotion as Tanu looked at him with fearful eyes. He said, 'It's going to be a busy night. Stephan will call me after the hearing tomorrow.'

***

Jennifer's flight had landed, and Cedric and Tanu were waiting for her in arrivals. She went to hug her friends and held them tight for a long time before standing back and asking where David was.

She was devastated by the answer, the airport suddenly turning into a vortex of fear.

Cedric and Tanu did all they could to calm her, but she kept repeating, 'He hasn't done it. He couldn't do anything like that. He couldn't, he couldn't...' Tanu held her hand in both of hers as they walked, and Cedric took her cases.

'Come back to our house. We'll look after you,' Tanu said.

They all walked to the waiting car in a daze and Cedric drove home silently while Tanu tried to comfort Jennifer with small reassurances.

They all remained together, fearful of leaving the landline or Cedric's phone.

Chapter 26

Search

David appeared in court at 9:30 am and was remanded in custody awaiting trial.

No date had been set as the judge had asked for further DNA tests to be completed in order to eliminate the potential of cross-contamination, as requested by Stephan Potgieter.

The judge had added, 'Considering this is a possibility, with examples in recent law, I need to be certain that there has been no further recurrence. If this can be cleared up before trial, then that process will be far less complicated for a jury to understand.'

Potgieter went to see David before leaving court. He explained the process to him. He also advised David that he would be allowed a one-hour visit the following day with a maximum of two visitors. He suggested that he gave some thought as to whom he wanted to visit and to inform the prison staff on his reception into the facility.

'Jennifer and Cedric,' he said, immediately.

'I'll tell Cedric when I call him,' answered the solicitor.

Potgieter left the court and rang Cedric. He made him aware of the committal hearing outcome and told him to expect a call from the prison. They'd be ringing to arrange a visit, he said, and David wanted him and Jennifer to attend, if possible. There could be only two

446

visitors and they would need their ID books or passports as confirmation of identity.

Jennifer was a little calmer now, and she'd had time to consider her options. She'd decided that the best way to support David was to put on a positive front and reassure him that she believed him, regardless of what the evidence might suggest.

'They must have missed something. I suppose he's still been driving round in that old car, which is a pity,' Jennifer said.

'Yes, he is. But you know what he's like. He hates waste, and I think he feels as long as it's running, he doesn't need anything else. Anyway, why is it a pity?' asked Cedric.

'A newer car might have had GPS, which would have tracked his movements,' she said, simply.

'They took his car and phone yesterday when they searched the house,' Cedric replied.

Jennifer's voice brightened. 'Perhaps they'll find something on his phone, then.'

Cedric shook his head. 'He mentioned on Sunday that he'd left it at home when he'd gone to the clinic. He'd forgotten it because of the pain in his thumb and wanted to get there as soon as he could. It feels like everything is stacking up against him. Which is why we've got to tell him tomorrow, that we know he's innocent.'

'Oh Cedric, thank God you believe in him too,' cried Jennifer. 'He's going to need to know that. In fact, we need to let Ethel know what's happening. Can you drive me over to see her, please?'

'Yes, of course,' answered Cedric.

They drove to Simeon's house and told Ethel what little they knew. Ethel was still devastated and continued to castigate herself for telling the police about how David had been bullied by Father Seth as a child. If only she'd had the wisdom at the time, perhaps this would never have happened, she said, tearfully.

Jennifer said, 'Ethel, I know you raised your concerns about that the day you told me about everything. But David never mentioned it, and I never felt it appropriate to discuss it with him. The opportunity never arose. I so wish he'd felt able to talk to me about it.'

'You know how timid he used to be, child? Also, he has always been extremely loyal. But you'll know that because of your closeness to each other. He quietly got on with it,' said Ethel, dabbing her eyes.

'Having said that, he was, I mean is, always very sensitive and thoughtful to the needs of others. I suppose that when you're always searching for acceptance, it's likely that you'll be prepared to put up with the worst of behaviour in those you most want that acceptance from. I blame myself for not challenging Father sooner than I did, but while I had my suspicions, I couldn't put my finger on it for a long time. In hindsight, I guess he used to do it mostly when I was out of the presbytery.'

Jennifer said, kindly, 'It serves no purpose to punish yourself for telling the truth, Ethel. David wouldn't want you to have compromised yourself with your witness statement, even if you believed that it would help his predicament. But I'm sure David is completely innocent, and they will find that out.'

'Oh, I am too,' Ethel responded. 'I do hope so. We must pray.'

Cedric said, with an attempt at optimism, 'The news is on soon. Perhaps we should watch it to see if we can find anything out?'

They turned on the TV. As the news came on, 'Jo'burg Priest Murder: Man Charged' was the first item. There, outside the presbytery, was a news reporter.

Her face was familiar to them all. The facts of her report, delivered with the same, cold efficiency she used for motorway pile ups or political stories, were today frightening and disturbing in the extreme to the listeners crowded round in Ethel's clean and comfortable sitting room, with its plumped up satin cushions and polished surfaces.

In practised and professional tones, the reporter spoke into her microphone. 'A close friend of recently married African Nations Gold 100 metres medallist Cedric Kai appeared in court on a murder charge this morning.

'The twenty-four-year-old IT company owner was Kai's best man at his high profile wedding just weeks ago. He is accused of killing the parish priest in the building behind me, a man with whom he lived for most of his life, almost as an adopted son.

'David Blind, CEO of the successful software company Blind Techno Solutions, based here in Johannesburg, was charged with the killing of Father Seth Rossouw on Sunday morning between seven thirty and eight o'clock in this presbytery.' She turned to point at the front door.

'He entered a plea of not guilty. The priest's mutilated body was found by the son of his housekeeper, who entered the property to speak to Father Rossouw and found the alleged murder scene.

'The date for the trial is yet uncertain. Police are continuing their investigations into DNA evidence. Blind was remanded in custody without bail.'

Mutilated body. Alleged murder scene. They all recoiled at the words.

'Oh dear God, poor David' said Ethel. 'I just cannot comprehend what's being said. Cedric, what DNA evidence can they have? To charge him with murder? David is always in and out of the presbytery. His DNA must be everywhere.'

'All I know for sure is that David is innocent, and no evidence, DNA, or otherwise, will change my mind,' Jennifer said. 'Trust me, Ethel, David didn't murder Father Seth. I know he didn't. I just know.'

They all slept badly.

The next morning, after a hurried breakfast, Jennifer looked at Cedric and said, 'I hope this doesn't sound weird, Cedric, but I'm so looking forward to today. I can't wait to see him, even though it's going to be in that place. I just think he'll feel better knowing that we believe him.'

Cedric answered, 'That's not weird at all. I know exactly what you mean, Jennifer. Just because the place we're going to is a terrible place, it doesn't mean we shouldn't be happy to see the person we love.'

Jennifer nodded at his wisdom and beckoned him to leave with her.

They arrived at Johannesburg Prison's secure compound, booked themselves in, and were sent into a room where they were searched. They were told that they could have contact with 'Blind', but should their conduct be deemed at any time inappropriate, the visit would be immediately terminated. They accepted the terms without question.

They were led into a waiting room. Name upon name was shouted as Jennifer turned to Cedric and said, 'I never realised that waiting could be so painful. I'm just thinking how hard it is for the loved ones of prisoners. How they suffer too.'

'I think you mean us, we suffer too. We're amongst that number now,' Cedric responded.

Jennifer nodded sadly and looked again at the clock on the wall. Many minutes had passed.

'Blind,' shouted a grim-faced warder.

They stood up and nervously followed him, keys jangling at his belt, down a long corridor.

'Don't be nervous,' he turned to say, with surprising gentleness and understanding. 'It looks like it's your first time. Just be careful to greet him one at a time. He won't be allowed to stand to greet you. He'll be sitting down when you see him. If you need to get up at any point during your visit, just let me know. I'll be in earshot.

'If I feel it appropriate as you leave, I may allow him to stand then. I'll try to make this as painless as I can for you all.'

'Thank you,' they both responded, with some relief. A human being in this awful place.

They rounded a corner, and they could see David through the bars of an electronic gate. The gate opened as they neared it. Beyond was a second gate which opened as the first one closed with a loud clanging noise. They looked at each other as the second gate slowly opened and gave them a full view of him. A big smile came across all their faces. They entered and walked over as David raised his arms in Jennifer's direction. The tears started to roll down both their faces as they held each other tightly. Tighter than ever before.

David murmured into her ear, 'Jennifer, I didn't kill Father, I promise you. I didn't kill him. I know it looks like all the evidence says the opposite, but I didn't do it.'

Stroking his face and looking into his eyes, she answered, 'I know you didn't, my sweet man. No one will ever make me believe otherwise. Have faith. God will find a way of getting you out of here. How are they treating you?'

He managed a smile.

'The vast majority of staff are really good, and you can see they are dedicated to what they do. But like every walk of life, there are one or two who are power-crazy, so I'm trying to avoid them. I am in a cell on my own until they've completed my assessment.'

They let go of each other, and he then hugged Cedric.

'I'm so pleased to see you both. I didn't know if you'd come. Apart from Father dying in such a terrible, cruel way, the worst of this is not knowing if people believe me or the police.'

Cedric said, firmly, 'David, we all know you're not capable of such a thing. We trust you implicitly and know you didn't do this. Have you heard anything more about the DNA evidence they have?'

David looked down at his feet as the expected lump came into his throat. He braced himself for their reaction. 'An officer told me at lunch time that the second batch of tests have confirmed that Father Seth was my natural father. I had never suspected it.'

They held their breath at his words. They weren't expecting this.

Jennifer, her hand still covering her mouth, was first to speak. 'David, what do you mean? Father Seth your real father? How can that be? That's...not possible, surely...?'

David nodded. 'Yes it is. I had no idea. But I only ever tried to look at my birth certificate once, and it was too painful. I curse myself now.

'From what I've been told by Stephan, Father Seth was the person recorded as registering my birth. And I'm sure he didn't just pluck my date of birth out of the air. Yet days had passed before I was left at the presbytery and there was no mention of my date of birth in the note, yet he knew it, or at least it was a very good guess. Why didn't I pick up on any of this? It felt too painful at the time to engage with all that information.

'And my mother was called Maria, they said. Father Seth took advantage of his position and she became pregnant. There were letters from her in the papers I got from SafeRand bank. She just signed herself Maria and thanked him for letting me see me. How could I have ever known she'd seen me? It's too much to bear, too much...'

He choked.

Then, swallowing back his grief and looking at them both, he said in a different tone, 'But I now get the feeling that this will be twisted to being another motivation to kill him, but I didn't kill him. You've got to believe me.'

'We know you didn't. Stop worrying about that. We know you're not a murderer,' Cedric said.

The pent-up words continued to fall out of David's mouth.

'How are Ethel and Simeon?' he asked. 'I was so worried about them. It must have been horrible for them. First, with Simeon finding Father like that...'

He stopped and looked up at the ceiling. 'Father, Father! I've always called him Father! And he *was* my father. All the time, he *was* my father. He knew and I didn't, and I always called him Father. How screwed up is that!'

They could hear and feel his anguish. David never normally spoke like that. There were no words of comfort for this.

'My God, he even chose a cruel name for me! Blind. Verblinden in Dutch means blind. Then he kept me blind for most of my life. He meant me never to see the truth. I was even too scared to look at the letters he gave me. I made myself blind because it was what he wanted. Always what he wanted. What kind of a priest, what kind of a man was he?'

He wiped a tear from his cheek in despair. Then he thought again of Simeon's ordeal and the horror he must have witnessed. 'Dear God, poor Simeon. Having to tell Ethel, then being dragged off to the police station and being questioned about it. It must have been horrendous for them. Please tell them I am so sorry they had to go through that and I love them.'

Jennifer said, 'We went to see them yesterday. They are fine, but obviously very upset. Simeon has taken some time off work, just to get over the shock, but they are coping.'

David needed to get some of the ideas and words out that had been swirling in his head for many hours. It was all helping to take his mind away from the torture of knowing that he was the living remnant of Father Seth's DNA. He had been born from his seed, born from a priest's lust. Could it have been love? Was he capable of love? What desperate actions had led to that bare fact of profane paternity, presented to him in a police station by a pair of detectives? Their words had eviscerated him. The knowledge of it all and the questions it left him with was like a disembowelment, but of the soul.

He knew his time was short with Jennifer and Cedric, so he pushed away the pain and concentrated on the mundane.

'Can you make sure Simeon and Ethel are all right for money? Tell them if they need counselling, then I'll pay for it, and if you can contact my office when you leave here, can you ask Francine, Simeon's sister, to make sure Simeon isn't out of pocket, taking time off work?

'Also, ask her to ring Keith Van Dow, my counsellor, to arrange to see anyone who needs it. In the meantime, tell her I'll sort out power of attorney with Stephan Potgieter this afternoon when I see him, giving you both my consent to run my affairs while I'm here.'

It became almost like a business meeting, the kind David had become used to. He went on, 'If that's OK with you? It's just that I don't want anyone to have to worry about paying their bills. Also Jennifer, can you contact Ethel and the archdiocese and try to sort out her pension. Also, find out what Father...no, no, what *he* paid her, and ask Francine to pay her the same until her pension comes through, and make sure she can manage.'

Even in his hour of greatest need he was thinking about everyone else, Jennifer realised, loving him all the more because of it. The income to the company was regular as most of his contracts were paid every month directly to the company accounts, and the company was in a good financial state.

He added, 'I'm entitled to five visits a month, but only two people can visit at a time. So, if you can find out who wants to come to see me and let Stephan have a list, then I can make the correct requests each time. But if it's all right with you, Jennifer, I'd like you to come every time?'

'I should think so, too,' she laughed, but there was a painful hollowness to her teasing.

The visit ended with the officer allowing David to stand to hug them both before they left.

'I'm never going to give up on you, David Blind,' Jennifer whispered in his ear. 'It's payback time for everything you've done for me. Stay safe, and I'll see you next week.' She buried her head into his chest. Cedric hugged him and said, 'See you soon, brother. Don't worry. We'll sort everything for you.'

The two of them left the prison in a more positive state of mind than that which they had entered it.

Back at Tanu and Cedric's house, Jennifer had an idea. She said, 'I'm sorry to be so demanding but could one of you take me to the presbytery, please?'

'Yes, I'll take you,' Cedric said.

They arrived at the top of the cul-de-sac. It seemed there were television crews from every corner of the globe. David's connection with Cedric had heightened interest from many quarters, sporting, secular and religious. Jennifer said a silent prayer of thanks that knowledge of David's paternity was sub judice and had not yet been released. She imagined that things would turn even uglier if it was.

'I need to get as close to the presbytery as I can, but it's not going to happen today. Can you drop me off on the forecourt of the petrol station?' asked Jennifer. 'I'll walk back.'

'Let me drive you back,' said Cedric.

'No, thank you,' she answered. There are clues here somewhere. I just need to find them.'

***

Jennifer walked to and from the area of the presbytery every day for almost two weeks. Every hour of every day, she tried to understand how the relationship between Father Seth and David had worked. Why did he beat him, his own son? Why was he so cruel during his younger years? Why had he then provided for him materially, like any good father would, and become kinder? The mysteries deepened and there were no easy answers.

Some days she was out all day walking up and down Botha Road. She couldn't get near the presbytery for the media attention, but she was drawn there all the same. Tanu and Cedric started to worry about her state of mind, but she ignored their pleas to stay at home with them.

Then, one day, for the first time, interest had waned as the long wait for the trial kicked in, and the film crews and reporters had melted away. She walked down the length of the cul-de-sac and went through the familiar gates, up the drive to the presbytery door. To her shock, before she even knocked, the door opened. It was Father Duncan. Delighted to see each other, they hugged.

The young priest said, 'I'm sorry we haven't been in touch, Jennifer. We've been told that we shouldn't contact any of you as you need your space. We know the circumstances are very...sensitive.'

She looked at him with eyes blazing, and feeling uncharacteristically angry, she said, 'It has nothing to do with our needing space, Duncan.

'This is the church at work. Don't worry, I'm not criticising you, personally. I think the hierarchy just wants this to go away, and of course it will, eventually. It reminds me of that night with Dominic, and what we found in his room. Sweep the awkward facts under the carpet.

'Well, it's not going to go away, not on this occasion. Once Father's body is released, then it will be to his next of kin which, like it or not, will be David.' Duncan flinched at her candour. He hadn't known for sure, but this was confirmation of the rumours circulating among the clerics.

'He will no doubt ask me, Cedric, Tanu and Ethel to arrange the funeral in his absence.

'We have no intention of making things difficult for the church, but I know David would like Father Seth to be interred in the crypt here. Regardless of what everyone thinks, David is innocent, and we intend to prove that. So, please tell Luigi and Martin that we'd like the three of you to officiate at Father Seth's requiem mass and tell the archbishop he needn't attend if he finds it too embarrassing.'

Duncan looked ashamed. 'I'm so sorry Jennifer. We've let you all down. I'll contact everyone tonight. Please, will you come in for a cup of tea?'

He moved to welcome her into the presbytery. She stepped in. 'Thank you, Duncan, if you wouldn't mind. I must be honest and say that I've been trying to come to the house for two weeks, but it was impossible with that lot outside, without causing more headlines.

'I feel there must be something the police have missed. David is completely innocent, and a great injustice is being done. Maybe the answer is here, hiding in plain sight.'

While the gentle Duncan went into the kitchen and made tea, Jennifer's eyes darted across every surface, clocking every item that had been moved or taken. She looked up at the St Brigid's Cross in the hall and went to straighten it. Few people knew the exact angle it should be hung at, she thought, irritated.

She went into the dining room and the study, but nothing caught her attention.

The police had been over everything. She could see that. She went into the kitchen and saw that it had been forensically cleaned. Everything seemed in order, but it was soulless.

There was no Father Seth calling from the study. No Ethel bustling around, no smell of cakes in the oven. No David walking in from the garden, smiling shyly.

She drank her tea and tried to talk of lighter things. She asked Father Duncan how his priestly duties were going, and he told her little stories to interest and distract her troubled heart.

She thanked him and rose to go. 'Duncan, this has been lovely, but I hope you understand...there is much to do, and I can't rest. This is such a sad place to me now. But I hope you can make it into a happier one. I'm sure you will.'

He nodded and rose to see her out.

She asked, 'Are you now parish priest here?'

'No, he smiled. 'Father Vries, my superior at St Benedict's is parish priest for both parishes. But he's sent me here to keep everything running.'

'Oh, I see. Well, don't worry. I know lots of important people. I'll get you to the position of pope in no time,' she quipped.

They both laughed.

'Duncan, I know the parish is in good hands.'

'Thank you, Jennifer.'

'Well, I must get back,' she said, smiling.

'Bye, Jennifer. I'm truly sorry.' Duncan walked with her through the hall, hugged her again as she left, and closed the presbytery door after her, quietly and thoughtfully. There were indeed questions about the church's position on all of this to consider, he reflected, and said a silent prayer.

She made her way up the slight incline to the top of the close. It was then that she saw it, hidden behind the trees, but extending high above them.

Outside the garage was a post that stood 35 or 40 feet tall. On top of it were two CCTV cameras pointing either way down Botha Road. Excitement started to well up inside her. CCTV! This might be the answer to David's plight.

She whispered the well-rehearsed words she knew from the Gospel of Matthew.

Ask, and it will be given you; search, and you will find; knock, and the door will be opened for you.

She stood for a moment on the forecourt of the petrol station, taking deep breaths. Here must be the answer.

She walked purposefully into the garage shop. Mr De Bruyn was sitting in a chair behind the counter. He looked up and could see immediately she wasn't there to buy anything. She looked him straight in the eyes, the question burning in her.

'Good morning. Can I help you?'

'I really hope so. I see there are two CCTV cameras outside on top of the post. Do you actually own them, or are they owned by the authorities?'

'They're mine,' he answered, intrigued by her question. 'I had them installed several years ago...'

He paused as she started to cry and then to sob, holding her ribs in pain. He was at a loss.

'Sit down miss, what on earth is the matter?'

She sat down on a chair by the counter. It took a while, but thinking of what the cameras might reveal, she was able to compose herself. Mr De Bruyn had gone into the back to get her a glass of water.

'Father Rossouw,' she said, looking up when he came back, 'I expect you know what happened.'

He nodded his head. 'Yes, it's a terrible tragedy. I knew them both, both him and David. They were good friends of mine. I'd known Father Seth for years. This is a terrible, terrible thing. 'I also remember the excitement at the time young David was found on the steps of the presbytery. But it was nothing compared to what we've all experienced in the last few weeks. All the television cameras!'

He added, quietly, 'I was so shocked to hear that David...murdered him. He always seemed to be such a nice boy.' She looked dismayed at his words but said nothing. She wanted to hear what Mr De Bruyn might have to say.

He continued, 'But, you know, I suppose we all have it in us, especially if you find out that the person who's brought you up has kept you away from your mother, and then the other terrible thing about this, you know, the thing everyone is saying round here, and I don't know if it's true, but that Father Seth...was his real father.

Jennifer tried to keep her expression neutral and sympathetic, although inside she wanted to scream at the things that people round about must be saying. Poor, poor David. This was his life they were dissecting.

The shopkeeper went on, 'I can understand why he snapped. Poor boy, he must have been in turmoil. I know it's wrong to kill, but in those circumstances, you can only imagine what someone would do. Did you know them too? Well, you must do, or you wouldn't be so upset.'

She replied, holding out her hand, 'I'm Jennifer O'Broin. Pleased to meet you. I lived at the presbytery too a few years ago. I was preparing to take my vows as a nun back then. You might have recognised me in my habit.'

He suddenly realised who she was.

Looking straight at him, she fixed him with her gaze. 'I really think the police have it wrong. I've been trying to find some evidence to prove David's innocence since I came back, and I think your CCTV might provide that evidence. Did you have a visit from the police when it happened?'

'Yes, I did. But Jennifer, I'm so sorry to tell you. The cameras are dummies. The real ones were far too expensive for a little shop like mine. The police did come and ask me about CCTV images, but I had to tell them that too. Obviously I don't tell just anyone, for security reasons. I'm really, really sorry.'

Jennifer stared at him, disbelieving, for a moment. Then the reality sank in and she held her ribs again. It was like she'd been punched in the stomach.

'Thank you anyway,' she said, her voice suddenly flat and emotionless, to keep her panic and despair at bay. 'It can't be helped. There will be an answer, there has to be. Bye, Mr De Bruyn.'

'Bye, Jennifer. I am so sorry,' Mr De Bruyn answered, sadly.

She felt drained and desperate. Too emotionally and physically exhausted to walk back, she went to stand at the bus stop to get the bus back to Cedric and Tanu's. She was there about ten minutes, whispering prayers, her mind wandering and from time to time staring hopelessly at the dummy cameras on the post, when a taxi pulled up in the lay-by. It was Simeon. God bless that man, she thought. Always there, always strong. Like a guardian angel. She very much needed a guardian angel.

'Where are you going?' he asked.

'Back to Tanu's,' she answered, finding it hard for once to fully return Simeon's friendly smile.

'Jump in. I'll give you a lift.'

Gratefully, she got into the taxi. Simeon wanted to know how she was and asked about David. She answered his questions mechanically as best she could. He could tell she was distracted.

She was privately praying, and her mind was working overtime. She knew there had to be an answer. An answer. And it might just be staring her in the face. Somewhere. She reached out a hand. There, in front of her, in Simeon's car, was the array of dashboard equipment, different devices flashing different colours, connected by USB, cameras, screens, microphone.

She hardly knew why, but she asked Simeon to explain what each of them was for. He explained about the meter which he used for fares and the satellite navigation he used for finding addresses. Finally he explained about the Cloud dashcam that not only recorded all his journeys digitally, in video and sound, front and rear, for his and his passengers' safety, but was also used by his boss to calculate the private journeys that he made in order to deduct the cost of the fuel.

'How do you get to the presbytery from home?' she asked with reawakened hope and excitement.

He answered, 'I drive in the opposite direction down this road, so it records all those journeys, and then the boss looks on the Cloud, and he can see if it's official or private business. So, for example, everything we're saying right now is being recorded, and it has two cameras, one pointing into the cab so he can see who's in the cab and the other pointing onto the road. Some drivers don't like it because they feel they're being watched all the time, but not me. It's great for security, and I don't do anything I'm not supposed to.' He laughed his warm, throaty, reassuring laugh.

She hardly dared ask the next question as they neared the street of houses where David, Tanu and Cedric lived.

'Did you drive this way on the morning of Father's death, Simeon?'

'Yes, I did, I always do. It's the quickest route, and on some occasions in recent months, I've picked David up from his house on the way if he hasn't had his car for any reason. The police asked me about it in great detail.'

'And you definitely didn't see David driving home? It must have been around the time you drove up Botha Road. It must be possible you passed each other,' she said.

'I thought that, too,' said Simeon. 'But I definitely didn't see him. I usually keep both eyes on the road ahead, Jennifer, and, if I say it myself, I'm pretty sharp on spotting people. This is my city, my workplace, if you...'

He stopped suddenly, a memory hitting him right between the eyes, one that had escaped his mind in the trauma of the event of Father Seth's death, until now.

'There's just one thing, one thing I'd completely forgotten...' He said, a cold shiver running through him.

'What's that?' asked Jennifer.

'I'd completely forgotten this, and it's a bit of a long shot, but well, I asked my mother to get me some mints from the glove compartment and she was struggling to find them. I'm afraid to say I got irritated and leant across her. She told me off. Quite right, too. So to be safe, I pulled over a few metres up the road and got them myself. Mother's knees were hurting her, and she was just in the middle of deciding not to work that day, I think.

'But the thing is, Jennifer, I did take my eyes off the road for a few seconds, but that's all. I'm so sorry, how could I have forgotten that?'

She gulped down her excitement, hardly daring to hope, but what else was there? She had to try everything. 'Can we go and see your boss now please and ask him about the video? I really need to speak to him.'

'Let me call and see if he's in the office,' said Simeon, shocked at his own faulty recall of the morning in question. He rather hoped his boss was in a good mood. Simeon was an excellent driver for the company, hardworking and trustworthy, but his generosity to family and friends did take him away from official duties at times, even though he always made up the deficits.

He pushed a button, spoke into the hands-free radio and explained the reason for his call. His boss, aware of the possible importance of the video record, answered, 'No problem, Simeon, bring the lady into the office now, and I'll have burned a DVD by the time you get here.'

They entered the office and, as good as his word, Simeon's boss Johann had made the DVD but had also left the picture on the screen that he thought most important. It was a picture of David's car turning into his street at 7:53 am on the 27th of August. She stared at it in awe. The clarity was startling. She asked him to play the video. He played the short clip, and with the high-definition picture quality, it was plain to see that David's hands were clean, his white shirt spotless, and his face easily identifiable.

She almost screamed into Simeon's ear. 'Yes! I think we've done it, Simeon. I think David's coming home! This must prove his innocence. It must.'

Simeon looked at her questioningly. 'Don't you see?' she cried. 'David couldn't have murdered Father Seth. It isn't possible for him to have driven down Sobukwe

Close, park up, enter the presbytery, commit a brutal murder, clean himself up and arrive where he is in this video, and all with a couple of minutes to spare, it just isn't possible!

'Look at his shirt, look at his hands, look at his face, he's spotlessly clean, *I knew it, I knew it,* David *is* innocent, David *is* innocent!!!'

Then it was all just too much for her. She burst into tears, but this time they were tears of thanks and exultation and Simeon hugged her, hardly daring to believe that what he had just seen would rescue his friend from a murder charge, but praying that it would.

Jennifer recovered her composure, asked Simeon's incredulous boss if he could burn another DVD and call the police. Then, armed with her copy of the evidence, Simeon dropped her off at Cedric's.

She ran like the wind into the house, shouting, 'Tanu! Cedric! We're going to watch a movie, and we're going to watch it now!'

'A movie?' asked the puzzled Tanu, walking into the hall with a tea towel in her hand, but immediately followed Jennifer into the living room when she saw the look on her face.

Tanu, Cedric and Jennifer were ecstatic as they watched the clear video of David's car driving down Botha Road, and turning into the street, heading in the direction of his home. The recorded time on screen was 07:53 am on the 27th of August. This must now, surely, be the evidence to clear David's name and detach it from the murder of Father Seth Rossouw. He was indeed an innocent man.

Jennifer called a weary Stephan Potgieter and told him what she'd found and how she'd found it. In barely concealed delight, the solicitor immediately arranged to come round to view and pick up the evidence.

***

It was just past half seven in the evening as the gate of Johannesburg Prison opened, and David walked out.

Press and TV had got wind of his release, and the shutters and flashes of their cameras filled the evening air with the clicking noises and the flashing lights of freedom. David blinked in their brilliance, only half smiling, and held up a hand shyly as Potgieter read out a prepared statement.

'My client, Mr David Blind, has been released and all charges against him have been withdrawn...' he began. The shutters rattled again at every movement of his head. They followed the figures trying to make their way through the throng.

David and Jennifer were escorted to Cedric's car by police officers, and police outriders accompanied them back to Cedric and Tanu's home.

Chapter 27

Family

Free, but not free.

David fought the emotions that swirled through his body as he walked to the waiting car. Joy, grief, relief, dereliction, which should he feel most?

While he was pleased to be returned to those he loved, he had now to come to terms with the loss of the man he'd known as Father Seth.

He'd lost his life's companion, the man who had punished him for no reason, brutally at times, but the man who had also looked after him and protected him. He'd lost Father. He'd lost *his* father, now. There were questions he would never get the answers to. It was going to be a long and painful journey, he knew that. But then, he knew about long and painful journeys.

He hoped he could talk it all through with Jennifer. She would help him understand and come to terms with it all, but in the meantime there was much to be done, many practicalities to deal with, as there are after all deaths, in all families.

The police, in the absence of any unexplained DNA in the presbytery, had set in motion the usual process for sudden deaths, referring the case to the coroner with the evidence now suggesting that there had been a fatal accident.

The evidence of paternity was to remain his private business, they had said, recognising the psychological and emotional issues it would inevitably raise. It was up to David who he told and when. His mother's letters to Father Seth would be released to him in due course, but it might take many weeks or months, they said.

Cedric drove into the drive of his and Tanu's house. Tanu, Cedric and Jennifer were jubilant and bursting with energy to celebrate. David could see it was a big relief for them, and no more than for himself, but he needed time on his own to think, to let his turbulent thoughts take shape.

He quietly told them that he was desperate for a little time on his own, and to toast him in his absence. 'Just an hour or so,' he added apologetically. Jennifer understood immediately and caught Tanu's eye before she said anything to try to persuade him otherwise.

'Of course you do, lovely man,' said Jennifer. 'Go to your own space and rest. We've so much to talk about, but it can wait. I'll check on you later if that's ok?'

David nodded, and they watched as he crossed the road, turned to give them a thumbs up, then disappeared into his house.

He went straight to the kitchen, made himself a coffee, and automatically went to his desk to switch on his computer. It was always what he'd done when he was younger, finding refuge and comfort in a screen that he could control, whether it was some online research or designing a spreadsheet. The computer might swallow his pain, for now, and the house was a place of silent solace.

He punched the letters DNA into a search engine. Up came a panoply of results, the top ones being DNA testing companies offering this offer or that offer, 25% off just this month, or which kits were the best to buy. Further down were the scientific sites, describing the chemical makeup of deoxyribonucleic acid and explaining its structure.

My DNA. Seth Rossouw's DNA. I have half his DNA, he thought.

And Maria.

Her name exploded into his head. Maria. Mamma. Mother. Mother of mine. Who are you? Where are you? What happened to you? How can I find you with only your first name to work with?

The only chance there might be, for now, was probably to take one of these heritage tests. He might find out which country his Hispanic blood came from, at the very least, even if he didn't find relatives, as had been the case for Jennifer. It might give him clues, though, and when he eventually got to see his mother's letters, he might be able to make sense of the story.

He clicked on FindMyFamily DNA. He recognised the name and that Jennifer had mentioned they were the biggest company and might therefore give more accurate and wide-ranging results.

A few clicks later and he received an email to say his test kit was on the way. He relaxed and left the computer. That was all he could do right now. He lay down on the sofa and, in spite of the strong coffee, drifted off to the most healing sleep he'd had in many days.

An hour and a half later, his doorbell rang and he stumbled across the room and hall to answer it. Jennifer and Tanu stood there with beaming smiles.

'We saw the light of the computer through the window,' said Tanu. 'Oh, it's so wonderful to see you!'

Jennifer couldn't say anything. She threw her arms around him and then the three of them embraced and wept with joy.

***

Father Seth's body was released the next day, and David called Duncan to make arrangements for the funeral.

Duncan asked if they could meet since there was the question of the priest's personal effects to discuss. David was aware that this was going to be hard for the young priest, so he suggested that Duncan, Martin and Luigi should visit him at his home.

He wanted to include them, fully. They had been among the closest of his friends, and he didn't want that to change. Not only that, but he wanted them all to be part of Father Seth's requiem and memorial. It needed to be a mass of healing for so many people.

Two weeks went by, with much activity and planning by all of the people closest to Father Seth, including Ethel. It was so important to get it right, they all knew that, especially in view of the media attention it might attract, but also for the many parishioners and colleagues who had known him over the years.

In the middle of the preparations, a small package from FindMyFamily DNA arrived for David, and he sent his saliva sample off by return post. Mamma, this is for you, he thought as he put it into the letter box. So slick, this operation, he reflected. Such a well-designed website, and the test itself, so easy to do. Now all there was left was just to wait.

***

It was the day of the funeral, and the archbishop had agreed that Father Seth could, like his predecessors, be interred in the crypt at St Brigid's. There had been much discussion about the arrangement between senior clerics and the archbishop, since the prelate had taken a dim view of how Father Seth had led his life. But, they decided, it was to be a private funeral, and therefore the official judgement of the church was suspended.

Even so, St Brigid's was packed with parishioners and Father Seth's many clerical colleagues and friends, and the mass was outwardly a celebration of his life, and of all the good things he had done.

Monsignor Prince gave the eulogy. He spoke of the priest's unerring duty to the church and his parishioners, his devotion to Our Lady, his love of learning. He outlined his sacrifices in not pursuing a professional career, in spite of being a highly intelligent and talented man. He mentioned his prowess as a footballer when he was young. He spoke of David, and the fact that Father Seth had taken him in as a foundling, and selflessly looked after his interests, all his life.

David and Jennifer listened with new ears to the monsignor's *official* narrative of Father Seth's life. Their grief was bittersweet. David had asked if he might simply read a sonnet by Father Seth's favourite poet, Gerard Manley Hopkins. The small volume of works had always been on the desk in the study, and David had always been aware of it, but had never picked it up until after Father Seth's death. The title page was inscribed with handwriting he didn't recognise, 'To you, from me, Christmas 1979.' Who was it who'd given him the book, he wondered. Would he ever know the full list of people who had been of significance to his father? It was yet another mystery in the mountain of mysteries that made up the person of Seth Rossouw.

David had almost devoured the poems and researched the poet's life hungrily, looking for clues to his father's psyche. He discovered that the Oxford-educated Hopkins had burned his early works when he became a Jesuit priest because he believed them to be born of vanity, and they were lost to the world forever. It was like self-flagellation, thought David. Self-chastisement, punishment of the soul.

Of the surviving sonnets in the anthology, David thought the words of 'God's Grandeur' seemed most appropriate to the occasion. He paused at the microphone and held up the book, explaining its importance to Father Seth.

As he finished reading, he looked up over the silent and appreciative congregation. They had no idea, though, had they? Most of them had no idea of the complexities of the man who had loved this poetry.

As they filed out of the church and entered the vestibule at the end of the mass, a fine-featured blonde woman approached Jennifer and introduced herself. She whispered in a Dutch accent, that she didn't want to impose on David in his time of grief, but she had flown in from Amsterdam for the funeral.

Jennifer smiled and thanked her and asked how she had known Father Seth. She must be in her late thirties, she thought.

The woman answered, gently, 'My name is Anneke de Groot and I'm related through my mother's side of the family. She died three years ago, unfortunately, or she would have been here today. She always thought a lot of Father Seth, and was very proud of him, although I never met him myself. So I've come to represent her.'

Jennifer, aware that Father Seth was the youngest by far of his family and no siblings were able to make the long journey, welcomed her with delight. 'Thank you so much for coming, Anneke. How lovely. I'll get David to come and speak with you.'

David had seen them in conversation and went over to them, offering his hand and said, 'Hello, will you join us in the presbytery for refreshments? You are very welcome.'

Anneke took his hand and smiled.

Jennifer gestured towards her and said, with great deliberation, 'David, this is Anneke De Groot who has travelled from the Netherlands for Father's funeral. She's related to Father on her mother's side.'

'Oh, really? I'm very pleased to meet you,' said David, suddenly aware of the implications of meeting a member of Father Seth's extended family, however distant. 'I very much hope we can get the chance to speak properly later. I'm so sorry, but please excuse me just now. There are people who are leaving who I must say goodbye to.' He moved on, shaking hands and greeting the other funeral-goers, as Jennifer walked with Anneke to the presbytery.

As they entered, the heady smell of fresh paint filled the atmosphere. The new carpets and décor had overcome the physical reminders of the tragedy of Father Seth's terrible last day, and the sun shone through the presbytery windows to brighten heavy hearts and remind them that life went on. It had to.

David followed into the presbytery and went over, increasingly aware that Anneke had to be one of the few living links to his biological father and he wanted to know more about her, without revealing to her his own very personal reasons.

'I'm very glad to meet you, Anneke.' He held out his arms to her, and she gratefully returned his embrace.

'Please, would you tell us about your mother and Father Seth?' he asked, indicating the chairs by the wall. They sat down together and Jennifer joined them.

Anneke smiled and slowly began.

'So, my name is Anneke De Groot. I was born near Arnhem, in 1980. My mother was a nun, actually, and then she left the convent. It's a bit of a long story, but anyway, I was born and my mother brought me up as a single parent. She always spoke of Uncle Seth to me. The whole family was very proud. I never met him, so in my mind I made him into a father figure because I never knew my real father.

'My mother never married. I loved her very much. She died three years ago...'

Jennifer said, 'Oh, I'm so sorry to hear that, Anneke.'

Anneke nodded and went on, 'When I saw the terrible things on the news, awful things...I thought I should come and just be here for her, really. I know she would have come herself if she could have. I didn't want to impose on you.' She started to cry and reached in her bag for a tissue.

'Do you have a family yourself, Anneke?' Jennifer asked as memories of her own father flooded her head, and she put her arms around her.

Anneke answered, 'No, I'm not particularly good in relationships, and it's been a difficult few years, so I'm happy to stay single.'

She added, quickly, 'Don't worry, I don't want or need anything from you, either of you.

'But, when I saw the story on the news back home, and I saw the photographs of you and Seth, I recognised him immediately from Moeder's photographs, and I then felt compelled to come. He seemed a wonderful man. We have both been cheated of our fathers, David.'

Jennifer couldn't stop the image of her own father filling her head. What was it with fathers?

David swallowed hard and nodded. 'My life has been turned upside down these last few weeks, Anneke. I'm so sorry to hear what you've said. It must have been very hard for your mother, and you.'

'Thank you, David. Can I give you a hug?' Anneke reached out to him.

'We must exchange numbers,' said David, as Jennifer and Anneke embraced. 'It would be great to meet up and find out a little about Father Seth's family tree.'

'Of course!' said Anneke. 'I'm in Johannesburg for a week or so. This is my first time leaving home for a long while, and I've never been to South Africa, although I have always wanted to. I am going to see all the sights, I hope.'

'Where are you staying?' asked David.

'At the Europa Hotel. It's not far from the park,' said Anneke.

'Wonderful,' he replied. 'Actually, the Europa restaurant was Father Seth's favourite. We ate there the day before he...' David tailed off, unable to finish the sentence. 'We can all meet there if you want to, in his memory.'

They shared their phone details and David promised to text her when they could meet up for a meal in the next couple of days.

***

The wake was over. The people had left. The presbytery was once more in silence as dishes had been cleared away by parishioners and chairs put back where they belonged.

Ethel wiped away a tear as she turned to look once more at the house she had cared for over so many years, hugged David and Jennifer, then sadly made her way with Simeon to his car.

David and Jennifer walked back together to Tanu and Cedric's house, and Jennifer was hoping they could all sit and talk together about the day, but David stopped on the drive and suddenly turned away from her.

'Jennifer, I'm sorry. I just need to be on my own for a while,' he said. 'It's been a hell of a day.' She was taken aback for a moment as he left her side and the distance grew between them.

As he walked across the road, the immediacy and abruptness of his action suddenly reminded her of when she was seven, and the moment her father walked out of her life. She was back there in that moment, an abandoned child, with all the hurt and longing, and not knowing what to do.

Life's too short, she suddenly thought, to waste another minute. She immediately wanted to run over and comfort him and talk to him, and bring him back to her. But she let him be. He needed to hear his own thoughts. She had made her decision, the biggest decision of her life and she had to tell him of it, but not now. As much as she needed to speak to him, she knew it would have to wait.

She went into the kitchen with Tanu and Cedric and helped them to prepare the evening meal. A couple of hours had passed when she went across to see if David was going to join them for dinner. The decision was made, and it was tearing her apart inside. She needed to be honest with him, and she needed to give vent to her pent-up emotions.

'I need to talk to you David.'

'Sounds ominous,' he smiled, as they sat together on the sofa, and she held his hands in hers. This was going to be it, he thought. She was about to say she was going to re-join the convent and take her vows. It was a conversation he'd been expecting for a long time.

Jennifer began. 'I've been thinking about my Daddy a lot and other relationships in my life, David. There's a long-overdue decision that I've been praying about for what now feels like a lifetime.'

Here we go, he thought, steeling himself, and nodding, trying to listen happily to what was coming.

Jennifer saw him tense, but carried on, 'It's hard to say it, David, because I'm not sure how you'll respond. But there's something I have to tell you, and it's something you, above anyone, have the right to know. Please try not to get angry because I'm aware that the timing of this is short of perfect.'

David steeled himself even further. He'd known this was imminent, so now was as good a time as any to hear it. 'It's OK,' he said. 'You know I love you, and I want you to be happy. I'm always going to be here for you. You've wanted this for a very long time.'

She looked into his sad eyes and watched as a solitary tear fell on his cheek, and moving forward to kiss it, she whispered, 'I feel like I've wasted so much time, David.

'I love you. I'm *in* love with you, David. I hope...' she broke off, in response to his silence, uncertain of his reaction.

At her words, it seemed as if time stood still for David, then crashed, like a great clock falling off a wall. He blinked. He looked away for a moment, looked back and blinked again.

'Just say that again,' he said with a tone in his voice she'd never heard before.

'I'm sorry, I shouldn't have said anything,' she said, the tears welling up in her eyes as she turned away.

'Wait, wait. Let me get my breath,' he interrupted, pulling her back.

'Right, say it again please. Please say it again,' he said, in his usual soft and gentle tone, looking deep into her eyes.

'I'm in love with you David,' she answered, slowly and nervously.

He took her face in his hands and kissed her on first one cheek then the other. Then on her forehead, and her nose. And then on her lips. It was a long and beautiful kiss that banished every bad thing they had ever known in their lives.

It seemed endless.

Eventually they pulled away from each other, still in their embrace, smiling into each other's eyes in wonder and delight.

Then he held her close and said, 'Jennifer, my dear, sweet Jennifer, have you any idea how long I've hoped, prayed and waited to hear those words?

'Jennifer, I've loved you since the first time I looked into your eyes. The number of times I've wanted to hold you and tell you I'm in love with you, I've lost count. I'm the happiest man alive Jennifer, do you realise that? Jennifer, Jennifer. Jennifer. My Jennifer.' He held her even tighter.

'So...you're all right with this then?' she said, laughing and wiping a tear from her eye.

'You have no idea, Jennifer. I love you. I love you. I love you, I love you.'

He cried out in a great whoop of joy.

She looked deep into his smiling eyes. 'I was so certain that my life was all mapped out for me, David. How wrong could I have been? I'm coming to terms with the fact that what I thought of as my vocation was never really that at all. It was a means of self-preservation, an escape from the cruel reality of my childhood, the loss of my Daddy. I suppose in some weird sort of way, I was trying to manage my deepest vulnerability, when all I was doing was avoiding my reality.'

Her eyes were full of emotion and she choked before she was able to carry on. 'Then, I met you, my lovely David, and you, you challenged everything I *thought* I knew about myself. Uncle Malachi did that too. He challenged me, not in a direct way, but he was so clever in how he would always leave me with a question in my mind, something I had to work through, something I had to think about. I don't know how he did that, but he's brought me to where I am now. He's brought me back to you, as you did when you sent me to him. Thank you for doing that David, knowing what I do now, that was so selfless of you, but so typical too.'

'Thank God for his intervention.' David said, delighting in her words. 'It's time to move on now, move on together, create a future for us and each other. We can't replace our losses, Jennifer, but we can build ourselves a happy place, a relationship to stand the test of time.'

'That sounds like a proposa...' She stopped herself, worried that it might not be what he meant.

'Actually, it is!' he said with his broadest smile.

'You mean you would... ask me to...?'

'Yes, I would, I will, I do.'

Going down on one knee, he said, 'Jennifer O'Broin, I haven't had chance to organise this properly, and I haven't got a ring for you, but...will you be my...will you marry me?'

She burst into tears of happiness and bent down to kiss him.

'David, oh my dear Lord, I love you too. So much. Yes, yes, of course I will marry you. You are the most special human being I have ever met, David Blind, and I don't even mind taking your very odd name! Well, I might have to tag it onto O'Broin.'

He laughed at that. 'Well, it's not really my name, either remember. We could both be O'Broin if you like.'

They sat, holding each other for long minutes, unable to speak, unable to comprehend their own happiness, not knowing fully how it had come to be, but content to glory in it and the gentle caress of their love.

David eventually broke the silence. He said, 'Jennifer, I love you beyond anything I've ever known in my life, beyond anything I can understand, and I'm longing to tell the world that I do, but I don't suppose now is the right time to tell anyone, is it?

'Everyone has been so focused on the funeral, and Father Seth. I don't think people will understand. They don't know the depth of our love, over many years, like we do.'

She looked at him and nodded silently.

He went on, 'There's only Ethel, Tanu and Cedric who'd really understand. And Simeon. I think everyone else would be shocked, even scandalised. You were going to be a nun, for heaven's sake!'

She buried her head against his shoulder. 'You're absolutely right, sweet man, my sweet David. We'll have to go cautiously.

'You see why I love you so much, David Blind,' she said. 'Your capacity to love is amazing. Your ability to consider everyone else is such a beautiful part of who and what you are. I'm so happy that you, the man who has always put my needs before his own, did so because of his unconditional love. You're the best.'

Nursing their secret joy, they went over to Cedric's and Tanu's for dinner.

Chapter 28

Anneke

David and Jennifer arranged to meet Anneke at the Europa restaurant two days later. They had a table by the window overlooking the gardens and Anneke had ordered wine and fruit juice for David.

'Just so you know before we start, this is my treat,' she said.

David protested but Anneke wouldn't hear of it. 'No,' she said. 'I have wanted so much to have this opportunity to speak with you both, so I feel very happy right now.'

Jennifer said, 'Well, I am sure I can speak for David and myself in saying this feels a very special moment. As you know, Father Seth was almost like a real father to David, quite a strict father when you were young, David?'

David nodded and half smiled. Jennifer continued, 'And he was just like an uncle to me, but in all the years we knew him, he never really spoke about his family, and they never came to visit, as far as I know. That's right, isn't it, David?'

David said sadly. 'Yes, Father Seth loved this place. He loved the Italian food, one dish in particular. I'll show you on the menu...' He reached over for the menu and quickly found pasta al forno con pollo.

Anneke read the description and said, 'Then that's what we must order. With insalata mista and pane all'aglio. Magnifico!' She signalled to a waiter and he took the order.

'You come from Arnhem, is that right, Anneke?' asked David. She nodded. 'Just outside, actually. It's really beautiful. You must visit sometime.'

'Oh, thank you. That sounds great,' said David. 'Also, it's really interesting, because I know what happened in the Second World War must have meant a lot to Father Seth. There was a film about trying to capture a bridge in Arnhem, with thousands of paratroopers being dropped over Holland. He watched it more than once.'

Anneke smiled. 'Yes, I know that very bridge very well. It's over the Rhine. It was rebuilt after the war to look just like the old one. You must come to see it. It was a disaster though, the operation, wasn't it? I think it was called Operation Market Garden. Many people died trying to liberate my country.'

They nodded in sympathy.

Anneke smiled. 'But we have much to be grateful for these days. The older generations suffered greatly, I think,' she added.

'Indeed we do, Anneke,' answered David, reflecting solemnly on the truth of her statement.

'Sorry to change the subject abruptly, but do you know how exactly you're related to Father Seth? I know cousins can get a bit vague down the generations in families, but I would be really interested to know more about the Rossouws in Holland. Maybe you could draw us a family tree?' He smiled in anticipation of her answer.

'Ah, yes. Well, I do know how I'm related, actually,' said Anneke, taking a sip of her wine, and taking her time. 'This may come as...something of a surprise.

'But, before I tell you, I just want to make it clear that no-one else knows this except you both and me. Until my moeder died, it was just her and, since then, just me.'

David and Jennifer held their breath for the next words to come out of Anneke's mouth.

'Seth Rossouw was my biological father.'

They gasped. Anneke paused for a moment as they tried to take it in.

'My moeder kept it a secret all her life. She always told me I was the result of a relationship with someone she lost touch with, a handsome man she cared deeply about, but he left her and she never knew where he was. I grew up thinking that almost my whole life. She was a wonderful moeder, though, and I loved her very much. I think she was very lonely, but we did a lot of things together. We had each other.'

'But how, how did you find out?' asked Jennifer, unable to hold back her burning question.

Anneke's eyes glittered with tears. 'When she died, I was going through her papers and I found letters from Father Seth, and photographs. There was a photograph of Mama and him together near the Trevi Fountain in

Rome, taken on Christmas Day 1979. She produced it from her handbag, handing it to Jennifer.

'That's how I knew it was him when I saw the television reports. I knew his name, and I recognised him. He even came to see me, once, when I was a baby. But never after that.

'The scandal would have been too much for Moeder to bear. I knew her so well. She could manage being a single Moeder, but not…not with a priest's baby, when the priest wanted to remain a priest. And she had been a nun. She was very ashamed, and I know that because it said so in his letters. Well, actually, it was something like Seth saying she mustn't be ashamed, she mustn't go on loving him, and she must make a different life for herself. She just couldn't.'

Jennifer shook her head, unable to take it in. 'That is so sad. So sad, Anneke. I'm very sorry to hear such a story. Your poor mother. And how painful for you, never knowing, then finding out like that…' she tailed off, hardly knowing what more to say for the best.

David had been sitting silently, the obvious truth now staring him in the face, neon lights flashing. He had a half-sister. Here she was. His flesh and blood. The penny hadn't seemed to have dropped for Jennifer yet.

But more than that, the awful knowledge dawning on him, that Anneke and he were both the products of a vain and lustful man who had either abandoned his offspring and their mothers or played games with them for his own grotesque pleasure. For nearly forty years.

Anneke couldn't know it yet, fully, but she was about to.

Slowly he told his story, and Anneke listened in turns with amazement, shock and then horror, as the awareness in her grew that both of them, sitting here, were the residue of one man's selfishness. One man's pride, greed, lust, envy, wrath, most of the deadly sins. They were even about to eat a meal together that he had gluttonously devoured on many occasions, David thought, the anger suddenly rising as he remembered Seth's obsession with good food and the best wines.

And what about cruelty? Cruelty wasn't one of the deadly sins, but it ought to have been, he raged. Seth Rossouw, the priest, had shown cruelty on an industrial scale, right up to his last years, when he might have thought the game was up once David was old enough and strong enough to take him on. Then Jennifer was on the scene and he even managed to change his personal behaviour. Seth had always been careful to show his best side, his avuncular side to Jennifer...but then he had always seemed, after all, to be attracted to young, pretty nuns, didn't he, thought David, looking at the photograph of Seth Rossouw and the beautiful young nun, Anneke's Moeder.

Fury ran through him at the realisation, piercing his memories and splintering the final image he had built up of the man who had laid upon him a curse in his childhood. It was all about power.

Suddenly, then, like a bright fire burning, the clearest thought he had ever had in his life shone as a beacon in his head.

Even as he spoke the final words to Anneke, he pledged that no more would he let Seth, yes, that man, Seth Rossouw, that so-called man of God, that liar, that cheat, that power-crazed priest, that sadist, no longer would he let him rule the direction of his life or dictate the terms and redemption of his soul.

He would live for goodness alone now, and Jennifer, and this lovely woman, his half-sister, who had come to share her personal journey, asking for nothing, and not previously knowing the true situation and how it would impact on her.

Anneke, his sister. His sister. Together they could rise above all this. They would. They were better than their father. Their ability to love would eclipse his wrongdoing. Their mothers would be avenged...no, no, not avenged, appeased. Vengeance was something Seth Rossouw would seek.

When David had stopped speaking, his story told, Anneke stretched out her hand taking David's and looked into his eyes with the full depth of her understanding. Jennifer wept with relief, looking from one to the other, waiting for Anneke.

'You're my brother. My little brother,' Anneke said, simply, with a smile. 'This is a new beginning for us both, David.'

The three of them talked for hours over their meal. The pollo was delicious.

***

The next day Tanu, Cedric, Ethel, Amahle and Simeon were expected at David's house for dinner and in the morning Jennifer and David went out to shop for ingredients.

They had bade farewell to Anneke after walking her back to her hotel and promising to meet up again in the city and to spend as much time together as possible before her flight back to Amsterdam.

David felt emotionally bankrupt, but he knew it was good to channel his energy on planning an evening in the company of good, old, trusted friends. He and Jennifer spent the afternoon preparing food and talking endlessly about Anneke and the massive implications of the revelations about Father Seth's life, and what their guests would make of it.

Anneke had told them she had no objections to their sharing her news, but she'd rather not be there when it happened, so together David and Jennifer planned how to reveal it. They knew it would be something of a bombshell, and both of them knew David had a long road ahead of him, dealing with his shock, anger and his new feelings towards Father Seth.

But, they agreed, it was also time to be hopeful and new. Time to rise above the darkness and go into the light. One step at a time.

'Well, there's nothing like a pile of mushrooms, onions and courgettes to concentrate your mind', said Jennifer, smiling across as she watched David tackle the chicken.

'You're not wrong there,' he answered. 'I'm secretly glad we don't have to do a vegetarian dish as well. Not quite feeling the full chef today.'

Jennifer grinned and nodded. 'I'd have loved to talk about our wedding plans tonight, but I suppose that's better left to another time, considering what we have to tell them about Anneke. They are going to be amazed.'

'That will be the least of it, I imagine,' said David, ruefully.

Jennifer saw his expression and said, trying to keep things light, 'Well, Cedric is obviously going to be first choice for your best man, since you have to return the compliment.'

David wagged the knife at her, grinning. 'I can see you've been giving this much attention, the future Mrs Blind.'

'The future Mrs O'Broin-Blind, if you don't mind,' corrected Jennifer. 'And now, it's even more obvious to me who else will be in our wedding line-up. Anneke and Tanu will have both to be my bridesmaids.'

The pair of them laughed at the pleasant proposal, though both knew that announcing their wedding date would have to wait until the time was right and they could share their happiness with people who wouldn't judge them.

'That's a very good idea,' said David, opening the fridge. 'But don't get carried away with all the plans just yet. I might have to personally vet several possible honeymoon destinations...'

She threw a mushroom at him, laughing.

They cooked and talked until it was time for dinner and their guests were due to join them. Jennifer watched the oven and David tidied round, set the table and lit candles. They knew it would be an uproarious gathering, over good food, wine, and old, shared jokes.

The doorbell rang. Jennifer touched David's cheek and said, 'We have a lifetime ahead of us to enjoy what we have, so concentrate on the relationship of you and your sister, tonight. You deserve to be happy, and I want you to experience it in as wholesome a way as possible. You'll never get the opportunity to relive these moments, so you should savour them.'

He kissed her forehead and went to answer the door.

First to arrive were Ethel, Amahle and Simeon. David greeted them with hugs and showed them into the sitting room for a drink when Cedric and Tanu arrived. Chatter and bursts of laughter carried through to the kitchen, most of it from Tanu and Amahle. Ethel was quieter than usual, finding it harder than the younger ones to step out of her grief.

They sat down to dinner, and for the first time since Father Seth's death, everyone was smiling.

When they'd eaten the main course, David said, tapping his glass with a spoon, 'I have something to tell you all, something I only found out yesterday.'

They all looked at him and waited with interest.

He glanced at Jennifer and then began. 'On the day of Father Seth's funeral, a very lovely Dutch lady approached Jennifer as we left the church. During her conversation, she said she was related to Father Seth through her mother.'

He paused for the reaction. The table fell expectedly silent.

Tanu said, 'Oh, that's really interesting David. Do tell us more!'

Ethel spoke up. 'Well, I never. In all the years, Father hardly ever spoke of his family. Only to say they came from near Am..Arm, Armham, I think, something like that. I didn't like to ask in case there was something painful he couldn't talk about. So who is she?'

David knew this was going to be sensational news for the small gathering. He almost grinned. 'Arnhem, Ethel. The family was originally from near Arnhem. So, Jennifer and I met up with her for a meal at the Europa. She's called Anneke. We had a lovely time. But, to cut a very long story short, well, it turns out that she's my half-sister.'

Tanu mouthed, 'What?' and turned to Cedric incredulously, eyes wide open. He put his hand on her arm to tell her to keep quiet.

David continued. 'I...couldn't be more delighted. We are going to have a lot to talk about, as you can imagine. There are obviously a lot of implications.'

Ethel slowly got up from her chair and made her way around to David. Putting her arms around him, she said, 'Oh child, you've had so much to deal with in your young life. I'm so proud of you and how you've carried yourself with dignity. You and your sister's new relationship will flourish because of that. God in his mercy has sent your sister to help you to come to terms with everything you have had to deal with. Thank God for his intervention.'

Tanu had been bubbling with reaction and she couldn't keep it in any longer. She chose her words carefully, knowing she might run away with the explosion in her head.

'David, that's incredible news. I can hardly believe it. What on earth does it mean, though? We'll help you in any way you want us to, won't we Cedric? Just ask, please, just ask. We don't want to pry or interfere, but if we can be of use, David, you mustn't hesitate.'

Then she couldn't resist. 'Hey, a half-sister! I really want to meet Anneke. And if you like her, both of you, then sure as eggs are eggs, I will too. We can go shopping together. I've always wanted to go to Amsterdam! The canals! The bikes! The Van Gogh Museum! I love Dutch cheese! Jennifer, we can have a girl trip!'

Jennifer couldn't help the chuckle that escaped. 'We feel so blessed to have all of you, and we want to share you all with her too. She's a lovely person, and she hasn't had an easy life. I know she and David will work together to help each other to move forward. I'm delighted too. Anyway, David, tell everyone a bit more about Anneke.'

He told them all he knew about his half-sister, and they listened with great sympathy, and not a little shock at the new window they were being given into the private world of Father Seth Rossouw.

When he'd finished, Jennifer proffered, 'Tanu, you might get your wish. I'd love for Anneke to visit here and for us to go there.'

Chapter 29

Result

Jennifer and Evie boarded the plane at Johannesburg Airport and, as usual, Jennifer passed the time people watching. A young family entered the cabin from the front. A mischievous little girl, about five years old, with auburn hair, ran down the aisle, followed by her parents. Her adoring father was trying, badly, to hold back his smile so that she couldn't see that her naughtiness was making him laugh. He gently shouted in a familiar Dublin brogue, 'Aoife!'

Jennifer was startled at the sound and tone of his voice. It sounded like the last part of her own name, and so like her memory of her own father calling her. She swallowed hard to hold back the tears that were welling up. The child's mother smiled, half stressed by her daughter's antics, half embarrassed, as she made her way to the window seat across the aisle from her.

The girl was carried to her seat by her father and placed securely between her parents. Jennifer looked across and played peep, loving the delight and mischief in Aoife's eyes. The father kept apologising, but she protested each time that all was fine, and what a lovely child she was. He smiled in appreciation, said she was very patient, and asked her where she was travelling to. Jennifer answered him fully and pleasantly, but there was a part of her that wished he'd just stop talking, because every time he opened his mouth, he sounded just like her own father. It started to become painful. Evie seemed oblivious, and it wasn't a topic of conversation Jennifer wanted to open with her.

The long flight continued, Aoife fell asleep, and Jennifer eventually lost herself in the TV screen in front of her, snoozing and looking at the earth far beneath, whenever there was a break in the clouds.

They changed flights at Schiphol and found themselves in seats across the aisle again. Aoife was delighted to begin her game of peep again, to remonstrations from her father.

Jennifer tried to screen it out, but she was finding the sound of the man's voice, just talking to his own daughter, more and more painful as they crossed the North Sea, then over the green hills of England, and then the Irish Sea.

As they landed in Dublin, her heart nearly bursting, she couldn't wait to alight the plane. Her last glimpse of the lovely little family, walking off towards passport control with their suitcases from the carousel, left her with sharp pangs of hurt, like little daggers in her chest. Or was it hurt tinged with envy? Envy? Yes, probably envy, she thought. And a sad wish that things could have been different in her own life.

They arrived at Malachi's house, and Oliver and his mother were just leaving. Oliver ran to them both and gave Jennifer a welcoming hug, greeting her like the old friend she was.

'We've made a fire and made your beds. There's milk, bread and a few other bits in the scullery,' Bernadette O'Callaghan said, beaming and welcoming them into the cottage with their luggage.

Before they could sit down, she took a letter out of her pocket and continued, 'I must give this to you now. We got this from Finbarr Casey, the solicitor. It says for us too to go to his office tomorrow for the reading of Malachi's will. I hope neither of you minds?'

'We don't mind at all. Great Uncle Malachi adored Oliver, and we both know you were all very kind to him,' answered Jennifer.

'Then we'll see you both tomorrow,' said Bernadette. 'I'll let you get settled.'

Evie and Jennifer hugged her and she made her way out of the cottage. The place smelt slightly damp, but it had been aired and was warm, and the memories of Uncle Malachi made it a welcome place to be.

Soon after breakfast the next day, they left the cottage and took the short walk to the solicitor's office. They sat in the waiting room with Oliver and his parents and three men they'd seen at his funeral in January but didn't know personally.

Casey introduced everyone, starting with Evie, Jennifer, Oliver and his parents Feargal and Bernadette O'Callaghan, and finally Daragh O'Halloran and his sons, Finn and Cormac.

The solicitor began the reading of the will. The assembled company listened politely and without comment.

Malachi had lived a remarkably simple life, so it came as a great shock to Evie, Jennifer and the O'Callaghans to hear that he had been the wealthy owner of the local whiskey distillery. He had never spoken of it, ever. Malachi had enjoyed the odd dram or two at night 'to warm the cockles' as he put it, but never in their wildest imaginations did they think he'd owned a distillery.

The Trout River Irish Whiskey Distillery was managed by Daragh O'Halloran. His son Finn was the master blender, and Cormac was the sales and marketing manager. Along with Casey, these were the only three people who had known of Malachi's involvement in the popular local brand of whiskey, and they had kept his secret for decades. Because of this, he had given them all a five per cent interest in the company, providing that they continued to maintain their positions within it.

A further five per cent had been bequeathed to the O'Callaghans on the understanding that they would receive an annual three per cent dividend and their five per cent share was to be left to Oliver at the time of their deaths. The O'Hallorans listened with delight and respect. The O'Callaghans looked at each other in amazement.

Oliver had looked up, startled, at the mention of his name, but Bernadette quietened him with a look.

A €500,000 trust fund was to be set up for him, and the remainder of the company and his estate equally shared between Evie and Jennifer.

Casey asked the O'Callaghans and O'Hallorans to return to the waiting room as requested in the will. They left the room, and he explained to Evie and Jennifer the value of the estate. The total of their shared inheritance, including the business, the cottage and personal funds, was valued at €6.74 million after taxes. They stared at each other in disbelief.

The solicitor invited everyone back into his office to complete the paperwork. He then explained that Malachi had requested that a table should be booked at a local restaurant that evening for all to eat together in his memory.

As they left the office, Oliver took hold of Jennifer's hand and pulling her to one side, tears filled his eyes as he said, 'I loved Malachi, Jennifer. He was always very good to me, and he taught me a lot about all kinds of things. He used to tell me all the time that I had good and kind parents, and one day we would all be rewarded. But I thought he meant God would reward us for being good Christians. I didn't understand what he meant until today, but I wish I could have him back rather than have the reward.'

Jennifer stroked his face as she wiped away his tears and said, 'Oliver, Malachi also taught you a lot about the value of humanity and love, and along with those lessons and moral values you've learnt from your wonderful parents, he has helped to set you up in life with everything you need beyond the material, I mean the money and everything.

'I'm sure he'd want you to remember that people are always far more important than things, and I'm sure you will.' The boy nodded and hugged his grown-up friend, the friend who felt more like a big sister.

They were due to return to South Africa in a couple of days, so over dinner in O'Reilly's restaurant that night, Jennifer asked whether Finbarr Casey and the O'Hallorans might arrange for the cottage to be sympathetically refurbished, using some of the money from Malachi's bequest. She and Evie would return to it regularly, she told them, and intended to keep it in the family.

She spent the last day packing, and to bring lightness to the proceedings, playing some of the old games with Oliver that he used to play with Malachi. He told her that the old man's favourite game was dominoes, and stacking the little black blocks transported her back to happy memories of playing with her own father. It was his favourite game, too, at least his favourite to play with a seven-year-old daughter. The mental videos she had of her last times with her father just wouldn't go away. She couldn't switch them off.

They returned to South Africa the following day and David was at the gate to meet them. Jennifer had to restrain her natural feelings because Evie still wasn't aware of their deep love for each other. Jennifer wished with all her heart that she could have trusted her mother enough to confide in her, but she knew the emotional divide was too wide. Evie needed time to get used to new situations. She had always liked things in boxes, and Séan O'Broin was definitely in a box she had locked and kept hidden out of sight.

Maybe in time, things would become clearer and she'd know what happened to her father. Perhaps he would feel he could once more be in her life.

They went back to David's house and he made them food. It was so good to be back, just breathing the same air, Jennifer thought, her eyes never far from his face.

They went to sit in the living room together and Evie opened a book.

'So, dying to ask, what's the latest with Anneke?' Jennifer asked, after a few minutes of talking about David's work, and the latest goings on with Ethel, Tanu and Cedric.

'Couldn't be better,' he replied. 'Well you know we're talking every day, and she said yesterday she's hoping to fly over just as soon as she can get some leave from work.'

'Wow, that's great news. I can't wait to see her again, and Tanu will be beside herself. We're just talking about Anneke Mammy…' Jennifer said, turning to her mother, whose head had fallen to one side, the steady low burrs the first breaths of sleep. 'Too late,' she giggled, 'Mammy's shattered.'

'I love you,' he whispered.

'I love you more,' she said.

***

David was due at a two-day information technology convention in Kimberley the following day and left her somewhat regretfully early the next morning, protesting that he would cancel it right until the last moment when Jennifer playfully pushed him through the door. She kissed him on the cheek, told him not to worry, to enjoy it, and waved him off cheerfully. He'd already cut the two nights to one and so would miss the first session, but he would be there by mid-morning, and return the following night.

She was looking forward to relaxing, but no sooner had his car disappeared round the corner than Tanu ran across the road. They sat, drank coffee and chatted animatedly for a couple of hours until Tanu's phone rang. It was the deputy manager of her boutique with a problem she couldn't solve. Tanu raised her eyes and knew her time with Jennifer was at an end for the moment, so she blew a kiss, took her leave still talking into the phone and drove into the city.

In the course of their chat, Tanu had expressed a desperate wish for a new dress to wear the following evening because she was due at a presentation event with Cedric, and she knew there was nothing suitable in her own boutique. She had suggested a trip first thing in the morning with her favourite personal shopper, Jennifer. Jennifer had laughed at that grandiose description but recognised that it had probably been true on many occasions. Tanu was excellent at choosing stock for her boutique, but somehow very little of it reflected her own personal fashion choices.

The trip would also be a chance to spy on the competition in Jo'burg city centre's other fashion shops, Tanu had said, excitedly. And Jennifer's advice was always invaluable, apparently. Jennifer had smiled at her friend's generous and persuasive compliments and agreed amiably to the outing in the full knowledge that it was going to be anything but relaxing. She knew only too well what Tanu's expeditions were like. They'd walk around all day from shop to shop trying on this dress then another. Then it would be onto the market boutiques, going through the same routine time and again throughout the day, before returning to the original shop just before closing and buying the first thing Tanu had tried on at the beginning of the day. It was almost guaranteed!

But for now, she could relax. She grabbed a book from David's extensive bookshelf, something intriguing that had caught her eye. It was about the Shakespeare authorship question, said the blurb. What was that? Didn't we know who Shakespeare was? It looked interesting, anyway. Had David read it, she wondered? He hadn't mentioned it. He was often picking up books in bookshops with the full intention of reading them and then getting carried away with his computer work.

She'd always intended to read more Shakespeare, in particular the Sonnets. The words of the beautiful sonnet David had read at Tanu and Cedric's wedding came back into her mind.

'Let me not to the marriage of true minds
Admit impediments. Love is not love
Which alters when it alteration finds...'

Going to Stratford-upon-Avon in England was definitely on her list of must-dos, she decided. She spent the rest of the day completely absorbed, swapping between book and search engine. She soon began to wonder if Stratford-upon-Avon was a good idea after all. Shakespeare might not have been born there at all, according to this huge amount of evidence, all new to her, presented by Shakespeare scholars, professors and historians of high regard. She was dying to tell David all about it and see what he thought.

Jennifer had an early night, taking her book to bed and slept more soundly than she had done in weeks. She woke early, grabbed a quick breakfast, and so the challenge of the day began. Jennifer was almost bracing herself because she was still so tired after the trip to Ireland. But being with Tanu always lifted her spirits. The day turned out to be pure fun and joy, and they laughed and lunched and had coffee en route through the city. The usual outcome was achieved, on this occasion in the form of a beautiful shift dress in shades of mauve and green, with a matching bolero, bought from the second shop they'd visited. They'd eventually got back just in time for Tanu to shower before going out with Cedric.

Jennifer hadn't looked at her phone all day, so immersed was she in Tanu's happy, mad world.

She returned to David's, and comforted herself with the fact that David would be home in a few hours and she could have a lie down, a nap, maybe. She left her mother watching TV and went to her room to take a shower. It was as she was undressing that she noticed the email icon on her laptop.

It was from FindMyFamily. They sent updates from time to time. None of them had revealed anything of importance, nothing at all to give her clues about her father.

But maybe this would be the lucky one. She allowed the small hope to flicker for a moment then clicked the link desultorily and read through the information, expecting the usual disappointment. Then she read it again. And again.

Everything in the room was swimming. She got up and went unsteadily to the open window, gulping the fresher air. She returned in a trance and stared at the screen. The contents of the email were rippling in front of her eyes.

It was devastating in its simplicity.

Dear Jennifer, Here is an update on your DNA sample.

We are pleased to advise you that our system has identified one or more DNA matches. Please see below.

Jennifer O'Broin
DNA match: David Blind. Location: Johannesburg, South Africa. Approximate shared DNA: 29.2%. Relationship: Close relative, suggested half-sibling. Click here to message David Blind

She turned back to the screen, willing the words to disappear. No, no, no, this had to be wrong. It could not be. David was Anneke's half-brother, not hers. This was just stupid, stupid, not right at all.

She knew David had sent off his sample three or four weeks before and was waiting for the results to give him clues about his mother. She was excited to see them too. Clues about his mother. His mother.

But this says that I'm...*suggested half-sibling*. She read the words over and over. Her heart wrenched. Pain gripped her in the chest and the stomach. She had to turn away, holding herself tightly for fear she might fall.

This was never meant to be. This was monstrous. This was grotesque. The thoughts ran in a loop. It's got to be a mistake, they've mixed things up, they've mixed things up. But then she remembered that when her own results came the first time, they included distant cousins with surnames she recognised. So she knew they were her results. Definitely her results.

And DNA can't lie, can it? These tests are neutral, scientific, she reasoned. This information, staring back at her in its scientific neutrality, was irrefutable.

Something in the centre of her brain screamed.

The lab doesn't know we are in love! The lab doesn't know we are Jennifer and David, that we love each other, that we want to spend the rest of our lives together.

She flung herself in despair on the bed and moaned with the pain of the realisation that they no longer could. They couldn't ever be lovers. Not now. They'd burn in hell. She felt trapped. She writhed in a foetal position, crying like a wounded animal, searching her mind for means of escape.

So, there are three of us, her brain whispered to her, some corner of rationality returning. Anneke. David. Jennifer. Three different mothers. One father. She felt like her heart was cleft in two. She yelled, wailed, screamed, into her pillow, not caring that anyone might hear. Her mother, watching a film downstairs at the back of the house with the sound turned up, didn't hear.

When her throat began to burn and the screams had quietened, the sobs grew less and she needed to gulp for air. The questions started to switch round in her head. So Mammy had lied to her all these years. Like Anneke's mother had lied. Surely she must have known who her father was? Was that why Daddy left?

Oh, Daddy, Daddy. My Daddy! But, he wasn't her Daddy, was he? Not now. She wasn't his child. She was Father Seth's child, like David, and Anneke, she had to be. These results were telling her that, unequivocally. This was beyond, far beyond, her understanding. How could she go on, now? How could she live her life, now, knowing this? The mental image of Father Seth flashed in front of her. She retched.

Father Seth. Priest! What kind of priest was he? What had he done, what vows had he broken, that she should exist, that David and Anneke should exist? What had she done that was so bad that God would want to punish her in this way? To let her love David, and for him to love her. They were to have been married! What had David done for God to want to punish him, too? Hadn't he had enough pain and suffering in his life already?

They'd both been betrayed. She'd been betrayed by God, by her Mammy, by her Daddy, by that evil, wicked, damnable, damned, despised creature of some stinking swamp in hell, Father Seth.

Father Seth? No! She would never, could never, call him that now. She couldn't even bear to think of his face, his voice, or his smell, the smell of his aftershave mixed with candlewax and incense. Dead! Dead! Dead, in a swamp of his own blood.

But, dear God, wasn't she his blood? And David? And Anneke? His blood lived on in them. She felt unclean, despoiled. She needed to shower, to wash him off her, out of her.

She remembered her mother. Her mother! How in God's name had she borne a child for a priest? What did my Daddy know? Is that why he left? Daddy. My Daddy. So many questions. Oh, I can't bear it. Dear, dear God, please end this torture. End it. Please.

The pain was too intense to bear. She needed it to go away. She needed to be numb, completely numb, but her brain wouldn't let her. My God, Seth Rossouw, old friend of the family! Some friend! He knew all along, didn't he? He must have known that she and David were brother and sister when he made them share that bathroom, and encouraged their relationship, right back in the beginning. He was playing with them!

Oh, dear Christ, what wickedness had dwelt in that building, that cursed place, St Brigid's presbytery? She had felt safe there, felt joy there, learned to love David there, and within its thick, wood panelled walls and safe, comfortable rooms was where he had fallen in love with her. That building would never now be free of that evil presence, his unforgivable sins...

David said the curse of St Brigid's was the staircase. But this, this was the real curse. How she longed for the time she had spent with David that innocent day in the church, before she knew this dreadful truth, all these truths. When she and David were pure and unadulterated, finding love for the first time.

Theirs was a love that could never be. Not now. How could they ever live with this eviscerating, gut-spilling truth?

Seth Rossouw died so horrifically because it was the way he had lived, she thought, fury surging again hot through her veins. He'd bled others of the truth. He'd torn out their insides for sport. He'd tortured them. She and David were pawns in his pleasure. Torn, torn to pieces. Why? Simply for his amusement?

This was darkness, blackness, utter evil...shut it out, shut it out.

She couldn't. He died in carnage, in pain, alone, desperately seeking help. It was what he deserved. But they, too, were left in carnage and they were slipping around in the blood, the familial blood, the Rossouw blood, writhing in it, drowning in it, his blood.

The world she had known was out of reach to her. She thought of David's handsome face, the face she loved, the beautiful brown eyes she had lost herself in, and then his face merged with her own face and Anneke's face and Seth Rossouw's.

She didn't know she could feel these things, pure rage and disgust for another human being. An abomination of a man. He didn't deserve to be called a human being. She wanted him to burn, roast, shrivel, scream in hell for all eternity.

It seemed everything good in her life had been torn away from her. She needed peace from this living nightmare. She needed comfort from somewhere, and she needed it quickly. For a desperate moment she thought about taking the strongest painkillers she could find and some whiskey to sleep, sleep, sleep, and never wake up. She banged her head down into the pillow again and thumped it with her hands. It was all useless, useless. Pain and more pain seared through her. She couldn't make sense of anything anymore.

She lay there for hours, blanking out her thoughts and turning her mind into numbness.

***

David packed his laptop back into its case and tidied the papers on the table in his hotel room into a folder. He looked at his watch. It was time to check out and hail a taxi to the station.

The conference had been a good one. His mind was buzzing with new ideas to develop his business, and he was eager to get home and get started. Three hours and he'd be there if all went well, he thought, optimistically.

Jennifer. He would soon be with her, back in her arms, back in the safe comfort of her love. He imagined her face, the warmth of her embrace, then he opened his phone just to see her smiling back at him again on his home screen, her eyes bright with mischief and love. Can't wait, he thought, reaching for his trolley case.

The phone pinged. Just an email. He'd check all his emails on the train, he decided, grabbing his room card and opening the door. The notification scrolled down for a couple of seconds, and he caught it in his peripheral vision. It was from FindMyFamily DNA. *Dear David...*